CYTONIC

SKYWARD: BOOK THREE

BY BRANDON SANDERSON

THE STORMLIGHT ARCHIVE

The Way of Kings
Words of Radiance
Edgedancer
Oathbringer
Rhythm of War

THE MISTBORN SAGA

The Final Empire
The Well of Ascension
The Hero of Ages
The Alloy of Law
Shadows of Self
The Bands of Mourning
Misborn: Secret History

LEGION

Legion
Legion: Skin Deep
Legion: Lies of the Beholder

COLLECTIONS

Legion: The Many Lives of Stephen Leeds
Arcanum Unbounded: The Cosmere Collection
Legion and the Emperor's Soul

ALCATRAZ VS THE EVIL LIBRARIANS

Alcatraz vs the Evil Librarians
The Scrivener's Bones
The Knights of Crystallia
The Shattered Lens
The Dark Talent

THE RECKONERS

Steelheart
Mitosis
Firefight
Calamity

SKYWARD

Skyward
Starsight
Cytonic

Elantris
Warbreaker
The Rithmatist
Snapshot

GRAPHIC NOVELS

White Sand
Dark One

SKYWARD: BOOK THREE

BRANDON SANDERSON

First published in Great Britain in 2021 by Gollancz
an imprint of The Orion Publishing Group Ltd
Carmelite House, 50 Victoria Embankment
London EC4Y 0DZ

An Hachette UK Company

1 3 5 7 9 10 8 6 4 2

A CIP catalogue record for this book is
available from the British Library.

ISBN (Hardback) 978 1 473 21793 5
ISBN (Export Trade Paperback) 978 1 473 21794 2
ISBN (eBook) 978 1 473 21796 6
ISBN (Audio Download) 978 1 409 16740 2

Printed in Great Britain by Clays Ltd, Elcograf S.p.A

www.brandonsanderson.com
www.gollancz.co.uk

For Darci Rhoades Stone,

Who deals with my made-up physics
better than any physicist probably should.
Thanks for all the help on this series!

Lightburst

The Solitary Shadow

Surehold

SUPERIORITY TERRITORY

Arena

JOLLY ROGER TERRITORY

Second Ruins

CANNONADE TERRITORY

BROADSIDER TERRITORY

Broadsider Base

Starting Jungle

Map of the
Nowhere
(not to scale)

First Ruins

PROLOGUE

A dark sphere appeared before me in the center of the room.

Scud. Was I really going to do this? In my hand, Doomslug fluted nervously.

The sterile whitewashed walls, enormous one-way mirror, and metal tables marked this as some kind of scientific facility. I was on Starsight: the massive space station that housed the regional offices of the Superiority. Up until this past year, I'd never even *heard* of the Superiority, let alone understood the nuances of how it—as a galactic government—ruled hundreds of different planets and species.

To be honest, I *still* didn't understand those nuances. I'm not exactly a "there are nuances to this situation" type of girl. I'm more of an "if it's still moving, you didn't use enough ammunition" type of girl.

Fortunately, nuance wasn't needed at the moment. The Superiority was undergoing a violent military coup. And the new people in charge did *not* like me. The shouts of the soldiers calling to one another as they searched the facility for me grew louder.

Hence the dark sphere. My only way out was to open a portal to another dimension. I thought of it as the nowhere.

"Spensa," M-Bot said. "My thoughts . . . they're speeding up?"

He hovered nearby, having stuffed himself into a little drone. It was shaped vaguely like a box with wings and a pair of grabber arms on the sides. Two tiny acclivity rings—blue stones that glowed when powered—allowed it to hover, one beneath each wing.

"Um," he said, "that does *not* look safe."

"They use these nowhere portals to mine acclivity stone," I said. "So there must be a way to return once you go through. Maybe I can get us back with my powers."

The shouts outside were getting closer; there were no other options. I couldn't use my powers to hyperjump out of this place, not with the shield that protected the station.

"Spensa!" M-Bot said. "I feel very uncomfortable with this!"

"I know," I said, slinging my gun over my shoulder by its strap so I could grab his drone by the bottom of its chassis. Then—M-Bot in one hand, Doomslug in the other—I touched the dark sphere, and was sucked through to the other side of eternity.

In a flash I was in a place where time, distance, and *matter itself* didn't exist. Here I was formless, a mind—or an essence—with no body. It was as if I were a starship floating in an endless blackness with no stars—with nothing at all to interrupt my view. Every time I hyperjumped using my powers, I briefly passed through this place. I was accustomed to the sensation, but it wasn't familiar. Just . . . slightly less terrifying than it used to be.

Immediately I reached my mind out, searching for Detritus—my home. I'd begun to understand my powers in the most basic of ways. I couldn't go many places with them, but I *did* know how to get home. Usually.

This time . . . I strained . . . Could I do it? Could I hyperjump to Detritus? The blackness around me seemed to stretch, and I could see white spots in the distance. One of those was . . . Gran-Gran?

If I could connect with her, I thought I could pull myself to her. I pushed harder, but grew worried that I'd draw attention.

The delvers lived here. And as soon as I thought of them, I became aware of their presence out there in the darkness. All around me, yet invisible for now.

They didn't seem to have noticed me yet. In fact . . . they were fixated on something else.

Pain. Terror.

Something was in *pain* in here. Something familiar.

The delver. The one I'd prevented from destroying Starsight. It was here in this place, and it was afraid. As I focused on it, it appeared as a white point much brighter than Gran-Gran. It had noticed me.

Please . . . help . . .

Delver communication never manifested as actual words; my mind simply translated the impressions, the images, as words. This one needed my help. The others were trying to destroy it.

I didn't think. Instinctively, I shouted into the nowhere.

HEY!

Hundreds of bright white spots opened around me. The eyes. I could feel their attention on me now, knowing me. The one they'd been fixated on hovered around the outside.

As always, the sight of all those eyes intimidated me. Yet I was a different person now. I'd spoken to one of their kind, *connected* with it. I'd persuaded it to turn its appetite away from the people of Starsight—by showing the delver that they were alive.

I just needed to do the same thing here. *Please.* I projected my thoughts toward those eyes, showing them calm understanding, not fear: *I am a friend. I am like you. I think. I feel.*

I did exactly what I'd done before. The eyes stirred and quivered, agitated. A few drew closer, and I could feel their scrutiny. Followed by . . . an emotion, so much more powerful. Pervasive, overwhelming, omnipresent.

Hatred.

The delvers—there was no telling how many—accepted that I was alive. Because of my cytonic abilities, they understood *me* to be a person. Their hatred changed to disgust. Anger. It was *worse* to know I was alive. It meant the things that had been encroaching upon their realm—persistently bothering them—were self-aware. We weren't mere insects.

We were invaders.

I tried again, more desperate this time. They rebuffed me. As if . . . they'd seen what I'd done to the one of their kind, and had prepared themselves to resist the same sort of approach.

I recoiled at the wave of their terrible anger. And I heard a terrified scream. Doomslug? Her shout projected something into my brain, a location.

Home.

The delvers withdrew. I unnerved them, it seemed. They hadn't expected to find me here. That gave me an opening.

Thanks to Doomslug, I could feel the path. I could get to Detritus. I could see Gran-Gran, and . . . and Jorgen. Scud, I missed him. I wanted to be near him again, talk to him again. I needed to get home to my friends and help them. The war was going to escalate now that Winzik had seized control of the Superiority.

I almost hyperjumped. But I lingered. Something held me back. An impression, an instinct.

What am I? that singular delver projected in a pleading tone. *What are WE?*

I'm Spensa Nightshade, I sent to it. *A pilot*.

Is that all?

It used to be all I cared about. But now . . . now I'd discovered another side to me. Something frightening, something I didn't completely understand.

There is a way to learn, the delver sent. *In this place. We call it the nowhere. You sensed that, didn't you?*

Yes, I had. But I didn't want to stay here. I tried to put that option out of my mind. I needed to go home.

But . . . did my people need me? Just another pilot? I visualized something then. A projection of my own fears? Maybe it was an effect of the nowhere. I saw myself return and rejoin Skyward Flight, fighting . . . and failing. Failing when the delvers inevitably returned, because a fighter pilot—no matter how skilled—couldn't defeat them. Failing when the Superiority marshaled the power of its cytonics, hyperjumping whole fleets. Worse, they could manipulate cytonics such as me, exploit weaknesses in our powers.

They'd done that to my father. Turned him against his own flight. Led him to death.

I was a pilot, yes. But pilots weren't enough.

We knew so little about any of this. We didn't understand what the delvers were. How could we hope to fight them? We didn't understand cytonics—up until recently, we'd considered those who had these powers to be "defects." How could I face opponents like Brade, skilled with their talents, if I ran from who I was?

Home called to me, and I yearned to return. But home didn't have answers.

Can you show me? I asked the delver. *What I am?*

Maybe. I don't even know what I *am. There is a place we can learn, a place in the nowhere. A place where . . . we were all . . . born . . .*

There are no places in the nowhere, I sent.

Not in its heart, no. But at the fringes there are settlements.

I saw the meaning—the delver spoke of a region where acclivity stone was mined. Another mystery I had never quite understood. How did people go into the nowhere and harvest that rock, if the nowhere was a formless void?

Yes, there were actual places on the fringes. Places important to cytonics. Important to me. The delver put one of these locations into my mind.

I hung trapped between two opposite pulls. One, my desire to go home, to hold Jorgen, to laugh with my friends. The other, something frightening. Unknown. Like the frightening, unknown things in my own soul.

If you come here, the delver sent, *it will be difficult to return. Very difficult. And you might get lost . . .*

I felt Doomslug's mind trembling. The rest of the delvers began to reappear, eyes opening—piercing white holes in reality, burning and *hating*. They did *not* want me going where that delver directed.

In the end, that was what prompted my decision. *I'm sorry, Jorgen,* I sent—hoping he could at least feel the words. I had to choose the path that led to answers. Because in that moment, I was absolutely certain it was the only way to protect the people I loved.

You go home, I told Doomslug. *I will find my way later.* I grabbed hold of the destination the delver had sent me.

Thank you, the delver projected. I could feel its sincere relief. *Seek to walk . . . the Path of Elders . . . and remember to not get lost . . .*

Wait! I sent. *The Path of Elders?*

But the delver withdrew, and I felt the others preparing to attack. So I gave Doomslug a final push to go home, then activated my powers and threw myself into the unknown.

PART ONE

1

I dropped out of a wall.

Like, I emerged straight from the stone. I flopped forward in a heap of tangled clothing and limbs. M-Bot made a grunting noise as his drone body fell out beside me, but there was no sign of Doomslug.

I scrambled to my feet, orienting myself, looking around to see . . . a jungle? Like, a real jungle. I'd seen pictures in school of Old Earth, and this place reminded me of those. Imperious moss-covered trees. Branches like broken arms, twisted and draped with thick vines like power lines. It smelled like the algae vats, only more . . . dirty? Earthy?

Scud. It truly was a jungle—like where Tarzan of the Apes had lived in Gran-Gran's stories. Were there apes here? I'd always thought I'd make a good queen of the apes.

M-Bot hovered up, turning around to take it in. The wall we'd fallen out of was behind us. A flat stone freestanding in the jungle, like a monolith. It was overgrown with weeds and vines, and I recognized the carvings in it. I'd seen similar carvings on a wall in the tunnels on Detritus.

I knew from the delver's impressions that this *was* the nowhere.

That *felt* right to me, for reasons I couldn't explain. Somehow I had to find answers in this place. Which seemed a whole lot more daunting to me now than it had moments ago. I . . . scud, I had barely escaped the Superiority with my life. Now I thought I could find answers about the delvers, one of the universe's greatest cosmic mysteries?

Not merely about the delvers, I thought. *About myself.* Because in those moments when I touched the nowhere, and the beings that resided in it, I felt something that terrified me. I felt *kinship.*

I took a deep breath. First order of business was an inventory. M-Bot looked fine, and I still had my stolen energy rifle. I felt a ton more safe holding it. I wore what I'd escaped in: a standard Superiority pilot's jumpsuit, a flight jacket, and a pair of combat boots. M-Bot hovered up to eye level in his drone, his grabber arms twitching.

"A jungle?" he asked me. To him, the time I'd spent communing with the delver would have passed in an instant. "Um, Spensa, why are we in a jungle?"

"Not sure," I said. I glanced around for any sign of Doomslug. She was cytonic like me—slugs were what made ships able to hyperjump—and I hoped that she'd done as I'd asked, and jumped to safety on Detritus.

To be certain, I reached out with my powers to see if I could sense her. Also, could I jump home? I stretched outward, and felt . . .

Nothing? I mean, I still had my powers, but I couldn't sense Detritus, or the delver maze, or Starsight. None of the places I could normally hyperjump to. It was eerie. Like . . . waking up at night and turning on the lights, only to find infinite blackness around you.

Yes, I was *definitely* in the nowhere.

"When we entered the black sphere, I felt the delvers," I said to M-Bot. "And . . . I talked to one of them. The one from before. It said to walk the Path of Elders." I rested my fingers on the wall behind us. "I think . . . this is a doorway, M-Bot."

"The stone wall?" M-Bot asked. "The portal we entered was a sphere."

"Yeah," I said, looking up at the sky through the trees. It was pinkish for some reason.

"Maybe we passed through the nowhere and came out on another planet?" M-Bot said.

"No, this *is* the nowhere. Somehow." I stomped my foot, testing the soft earth beneath. The air was humid, like in a bath, but the jungle felt too quiet. Weren't these places supposed to be teeming with life?

Beams of light filtered in from my right, parallel to the ground. So was it . . . sunset here? I'd always wanted to see one of those. The stories made them sound dramatic. Unfortunately, the trees were so thick that I couldn't make out the source of the light, merely the direction.

"We need to study this place," I said. "Set up a base camp, explore the surroundings, get our bearings."

As if he hadn't heard, M-Bot floated closer to me.

"M-Bot?"

"I . . . Spensa, I am *angry*!"

"Me too," I said, smacking my hand with my fist. "I can't believe that Brade betrayed me. But—"

"I'm angry at *you,*" M-Bot interrupted, waving an arm. "Of course, what I feel is not *real* anger. It's just a synthetic representation of emotion created by my processors to present humans with a realistic approximation of . . . of . . . Gah!"

I set aside my own concerns and focused on how he sounded. When I'd first found M-Bot in the little drone, his speech had been sluggish and slurred—like he'd been on heavy pain meds. But he was speaking clearly now, and quickly, more like his old self.

He buzzed back and forth in front of me like he was pacing. "I don't care anymore if the emotions are fake. I don't care that my routines simulate them. I am *angry,* Spensa! You abandoned me on Starsight!"

"I had to," I said. "I had to help Detritus!"

"They ripped my ship apart!" he said, zipping the other direction. Then he froze in place, hovering. "My ship . . . my body . . . It's gone . . ." He drooped in the air, sagging down almost to the ground.

"Uh, M-Bot?" I said, stepping up. "I'm sorry. Really. But look, can we have this conversation later?"

I was pretty sure that jungles like this were full of dangerous beasts. At least, in Gran-Gran's stories people always got attacked in jungles. It made sense: anything could be hiding out among those shadowed trunks and deceptive ferns. I remembered how intimidated I'd felt when I'd first stepped out of the caverns and seen the sky. There had been so many directions to look, so many open places.

This was even more unnerving. Something could come at me from *any direction*. I reached down to touch M-Bot's drone, which still hovered near the ground. "We should map the area," I said, "and see if we can find a cave or something for shelter. Does that drone of yours have any kind of sensors? Are you picking up any signs of civilization, like radio broadcasts? There are mining operations in here, I think."

When he didn't reply, I knelt beside him. "M-Bot?"

"I," he said, "am *angry*."

"Look—"

"You don't care. You never care about me! You left me!"

"I *came back*," I said. "I left you because I had to! We're soldiers. Sometimes we *have* to make difficult decisions!"

"*You're* a soldier, Spensa!" he shouted, hovering up in the air. "*I'm* a survey AI designed to search for mushrooms! Why do I keep letting you push me into doing things? I didn't want to even enter that sphere, and you pulled me in! Aaah!"

Scud. That drone had surprisingly powerful speakers. And as if in reply to his shouts, something roared in the distance. The sound echoed in the forest ominously.

"Look," I said softly to M-Bot. "I understand. I'd be a little angry in your place too. Let's—"

Before I could finish he zipped away into the jungle, sobbing softly to himself.

I cursed and tried to follow, but he could fly—while I had to deal with the underbrush. I leaped over a fallen tree trunk, but on the other side I had to wiggle through a tangle of vines and fronds. After that something caught my foot, and I ended up tumbling to the ground.

When I finally managed to right myself, I realized I had no idea what direction he'd gone. In fact . . . what direction had *I* come from? Was that log over there the one I'd climbed over? No . . . that had been before I'd pushed through the vines. So . . .

I groaned, settling into the hollow of some overgrown roots, gun in my lap, and sighed. Well, my quest had started in a traditional Spensa-like fashion: with everyone mad at me. I realized that I needed a moment to decompress. M-Bot wasn't the only one with a lot of powerful emotions.

I'd gone from confronting a delver to floating in space thinking I was dead, to waking up in a hospital, to escaping a hit squad sent to kill me. Now I'd had to make a snap decision about coming to this place, and I worried I was wrong.

Maybe I should have gone home and found a way to send someone *else* into the nowhere to find answers. Someone smart, like Rig. Or someone careful, like Kimmalyn. Right now I felt lost. I didn't know what had happened to Cuna, and I worried about my friends.

I was alone, isolated, lost. And to top it off, my only companion—who was *supposed* to be the emotionally stable one, by programming *design*—had just thrown a tantrum and left.

Did people in Gran-Gran's stories ever feel like this? I wished I knew what Khutulun of Mongolia or Calamity Jane of the Wild West had done when feeling overwhelmed.

I don't know how long I sat there. Long enough to notice that whatever was providing the light here didn't seem to be moving.

I let myself fixate on that instead of my mounting anxiety about Jorgen and my friends.

I'd made my decision. Now that I was here, I needed to learn what I could, then find a way home. "M-Bot?" I said to the trees, my voice coming out as a croak. "If you can hear me, would you please come back? I promise to apologize—and I'll even let you have the first insult."

No reply. Only the sound of faintly rustling leaves. So I forced myself to focus on a more detailed inventory of my assets. A way to do something about my situation—no matter how small—in order to start reasserting control. Cobb had taught me that.

Scud. I'd told Cobb that Cuna's faction wanted peace. Winzik and Brade could use that to lure Cobb into talks—then double-cross him.

No, I told myself. *Inventory.*

I gave my rifle a quick once-over. I'd barely used up any of its charge during my escape, which meant I had a power source—and roughly five hundred shots, depending on whether I used standard energy rounds or amped rounds.

My jumpsuit didn't include a medic belt, unfortunately, or a pilot's survival kit. I did have the translator pin I'd been using at Starsight to understand alien languages. I fished in the pockets of the jacket, hoping maybe I'd shoved a knife or something into one of them without remembering. Instead I pulled out a handful of glowing sand.

Glowing. Sand.

Silver, like it was made of ground-up starfighter hull, and glistening. It was such an incongruous sight that I sat there staring at it as some dribbled between my fingers.

Saints. What was it? I closed my hand and returned it to my pocket, where I noticed something else. A lump at the bottom of the sand? I dug down and pulled out my father's pilot's pin. The one I'd kept hidden away since his death. Yet I *knew* it hadn't been on me when I'd jumped into the portal. I didn't even have it on Starsight. I'd left it on Detritus, in my bunk. So how was it suddenly in my pocket, surrounded by silver sand?

Weirded out by its appearance, I tucked the pin away. I didn't find anything else hiding in my pockets, but I had one other asset I could think of: my powers. I knew I couldn't hyperjump home—I couldn't even *feel* home in here. But I had other abilities; the first I had ever manifested was the power to "hear the stars." Which in practical terms meant I could communicate across long distances. Maybe I couldn't hyperjump out of here, but could I reach Gran-Gran mentally?

I settled back against the tree and decided to give it a try. I just closed my eyes and . . . listened, extending my mind. That sounds silly, but I'd spent hours with Gran-Gran practicing this. And today I felt something.

There was a mind near me. It was familiar, like a presence I'd once known. Who was it? Not Gran-Gran . . . not Jorgen . . . not even the delver. I tried contacting the mind, and I got . . . a sensation of contentment? That was odd.

Then I felt something else. A second mind nearby. They were cytonic, whoever they were, because the moment our minds brushed a voice popped into my head.

Ho there! it said. *Another cytonic, in the belt?*

Yes! I sent. *I'm lost. Can you help?*

Careful now, the voice said. *Dangerous things can hear you in here if you use your powers! Where are you? Describe your fragment, and I shall endeavor to locate you.*

Fragment? I sent. *I'm in a jungle. By . . . um . . . a tree?*

I needed to find a better landmark. As soon as I considered it though, I hesitated. What if this was an enemy? How did I know the voice could be trusted?

At that moment, I got attacked.

2

There were three of them. Two birdlike humanoids with wing-arms leaped around the tree from the right to tackle me, and a blue-skinned dione came in from the left—probably to go for the rifle, which I had slung over that shoulder.

It was a good plan, but man were they *sloppy*. The first avian slipped as it jumped, tripping the other one and giving me enough warning to turn and start raising my weapon. That *almost* let me shoot them—but the energy blast went wild as the dione got a hand on the gun.

They grunted, trying to brute-force wrestle the rifle away. The wrong move; even I knew that from my limited DDF training. They should have slapped the barrel, controlled the weapon with one hand, and then gone for my face with the other.

I shoved the dione away, but the two avians tackled me. Grunting, I rammed the butt of the gun into one of them, earning me a squawk of pain. I pulled hard, twisting, and started to wiggle free.

Unfortunately, just as I was about to slide out of the writhing mess of people, someone else grabbed me from behind. A feathered fourth enemy? The group had apparently been smart enough to leave someone in reserve.

I struggled against the fourth attacker, disoriented, as a fifth creature bodychecked me. I didn't get a good look at this last guy—he was furry, and roughly the size of a refrigerator. While I'm . . . well, *not*. I'd stretched the truth to get 152 centimeters listed on my pilot records.

Being small is an advantage in a cockpit. Not so much in a fist-fight. I'd like to think I gave a good showing, but in seconds I was lying on the ground completely disarmed, with the furry one sitting on top of me and one of the avians pointing my own rifle at my head.

"So," the avian with the gun said, the translated words chirping out from my pin, "what have we here? A Superiority soldier? Well, *that's* a nice surprise. A human even! I'm not afraid of your kind, human—but keep struggling, and I'll shoot you and be done."

I groaned and stopped fighting. I reached my hands out to the sides, where they were roughly grabbed and held down. At last I was released from the buttward side of that alien and was able to get a deep breath of fresh air.

My captors pulled me to a sitting position and bound my hands behind my back. I focused on the avian with the gun. I'd heard of this species. The heklo, I thought they were called? They had long beaks, kind of like a stork, but their feathers were of radiant colors. The combat fatigues they wore had no sleeves, but the feathers on their arms didn't seem large enough to support flight. They seemed . . . more a vestige, like how humans had hair instead of fur.

"What do you want to do with it, Vlep?" asked the furry alien. It was vaguely gorillalike. I'd seen this species too. Burls, if I remembered their name correctly.

"That depends," Vlep—the armed one, and the obvious leader—said. "Human, why did they send you through? This portal is for exiles, yet here you are, uniformed and armed."

Right. I was wearing a Superiority jumpsuit and jacket. That, with the weapon, had led them to assume I was working with the enemy. The comment also told me something else: the wall *was* a portal, and this place was where people appeared once the Superiority exiled them. I'd seen that happen. In fact . . .

I looked at the burl. "Gul'zah?" I asked. I'd watched a burl get exiled into the nowhere a few days ago.

"Ha," the burl said. "We grabbed him when he came in."

"So that's why you're here," Vlep said. "Hunting that specific fugitive? Curious."

I wasn't, of course. But I could now see that the burl who had captured me had slightly different features. I wasn't the best at distinguishing one alien from another, but this burl was shorter, more stout, and had a wider face.

So, this group—whoever they were—had an outpost here and captured people who were sent in. Why though? Exiles wouldn't have anything valuable on them. And who was the cytonic I'd contacted? Had I led these to me by using my powers? Or was I just jumping to conclusions?

I reached out with my senses again, seeking that mind. It *wasn't* one of these . . . It was a little farther away.

What? the voice said as I brushed it with my mind. *I told you to be quiet.*

I've been taken captive, I said. *By a group of raiders or something, who were watching the portal where I came in.*

Pirates, the mind sent. *This is Cannonade territory. They're a rough group. Hold your tongue; don't let them know what you are. And please stay quiet cytonically. You'll draw the delvers!*

"Not talking, I see," Vlep said, pulling my attention back. "Hold her tight."

The dione and another heklo grabbed me while Vlep began rummaging through my pockets. I struggled again—it felt violating to have their hands all over me—though I'd expected to be searched.

Soon Vlep pulled some of the silver dust from my pocket. "Ha! A nice haul." He dug in it, then brought out the pin.

His eyes went wide, which seemed to be an expression of surprise for his species. The burl let out a low growl, which . . . might also have been surprise?

"A reality icon?" Vlep asked, then looked at me. "You must be someone important."

My heart leaped as he closed a feathered hand around the pin, but it seemed like a bad idea to show how important that pin was to me, so I forced myself to relax. "I really have no idea what you're talking about."

"Well, thanks for the treasure," Vlep said. He tucked the pin into a small pouch.

"Do we shoot her now?" the burl asked. "I don't like the idea of taking a soldier as a servant. Too dangerous."

"Could be useful in a fight," the dione said, "if they join us. Imagine having a human on our side."

"Broadsiders have one," Vlep said, "and he's useless. They don't live up to their reputations. Trust me. But we're not going to shoot her—the Superiority sent her in armed. So she's valuable to them. We'll ransom her back to the mining base."

So there *were* mining stations in here. At least that gave me a good lead on how I might get out, once I accomplished what I needed to in here.

Right now, my best chance at escape was to get the pirates to underestimate me. So I slumped down. "I'm going to get into so much trouble for this . . ." I moaned.

"Ha!" Vlep said. "Well, good news! Now that we know Gul'zah is valuable, maybe we can ransom him too! *Double* the haul." He looked at the pouch. "Triple. Or more. Stand her up. Let's get moving. Judging from that roar earlier, there's a grig in here somewhere. I'd rather not run into it."

He started off through the jungle, and the others pulled me along. I made a few token complaints and struggles, then slumped as I walked, pretending to be defeated.

Secretly I studied them. These pirates clearly weren't trained soldiers. Vlep didn't understand muzzle control; he turned and absently swung the weapon toward the others when they spoke to him. I wasn't surprised. The Superiority denounced what they called "aggression," and its people were unlikely to have combat training. Winzik and his cronies liked it that way. It made people easier to control.

So maybe this group had formed from exiles? A couple had weapons at their hips—a knife on the burl, and what appeared to be a pistol at Vlep's side. But they hadn't used those on me. They'd purposely taken me alive. Though perhaps they'd been surprised by how well I fought, and how well I'd been armed.

I could probably exploit their ignorance. At least, someone more capable could have exploited it. I didn't have the training for this kind of thing, I . . .

I couldn't really use that argument anymore, could I?

I hadn't been training as a spy, but I'd infiltrated the Superiority. And arguably I'd done a pretty good job. At least until everything had gone wrong at the end.

I'd *chosen* to come here. It was time to stop complaining about my situation.

"Hey, Vlep," I said, trying to hurry up and catch him at the front of the group. I stumbled almost immediately, nearly tripping on hidden vines. Running away wasn't really an option, not while my hands were tied.

I righted myself with some help from the dione, then called again. "Vlep. You all, you're exiles, aren't you? Making the best of a bad situation? I can help you. I'm not your enemy."

"In here," the heklo said, "everyone's our enemy."

"I'm a soldier," I said. "I can train your people. Help you. I just need a little information. About this place, and about—"

He stopped and turned his gun on me. "No talking unless you're asked a question. You're in Cannonade territory now. Keep your head down and hope I don't decide you're too much trouble to be worth keeping alive."

"You know, Vlep," one of the other heklo said, "I think I might know her. Is that . . . Winzik's pet human?"

"Winzik?" Vlep snapped. "Who is that?"

"Sorry," the heklo said. "I forget how little about the outside gets in here. One of the high officials of the Superiority keeps a human bodyguard. I think that's her."

"Curious," Vlep said, narrowing his eyes at me. "Why would they send you to chase an exile, human? Or did you finally cross the Superiority and earn your inevitable reward?"

They'd mistaken me for Brade? Guess I wasn't the only one who had trouble distinguishing one alien from another.

As soon as I thought of Brade, I winced. I'd failed so badly in trying to recruit her. She was cytonic, and was the one who had summoned the delver that had gone on to attack Starsight. If I'd been able to get through to her somehow, all of this would—

A terrible monstrous call tore through the jungle. It was so deep and sonorous, it made the trees vibrate. The entire group froze in place and peered outward through the trees and vines. What in the unholy universe could make such a sound?

"It's getting closer," Vlep whispered. "Quickly. Back to the ships."

Wait.

Ships?

Dared I hope they had starfighters in here? I sure would feel more confident in the cockpit of a ship. When they started walking again, I hurried along with them. And gloriously, like debris parting to reveal heaven itself, the trees fell away and we entered a small clearing—with three ships in it. Two midsize civilian craft and a sleek, dangerous-looking starfighter.

It was like fate had seen me struggling and decided to send me a little gift—in the form of an interceptor-class ship with twin destructors. I was so captivated by its beauty that I missed something important. The group had halted around me, and they weren't looking at the ships—but at the two pirates who had presumably been left to guard them.

One was a dione, who seemed panicked and was trying to administer some kind of medical kit to the other—a burl, who was sitting on the ground by one of the ships. Female, I assumed from her size.

And her face was melting.

3

The strange visage made me gape in shock. Though her body was gorilla-shaped, and she was wearing utilitarian clothing like the others, she had no nose, just a small lump where one had been, and a thin slit for a mouth. Her cheeks sagged to the sides, and her eyes—a milky white—were open and staring forward.

There was something distinctly unnatural about that face. What had happened to her?

"Tie down the prisoner for now," Vlep told the dione—who yanked me over to the side of the clearing. There they anxiously tied my hands—still bound behind me—to part of a tree to hold me in place. A root perhaps? Then the dione ran over to join the others gathering around the burl.

I immediately started trying to worm free. Unfortunately, their knot-tying skills were superior to their combat abilities. I was secured tightly, so I resorted to rubbing my binding against the bark in hopes of making it fray.

"What happened?" Vlep demanded of the dione guard. "What did you do to her?"

"Nothing! I just wandered out into the trees to relieve myself, then came back to . . ." The confused dione gestured at the figure.

Scud. That melty-faced alien was getting unnerving. The others argued for a moment, then one suggested they try the "reality ashes," which turned out to be the silvery dust from my pocket. Vlep began sprinkling it on top of the burl.

As I watched, her eyes started to glow. Beneath the skin, as if there were something inside her. A pure white light. It reminded me . . .

Of the eyes. Of delvers.

Oh, Saints.

I tried to yank free of the root, and it did have some give to it—but I wasn't quite strong enough to pull it out of the ground. So I returned to rubbing my bonds on the bark.

"A little to the left," a peppy voice said from behind. "There's a rougher part there that might help."

I paused, then twisted to look over my shoulder. To where a small drone hovered, hidden among the underbrush.

"M-Bot!" I said, then hushed, glancing at the pirates. They were only about seven meters away, but fortunately they didn't seem to have heard. "You found me!"

"Well, you weren't exactly quiet, Spensa," M-Bot said, hovering closer. "I see you found some friends. That's . . . nice. Look, we need to talk. A heart-to-heart. Heart-to-processing-unit-simulating-a-biological-function-like-a-heart."

"Now's not a great time!"

M-Bot shook a grabber arm at me. "The emotions of biological beings often come at inconvenient times; I've dealt with yours on many occasions. And Spensa . . . I think I have *feelings* now."

"That's . . . not surprising. You had them before, no matter what you said."

"Spensa," M-Bot continued, "I've been thinking. And . . . and feeling. I really *was* angry that you left me behind to be ripped apart, gutted, and killed. But I understand *why* you did it. I shouldn't have been so angry at you. I . . . overreacted."

"Great," I said, struggling to get loose. "I'm sorry too, and I forgive you."

"You *do*?"

"Yes, of course," I said, twisting to the side to show him my bound wrists. "Look, can you—"

"Oh, thank you, Spensa!" he said. "Thank you, thank you. I feel so warm! Maybe my power matrix is overheating. But, but, it's *marvelous*! I feel like I'm going to cry, though that's physically impossible for me."

"Could you—"

"Maybe I could have mechanical tear ducts installed on this drone. So I could be like you, and leak? You become less efficient with your secretions when you're emotional."

I took a deep breath. In the stories, the heroines always had trusty steeds—who could not talk—or loyal, *quiet* sidekicks. I could see why. The Lone Ranger probably wouldn't have accomplished much if his horse had been a mushroom-obsessed blabbermouth.

Still, I was really glad to see him. I glanced toward my captors. They were holding down the sick burl, who seemed to be having a spasm. My heart went out to her, but her distress was timed perfectly. The pirates would have noticed M-Bot for sure otherwise.

"Spensa?" he said. "Oh! Are you tied up?"

"You're only *now* noticing?" I growled. "What did you think I was doing with these ropes?"

"I thought you were trying to scratch an itch! That's why I pointed out the rough part of the root. You biological beings are always scratching things. Skin must be awful." He hesitated. "To be honest, I *should* have figured out you were captive. It's actually rather obvious. I was distracted by all these emotions my processors are inexplicably simulating. Hmm . . . Yup. Those are ropes."

"Help get me out of them?"

"Uh . . . right. I will . . . search for knot-untying solutions in my database . . ."

"Or you could untie them!" I hissed.

"I'm not sure how."

"It's not that hard."

"For you, maybe. I'm not exactly used to being able to *do* things, Spensa. I'm an information-support AI. I . . . don't know how to *act*. In fact, I've needed to send my self-shutdown protocols into an infinite loop. They don't like me being able to fly myself around."

The people who had made his old ship had implanted deep controls on his personality. It said a lot that he had progressed enough to circumvent some of those.

An outburst from the pirates pulled my attention back to the sick burl. She was struggling and thrashing, and had thrown one of the heklo away with incredible strength.

"Quickly," I hissed. "Do you have *anything* that could help me escape?"

"I have a light-line," M-Bot said. "I found one in the shop on a worker drone and moved it to myself. I was planning to use it in my escape. Maybe I could drag you away?"

A light-line was a plus. Though his acclivity rings were small, and the drone was only about the size of a lunch tray, if quite a bit thicker. It wouldn't have a lot of power.

"Attach the light-line to the ropes on my hands," I said. "Maybe with your added strength we can rip this root out of the ground and I can pull myself free. Get ready. We have to do this before the pirates notice what we're doing."

"Yeah," M-Bot said. "About that . . ."

The pirates were running for their ships, having apparently decided to abandon the one with the melting face. The male burl didn't like this. "Give me the icon, Vlep!" the burl shouted. "We have to try! Maybe it will work!"

But Vlep wasn't listening. As the others were running for their ships, he'd turned to look at me. He'd seen M-Bot. He immediately raised the rifle toward us, apparently deciding I was too dangerous to let live.

Get ready, a voice said in my mind.

Ready? I thought, staring down that rifle. *For what?*

The ground started shaking. Trees trembled. Vlep swung the gun away from me and pointed it toward the approaching sounds.

Then a scudding *dinosaur* came rampaging into camp—with a mustachioed human man riding on its back.

4

Yes, a dinosaur. I mean, I'd never seen one before, but this thing was reptilian, walked on two legs, and had a long tail trailing behind it. Yeah, the eyes appeared to be on its shoulders, and its "neck" was long like a trunk and ended in a toothy mouth. So maybe "enormous demonic anteater" would have been a better description. But I'm going with dinosaur.

The human was almost as baffling to me. He wore a flight jacket and combat trousers, and looked to be in his fifties. He was square jawed, muscular for his age, and his mustache stuck out a good fifteen centimeters to either side. As the dinosaur stormed forward, the man slipped expertly down the animal's flank, then hit the ground and rolled.

It was just about the most incredible entrance I'd ever seen. Why hadn't *I* ever been able to ride a dinosaur into combat, then dismount with a flourish?

Oh, wait. Escaping. Right. The stranger's arrival had taken all attention off me.

"Now!" I shouted at M-Bot.

I heaved up to a squatting position, then tried to stand, pulling with all my strength to snap the root I'd been tied to. M-Bot hovered up beside me, towing the root with his light-line as I'd asked. With his added strength, the root gave and I stumbled free.

I found my balance and pushed my hands down my back and squatted, then pulled my bound wrists under my feet to get my hands in front of me. There *are* advantages to being my shape and size.

"Excellent to meet you in person, my cytonic friend!" the stranger said, bounding up to me and yanking out a hunting knife. I proffered my hands, and he sliced the ropes with a single cut. Then he offered his own hand in a gentlemanly sort of way. "Chet Starfinder! Interdimensional galactic explorer!" He had to shout over the sound of the monster rampaging through the camp. The ground shook with its thundering gait.

"That's an awesome name!" I shouted at him.

"Thanks! I made it up myself! What now?"

"Fancy stealing a starfighter?" I said, pointing.

"Music to my ears, young lady!" he shouted back. "It's been far too long since I've had the chance!"

Unfortunately, the sleek ship was already taking off. The pirates had scattered. Only three remained: the male burl, the glowing-eyed female burl he was trying to pull to safety, and Vlep. He was shooting at the dinosaur—which remarkably didn't seem to be hurt by the energy blasts.

We still had a chance to grab one of the civilian ships, a shuttlecraft. I hesitated though, eyeing Vlep. The feathered alien had the pouch with my father's pin.

For some reason, in that moment the pin felt more important. "Change of plans," I said, running for Vlep.

Chet joined me in my charge. Vlep continued firing at the dinosaur, which was ignoring him in favor of snapping toward one of the ships as it took off. I hit Vlep from behind, right at the knees, sending him sprawling. Chet scooped up the gun while I pulled at the struggling heklo's uniform coat, eventually yanking the pouch out of his pocket.

"Freeze!" a voice said from behind.

I spun and found the sleek ship hovering nearby, destructors pointed at me. Vlep took the chance to scramble away, leaving me without a captive. Chet dropped the gun and threw his hands up. Ship-mounted weapons would be powerful enough to vaporize us completely.

Fortunately, the pilot had forgotten the dinosaur. It seized the wing with a furious bite. I dove for the underbrush, and Chet was only a moment behind me. M-Bot belatedly swooped over to us.

I glanced at the last ship, but Vlep was climbing aboard—and the others were firing on the dinosaur. Crossing that clearing would be risking death from a stray shot.

"I believe," Chet said, "Operation Ship-Steal will have to be canceled. My regrets."

"It's all right," I said.

"Shall we?" he said, gesturing into the jungle. "I'd rather not remain in the line of sight of those vessels."

In the clearing, the female burl had come out of her daze and slammed the male against a tree. He slumped to the ground, his eyes closed, and she turned immediately toward me—as if she could sense where I was. Her eyes looked like they'd grown over with skin, smoothing the sockets. But deep within her skull, two white dots—glowing with what I could feel distinctly was an intense hatred—shone through.

My breath caught in my chest. Then the burl pointed and screamed at me.

Scud.

I gave up any last hope of getting one of those ships. I joined Chet and dashed into the jungle, chased by the sounds of destructor fire and monster roars.

5

Chet ran in front of me, and he seemed to have a sixth sense for where to step—I was able to follow him fairly quickly, avoiding any pitfalls or hidden tree branches. I supposed jungle survival was part of an interdimensional space explorer's standard repertoire.

M-Bot hovered along beside me. "Spensa!" he said. "I think I'm simulating fear! Or . . . No. It's time to stop talking like that. I *feel* afraid. I *am* afraid!"

Well, that seemed like progress. The shouting faded behind us, and I was glad to put a large distance between me and that creature with the glowing eyes. Though I did feel another stab of worry for Doomslug. I assumed she'd hyperjumped home, but what if she'd only jumped somewhere nearby in here instead?

I felt terrible for not being able to do a longer search for her. But . . . well, hopefully if she *was* in here, she was safe. Honestly, if I had to lay bets on me, M-Bot, or the slug surviving in this jungle alone, she'd top the list.

We ran until we could no longer hear gunfire. Finally Chet nodded to me, and the two of us huddled down beside a moss-covered log. This place felt so alien. What did you do surrounded by all this *life*? Planet surfaces were supposed to be barren expanses of rock and craters. That was natural and normal. Not this greenery.

"Alas," Chet said quietly, "the pirates finally seem to have noticed that the beast feeds on energy. You can't hurt them with such weapons, but approach with a small power matrix as an offering and they become quite tame! Grigs are used as pack animals, for all their fearsome appearance. She should be full from all those blasts—I bet she'll wander off and have a sleep now. Still, I think we should proceed as silently as possible, because of that thing with the shining eyes. I didn't like the look of that at all."

I nodded in agreement. "Thank you," I whispered. "For your help. I didn't get a chance to introduce myself. Spensa Nightshade."

"Excellent name!" he whispered back. "As for my help, it was a pleasure! I was already prowling Cannonade territory looking for some action, you might say. And I found it, yes I did! Helping a fellow cytonic is a hearty reward on its own. That said . . ." He trailed off, glancing at M-Bot. "Now I don't want to pry, but . . . did I hear you *speaking* to that drone?"

"Oh, right," I said. "This is M-Bot."

"Hello!" M-Bot whispered. "I'm not so scared any longer. That feels nice."

"Ah," Chet said. "You, um, brought an AI into the nowhere, did you?"

"That's . . . bad, I take it?"

"Yes, well, I believe that word to be an understatement, Spensa Nightshade. Do your people not know about the delvers?"

"We met one!" M-Bot exclaimed. "Well, Spensa did. I was being murdered at the time. But I heard about it on the news! Sounded scary."

"Ah yes, well then." Chet looked at me. "Your AI has gone fully sentient, I see? I thought you were newly arrived, but full sentience usually takes a few weeks."

"Technically," M-Bot said, hovering a few centimeters closer to him, "the word 'sentient' just means an ability to perceive and/or feel. Many people misuse this word. Instead, 'sapience' is the word for self-awareness—or intelligence like a human being. Which if you think about it is a human-centric definition. Those rascally humans and their linguistic biases.

"At any rate, my programming is telling me to explain that I'm not sapient, merely programmed to simulate sapience for my pilots. However, my programming was written by people who smell of cheese and have noodles for brains. So I'm ignoring them right now."

". . . Noodles for brains?" I asked.

"When I copied my personality to this drone, I had to leave behind several nonessential databases for space reasons. I assume my collection of keen, brilliant insults was among them."

"Yeah," I said. "You never had one of those, M-Bot."

"Really? Guess I'll have to start one up. On a scale of one to ten, how would you rate 'noodles for brains'?"

"Miss Nightshade," Chet said, "I . . . must warn you. This is incredibly dangerous. Fully sapient AI are abominations, you see. Not that I'm one to shy away from danger! But I . . . well, I suggest you keep an eye on the thing."

"Noted," I said.

"Noted," M-Bot said. "Noodle-brain."

We both looked at him.

"I'll keep using it until I have a rating," M-Bot said. "One to ten. What do you think? I need some data."

I sighed, glancing back at Chet. "You said you're an explorer?"

"Interdimensional galactic explorer," he said. "I've only been to two dimensions so far—the ordinary universe and this place. But I figured the title was fitting regardless."

"I could use a guide," I said. "And maybe some help understanding cytonics."

"Well," he admitted, "on the second I'm not going to be terribly helpful. I didn't know I *was* cytonic before falling in here, and I've had to pick up what I can on my own. I can contact people through their minds, but that's about all I can do. I hear we're supposed to be able to teleport. Wouldn't that be something?"

I didn't say anything. To be honest, I wasn't a hundred percent certain I should trust him. Something about his arrival seemed convenient. I mean, yes, awesome dinosaur antics—*so awesome*—but still . . .

"I would love to be employed as your guide, however," Chet said. "I know these fragments like I know my own boots. But tell me, before we continue. Why was that pouch so important that you gave up capturing a ship to steal it?"

I hesitated. I had a hundred more questions. Where did he come from? Were there lots of humans there? What was a fragment? I put those off for the moment, settling on something else instead.

I retrieved the pouch, then pulled out my father's pin. "What," I said, "is this?"

Chet's eyes went wide. And I felt a distinct *longing* from him. An *envy*. It was gone in a moment—he seemed to be able to cover his emotions—but it had been there, and it made me wary.

"That, young lady," he said, "is a reality icon. An important relic from your old life, imbued with your attachments to places and people you love. Those are exceptionally powerful. They create reality ashes. That silver dust? Without those, or without groups of people nearby . . ."

"What?" I asked, resisting the urge to tuck away the pin. I didn't like how he stared at it.

"We're at the fringes of the nowhere," he said, "in a region known as the belt. It's rather difficult to explain, but the longer you stay in here, the more likely you are to forget yourself. Your past, your memories, even your identity." He paused. "I remember almost nothing about my life before I came in here. It's a blank . . . nothingness.

"But I'm lucky. I've been able to trade for ashes often enough to keep myself mostly . . . well, myself. Many people forget everything quickly—including their own names. That's why the pirates grab newcomers, you see. Put them to work, keep them close. The more minds nearby, the more your memories and identity stay safe. Unless you have reality ashes. Then you can go anywhere without fear."

"And this thing makes them," I said.

"Yes," he said, oddly solemn. "The only other way is to get them off people or objects when they first arrive in the nowhere. And the ashes fade over time. It takes . . . a while. Months, maybe? Hard to keep track sometimes. So if you want to go out on your own, you need a constant supply."

Well, that explained why everyone had been so excited about my pin. I dropped the pin in the pouch and tucked it into my pocket.

Chet's eyes followed it the entire time. Then he grinned, and some of his earlier perkiness returned. "Well," he said, "a guide you want, and a guide you shall have! I fear that I've played my hand, explaining how valuable those are. But if you'd be willing to trade me some—just the ashes, not the icon—for my services, then I shall dutifully be in your employ. Shall we say, a single ash per day of service?"

Scud. I had hundreds. They might be valuable, but that deal felt like a bargain. "I'm in," I said. "I need information about this place. And I need to find . . . something called the Path of Elders?"

He cocked his head. "Where did you hear of that?"

"I'm not at liberty to say."

"Ah, espionage, is it! Well, I shall keep my tongue then, Spensa Nightshade. I know of the Path of Elders. Following it leads one to some of the first entrances into the nowhere, left by the most ancient cytonics. Traversing it won't be easy, but—"

He was interrupted by the sound of branches snapping in the forest. The ground began thumping.

"I thought you said it would go to sleep," I said.

"It . . . should have." Chet turned his head toward the noises. "I say. It *is* coming this way, isn't it? Never fear, I can tame the beast again. It is not . . ."

He trailed off. A coldness emanated from the same direction. A kind of . . . chill that penetrated my soul. And a sound reverberated in my head. No words. Just a low hiss, accompanied by an intense wave of hatred.

"I think," he said, "perhaps we should be away. With haste."

"Agreed," I said, jumping to my feet.

Chet took the lead, faster this time, and I followed as best I could. He slid across a fallen log, then hit the ground and moved with a light, quick step, ducking through a group of fronds. M-Bot zipped after him. I slid over the log awkwardly, then stumbled through the same plants, barely staying upright.

We fortunately hit a patch of less dense jungle, letting us pick up our pace further.

"Spensa," M-Bot said. "I'll note a nine from you on the rating for that insult of mine. Great, with a little room to improve. How does that sound?"

I grunted. The noises behind us were getting closer.

"Chet said that thing eats electricity," M-Bot said. "It . . . won't eat *me,* will it, Spensa?"

I just focused on trying to keep up with Chet, who waved me forward, then hurried through the underbrush. I barely avoided tripping.

"You know," M-Bot said, his volume turned down low, "it's rather inconvenient that you humans need your aspiration apparatus in order to communicate. Often when you're working hard, you also have important things to say. But you can't say them, or risk interrupting your oxygen intake."

"Point?" I asked, puffing as I ducked under some vines.

"Oh, no point," M-Bot said, doing a loop-de-loop through the vines. "Merely making small talk. With a small voice. Ha! You know, I'll bet that given some more time to evolve, your species would have fixed that problem with your lungs. I can appreciate making use of existing hardware and giving it a new function, but there *are* other areas of your body that make noise when air is pushed through them. Wouldn't it be so much more efficient if you could communicate *that* way instead?"

It was best not to encourage him when he got like this, though I *was* happy to hear him acting more like his old self. When I'd first found him in the drone, slow of speech and feeling betrayed, I worried I'd never get him back. Then after his bout of angry emotions . . . well, hearing him making fun of human biology was a relief.

The sounds from behind us grew even louder. I charged forward and met up with Chet, who had paused to wait for me. He took off again as soon as I reached him.

"Something's wrong," he said quietly. "The grig shouldn't be following. This is bad, Spensa Nightshade. Very bad . . ."

A loud snap sounded behind us. It was closer now. Too close. Terrifyingly close.

Don't look, my warrior heritage whispered to me.

I looked anyway.

The thing was back there, moving with an incongruent grace. It slid its mouth-neck among the trees, whiskers along its length feeling the way for its larger body to follow. The eyes on its torso at the base of its trunk were now glowing white. Just like the eyes of the wounded alien. And the delvers.

I felt the cold sensation increase, a pressure on my mind, as if it was reaching toward me, *searching* for me. It *knew* me.

"Chet!" I shouted, turning toward him. Somehow I'd managed to avoid tripping. "It's *right there*!"

He leaped through a line of shrubs. I followed and broke out of the jungle, then pulled up hastily as I realized I'd not only reached the end of the trees, but the end of the *land itself.*

An expanse of open air extended before me, broken by distant masses of earth and stone that were *floating* there, idly drifting. We hadn't been in an ordinary jungle, but one that grew on a giant floating chunk of ground.

And there was no path forward that I could see.

6

Chet immediately took off to the right, running along the edge of our fragment of land. "This way!"

I scrambled after him but risked a glance back. I was rewarded with an encouraging sight: though there was a meter of open space between the jungle and the cliff, the monster was wider than that. So while we could run on a straightaway, it had to maneuver around trees and tangles of foliage, its trunk-mouth-nose thing wagging angrily.

"Spensa," M-Bot said, hovering along beside me, "I am not enthused by my first experiments in self-determination. My chronometer details that since my awakening, I've spent a frightening amount of my time lost, pouting, or being chased by interdimensional monsters."

I nodded but kept running, trying to save my breath.

He zipped out a little farther ahead of me. "If you were to rate my mastery of emotions on a scale of one to ten, what would you give me?"

I grunted.

"I'll pretend that was a three," M-Bot said. "I know it wasn't optimal, but for a newly awakened robot, you have to admit that I did a fine job. In fact, all things considered, I think I deserve higher than a three. I feel bad that you'd rate me so low, Spensa."

I glanced over my shoulder again. The beast had fallen behind, but I could still see those eyes glowing on either side of its trunk.

What . . . I felt the word pushed into my mind. *What have you . . .*

I redoubled my efforts anyway, and with a burst of speed caught up to Chet. "Where," I managed to say. "Are. We. *Going*."

He pointed ahead. "Another fragment up there. You see it? I'm hoping we can leap from this one to that one, and thereby escape the beast."

Tons of these fragments hovered about, all on the same plane, at the same elevation. Like they were scattered pieces of a puzzle on an invisible table. Ahead, a tan chunk of ground was drifting near, separated from our chunk by only a few meters. Seeing it highlighted to me that there wasn't much rock under my feet. Did sections of these masses break off? Was it dangerous to be this close to the edge?

We ran anyway. And as we drew closer, I saw that the distance between our fragment and the tan one was larger than it had looked. Clearly farther than a person could jump.

Chet ran beside me, and his expression fell as he obviously realized the same problem. "Miss Nightshade," he said, glancing toward the monster, "I fear I might have led us both to our dooms. Would you prefer to try to hide in the forest or stand and fight?"

"Neither," I said, feeling that beast's *mind* pressing against mine. "M-Bot? Want to earn a ten out of ten on saving my life?"

"Ooooh," M-Bot said. "Ten is way higher than three. I mean, depending on your frame of reference, of course."

"Go attach your light-line to that other fragment," I said, panting, "then come back! Meet us by that boulder up ahead, where the two fragments are closest to one another!"

He zipped off. I wasn't certain how much mass that little drone's acclivity rings could support, but a good light-line could bear my weight and more.

"Excellent idea!" Chet said. "Keep running! We can make it!"

Behind, the beast roared, but the voice was different now. It sounded like a hundred different versions of the same roar, overlapping. I glanced over my shoulder and saw it charging toward us, nearly upon us.

Scud. Couldn't it see I wasn't worth the effort? That had to be one advantage I had over someone like Conan the Barbarian. I would barely constitute a snack. But I didn't think it was my flesh it wanted to consume.

Fortunately, M-Bot's drone moved at a good speed. He was already attaching the light-line to the other fragment. That accomplished, he streaked toward us, trailing the glowing reddish-orange line of energy.

The monster's footsteps shook the ground just behind us. I could practically feel its breath.

Come on . . .

M-Bot soared back—then pulled up short right before reaching our fragment. He jerked to a halt in the air. The light-line wasn't long enough.

He was so close though . . .

I glanced at Chet. He nodded.

Only one thing to do.

We reached the part of the fragment nearest M-Bot and—together—we jumped.

We probably made a dramatic sight, the two of us hanging in the air as the monster arrived and snapped at the place where we'd been standing. We soared over an infinite expanse and . . .

I managed to grab M-Bot's drone.

Chet missed. He'd aimed too low and ended up slamming into my waist. We all started to plummet, as M-Bot's acclivity rings proved far too weak to keep us in the air. I was almost jolted free as Chet got a grip on my leg, and we swung like a pendulum away from the jungle.

I hung on for dear life, my eyes squeezed shut, concentrating on keeping my grip on M-Bot's drone. We swung back and forth a few times before slowly coming to a rest.

I opened my eyes. M-Bot's light-line was attached to the fragment some fifteen meters above us. I held to the drone with everything I had, and Chet clung to my left leg.

"Well," M-Bot said, "you don't need to rate this rescue on a scale. I figure it's pretty much pass/fail, right?"

I grunted, hugging the drone tighter to my chest. I was really glad I was in a jumpsuit, because otherwise there was a good chance Chet would have ended up falling for eternity, his only company a pair of women's trousers.

M-Bot began to retract the light-line. Fortunately, the mechanism proved strong enough to hold us as we inched upward. I glanced behind me, where the monstrous creature stood at the edge of the jungle, watching. Those haunting eyes glowed so brightly they consumed its other features.

Vast, terrible, they intruded on my mind. *What . . . have you done . . . to the Us? WHAT HAVE YOU DONE?*

That was the delvers. I recognized their minds.

"Can you hear that?" Chet asked softly.

"Yeah," I said, squeezing my eyes shut again. I forcibly *pushed* the delvers away.

When I opened my eyes, I saw the beast retreating into the jungle, vanishing in the shadows.

"I sure am glad everything turned out all right," M-Bot said as we slowly moved upward. "Actually, that's me lying. Look at how good I've gotten at that! In truth, Spensa, I'm *still* frightened. Even though we're safe now. Why is that? Shouldn't I be relieved?"

I shook my head. "It sometimes takes a few minutes for nerves to settle. Chet, how you doing down there?"

"Contemplating my life's choices, Miss Nightshade," his voice said from below. "How is your grip, if you don't mind me asking?"

"Solid, for now," I said.

"If you start to slip, I'd request that you inform me. As your would-be rescuer, I will not allow my weight to hasten your demise! Better that one should fall than two."

"Don't talk like that!" I said. "What would happen? Would you fall forever?"

"At least until you cleverly acquired a ship and came to my rescue!" he said. "I'd hope my performance up to this point would earn such a turnabout. But let us simply hang on!"

Fortunately, I'd positioned myself to grip not just with my fingers but my whole arms. I was fairly stable, all things considered.

We eventually pulled to a halt near the rim of the fragment, where M-Bot had stuck his light-line. There were a few centimeters of slack left, but he couldn't retract that while I was clinging to his boxy form.

"You'll have to climb up first," I said to Chet.

"Right, then!" Chet said. "Sorry in advance!"

He started pulling himself up by my jumpsuit. I focused on keeping my grip. My hands were slippery from my sweat, and Chet's weight as he climbed threatened to jostle me free. Eventually however, he was able to grab something on top of the fragment and haul himself up over the side. I sighed in relief.

His hand reached down a moment later, and I accepted the help, letting him heave me up onto the surface of the new fragment. Bits of dirt and sand rained off the side, sprinkling against M-Bot's hull as he hovered up. We were on some kind of desert fragment—it was covered in sand, broken only by occasional bits of scrub plant life.

Nothing here appeared immediately threatening. Chet and I looked at each other, then both of us deliberately scooted away from the edge before collapsing and letting out exhausted sighs. My arms ached and my heart was still pounding. But when I glanced at Chet, I discovered he was *grinning*.

And . . . scud. I felt the same way. There was something incredibly thrilling about our wild escape. My friends called me crazy for this sort of reaction, but Chet seemed to get it.

"We had *no* business surviving that," I said to him.

"None whatsoever!" he agreed. "But it *is* the most fun I've had in ages."

M-Bot's drone turned from me to Chet, then back to me. "You're insane!" he said to us. "Both of you!"

"We simply appreciate life, abomination!" Chet said, dusting his clothes off and standing up. "Nothing brings you more of said appreciation than nearly losing that which you value." He walked back to the edge of the fragment and put one foot up on a rock, leaning forward as he studied the jungle fragment. It was drifting away from us at a slow speed.

Standing like that in his flight jacket, I had to admit he cut an impressive figure. He reminded me of . . . well, someone from one of the stories. The people I'd dreamed about meeting, even imagined myself joining in an adventure.

But I couldn't help being wary. Running into him here so quickly seemed coincidental. But what did I know? Maybe this strange place was full of heroic adventurers. You couldn't ask for a better ambiance. Because as Chet stood there staring outward, the jungle fragment drifted far enough to the side for me to finally make out the source of light in this place.

A gigantic, expansive bright sphere of light rose halfway over the horizon. It looked like a bomb frozen mid-explosion. Though it was difficult to tell from my vantage, it felt like hundreds—maybe thousands—of fragments led toward it, each with a different terrain.

A thousand little worlds of adventure, leading like a broken roadway toward that enormous sphere. Was that a sun? It looked far too big, and was too close. I mean, yes, it was probably hundreds and hundreds of kilometers away—but suns were supposed to be millions upon millions of kilometers away.

Plus, it didn't seem to be producing any heat, and I could look directly at it without trouble.

"We call it the lightburst," Chet said, turning back to me. "It's where the delvers live. The center of everything, in here. I assume from your expression that you'd like some answers?"

"That sure would be a nice change . . ."

"And you still intend to follow the Path of Elders?" he asked.

"That's why I'm here."

"Then our journey begins," he said, walking over and offering a hand to pull me to my feet. "Join me, Spensa Nightshade, as we head toward adventure and I do some explaining."

7

"All right," I said as we started across the desert. "First question. *How* can this place be the nowhere? I've been in the nowhere before during hyperjumps. I think I'd remember flying chunks of stone and monsters with teeth in their noses."

"An astute observation. What you experienced before is the *inside* of the lightburst." Chet spun around, both arms extended as he walked. "We are outside it now—in the belt, which is a boundary area. Things of our world—like time, individuality, matter itself—have leaked into the belt. Like how you get brackish water between an ocean and a river."

"I've . . . never seen an ocean," I said.

"Tragic!" he said. "Perhaps imagine two countries next to one another. Over time, the people living near the border might pick up the other country's language. Start to practice some of its habits, customs, traditions. Well, that's the belt: the part of the nowhere that abuts the somewhere—the ordinary universe—so has some of the same rules. Those who tossed you in here didn't warn you?"

"I wasn't thrown in," I said. "I jumped in on purpose. To escape being captured."

"Some might call that extreme," Chet said.

"It was my warrior's duty," I explained, "to avoid capture, so that I could not be tortured into betraying my friends."

Chet grinned. "I like the way you think, young woman. Honor, valor. From those I've met in here over recent years, I worried such ideals had been lost!"

"There is this galactic empire," I told him, "called the Superiority. They . . . have a different perspective on battle."

"I know the Superiority," Chet said. "They have a large base in here for extracting acclivity stone."

"And so they must get the stone out," I said.

"Yes, but the only active portals for that are operated by the Superiority," Chet explained. "From what I know of them, they are unlikely to allow access. They seem a rather controlling bunch, led by . . . some unsavory individuals."

"They're absolute jerks," I agreed. The word made me sentimental and think of Jorgen. It was a stupid reaction, but it felt like years since I'd last heard his earnest voice.

I'd almost been able to go back to that. Instead I'd come here—a decision I desperately hoped was the correct one.

Please, Jorgen, I thought, *stay safe. And be smarter than I've been.*

Chet snapped a branch off a nearby dried-out shrub, and we stopped walking for a moment as he drew a wide circle in the sand, with a smaller circle at the center.

"Imagine this as the nowhere," he said. "The lightburst is this circle at the center. All of this larger portion is the belt—where the fragments float. I've always thought it resembled a sunny-side-up egg, the yolk being the lightburst and the white being all the fragments."

"Got it," I said. "Where are we?"

"Right at the edge," he said, stabbing the stick at the very rim of the drawing. "This is pirate territory. Specifically, we're in the region claimed by the Cannonade Faction, near the border of Broadsider Faction territory. That's where we can start the Path of Elders."

"Which is . . ."

"When people come into the nowhere, they leave an impression," he explained. "Memories, embedded into the stone of the portals. You can view these—and a long time ago, some cytonics organized a few of the portals into a kind of narrative. One walks the Path of Elders to see firsthand the lore of the ancient cytonics." He hesitated. "I've never done it, but it supposedly requires you to travel all the way inward to the lightburst."

I turned toward the enormous glowing sphere. "That . . . seems like quite a distance."

"It's a trip of roughly fifty thousand klicks."

That was a daunting distance. Even in a Poco starfighter at full speed, it was a trip that would take many hours. On foot . . . Well, scud. We were talking years.

"So," I said, "we really are going to have to find a way to steal a ship."

"I'm looking forward to it!" Chet said.

"I'll try not to distract us by going the other direction this time."

"You made the correct choice," he said. "Reality icons are worth more than ships. Unfortunately, I fear that even with a ship our journey will be difficult." He drew a little more on his map of the nowhere. "I know where the Path of Elders starts—here in the rim, inside Broadsider territory. I can get us there. But to get any farther inward, we're going to have to move through Superiority territory, which will be *very* difficult. They have long-range scanners and dozens of starfighters. If we try to fly through, they're likely to intercept us."

"I'm pretty handy with a starfighter," I said.

"Well, I'm excited to see you fly, then!" he said. "The Superiority forces aren't the best pilots. In fact, everyone in here tends to be people the Superiority *forced* in. Not all are exiles, but the workers are pressured into their jobs at the acclivity stone quarries at their base, Surehold.

"Most of the pirates are miners who have defected. The entire place is a mess, Spensa Nightshade. Full of desperate people trying to survive. To move inward along the Path, we're going to have to sneak past them all. And then . . . Well, if we have to approach the lightburst, it's going to get even worse."

He pointed at the remainder of the space, past Superiority territory, inward toward the lightburst. "This is No Man's Land. The fragments are more stable through this section, with less bumping or colliding. But this is delver territory."

"Isn't all of the nowhere delver territory?" I asked.

"Yes and no," he said. "Out here in the belt, things are too much like the somewhere for them. They can't see into this region well, and you can hide from them here. But if you get into No Man's Land . . . well, it will be impossible to avoid their attention. I've heard of pilots in No Man's Land seeing things that aren't real. Or crumbling to dust."

I thought it through, surveying the crude drawing. M-Bot hovered over, inspected it, and took a picture.

"What's to the far right?" I said, pointing. "And the far left? Can you go all the way around?"

"Possibly," Chet said, "but in those directions there are large expanses with no fragments. Empty sections are dangerous to cross, even with a ship. But the Path of Elders is forward, not to the sides. Still determined to walk it?"

"Absolutely," I said.

"That's the spirit!" he said, standing.

"Once we do all this, there will still be one problem," I said. "I'll need to get home. If the Superiority doesn't let me use their portals, then what?"

"Well . . ." Chet said. "Theoretically there's a way out. A quite simple one." He turned and looked toward the lightburst.

Right. That was the center of the nowhere—the place where I traveled when I hyperjumped. "If I get into the lightburst, I can jump home?"

"I believe so," he said. "I've never dared get close enough. But it should work—it's like a giant portal between dimensions, after all. I'll admit, though, the lightburst intimidates me. Inside, there is no time. There is no place. It's like . . . a single point somehow as vast as a universe."

Scud, that broke my brain to think about. I took a deep breath. "Let's get on the Path first."

"Onward we go, then!" He pointed with his stick, like some general with a sword. "We'll need to cross eight fragments to get to where the Path starts. But in relative terms, that's right round the corner!"

We continued across the sand, and M-Bot went hovering off to investigate some of the local plants. Just walking was harder to do than I'd imagined. It took extra effort to move when the ground kept shifting beneath you. Yet I was excited. This was all so new, so *interesting*.

I fished in my pocket and brought out my father's pin. I felt . . . serenity, having it in my hand. How odd.

Chet eyed it as he had before. Hungry. As if he physically *couldn't* tear his eyes away from it. I trusted him well enough, but . . . well, that hunger made me tuck the icon away. Instead I brought out one of the reality ashes and handed it to him. It was merely a speck, but he took it reverently and tucked it into a pouch from his pocket. Then he held that pouch, breathing in and out, and visibly relaxed.

"You said people lose themselves in here without those," I said. "Is that what was happening to that burl? The pirate whose face was . . . melting?"

Chet shook his head. "I don't know *what* that was. It felt like something far worse. Like . . ."

"A delver was possessing her."

"Indeed. I normally enjoy new and exciting events, yet I would not wish to repeat that one! But thank you for the ash. It is . . . comforting to hold."

There was a haunting tone to his voice. "Do . . . you remember *anything* of who you were?" I asked. "Before?"

"No," he whispered. "I have forgotten myself entirely. I remember some few things about the last few days before I entered—some caverns, and old ruins—but that time is so vague to me. Even my early days in here are fuzzy. That's not surprising, I confess. I've been here a long time—almost two centuries, I think!"

"Wait, two *hundred* years?" I asked.

"Well, around a hundred and seventy," he replied. "Best I can count. Time is hard to track in here, but I wrote down the date—and have been able to confirm it a few times in order to help me keep track. Yet I haven't aged a single day.

"I haven't always been able to get ashes, so during those times I took work for one group or another, since people staying together can replicate the effect of ashes."

I found it daunting to think about what had happened to Chet. If I stayed too long, would I forget Gran-Gran? My father? My friends? Scud, I needed some time to process that.

Unfortunately, M-Bot chose that moment to come hovering up, jabbering excitedly. "Did you see those things over there, Spensa? Those are cacti! They're *so beautiful*. Is it normal to see something like that, and feel so overwhelmed? I . . . I want to write *poetry* about how pretty they are."

"Uh . . ." I said.

"Cacti are so neat, they make me want to dance. Is that a good poem? Will you rate it on a scale of one to ten?"

"Poems don't deserve numbers, M-Bot. But if you like it, then it's wonderful."

"Great! Let's see what my rhythm and rhyme analysis protocols say . . . Oh, Spensa. That's a *terrible* poem. You should be ashamed for liking it. You know, 'cacti' is such a funny word. I think 'cactuses' would have been less funny, don't you? And easier to rhyme?"

I just wanted a break right now—though I loved the robot, he could be a bit much. "Hey, I think I saw a mushroom," I said, pointing.

"What, *really*?" he said. "Where!"

"Between those two bushes over there, in the distance."

He zoomed off. I found myself thinking about what Chet had said about his age. Two *hundred* years?

"So . . . are we immortal in here?" I asked.

"No," he said. "And I think my not-aging might be due to my powers. Other people do age, and unfortunately, ordinary wounds can still kill us. But our biological functions are odd. You won't need food in here, for instance—and after a few days you won't even need water. We do need to sleep, but it doesn't seem to be required as often.

"Night never falls. The lightburst doesn't move. And the longer you stay, the more the passage of time will all blend together. Days. Weeks. Years. Centuries . . ." He shook his head.

"I'll admit," I said, "I'm starting to feel a little tired. It's been . . . kind of a long day for me."

"Well, then!" he said. "There is some shelter farther along this fragment! I suggest we take a break there."

We'd walked for another few minutes when M-Bot came zipping back up. "You didn't see a mushroom, did you?" he demanded.

"No," I said. "Just wanted to distract you."

"Why would you do that?"

I shrugged, not wanting to explain. "It's a joke humans sometimes play. You trick someone by sending them on a meaningless chase."

"What a terrible joke. Scanning culture databases. Oh. It's called 'made you look.' What an original name. Your kind has a terrible sense of humor, something I can authentically say now, as I am truly alive. But your prank is not important. It occurred to me that cacti are *desert mushrooms*. They look kind of the same. And act kind of the same. Except for the whole 'living in an arid location' part, which would kill most mushrooms . . ."

Great. After walking a little farther we crested a small dune, and Chet pointed ahead. "See those hills?" he asked.

I picked out some rocky chunks rising from the desert.

"That will be our housing for the 'night,'" Chet explained. "I'll jog on ahead to secure it and be certain the cave there is safe. Join me at your own speed! You're looking a little run-down, but certainly with good reason!"

I nodded, grateful as he jogged off. Once, I might have been angry at the implication I was too weak—but he had a lot of experience in this place, and I had practically none. I was woman enough to admit that pushing myself now was a bad idea.

So I followed at a slower pace, M-Bot at my side. "M-Bot," I said, something occurring to me, "you got a historical database from Superiority records, right?"

"Sure did!" he said. "I had to dump a lot of it, but I kept many text files, which are small. I now know when jazz music developed. You know, in case it's important—"

"Chet said he's around two hundred years old," I said. "Would he have been alive during the Second Human War?"

"Most certainly, if his guess of his age is accurate," M-Bot said. "The Second Human War began two hundred and fifty years ago, but lasted decades. It was characterized by the first attempts to weaponize the delvers, who had appeared near the end of the First Human War.

"The first war started when humans escaped Earth and found an entire galaxy full of people who enforced nonaggression by imprisoning, exiling, or executing those who showed aggressive tendencies. Let's just say they were *not* ready for your people. Boy, howdy."

". . . 'Boy, howdy'?"

"Cool, huh? I just made that up." He buzzed around me. "No, I didn't! That was a lie! Ha! I can say them *so easily* now. Anyway, if Chet there was born two hundred years ago, he'd have lived during the time known as 'the stilling,' when the galaxy was actively trying to stop using wireless communication. These were the times punctuated by the worst and most terrible delver attacks, and when the war was starting to end."

"When was the original colony on Detritus destroyed?" I asked.

"That's uncertain," M-Bot said, "as Detritus was a secret project, and the Superiority didn't have records of it. We can guess it was between three hundred and two hundred years ago."

"So Chet wouldn't have been alive when it was made?"

"A reasonable assumption," M-Bot said.

We reached the hills. Chet had disappeared into a cave there, but I could see his footsteps leading in.

"For further reference," M-Bot said, buzzing up beside me, "I crashed on Detritus a hundred and seventy-two years ago."

"Huh," I said. "Chet said he came in here right around a hundred and seventy years ago. He mentioned remembering some caves in the place he was before he came in here. And ruins . . ."

I trailed off. We looked at each other. Or, well, I looked at the box that contained M-Bot's circuits, and he focused his lenses on me.

Then we both took off toward the cave.

8

The cavern was small, barely as large as one of the bunk rooms on Detritus. A soft tinkling sound accompanied some water dribbling in through the wall and gathering in a shallow pool at the rear.

Chet knelt there, washing his hands. He looked up as I skidded to a stop, kicking up sand, my fatigue momentarily forgotten. "Chet," I said. "You said you remembered some things about the day before you entered."

"Just bits and pieces."

"Did you know someone named Commander Spears?" I demanded, naming the man who had been M-Bot's pilot all those years ago, when he'd crashed on Detritus.

Chet frowned. He shook his hands off, then stood up and ran them through his silvering hair. Slowly, he reached to the chest pocket of his flight jacket and took something out. A patch, as if from a uniform.

It said SPEARS on it.

"Oh, *scud,*" I said.

"I . . . think I crashed somewhere?" he said. "A place with caverns, and . . . metal platforms in the sky? It's so fuzzy, though I have a distinct impression of a wall full of strange lines. I now recognize that as a nowhere portal. I must have fallen through."

Scud. Scud, scud, scud.

M-Bot hovered at my side, and I could sense his concern. Like, *actually* sense it. I could *feel* his emotions. He was worried. Apprehensive. Shocked.

"I found your ship," I said. "It had an AI on it. You are M-Bot's old pilot."

"I . . . hardly think I could fit in a drone . . ." Chet said.

"He used to be in a ship," I explained. "An extremely advanced one. All he could remember about his pilot was the name, and some orders. That was *you,* Chet."

"Nonsense," he said. "Why, I find it difficult to say this without giving offense, but I would *never* have fraternized with an AI. They draw the attention of the delvers!"

"You have the patch," I said, pointing. "You remember Detritus, my homeworld. You *are* Commander Spears."

Yet another part of me rebelled against the idea. *This seems impossible,* I thought. What were the chances that we'd enter the nowhere and find M-Bot's original pilot within *minutes*? Something very suspicious was going on.

"We were friends, Chet," M-Bot said, flying closer. "I mean . . . I don't *remember* that, but I felt it. We must have been. I . . . I tried to follow your final orders, all those years. Kept trying until I ran out of power and shut down . . . Waiting . . ."

Chet sighed. "I don't know much, but I've heard that computers have severely limited processing speeds unless you let their circuitry dip into the nowhere for calculations. It's a trade-off. Either deal with a nearly useless computer, or . . ." He nodded toward M-Bot.

"They come to life?" I guessed.

"Everyone talks about it in here," Chet said. "The pirates who used to be Superiority? They whisper about it. You can't let a true

AI continue to function. They'll eventually draw the delvers to you. To keep an abomination like that is . . . well, it's certain death. I'm sorry."

"Why?" I asked. "Why would AIs bring the delvers?"

"I can't remember," he admitted.

I didn't know what to make of that. Or any of this. It *did* seem that Chet was Spears though. We'd wondered what had happened to him after crashing on Detritus and leaving M-Bot's ship in that cave.

It stood to reason that Detritus would have had a way into the nowhere, as we'd found abundant acclivity stone on the planet. The people who had built Detritus must have had mining operations, like the Superiority now had. Maybe they'd traveled here using that spot in the caverns that had carvings like the ones on the portals.

"I've tried to get back," Chet said, wistful. "Find the place where I entered, then go through? Seemed like quite an adventure! But I've forgotten the way to that portal—and every one I've found since has been locked. The people who made those portals, whoever they were, grew *exceedingly* frightened of what was in here."

He turned away from me and M-Bot. "Anyway, we should bed down! Camp for the night, such as it is. Tomorrow is a big day! With a solid hike, we can make it to the first portal in the Path of Elders."

He took off his jacket and began rolling it up, evidently to use it as a pillow.

It was *too* convenient. *Too* improbable. Perhaps . . . perhaps I'd been drawn to this location, when hyperjumping into the nowhere? Because of him? Could that explain the coincidence?

Unfortunately, I was starting to feel genuinely exhausted. I wasn't in much of a state to process this information. I pulled off my own jacket to use as a pillow, then hesitated as I noticed M-Bot was gone.

I cursed myself softly. Of *course* he'd left, after hearing what Spears had said. I forced myself to hike back out of the cave and found him focused on a small cactus.

"M-Bot—" I said.

"You know," he whispered, "I anticipated this. We even talked about it, remember? I knew they were afraid of me. Why else would my own programming forbid me from things like piloting my ship? So yes, ha ha! I was right. My pilot was afraid of me . . ." He trailed off. "It would have been okay for me to be wrong."

"Look," I said, stepping up to him, "it doesn't matter."

"It doesn't matter what the *one person* who *knows anything about where I came from* says?" M-Bot answered, his voice rising. "I think it matters, Spensa. I really think it matters."

For the first time I was glad he was in a drone rather than his old ship. There was a certain sense of personality and emotion to the way he moved now, the way he drooped in the air, his grabber arms dangling beneath him, limp. "It's like finding out," he said in an even smaller voice, "that your father hates you . . ."

"I don't believe him," I said. "About you."

"Why?"

"Because I haven't fought an evil wizard yet."

M-Bot twisted in the air. Then he rose up before me and tilted his drone sideways, perhaps in imitation of a cocked head. "You know," he said, "I was beginning to think I could follow your leaps in logic."

"No, listen," I said, leaning in. "In the old stories, there was almost *always* an evil wizard. Aladdin had to face an evil wizard. And Conan? He killed like a billion evil wizards. There are tons of other examples. But how long have *we* been fighting? With *no* evil wizards? We're bound to face one eventually." I put my arm around his drone and pointed toward the cave. "I don't know what's going on, but somebody or something *has* to be messing with us. We come in here and *immediately* find your old pilot? Run the numbers, M-Bot."

"Run what numbers?" he asked.

"You know. The statistics and stuff. Math it. What are the chances we'd run into him?"

"I have no way of calculating that," M-Bot said. "You assume I could devise a percentage chance for something with so many variables—most of which are unknown, likely unquantifiable?"

I didn't push. "Look, that might be Commander Spears. It makes sense that he could have fallen into the nowhere. But his memories are spotty; maybe he's *not* Spears, and this is some kind of setup. But even if he *is* Spears, my gut says we didn't meet him by chance. Trust me, M-Bot. In some way, in some form, we're facing an evil wizard. Or the modern equivalent."

"Perhaps," M-Bot said. "But you have to accept that there is evidence for what he's saying. About my kind being dangerous. My creators were *obviously* afraid of me."

"It doesn't matter," I said. "You're my friend. I trust you." I rubbed my forehead. "But right now, I'm *exceptionally* tired. Weak flesh body, remember? Let's talk about this after I get some sleep. Okay?"

"I will process this information," he said, "but I won't do anything with it until I consult with you."

"Good enough," I said, then paused. "Watch Chet and wake me if he gets up, all right? I trust him well enough, but just . . . let's be careful."

"Agreed."

We started back toward the cave. "Though," I added, really starting to feel my fatigue, "if any monsters arrive to eat me, kindly ask them to do it quietly. That might let me get a few extra seconds of shut-eye."

Inside I got a drink, then bedded down with my jacket as a pillow. I drifted off, hoping that my first "night" in the nowhere wouldn't turn out to be too weird.

I obviously should have known better.

INTERLUDE

I drifted.

And I searched.

Though my body was still exhausted, my mind quested outward, somehow conscious. This had never happened to me before, but it felt like a natural extension of my powers—my mind existing separate from my body, as happened when I entered the nowhere during a hyperjump.

I once again tried to hyperjump, with no luck. I wasn't completely "here," so to speak. So instead I expanded my mind, searching, listening. I felt more confident with this part of my powers. Not only had I been able to hear the stars since my childhood, I'd recently managed to contact Chet using that ability.

I pushed myself. I needed a destination. A location. A link.

There.

I found someone . . . who was searching for me?

I felt an immediate panic. Was it Brade? Some servant of the delvers? At the same time, I *knew that mind*. It wasn't Brade. It was . . .

I was suddenly inside the cockpit of a Defiant Defense Force starfighter, Poco model. I was awkwardly crammed in the rear storage area behind the pilot's seat. The Poco darted through outer space, destructor fire flaring nearby.

Jorgen was flying it.

I wasn't prepared for the rush of emotions that came from seeing him—longing, passion, worry. I reached to touch him, but my hand passed through the chair. I could feel the ship shake around me, hear him curse softly as he took a sharp turn, GravCaps barely compensating.

Was I actually here? Was this real?

His face reflected in the transparent canopy of the ship, lit from the glow of his console. There were a dozen tiny cuts on his face, and I wondered what could have caused that. The last time I'd seen him had been on that first day when I'd left Detritus for Starsight. While that had been only three weeks ago, it felt like an eternity. A part of me had worried I'd never see him again.

Now here he was. Serious as ever, almost too perfect to be real. His face a mask of concentration and sudden panic as he looked up and—

"Gah!" he shouted, jerking his ship to the side. He scrambled to look behind the seat. Though he stared straight at me, he didn't seem to find anything.

He turned around and hesitantly squinted at the canopy glass. As if trying to make out . . .

A reflection. When I'd seen the eyes—the delvers—in the somewhere, it had usually happened in a reflection. Could he see me the same way? To test my theory, I waved.

"Spensa?" he said. "Are you . . . Oh, scud. Are you dead?"

Right. That was probably what this looked like. I tried to speak, but I didn't have lungs here. So I tried another way, reaching out to him with my cytonic senses.

"No, I'm not dead," I said, hoping he'd hear. Or sense. Or whatever. "Though I probably should be, all things considered."

He cocked his head.

"Can you hear me?" I asked.

"I can . . . feel the meaning of your words. Where are you? What's happening?"

"I'm in the nowhere," I said. "The dimension where we go when we hyperjump. I . . . kind of fell in. On purpose. In my defense, I was being chased by half an army at the time."

He grinned, and the lines around his eyes softened. I could literally *feel* the tension melt out of him. He'd been worried about me. I mean, I'd expected he would be, but feeling it made me choke up a little. I'd spent my life being the person most others tried to avoid.

That had changed. I had a place where I belonged. With him and the rest of my friends in Skyward Flight. How I longed to return to them. How I—

A flash of red destructor fire slammed into his ship's shield, crackling. His low-shield alarm started throwing a fit on his dash.

"Jorgen!" I shouted. "Fly! You're in the middle of a firefight, idiot!"

"I'm trying! It's a *little* distracting to have your ship suddenly be haunted by the ghost of your not-dead girlfriend!" He steered the ship in a precise evasive pattern.

I melted a little. Girlfriend? Was that how he thought of me? I mean, we'd kissed. Once. But . . . I didn't think it had been formalized or anything. I hadn't even brought him any dead orc carcasses, which I was pretty sure was the way the stories said to show a guy you wanted to go official.

Apparently my feelings radiated, because Jorgen—still steering—continued. "Or . . . you know . . . whatever it is you are. To me. And I am, to you."

"It works," I said. "I'll get you an orc later."

"What?"

"It might look a *lot* like a rat. Fair warning."

He grinned, diving away from the destructor fire. Judging by his proximity monitor, he'd lost his tail.

I wished I could touch him. He looked up and met my eyes in the reflection, and I knew he felt the same.

"Nothing can ever be normal for us, huh?" I asked.

"I don't know," he said. "My life was pretty normal about a year ago. Then something remarkable happened." He smiled. "I wouldn't go back for the world. Here, let me get us a little breathing room."

He called in the flight to go on the defensive and give him time to reignite his shield. He flew his ship out of the main battle and some members of Skyward Flight stuck nearby, offering support and distracting enemies who drew too close.

I finally shook out of my stupor of meltiness. "Jorgen, what's the sitrep? How long has it been?"

"A few days since you came here, then vanished," he said.

Good. I'd spent a few days unconscious in a Superiority hospital, then one day in the nowhere. So it seemed that time passed at around the same speed in both the somewhere and the belt. Good to know.

"We've heard from your friend Cuna," Jorgen added.

"Oh, Saints! They *are* alive? I'd worried."

"Yeah," he said. "They're safe, but trapped. We're trying to figure out how to make the slugs work for hyperdrives."

"Slugs?"

"You missed that part," he said, diverting power from his boosters to the shield igniter. "We have a whole flock of them. Um, a herd? A pod? A bunch of slugs. They were in the caves."

"What, *really*?" I asked. "How did you find them?"

"I . . . um . . . heard them," he said. "As I'm hearing you."

"You're cytonic!" I said, pointing. "Your family feared it was in your bloodline! Ha! That must be why I could find you."

"I've been training with Gran-Gran," he said. "I'm . . . not very good at any of it." He grew solemn. "Spensa, it's bad. The war."

"How bad?"

"The entire Superiority is mobilizing. I had no idea how many planets they controlled. And we're isolated here. We're trying to get the slugs to work, but we have so much to learn, and . . ."

He again met my eyes in the glass. "And we need you. I need you. What can we do to get you out of there?"

I winced. Not because I didn't appreciate the sentiment, but . . . Well, he had to know.

"Jorgen, I came to the nowhere by choice," I said. "When I jumped through the portal, I realized I could come home, but I decided not to. Because . . ." Scud, how did I put this? "I have something I need to do here, Jorgen."

He frowned, looking at me in the reflection.

"I can't come back yet," I explained. "Not until I've learned what this place can teach me. I'm sorry, but if I did return, I'd be just another fighter. I need to be something more."

"You think they'll use the delvers again," he said, perhaps reading my emotions.

"I know they will," I said. "Winzik won't give up because of a single setback. And Jorgen, I *need* to be able to stop him. To do that, I have to understand what I am—and more importantly, what the delvers are. Does that make sense?"

"You think you can find these answers in the nowhere?"

"Yes. Jorgen, I'm on a *quest*."

He grinned. "That might be the single most Spensa-like thing I've ever heard you say."

"You're not mad at me?"

"I'm worried for you," he said. "But if you're right . . . if the delvers are still in play . . ."

I knew, from our research into the past, that this wasn't the first time someone had sought to weaponize the delvers. Every attempt I knew of had ended in disaster, but people continued to try. Because if you could control the thing that ate planets, who would dare stand against you?

"I trust you," Jorgen said, meeting my eyes reflected in the glass. "If you think this is important, then keep going. We will resist the Superiority until you return."

His confidence in me felt wonderful; I could feel it like a warmth radiating from him.

Jorgen unbuckled himself, then turned around, his knees on the seat. He closed his eyes, and I felt his attention on me. He reached out his hand, and I *swore* I could feel it cupping my cheek. I reached out to him too, and could *almost* feel his skin.

"We'll hold out, Spensa," he promised. "Until you find what you need. Which you will. I've learned never to bet against you." He smiled, his eyes closed. "After all, I might win the bet, but I'd still end up with a knife in my arm."

"Quick tip," I whispered. "Go for the thigh instead. Makes it harder for them to chase you down." I leaned forward, wanting to be closer to him, even if we could barely feel each other. But I began to fade.

Scud, I suddenly felt *exhausted*. It had been only a few minutes, but I soon faded completely, and ended up drifting in blackness. Try as I might, I couldn't find Jorgen again.

My mind began to fuzz. I knew I was heading toward true sleep, and started to relax . . .

A voice.

I pulled myself back to awareness. I *knew* that voice. "My, my," it said.

Winzik.

The words pierced the darkness, reaching toward something else. Beings. Entities.

Delvers.

I could sense them now—as an infinite number of white lights. The voice I'd heard was speaking to them. "No need to be so brutal," it continued. "So *aggressive*. I come to you with an offer! A trade. You have something I want, and I have something you want. They are not so different, are they?"

That voice . . . that wasn't actually Winzik's voice. It was *Brade's* voice—though of course the word "voice" was an approximation. She must have been relaying Winzik's words, like an interpreter.

I was overhearing them—listening in, spying, as I'd been trained for so long by Gran-Gran. My phantom sense to hear the stars.

You hurt us, the delvers said to Winzik. *You are noise. You are not a person. You are pain.*

"I am a noise that can *end* that pain," Winzik promised through Brade. "I can round up every cytonic in the galaxy. I can make it so none of them ever bother you again. Never . . . corrupt you again."

Oh, scud. They *wanted* that. I could feel it.

Speak, they said.

"I must be in control of my empire," Winzik said. "Once I am, I will find and stop every cytonic. I can't *be* in control, however, if you destroy my people when I summon you."

Leave us alone, the delvers said. *Stop yelling! Stop it all! Why hasn't it stopped?*

I sorted through the impressions, and *kind of* understood. To the delvers, all times and places were as one. But by interacting with us, they were forced to confine themselves to our way of existence.

That said, they couldn't truly see the future. Rather, they existed in all times at once, and so couldn't separate and distinguish future from past or present.

Yeah, it was tough to explain. Regardless, I felt their pain. That, it seemed, was universal across dimensions.

"My, my," Winzik said. "No need to shout. *I* can make the pain stop. But if I lose this war . . . Well, would you like a repeat of what happened to the delver who was corrupted? The noise who did that is among the noises I fight against."

It seemed he knew how I'd saved Starsight. I wanted to scream at the delvers, explain that I'd *helped* one of their number, not corrupted them. But suddenly I understood what they'd meant earlier, when chasing me. When they'd said "What did you do to the Us?" they'd been referring to the one I'd separated out.

We consider this trade, the delvers said to Winzik.

"Yes, take your time," Winzik said. "As much as you need."

We have no need of time. We hate it.

Yes, they did. But I could feel something more from them. Beyond their hatred of time and individuality, there was a hatred of something else. Something that was coming. Something they . . . feared? I pushed a little harder, to get more information.

They turned toward me. Scud.

I panicked and darted away, retreating toward my body. Thinking about the implications of what I'd heard would have to wait, for my mental fatigue seized control.

I found true sleep at last.

PART TWO

Autonomous Domestic Cleaning Drone (modified)

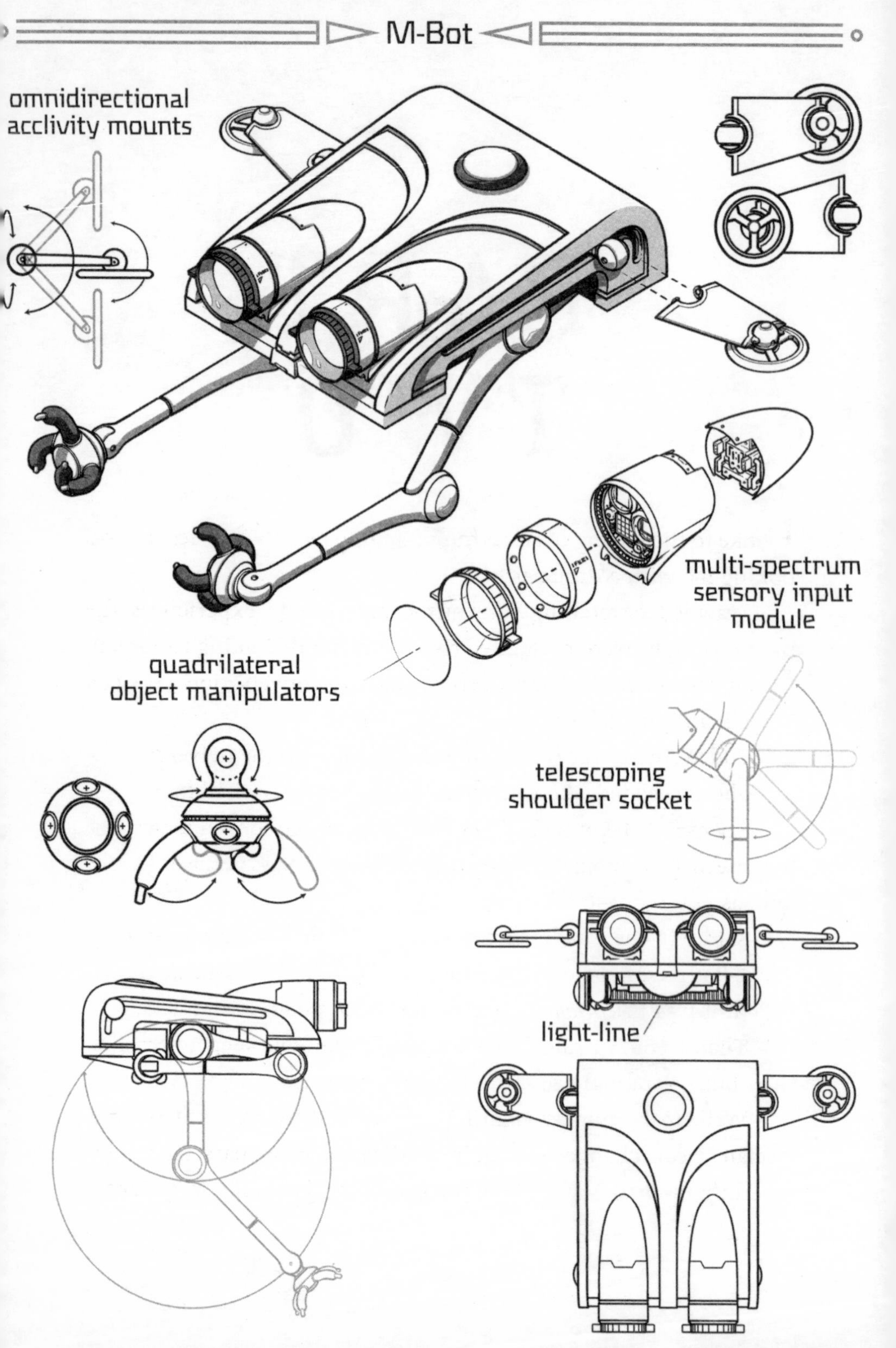

9

I woke to the feeling of something nudging me. M-Bot? Yes, he was poking me with a drone arm.

I yawned, stretching. Curiously, my strange experiences the previous night were perfectly crisp in my mind. Talking to Jorgen, *feeling* his concern. Then overhearing the conversation between Winzik and the delvers.

Scud. Winzik was trying to make a deal with the delvers.

If he succeeded, the war would take a very, *very* bad turn.

"Spensa?" M-Bot said. "You have been asleep for ten hours, per my internal chronometer. Chet just got up and left the cave. I woke you, as you requested."

I sat up in the dim light, my back stiff from resting on stone.

M-Bot hovered closer. "I," he said, "would like to be acknowledged. It was *exceptionally* boring watching you two all night."

"Thank you," I said. "I'm sorry to make you keep watch like that, but I slept more soundly knowing you were there."

"Well, to be honest, waiting isn't as bad for me as it is for a human. I can change how quickly time seems to pass for me by speeding up or slowing down my processor. I'm going to go take a cactus break. Let me know if you need me to do anything else super boring."

He floated off out of the cave, and I followed. Chet stood on some of the higher rocks of the hills here, looking outward. A heroic pose, focused, determined.

I climbed up beside him and adopted a similar pose, staring across the expanse of flying chunks to the distant lightburst. Home of the delvers.

"Two hundred years," Chet said. "And I'm finally going to do it. Walk the Path of Elders."

"Why have you never tried?"

"At first, I didn't know about it," he said. "After that, I didn't really understand what it was. Now . . ." He glanced at me. "I've never found a place I was afraid to travel, Spensa Nightshade. I always thought I'd be willing to explore everything and anything! But then I found something inside me, inside my head, that I didn't understand."

"I felt kind of the same way."

"It all worried me," he said. "Chet Starfinder, afraid to explore his own mind . . ." He glanced outward. "I can make a picture in my head of the *entire belt*. I can *visualize* it somehow, know my way to every fragment. That's how it manifests for me—other than speaking mind to mind. What about you?"

"I can do the speaking thing too, obviously," I said. "And more, I seem to be able to *intercept* thoughts that others send out, even when they don't want me to. I can use what I hear, interpret it, use it in battle by instinct. Plus, I can hyperjump—moving instantly from place to place."

"So it *is* possible," Chet said. "That sounds extremely useful."

I grimaced. "Less so when you're as untrained as I am. Regardless, being able to *see* the landscape around you? Like you have . . . sonar? That sounds pretty awesome."

"It's useful for an explorer, I must admit!" he exclaimed, then pointed. "The fragment you need to reach is in that exact direction, but we'll have to take a roundabout path, I'm afraid. We travel at the whims of the fragments, and can cross only when they bump against one another. I can see the route, fortunately. Eight fragments. We should be there in about a day's time." He looked at me and smiled widely. "Are you prepared, Spensa Nightshade, for an adventure?"

"Absolutely."

"Then onward!" Chet said, then slid down the rock slope and landed on the ground in an expert maneuver.

I followed almost as skillfully.

"Wonderful!" he said as I landed.

"I've got some experience caving," I explained.

He led us off then, M-Bot zooming along behind as we struck outward. Over the next little while, I got a fairly good picture of this place—at least on the small scale. The fragments were of different sizes, but on average took around two hours to cross. And there was such *variety* to them. The first we traversed was covered in strange tall weeds with red tips. The next was dominated by towering rock formations rising high like sentinels. The third had enormous waterfalls that tumbled from heights and then flowed straight off the side of the fragment in some impossible continuous cycle.

The travel challenged me to the extent of my physical abilities. On the second fragment, we had to rappel down the sides of cliffs using the light-line. On the third we forded a river, then crawled through a tunnel behind a waterfall. The fourth fragment was a prairie with many ravines and was populated by beasts that looked like rhinoceroses, only with two heads and fearsome teeth. It was touch-and-go as we hid behind rocks while they wandered past, seeking prey. Chet explained they didn't need to eat, but were instinctually driven to hunt.

The next fragment was rocky and barren, with only a few small trees for plant life. We had to wait on the far side to meet up with the next one—and while we stood there, Chet suddenly rushed us beneath the cover of a small scraggly tree with a thankfully thick canopy. Soon starships soared past—pirates on the lookout for slaves to capture.

Chet saw me watching them from beneath the trees, and must have noticed the hunger in my eyes.

"There is a pirate base a little beyond our first destination," he explained. "If you are still so bold as to want to try, I believe we can acquire a starship there—through roguish means, naturally."

I grinned at his phrasing, and then we scampered out—risking being spotted by the pirates—in order to catch the next fragment before it floated away. We skidded down the slope and leapt across together, reaching a swampy fragment with decaying trees and soft ground.

A *real* swamp! Places like I'd imagined from childhood, listening to Gran-Gran's stories. They were all here, each landscape in microcosm, inviting me to explore. As we traveled, I began to feel an exhilaration—and something more, something deeper.

Confidence.

It felt like it had been forever. I'd spent weeks uncertain of myself as I infiltrated the Superiority, trying to act like another person, lying and sneaking. I'd been terrified that my personality faults would cause me to fail the mission, and thereby doom my people.

It was so *satisfying* to be able to do something that I was good at. I'd spent a decade exploring the caverns of Detritus, and had trained physically for the task. I could tell, from the way Chet spoke and acted, that he hadn't anticipated my expertise in this—and he seemed to find it thrilling to be guiding someone who could keep up with him.

It made me feel wonderful. Like I could accomplish anything. I *would* walk this Path of Elders, and I *would* learn the secrets of the delvers. I'd bring this information back to my people, and together we *would* defeat the Superiority.

I could do it. I really could.

I loved that feeling.

"Spensa?" M-Bot asked as we moved around the perimeter of the swamp fragment—the footing was more solid here. "You appear more . . . alive than I've seen you recently."

"I'm merely confident," I said. "That we can do this."

"I'm not," he said. "It seems like so much. Chet says we'll have to travel all the way inward to follow this Path. Pirates, the Superiority, the delvers . . . It's a lot, Spensa."

"Focus on what we can accomplish right now," I suggested. "For the moment, all we have to do is get across this swamp."

"Well, that's easy for me," he said. "I can fly."

"See? One step at a time. You can do this. *I* can do this. Whatever it takes."

He nodded by wobbling his drone up and down. "Okay!" he said. "Whatever it takes. My! That feels *good*. To at least *pretend* we're in control! I like it. Is this how you feel *all the time*?"

I wished that were true, but I didn't contradict him as he zipped out over the swamp, looking down at . . .

"A mushroom!" he shouted, hovering above one growing in the bog. "A real mushroom, Spensa!"

I stopped to watch him buzz back and forth. Being in a drone suited him. There was an energy to his personality that came out as he flew around me in a circle.

Chet walked back to join me in watching M-Bot. I even caught him smiling.

"He's really not dangerous," I said to Chet.

"His energy *is* a little contagious," he admitted. "We're almost there—only two fragments to go. The portal you seek is in some ruins."

"Ruins?" I asked. "Like from an old mining operation?"

"No," he said. "Though we'll pass something like that on the next fragment. The ruins we're hunting are older. Perhaps as old as this place."

"Have you wondered how all of this got here?" I asked him. "This landscape, these fragments?"

"Indeed I have. There are legends, naturally. People think hyperjump accidents are behind some of it, or even the delvers. But lore says that some of this was here before either delvers *or* cytonics."

I helped M-Bot harvest a sample of his mushroom and store it inside his "specimen box," which was the cavity in the cleaning drone where it once held the dust it vacuumed up. The little drone hummed happily as we started out again.

We reached a larger river flowing over the side of the swamp fragment. Chet directed us inward instead of trying to ford it. Though the current wasn't swift, he didn't like the idea of potentially being swept off amid uncertain footing.

We continued on, leaping from one firm section of ground to another. After a half hour or so of this, Chet halted me by taking my arm. He narrowed his eyes at the next section of land, then shook his head.

"False land," he explained. "See how it ripples? Sinkhole underneath that patch. This way." He led me through some still water, where the stench of the mud was terrible. Soon we reached another long section of dry land.

"Are there any landscapes you haven't traveled?" I asked him, impressed by how easily he guided us.

"Oh, I'm sure there's something out there that I haven't seen," he said. "But I have traveled a great deal! I don't like staying in one place—you lose track of time in here that way. I prefer new sights, new experiences! I only stay with others when I'm out of reality ashes. Once I have a few, I'm off!"

After a little more hiking, I spotted our next fragment: the penultimate one before reaching our destination. This one turned out to be another desert, but with vast dunes as tall as buildings. I narrowed my eyes. Didn't sand worms live in dunes like that? Or at least giant scorpions?

Before we could cross over, however, Chet perked up. He turned, then pointed. There were more starships in the sky.

10

Used to this by now, I joined Chet in taking cover beneath a large tree with crooked branches but a decent number of leaves. The tips drooped so low they trailed in the water, making ripples.

"Broadsider markings," Chet whispered to me as we peeked through the canopy at the ships. "We've entered their territory."

"Are the factions that different from one another?"

"Generally, no," he said. "But the Broadsiders have a reputation for being more fair than the others. Then again, their leader is said to have once been in the Superiority security forces. I've kept my distance for that reason."

There were four ships in this formation. I didn't recognize the specific designs, but they were definitely military grade. As we watched, they clashed with another group of ships that darted up from beneath the fragment.

A quick firefight ensued, the various ships flying like hawks and prey from one of the pictures of Old Earth, twisting around one another as they soared down past the fragment.

Seeing them fight awakened something in me. I missed flying. It had been only a few days, but already I longed to feel a ship around me—its motion an extension of my body as I soared around obstacles and wove between enemies.

Being in the sky. Claiming the stars.

I missed it. Dearly.

"Soon," I whispered as the ships vanished from sight, chasing one another beneath the fragments.

"We should probably give it a few moments," Chet said, settling on a rock there under the tree. "In case they come back this direction."

"That was another faction, right?" I asked. "Cannonade?"

"Your eyes are keen!" he said. "Before long you'll know the proper markings for all six."

"Do they often fight one another?"

"Aggressively!" Chet said. "It's a pity. They could be out exploring and adventuring, but I suppose I shouldn't begrudge them a little sport. We all have our own ways of passing the time in here."

Well, if we were going to wait this out, it seemed like a good opportunity to arm myself. I'd cursed the loss of my rifle several times already, so I selected a sturdy stick from those fallen around the tree and began stripping it. Once finished, I found a good stone, properly oblong with a narrow portion in the middle.

I tried to affix it to the stick, but my first effort failed because the vines I'd picked snapped.

"If I may, Miss Nightshade," Chet said, unlacing his left boot. He pulled out a long shoelace, revealing another one still fastening his boot. "Always double-lace your boots when exploring! You'd be surprised how often an extra bit of string comes in handy. The uses are multitudinous!"

He showed me how to lash the stone in place—and then, surprised at my lack of knowledge, took out his other extra shoelace and proceeded to give me a short lesson on different knots and hitches. I realized, with embarrassment, that I'd allowed having a light-line to make me complacent in this area.

I listened with devoted attention. It felt like such a practical thing to learn—the sort of thing that . . . well, that I imagined my father might have taught me. If things hadn't gone so poorly.

Once we were done, I tucked away the shoelace—he'd told me to keep it to practice with—and picked up my club. I swung it a few times for good measure.

"A fine weapon," Chet said, hands on hips. "What shall you name it?"

"Skullbreaker, of course," I said.

"Excellent."

"Though . . . I don't know if sand worms have skulls," I said. "Maybe we should sharpen a rock and make a spear, in case I get swallowed and need to kill it from the inside."

"I doubt that will be requisite," Chet said with a chuckle.

"Say that when you're in a sand worm's gullet and *I'm* standing triumphantly on the corpse of mine, contemplating how to make a hat out of its skin."

"Ha!" Chet said. "I doubt I've ever met a young woman quite so . . . bloodthirsty."

I shrugged. "It's kind of an act. You know, bravado. But I do want to be able to defend myself against any beasts we encounter."

"If we must do so, then we have failed," Chet said. He held up a finger, adopting a straight-backed lecture pose. "No beast attacks a person unless that person has made a mistake. We trespass in *their* domain, and it is incumbent upon us to take the utmost care to avoid accidents."

"You don't hunt?" I asked.

"Heavens, no!" Chet said. "Not except for sustenance, which is unnecessary in here. I explore to see the wonders of the universe! Why, to leave that wilderness so desecrated . . . No. An explorer must *not* be a destroyer. He must be a preserver! But then, I'm rambling. We should continue. The pirates appear to have taken their squabbles elsewhere."

We continued on, barely reaching the desert fragment and leaping across before the two drifted too far apart. M-Bot seemed reluctant to leave his mushroom hunt, but he followed us.

Chet's comments about hunting and exploring left me intrigued—it was the opposite of what I'd expected from someone like him. The way he talked felt *liberating*. Exploring, traveling . . . he could do that and test his skills without needing to fight or kill. It was a new way of thinking. For me, the struggle to get better had always ultimately ended with the destruction of my enemies. Or at least the humiliation of those who had laughed at me.

I was changing though. It had begun on Starsight, as I met so many who were technically my enemies—but also just ordinary people. I wanted a way out of all of this now, more than I wanted to end the "Krell." Was there a way we could stop this war without destroying them or them destroying us?

Chet kept us to the valleys between the dunes. I watched the sand carefully as we walked.

"Um . . ." M-Bot hovered out in front of me. "Spensa? I had to leave behind *some* of my information databases, but I kept the fauna surveys for all known worlds in the Superiority and . . . I don't want to be a downer . . ."

"No sand worms?" I asked.

"Afraid not."

"Scud," I said. "What about giant scorpions? Orion totally killed one of those on Old Earth, so they've *got* to be real."

"There are several low-gravity planets with arthropod-like creatures that would probably fit that definition. Oooh . . . One has a poison stinger that, if it hits you, you grow *fungus* on your *tongue*. And in your blood. Basically, it kills you. But mushroom tongues!"

"Wow," I said. "That really exists?"

"Spensa?" M-Bot said. "Are you . . . crying?"

"No, of course not," I said, wiping my eye. "It's just . . . I'm glad something that awesome exists, you know? Like in the stories.

Maybe when this is all done, we can visit that place. You think maybe I could train one up from a baby to let me ride it?"

Chet chuckled from up ahead, leading us farther into the desert—and I allowed myself to grow excited. The next fragment would be the one with our destination, my chance—finally—to see what the delver had sent me to experience.

I should have been exhausted. And to an extent I was. It had been a difficult day of travel. It felt *good* though; there was something healthy and satisfying about being this type of worn out. It *was* odd that I wasn't hungry. And I'd been hiking all this way and was only mildly thirsty.

But . . . well, I was walking across a *literal* flying desert and had passed infinite waterfalls that were fed by no tributary. I doubted lack of hunger would be the oddest thing I experienced in here. I hurried up, joining Chet as we were forced to climb a dune—a difficult process, though he showed me how to do it at an angle, and while keeping somewhat solid footing by not walking in his footsteps.

"In snow," he explained, "step where the person in front of you did. That will save energy. Sand dunes, however, settle. And so the person in front of you will disturb that, which actually makes it *harder* if you step right where they did."

At the top, I picked out the proper fragment. "That one?" I asked. "The green one?"

"That's it," Chet said.

There was so much *life* on these. Plant life, at least. Even the desert had scrub stubbornly breaking from the sand and growing defiantly. Was this what it was like on most worlds? Plants just kind of grew, without anyone to cultivate them?

"Are you nervous?" I asked Chet. "About what we'll find?"

He thought for a moment, smoothing his mustache. "I feel . . . like it's inevitable. I knew I'd make my way to the Path eventually. To the point that when you mentioned it to me, I felt like I'd been drawn to you. Pulled onto this course."

"That . . . sounds kind of unnerving, honestly."

"My apologies; that was not my intent." He glanced toward the distant lightburst. "Still, I worry about the delvers' hand in this place. I never can quite trust that my will is my own . . ."

"Do you know anything about them?"

"They're not a group mind," Chet said. "People get that wrong about them. The delvers are all separate beings—but they're also identical. They live in a place where nothing ever changes, and where time doesn't exist. They exist in one moment, in one place, indistinguishable—and terrified of anything that isn't *exactly* as they are."

"Okay . . ." I said. "A lot of that doesn't make sense to me, Chet. But I'll try to pretend otherwise."

"Thank you," he replied. "All I know is that the not-making-sense part is why individuals like you can hyperjump through the nowhere! Time and space are irrelevant, and after slipping into the nowhere you can come out anywhere else. I worry, however. Every time we puncture the barrier between the nowhere and the somewhere, we corrupt the nowhere a little. Like how you can't walk through clean fresh snow without leaving tracks."

"Do you think . . . there is snow in here somewhere?" I asked. "I'd like to see it sometime."

"It exists, but is rare," he said. "Tell me, Miss Nightshade. Did you actually live your *entire* life on that barren planet? How did you survive?"

I shrugged. "We have algae vats and artificial light underground. And there is *some* life. Rats live in the caverns, eating fungi and algae that transfer heat into biological energy. It isn't much, but we make it work."

"You sound like an exceptionally courageous group," Chet said. "It is my honor to travel with you—though I must admit I find your home a strange place to have a society!"

"Oh!" M-Bot said, flying up beside him. "It is a *very* strange place, with a fascinating mix of technological advancements and backward ignorance. They have spaceflight, but not automatic soap dispensers, for example. So you could say their culture has had its ups and downs."

"It indeed sounds interesting, abomination," Chet said. "Come, Miss Nightshade and companion. We should hurry—there is a point of interest on this fragment I would like to show you before we leave it, but we will need to rush. It wouldn't do to miss the next fragment because we dallied!"

We continued on, Chet picking up our pace. A half hour later, we crested another dune and I got a better glimpse of our target fragment. It was covered with shimmering grass—it looked so *soft,* like the fur of a good blanket—and idyllic streams that dropped off the side, sparkling like drops of sunlight. It looked like paradise as described in the stories. Green, alive—there were even *butterflies.*

However, something felt odd to me. Chet had rushed us to get here in time, but that fragment appeared to be hours away. At the rim, Chet waved me along to the right. The dunes tapered off here, and in a few moments we found what he'd wanted to show me: a pit. The sand had blown away, exposing brown rock—and a vast chunk had been dug out of the fragment, going down at least thirty meters. The sides were tiered, like a reverse pyramid, paths running along them in a spiral.

"A quarry," I said. "For acclivity stone?"

"Precisely," Chet said. "This one is ancient, but I thought you might appreciate seeing an example of a quarry. The ones the Superiority runs farther inward at Surehold are much more massive affairs, but it's the same general principle."

"Too bad they didn't leave any acclivity stone," I said, searching the quarry. M-Bot zipped past me and went soaring down to look at the bottom. "Maybe we could have fashioned some kind of floating device for ourselves."

Chet shook his head, smiling.

"What?" I said.

"They left plenty of acclivity stone, Miss Nightshade," he said, gesturing. "What is it you think we're standing upon?"

"Rock," I said.

"Rock," he said, "that floats through the sky? These fragments all have acclivity stone in them. Unfortunately, it takes refinement and energy to make it work on a scale that's usable, so I doubt we'll be able to make any kind of device. Still, it is all right here."

I blushed at the realization. Of course the fragments floated on acclivity stone. It made perfect sense, now that I thought about it. I guess the blue coloring, like the light glowing underneath M-Bot's wings, came from the refinement process.

"Now," he said, "that other fragment." He gazed across at it, then frowned. "It should be here any moment."

"By my best guess," M-Bot said, "judging by its slow movement, our fragments won't touch for ten hours."

"Ten hours? Chet, why did you hurry us?"

"I . . ." He scratched at his head. "Ten hours, you say?"

"Yes," M-Bot said. "Though I have set my internal chronometer to the time used by Spensa's people, which is patterned after one hour Earth time. The same as used by my old ship, and thus also—presumably—by you."

Chet settled on a rock. "I apologize, Miss Nightshade. My sense of time is . . . not as reliable as it once was."

I let the conversation die, but I was baffled. How could Chet have such a poor sense of time?

"Well," Chet said. "Perhaps we should get some rest here, then attack the Path of Elders. Always best to hit a task fresh and awake! So that it can't hit back, you see."

I smiled. That reminded me of something Kimmalyn would say. But I agreed with getting some rest. It had been a wonderful day, though a long one.

As Chet took off his jacket to make a pillow, I checked on my reality icon, finding it had shed three motes of silvery dust today.

I proffered one to him and watched carefully so I could study the hungry way he eyed my pouch. Everything about traveling with him had been a joy—everything except that look.

I tucked away the pouch quickly. Chet took a little longer to put away his ash—instead staring at it for a time, glowing and twinkling in his palm.

"So, the Path of Elders," I said to break the odd mood. "Is there anything we need to do to prepare for it?"

"Not that I know of," he said. "I visited this first stop one time, but decided not to go into the cavern. I feel embarrassed to admit that, after seeing your excitement."

I stared out at the garden fragment. Yeah, it was moving more slowly than Nedd did at mess on an early morning shift. It would take a long time to get here. "It feels like the quests that happened in the old stories. That's why I'm excited."

"You put a lot of stock in those stories."

"My grandmother told them to me when I was a child. They kind of just . . . stuck."

"I find that admirable," Chet said. "But I warn you not to raise your expectations too much. Life isn't always like one of those stories."

"I know," I said, still staring over that beautiful field. "But . . . stories say something. About us, and about where we came from. They're a reminder that we have a past, a history. And a future."

When I was growing up, Gran-Gran's stories had been my shield. Against the names I was called, against the things people said about my father. Against my own terror that all those things—particularly the ones about me—were true.

In the stories, there was a sense of justice. Everything had a purpose; every little bit meant something. I thought if those heroes and heroines from the stories could keep going forward into the darkness, so could I.

I might have clung to them a little too tightly. With how strange everything had been lately, perhaps I was seeking some kind of stability. Or some kind of guide . . .

"I can understand that," Chet said. "It's odd—this place has stolen from me who I was, but I still *know* things. I know what a burrito is, though I've never eaten one in here. I can list the names of the first human colony worlds. And I remember . . . stories. I partially decided on my name due to the tales of the old hero Chet Cannister."

"Oh, those are good," I said. "But I like the older ones best. Heroes like Odysseus."

"Or Hercules."

"Yeah," I said, slamming my fist into my other hand. "Or *Satan*."

Chet blinked. "Excuse me?"

"Satan?" I said. "The hero?"

"The . . . hero."

"Yeah," I said. "Gran-Gran told me the story. Satan got thrown into a place of fire, but he was like, 'Hey, everyone. It doesn't matter, so long as we have each other. We can make this place as good as any paradise.' Then he volunteered to infiltrate the enemy's world and went on this big quest through the Abyss."

"Now, my memory—as I've warned you—isn't great," Chet said. "But that sounds like the old poem *Paradise Lost*. I . . . think you might have misinterpreted it."

"What? Who do *you* think was the hero of that story?"

"Adam and Eve."

"Those losers? They didn't do anything but sit around! Everyone else had flaming swords and dramatic battles!"

Chet grinned. "Well, that's one way to interpret it. And what do I know? I only know my own name because of the patch I found on my uniform."

I made a pillow out of my jacket. As I did, M-Bot hovered over beside me. "Ummm . . ." he said.

"What?" I asked.

". . . I think he might be correct about *Paradise Lost*."

"Read it again," I said. "You really expect me to believe that—in a story with people named *Beelzebub* and *Moloch* who live in *Pandæmonium*—the author wanted us to root for someone named *Eve*?"

Some things are obvious. Unless you're a robot, I guess.

"Do you want me to do what I did last time?" the robot asked me more softly. "Just in case?"

I nodded, then lay back, contemplating the day we'd had. I couldn't remember another day in my recent life that had been so thoroughly enjoyable. That made me feel guilty though. Jorgen and the others were fighting for their lives, and I was investigating swamps and playing explorer?

I would have to stay focused. Tomorrow we started the Path of Elders, and hopefully I'd finally have some answers. Or at the very least I'd learn the right questions.

11

M-Bot woke me the next "morning," and I stretched, finding the garden fragment hovering an easy step from our own. My memories of the "night" contained only ordinary dreams. I wished I'd been able to find Jorgen and at least deliver a report, but I was so exhausted that my attempt didn't get far.

Chet got up when M-Bot tapped him, and at his suggestion I searched out a nearby spring. I took a drink—one of the last ones I'd need in here—and washed my face and hands. Fortunately, I didn't stink as much as it seemed I should have, considering all the effort of the day before.

As I washed, I glanced at M-Bot, who quietly whispered, "He didn't get up. Slept until I woke both of you."

I nodded, then joined Chet at the edge of the fragment. "Ready?" I asked him.

"Forward!" he said.

We stepped across. And I realized this was my first time walking on grass. It felt so *strange* underfoot. Springy, like I was walking on a pillow.

This fragment turned out to be relatively small. All green grass and hills, with a lake in the center. Near that was a hillside with a hole cut into it—like a doorway into a mine.

The tunnels beyond weren't extensive: a little entryway followed by three small rooms with earthen walls. But walking through them, I felt an eerily familiar sensation. Scud. I'd been in places that felt like this before.

We found the portal at the rear of the largest room. It was much like the one I'd come out of in the jungle—a glistening surface of rock, slate grey, but carved with lines. Hundreds of them this time, in an intricate pattern.

M-Bot flew up to the wall, and the lights on his drone lit up the markings. "Hmm," he said. "I kept a database of all known scripts cataloged by the Superiority. This appears to be none of them."

I nodded absently, tracing a curving line with my finger. "They aren't a language, not really. I think I know what the lines mean though."

"How can you?" M-Bot said. "You just said the markings aren't a language!"

"They aren't."

"But they mean something?"

"Yes."

"Well then, what?"

My finger reached the end of the line. "Memory."

M-Bot hovered beside me. "Hmmm. Yes, I find this curious. I'm feeling a new emotion. It's like anger and frustration mixed! How interesting." With that, he hovered up, then came down directly on my head, whacking me.

"Ow!" I said, more surprised than in pain.

Chet immediately cursed, reaching to grab M-Bot, but I held up a hand to stop him. "M-Bot," I said, "what is wrong with you?"

"That is what my emotions said I should do," he explained. "Wow. I feel better! Curious, curious . . ."

"You can't just hit people."

"Didn't you hit Jorgen basically all the time?"

"That was different," I said. "First I hated him, then I liked him. So I had good reasons."

"Ah!" M-Bot said. "You say things like that, and I want to hit you again! Would you stand still so I can smack you with a grabber arm? That sounds fun."

"Abomination," Chet said, "you should—"

"It's all right, Chet," I said. "He's just having trouble dealing with emotions. They're new to him."

"I think I'm doing well, all things considered," M-Bot said to Chet. "I bet the first time *you* had emotions, you babbled a lot and soiled your clothing." He hovered back around to look at me. "Would you please *explain* what you meant by telling me this wasn't a language, then immediately interpreting it?"

"These are the memories of the people who used this portal, M-Bot," I said, kneeling and feeling at the grooves cut into the stone. "It makes a curious kind of sense. Cytonics are like . . . biological means of communication and travel. Hyperjumping replaces starships, and mind-to-mind contact replaces radios. So it feels right to me that there would be a way to store thoughts. A cytonic book, or recording."

"Yes," Chet said, kneeling beside me. "That is what I've heard. The Path of Elders involves a sequence of these portals—four or five total, from what I've been able to learn. Each is among the most ancient of ways into the nowhere, etched with the experiences of the first cytonics."

Yes, I'd seen these patterns in the tunnels of Detritus. I'd also seen them in a large space station—the shipbuilding facility in orbit around Detritus. And I'd seen them inside the delver maze, a place I was increasingly convinced was the corpse of a long-dead delver.

"What do we do?" I asked. "How do we begin?"

"I'm not certain," Chet said. "Admittedly, I thought we'd experience the memories as soon as we entered." He placed his own hand on the markings. "I . . . can feel something."

"So," M-Bot said, "these things are both memories *and* portals between dimensions?"

"Yes," I said, closing my eyes. The boundary was weaker than usual in this room. My pocket started to grow warm—my father's pin.

Time for a test. The somewhere, home, was on the other side of this wall. Could I open the way? I engaged my cytonic senses. With my hands on the wall here . . . yes, I could *feel* the somewhere—my reality—pulling on me, trying to suck me through. The rock became as if liquid, and I began to sink into it.

Strangely, I could again feel a presence near me. Like I had when I'd used my powers in the jungle. The one that . . . that I wanted to believe might be my father. Was it guiding me? Leading me to freedom?

I stopped with a thump. Like the sound your boots made on the floor when you kicked them off at night. I tried again.

Thump.

"What do you feel?" Chet asked me.

"The portal is locked on the other side," I said. "As you warned."

"I hoped I was wrong about that," he said. "And that your hyperjumping powers would let you use these portals to access the somewhere. Alas! Fortunately, that is not our primary endeavor here. There has to be a way to see the memories left for us. Can you . . . listen to the rock? Spy on it, as you say you can do to the delvers?"

I tried that, closing my eyes and listening. Opening my mind. Yes, there *was* something here. How did I access it? I asked the rock, pled with it, to open to me. But I failed. With a sigh, I opened my eyes.

To find that the cavern had changed around me.

I could make out the vague outlines of the rooms here, but they were ethereal, insubstantial. It was as if that world had faded, and another had sprung up in its place. In this one I felt like I was floating in darkness.

I stumbled, trying to get my bearings.

"Oh!" M-Bot said. "Spensa? You seem to be experiencing motor control problems. This isn't related to the rap on the head I gave you, is it? Oh *scud,* I directly disobeyed my programming mandates by doing harm to—"

"I'm fine," I said. "I'm seeing something."

"Well, you're probably *always* seeing something. Even when your eyes are closed, technically. Or maybe not because—"

"Hush," I said, turning around. Chet still knelt beside me, looking about in confusion.

"Do you see what I do?" I asked. "We're floating in darkness. Like when in the lightburst."

"Indeed," Chet said. "Only, look here. Beside me."

I knelt, unsteady. I could feel the floor, touch it. Yet it was faint, nearly invisible to my eyes. Near our knees was a small pinprick of whiteness. It was part of the vision. "Is this the lightburst?"

Chet shook his head, seeming baffled. But as we watched, something changed. A substance began to grow around the pinprick of light, obscuring it. Growing like a tiny asteroid, then flattening out, and . . .

"A fragment," I said, watching as stone grew. "We're witnessing the birth of a fragment."

"Yes . . ." Chet said. "I believe you are correct. We are watching it grow over hundreds of years, I suspect. It's as if . . ."

"As if matter is seeping through," I said. "That's what this is, Chet. A tiny weakness between the dimensions. The somewhere is leaking in, forming a fragment like a stalactite forms slowly over time in a cavern."

And I knew this was happening over centuries, as Chet had said. That information appeared in my mind, because . . . because it had been left intentionally to inform me. These thoughts, they were the thoughts of ancient cytonics.

"Yes!" Chet said. "I believe you've done it, Miss Nightshade! This is the past. The Path of Elders. The secrets of the ancient cytonics."

Scud, it sounded awesome when he said it that way. As we watched, the fragment expanded into a block of stone perhaps twenty meters wide.

"Look," Chet said, pointing behind me. "Was that there before?"

I turned around. I didn't see any other fragments, but I did pick out a faraway white spot. It was the lightburst, but it seemed to have appeared as the fragment grew.

"It's so small," I said. "And there are no other fragments around. This must be the distant, *distant* past."

I got a sense of this place at the time. A kind of silent tranquility. Nothing dangerous. No feelings of anger. No . . .

No delvers. The delvers either hadn't existed at that time, or had been somewhere else.

"How can we see this?" I asked. "You said this Path was memories of people who entered the nowhere, but presumably nobody was here to see this part."

"Time is strange here," Chet said, still kneeling. "I imagine that cytonics were able to uncover this somehow. Do you see this here? What do you make of it?"

A line had appeared in the ground—the illusory version. It was different from the rest of the fragment, shinier, a different color. As we watched, it grew up into a wall, just a few handbreadths high. But a tiny pattern appeared on it, a little swirl. It felt like some kind of natural occurrence. Like erosion.

Yes, that was it. A kind of interdimensional erosion. Only created when . . .

A figure appeared in the scene. A dione, with blue skin.

I felt the vision abruptly *slow*. Decades were no longer passing with each second; this was in real time. The dione stumbled to their feet.

"Preindustrial clothing," Chet guessed, pointing at the furs sewn roughly together.

The dione gasped and spun around, confused. They smiled, baring their teeth. Wait, no. That wasn't a smile. For diones that meant aggression, or maybe fear.

The dione didn't see us, and it felt eerie to have them look through me. They then dropped to their knees and started clawing at the tiny wall that indicated the portal.

Until . . . time seemed to speed up again. We watched the unfortunate dione as a blur trying to find a way off the fragment. They aged, then died. Their corpse turned to dust, leaving bones. It happened in seconds.

"That poor creature," Chet said. "Dying alone in this place."

I knelt beside the dione's bones. The fragment had grown larger, but only a little. "Matter leaks into here from the somewhere. You've said you suspected this, Chet."

"Indeed! Perhaps the belt formed because of weakened boundaries."

I scanned the darkness and thought I could pick out another fragment forming in the distance. And the lightburst . . . it was a tiny bit larger. "So the fragments grew around small weaknesses between this dimension and ours. The lightburst consolidated as a reaction—it became the uncorrupted region of the nowhere. A kind of . . . safe room in a quarantine zone, perhaps?"

"Yes," Chet said. "Yes, that feels correct."

There was another piece. Something more to this. "If the somewhere is leaking into here," I said, "did the nowhere in turn leak into our dimension? What shape would that take?"

The answer was right before us. Other diones appeared in the vision, coming through the portal, each leaving a tiny addition to the wall—more matter, and another swirl each. These learned to jump in and out, and no more died alone in here.

"Cytonics," Chet whispered. "This is how it happened. The nowhere leaked into our dimension, and it . . . changed people living near the breach. It made *us*."

"It's like . . . interdimensional radiation," I said, "that infuses people with the nowhere?"

I felt a surreal sense of disconnect as—in the near distance—another fragment grew in fast motion. Other people appeared on it eventually, but of a different species. Varvax. The Krell, though they didn't have their exoskeletons. They were little crabs, and . . .

I felt the two species connect, speak mind-to-mind before they even got close enough to shout at one another. The first two species to ever meet, at least in the nowhere, and long before either had access to space travel.

I tried to listen to them, tried to focus my attention. Like squinting, but with my brain. Cytonic metaphors are weird, but that's what it felt like. I pushed, and something in the memories encouraged me.

Further, it said. *Express your talent. Listen . . .*

I linked with it, and my brain interpreted what was being sent. Information, both verbal and nonverbal.

When I'd fought the drones on Detritus, I'd interpreted their instructions and responded before I consciously registered what I was hearing. This was the same. My mind, or my soul or whatever, knew what all this meant. And something clicked.

Ahh . . . I thought. *So that's how you do it.*

When I listened in on others with my mind, I did it by pretending I was something I wasn't. I somehow *spoofed* being the communication's intended recipient. It let me remain shadowy, unseen—a spy.

Good, the memories said. Then a soft impression appeared in my mind. A place. *Go here,* the vision whispered. Alongside the words came the image of a fragment with some ruins. Then the vision vanished.

I sank to the ground, my back to the portal wall.

"It *was* the hit to your head!" M-Bot said, hovering down beside me. "I'm so sorry!"

"It wasn't that, M-Bot," I said. "I promise."

"Oh, thank Turing!"

"Who?"

"One of the fathers of computing," he said. "It felt appropriate to say."

"You did not harm her, abomination," Chet said. "I saw the vision too."

"Did you feel that last part?" I asked. "Like a voice . . . helping guide me . . ."

"I didn't feel anything like that," he said. "I saw the first fragments, the first portals, and the first cytonics . . . then a hint of the next place to go?"

"Yeah, I saw that," I said. "Another fragment with ruins."

"Yes," Chet said. "That's a fragment deep inside Broadsider territory, I'm afraid. But . . . I know that we must go there. I feel . . . overwhelmed."

I felt elated.

Yes, *elated*. I realized that ever since I'd discovered my powers—what my people called "the defect"—I'd been worried they were something nefarious. I'd thought that maybe I was something terrible. A delver in embryo, or something monstrous.

But I *wasn't*. Cytonic powers were just a mutation. Granted, a bizarre one caused by my ancestors being exposed to the nowhere's leakage into the somewhere. But nothing terrible grew within me. I was just . . . well, me.

Saints. I'd *needed* to see that. A simple revelation, yes, but it changed everything. I knew what I was. I knew how I had come to be. And it was no wonder that powers manifested in our people—Detritus had one of these portals, perhaps helping activate the latent talent from our bloodlines.

This was part of the information the elder cytonics had left, the thing they'd wanted me to know. *You are not a monster,* the impression lingered. *You are one of us. You are wonderful. You are natural. You are loved.*

And along with that, a nudge to help me develop further in my talents. A push, and some understanding. I had the sense that if my talents had been different, I would have been nudged a different way, to develop those abilities instead.

I glanced at Chet, who was grinning practically ear to ear.

"I feel left out," M-Bot said. "You're both experiencing different emotions from the ones I am. And . . . this is all very confusing. What is one supposed to *do* with all of these emotions? What are they *for*? What's the purpose?"

"I don't think they have any specific purposes," I said.

"Of course they do. Otherwise they wouldn't have evolved in you and then been programmed into me. But . . . I suppose there are things that are evolutionarily neutral, and perhaps saying 'purpose' implies too much volition behind the process. Unless you believe in God, which I'm not sure that I do. I mean, I *was* created by someone. Hummmm . . ."

I took a few deep breaths, trying to digest what I'd seen. "Chet," I said. "Did you see those varvax on the nearby fragment?"

"I did indeed, and I find it curious. The two fragments were relatively near to one another. Diones and varvax."

"Well," M-Bot said. "I don't know what exactly you saw, but histories show that those two peoples traveled between worlds cytonically before they did it with starships."

"Yeah," I said. "The same thing happened to humans and the kitsen, and maybe other species. I never realized the hole in that. A cytonic usually needs a direction to go, instructions, to hyperjump—at least very far. But this explains how; they met in the nowhere before hyperjumping between worlds."

"Abomination," Chet said, "do you have a record on when the delvers first appeared in the somewhere?"

"The initial records of the delvers occur after the First Human War began," M-Bot said. "That was when the Phone Company—a human organization—gave hyperdrives to the people of Earth. Humans then spread throughout the galaxy. War began, and near its end the first delvers appeared. Before that time there were no reports of delvers, or even the eyes."

I looked to Chet. He'd sensed it too—no delvers had existed at the time of this vision. So how had they appeared? What *were* the delvers?

My contemplations were interrupted as an enormous jolt shook our fragment, accompanied by an overpowering *crash*.

12

I grabbed my makeshift club, which I'd dropped near the front of the cavern, and stumbled out onto the loamy ground. Chet joined me, unsteady on his feet, holding on to the wooden supports at the mouth of the cavern.

Another fragment had collided with the one we were on. It looked smaller than ours, but thicker and more dense. Like a battle-ship made of stone.

"How did you miss that?" I demanded of Chet, pointing across the green field to the place where the two fragments were mashed together.

"I have no idea!" he said. "Nothing like this has ever happened to me before!"

The ground shifted again as the "battleship" fragment shoved farther into ours, causing dirt to roll and stone to crunch. Our fragment was pushed along with it, like an old ship being pushed by a tug—a *really* aggressive tug with its boosters on overburn.

The chaos sent me to my knees. Scud, the entire fragment was shaking terribly. On Detritus I would have thought a thousand meteors were striking at once.

Chet grabbed me by the arm and helped me to my feet.

"How do we get off!" I shouted at him over the noise of rock crushing.

"I don't know!" he yelled back. "There aren't any nearby fragments!"

I struggled for balance but pointed at the "battleship" fragment. "There *is* one other place to go!"

"It's trying *right now* to destroy us," Chet yelled. "I don't know that I consider it an option!"

"I'm very angry too!" M-Bot shouted from behind me. "I thought you should know, since it seems like we're sharing!"

"Options?" I shouted at him.

"For being angry? I've always liked raw fury, but indignation has a certain bold flavor too, don't you think?"

"M-Bot!"

"Sorry!" he shouted. "My databases say the proper behavior during an earthquake is to either get outside—which we've obviously scored good marks on, since we're literally outside our own universe—or get to a place where nothing can fall on us. This seems to work. Yay us. Oh! And I'm not mad any longer. Wow. Do emotions always pass this quickly?"

Well, maybe the collision would subside now that we'd survived the initial impact. I looked up across the grass. The ground continued to tremble, and something else bothered me. Something I couldn't immediately define. It was . . .

"The water," I said, pointing. "The lake is empty. What happened to the water?"

"It must have drained out the bottom!" Chet said. "The fragments aren't made entirely from acclivity stone—some have more, others less. I have hypothesized that it influences how fast they move."

"The one crashing into us is more solid then?" I said. "It must have come up quickly, if you didn't spot it."

"Precisely!" Chet said. "Our current one looks to be mostly soil, so the bottom of the lake must have given out."

That bothered me. I mean, these fragments were *already* playing with my brain. I perpetually felt like I was walking across unstable footing. As I scanned the fragment, my fears became manifest.

Rifts appeared in the soil. Widening cracks like bolts of lightning moved across the once-tranquil prairie. In these lines the soil and grass vanished, sinking out of sight.

"It's breaking apart," I said, forcing myself to keep my feet despite the shaking.

"Scrud!" Chet said. Ahead of us an entire section of the grassland fell away, leaving a gaping hole. "I suggest a hasty actualization of your earlier plan. We must get onto that more solid fragment!"

We dashed away from the tunnel with the portal, and it collapsed in a roar behind me. The ground, which had once felt soft and springy, now felt treacherous.

"M-Bot," I shouted. "Stick the light-line to my back. If I jump or fall, pull upward with every bit of lift you've got."

"I'm not powerful enough to carry you!"

"I don't expect you to!"

As he complied, I tried to maintain a jog, but the tremors kept knocking me off balance. Chet wasn't faring much better; ahead of me a particularly violent quake sent him sprawling, and then a rift opened between us.

He glanced toward me with alarm.

I jumped.

Obligingly M-Bot moved upward, pulling the light-line taut. While he couldn't lift me completely, his efforts *did* add to my spring. I'd trained in low-g, and this wasn't much different, so I knew how to compensate. I spanned the widening chasm and landed next to Chet.

"Marvelous!" he said as I pulled him to his feet. Together we charged toward the fragment that was causing all of this. But abruptly Chet grabbed my arm and hauled me back, halting my run as a hole opened up right in front of us, dirt pouring down like it had liquefied.

Scud. I glanced to Chet with thanks, and he pointed to the side. We scrambled that direction, rounding the hole, and reached the far edge of the fragment.

Here the ground was bunched up, the earth piled in an enormous furrow. "Get that light-line off me and attach it somewhere up above!" I shouted to M-Bot.

He zipped up to the top and attached the line, then returned trailing the red-orange rope. I looked to Chet, who nodded, grabbing the light-line. "Just like climbing to the top of Mount Rigby!" he said. "Highest point on the fragments!" He glanced at the bunched-up soil. "Only perhaps more squishy!"

"Less heroic explorer talk!" I shouted. "More climbing!"

As if to punctuate my words, a vast section of the ground behind us fell away.

"Point taken," Chet said, then began ascending the high furrow of trembling soil. His feet sank in, making it an obvious struggle. Fortunately, there were chunks of stone to use as footholds; he proved his skill in climbing as he located them.

I followed him up, and my lighter weight was an advantage. When I'd been younger I'd imagined growing to Amazonian heights to become a fierce swordswoman—and then I'd run out of centimeters. Instead I'd taken to imagining myself as so small that giants underestimated me, so I could therefore scamper up their backs and stab them in the ears.

There weren't many giants to slay, but I got mileage out of my size today as I limberly scrambled up the mound of dirt, barely needing the light-line. Then I helped pull Chet out of a mire—it was tough with the dirt sliding around us. But together we managed to reach the top.

M-Bot hovered up from below. Worn out and filthy, the three

of us stumbled up to a high point on the new fragment. It looked like a blasted-out landscape, ashen and cracked—but it was solid.

The fragment we'd left was in utter turmoil. Little patches of grass peeked through the churning dirt—like sections of unburned skin on the face of a pilot who had died in a crash. Those were quickly vanishing as our current fragment pushed forward. Dirt fell away in vast swaths, with chunks of acclivity stone drifting off to the sides.

In minutes, the entire fragment was gone save for some chunks of dirt stuck to the front where we stood.

"I would not believe this if I hadn't witnessed it firsthand," Chet whispered. "Miss Nightshade, I've *never* seen such an event."

"Fragments don't often collide?" I asked.

"On occasion, they bump at speed," he said, "but I've never experienced anything more fearsome than a short jolt." He put his hand to his head. "It's as if the nowhere itself is trying to kill us."

Great. Jumping into a dimension literally controlled by beings that hated me might not have been my smartest decision ever. Then again, I had genuinely needed to see that vision at the portal. So . . . yeah. Frying pans, fires, all that. As long as there was some warmth and I could roast some rats.

"I feel bad about the portal," I said. "Those memories, lost . . ."

"All memories are lost eventually," Chet said. "I agree this is a tragedy—but I prefer to keep my head high." He dusted off his trousers, shook some dirt from his jacket, then smiled at me. "Think of it this way. We survived again, and we began the Path. I shall count it as a grand victory!"

"We need to get farther into pirate territory to get to the next stop though."

"Indeed," he said, pointing. "That direction." Our current fragment floated perpendicular to that, so I supposed it could be worse. "We'd have to cross dozens upon dozens of fragments, however, to reach those ruins on foot."

"So . . ." I said. "Time to restart Operation Ship-Steal?"

He smiled, turning and pointing a slightly different direction. "The Broadsider home base is perhaps two days' travel. I shall need a short time, Miss Nightshade, to use my powers and devise a path forward. We may not be able to go directly; it will depend on the timing of the intersection of the fragments."

"Let's hope," I said, "that no more of them intersect as violently as this one."

13

While Chet sat to figure out the route, M-Bot and I went to do a little scouting. This newest fragment was the most normal of the ones I'd been on. No strange grasses, no towering trees. Not even dirt. Just good, sturdy rock. It was darker than the stone on Detritus, and was cracked like it had been through a furnace, but the way it scraped underfoot reminded me of home.

We found a small wooden building, but it had been scavenged clean. While I was inside, M-Bot called to me. I peeked out to see three starfighters shooting past in the sky.

"I think they've come to survey the destroyed fragment," M-Bot said, hovering beside me.

Made sense. We stayed out of sight, and I had a spike of fear that they'd grab Chet. Unfortunately, I realized I'd misplaced Skull-breaker in the chaos of the exploding fragment. That gave me a surprising sense of loss. The club hadn't been impressive, but it had been special because Chet had helped me make it.

As the starfighters wove through the sky, flying away from our fragment and doing a few quick maneuvers, I got a feeling for their skill. Like . . . like how you can tell from watching someone's warm-up routine how athletic they are. Those pilots seemed fine, but not terribly skilled.

If I could get into a ship, I should have no trouble outflying them in the short term. But how would I get through pirate territory in general? We would need to land and study the next portal in the Path of Elders, and we couldn't do that if pirates were on our tail.

When the ships were out of sight, I hurried back to check on Chet—and found that he'd vanished. There was just the large pile of dirt heaped up on the front of the fragment near where the collision had happened.

That dirt stirred, then Chet appeared, digging himself out from where he'd apparently hidden himself. He brushed the dirt from his jacket, then spat out a little of it and grinned at me. "Not my most noble of escapes, but better than becoming a floor washer!"

"How goes the planning?" I asked him.

"A little more time, if you please."

I wandered a bit farther away—maybe twenty meters—and climbed up a small rock formation near the edge of the fragment. I stood tall, looking into the distance and admiring the view of the various nearby fragments, one of which was streaming water into the void.

Hands on my hips, I took a deep breath and couldn't help but grin. Scud, I was *loving* this. The feeling I'd had the day before—the joy of traveling with Chet—expanded. Now I'd seen firsthand that the quest was useful to me.

Exploring a strange frontier? Being forced to use some physical prowess for once? Running, climbing, jumping, and being chased by monsters? It really did feel as if I'd slipped into one of Gran-Gran's stories. Where I belonged. Where things were *right*. It was genuinely satisfying to have my life depend on whether I could escape a crumbling fragment—rather than on how well I could imitate an alien on Starsight.

I settled down on the rocks. My friends *were* in trouble, and I *did* miss them. Terribly. What I wouldn't give to be able to share this trip with them.

M-Bot hovered over, and I smiled at him. I had at least one friend here. I put my arm around his drone and pointed outward at the fragments. "What do you see?" I asked him.

"Chunks of matter."

"I see adventure," I said. "I see mysteries and striking beauty. Watch the water shimmer as it falls. Doesn't it look gorgeous?"

"Somewhat," he admitted. "Like . . . little bits twinkling on and off . . ."

"That's what emotions are for," I said. "Partially. It's not their only purpose, but it's an important one. Do you understand that part?"

"No," he said. "But I'm closer, maybe. I guess . . . I guess I wouldn't know how great mushrooms were without feeling something when I find them. Right?"

I smiled. "I'm glad I'm here with you, M-Bot. I know you were hesitant about entering. But thank you for being my friend, for joining me."

He wobbled in a nod. "But Spensa? I'm . . . still sad."

"Why?" I asked.

"I've spent years upon years' worth of processing time imagining what Commander Spears would be like. Now we've met him and . . . and he just calls me an abomination."

"He's coming around," I said. "The longer he spends with you, the more he'll see that he was wrong. But even if he doesn't, who cares? I'm your pilot now. And I think you're great."

"Thanks . . ."

"What?"

"I said thanks. I don't believe that statement requires qualification."

"Yeah, but you left it dangling," I said. "Something's still bothering you."

"You can tell that? How?"

"Gut feeling."

"I don't have guts," M-Bot said. "So I guess you're the expert. But . . . if you need to know, the bigger problem is that I'm still kind of mad at you."

"For leaving you behind when I left Starsight?" I asked.

"Yeah."

"I thought you forgave me for that."

"I thought I did too. But I keep remembering it. Is that . . . normal?"

"It is for humans. Sometimes it's too easy to forget the things you should remember—and far too easy to remember the things you really should forget."

"It's doubly so for me," he said, "since I literally can't forget things unless they're deleted, or at least commented out of my code."

I leaned back, putting my hands behind me to support myself as I sat and thought on what he'd said. Scud, he'd given up a lot in all of this—his wonderful ship body not the least of it. And now, to deal with all these emotions . . .

"I'm sorry," I said, "for what happened to you on Starsight, M-Bot. I truly am. It broke my heart to leave you like I did."

"But you'd make the same decision again, wouldn't you?"

"Yes," I said. "As much as it pains me to know I hurt you, if I were in that situation again . . . yes, I'd go save the people of Detritus."

"It makes logical sense," he said. "But I don't *feel* it. What do I do to get rid of these feelings? I don't *want* to be angry. So it's stupid that I'm angry. It makes no sense."

"It makes a ton of sense, actually," I said. "You don't have many friends—basically just me and Rig. When I left, you were being abandoned by everyone you'd known and loved. It's not the sort of thing you get over easily."

"Wow," M-Bot said. "You know emotions really well, Spensa. Particularly the stupid ones."

"I'll take that as a compliment."

"So what do I do?"

"Weather it," I said. "Get better. Learn to accept that sometimes what you feel isn't invalid, but that it doesn't mean you have to act according to those feelings either."

"Again I'm supposed to feel things, but then ignore those feelings. Act opposite of how they direct. Why is that?"

I shrugged. "It's just life. But sometimes talking about it makes it feel better."

"Huh. Yes, I believe that I do feel a little better. Strange. Why is that the case? Nothing has changed."

"Because I'm your friend, M-Bot. And that's what friends do. Share."

"And do they also abandon one another to certain death?" he said, then hovered down lower. "Sorry. It just kind of slipped out. I'll do better."

"It's all right," I said, climbing to my feet. "Again, it's okay to feel angry, M-Bot. But you're going to have to learn to deal with it. We're soldiers. We have responsibilities that are bigger than any one individual. So being friends doesn't mean I won't someday have to leave you behind again."

"What does it mean to be friends, then?"

"It means," I said, "that if something like that *does* have to happen, I'll do whatever I can to return to you once the crisis is over. And you'd do the same for me, right, bud?"

"Yes," he said, hovering higher. "Yes, because I can *move on my own* now." He turned, looking toward Chet. "And maybe you're right about him too. Maybe it *doesn't* matter what he thinks. It's hard to feel that, but I can say it. That feels like a different kind of lying. One that's not all untrue."

"We'll make a human out of you yet."

"Please no," he said. "From what I've read of it, I *really* don't want a sense of smell."

I smiled, intending to check on Chet. I hesitated, however, as I saw we'd drifted closer to the fragment with the waterfall. We weren't going to hit it—in fact, our current fragment seemed to have slowed to a normal speed. Serene and peaceful, as if it hadn't just been in a horrific collision.

Something was standing on the edge of that other fragment, near the waterfall. I couldn't make out much because of the distance, but it seemed to have . . .

Glowing white eyes.

I felt a mind pushing against mine.

What . . . did . . . you . . . do . . .

. . . TO THE US?

I backed up a few steps. The delvers had found me. Chet had said it was possible to hide in the belt out here, but . . . I supposed that in using my powers to initiate the vision on the Path, I'd drawn their attention.

Determined not to be intimidated, I quested out with my own cytonic senses. And I found . . . strength? I'd grown, here in the nowhere. I was able to brush that distant delver's mind as it projected anger at me. I picked out things it didn't intend to broadcast. They had indeed sensed what I'd done in activating the Path of Elders, and they'd sent the battleship fragment to destroy the one I'd been on.

That had taken a remarkable amount of effort, and was something they couldn't do often. It had actually been an experiment, as they felt they needed to push farther into the belt to try to find and stop me. These glowing-eyed things were the same. An experiment. Isolated individuals, who had lost a lot of their memories, were susceptible to the delvers' touch. But only non-cytonics, for this particular thing they were trying.

Saints . . . I felt so much more in control now, even after only one step on the Path of Elders. The experience had opened something in my brain, showing me how to hide and not draw attention while spying with my cytonics.

This delver still wasn't aware of how much I'd gleaned from it. I felt like gloating, but then I sensed it trying to attack my mind.

That manifested as coldness and pressure; it was as if I'd been plunged into an icy lake, the cold seeping like water through my skin, toward my heart.

And those voices . . .

What have you done . . . to the Us . . . to the Us . . .

"The Us" referred again to the delver I'd changed. The others were angry, *furious* at me. Because I'd touched and spoken to that one delver I'd persuaded not to attack Starsight. In so doing, I'd corrupted it forever. Essentially destroying one of their kind.

That made me feel sick. The friendly delver and I had connected in a beautiful way; I'd thought my actions would change things. But if the others refused to listen to me . . . I shivered as our fragment drifted farther from the one with the waterfall.

Chet stepped up next to me then, and jarred me from my thoughts. "You felt it too, I presume?"

"The delvers possessed someone over there," I said.

Chet nodded. "Whatever we did with the Path attracted their attention," he said. "I find it amazing they'd risk individuality by entering the belt, but it is obviously happening. We will need to be careful moving forward."

"Agreed." I took a deep breath. "You finished planning our route?"

"I did indeed, Miss Nightshade," he said, a twinkle in his eye. "Tell me. What is your opinion on sailing?"

14

Chet led me back to the small wooden building I'd discovered, saying that we needed to salvage some supplies. I tried explaining that it had been picked clean, but once we arrived he proceeded to take the *doors* off their hinges.

We each carried a door to the edge of the fragment, where we waited an hour to jump across to the next approaching fragment. It was a tropical one, full of tall trees with bare trunks and leaves only at the tops. We took our time crossing this one, scavenging for some strange oversized nuts the size of a person's head. They weren't coconuts—I knew those from my studies on Old Earth—but were similar.

We spent the evening hollowing the nuts out by prying off the tops and pulling out the long, stringy pulp by hand. Afterward we stretched the interior membrane of each one over the hole we'd made and set it to dry.

That night, I again failed at contacting Jorgen. But I woke up eager and excited for the day's trek—because while we'd slept, our next fragment had approached.

An ocean.

It was the most bizarre thing I'd seen here yet. The sides were stone like the bottom, but they were only about a meter thick. Beyond was water; essentially the fragment was an enormous bowl. It seemed larger than most fragments we'd traveled on, extending for kilometers into the distance.

Chet showed me how to use the pulp—which had become cordlike as it dried—to tie the doors together and lash the hollowed-out nuts to them. The nuts were watertight and filled with air. So when we shoved off into the ocean, we had a functional raft.

It was awesome.

Even M-Bot was impressed. He buzzed around us, complimenting the raft's "structural integrity" and "remarkable buoyancy." We named the ship the *Not-ilus* and I stood proudly at the prow—well, the flat front end I declared the prow. Chet chuckled softly, weaving oars from bent reeds and leftover nut-guts.

It was slow going, but I still felt like I was some ancient Polynesian hero sailing the ocean for the first time. Plus it got even *better*. Because the ocean had sea monsters.

I saw them swimming below as sinuous shapes and immediately fell to my knees, worried. And excited. Because, you know. *Sea monsters.*

I glanced at Chet, who was whistling softly and braiding some nut-guts into a stronger cord. One did not act so cheekily nonchalant by accident; he wasn't worried about the sea monsters, whatever they were.

"Oh!" M-Bot said, hovering past me. "Look! Ah! Um, turn around! About-face! Reverse rudder or whatever! We're going to *get eaten*!"

Chet calmly tossed me the rope, one end of which he'd fashioned into a loop. Then he handed me a small red fruit he'd harvested somewhere.

"Float that out beside us," he said, "then set the loop around it in the water and get ready to pull."

I could hardly contain myself as I did what he said. I stood at the ready as a blue serpentine head came up and snatched the fruit.

I yanked with a mighty pull, looping the thing around the neck, which let out a gaping . . .

. . . yawn?

Well, it *was* a sea monster, even if it barely noticed that I'd captured it. Instead it chewed on the fruit, bringing up another coil of its body from the depths below. It was like a snake, perhaps as thick as a man's thigh, but had little flippered legs along its very long body. It bit happily at the fruit, then looked up at me with pleading eyes, its head wagging in the water.

"You," I told it, "shall be known as Gnash the Slaughterer."

It made a bubbling sound, then turned eagerly as Chet tossed another fruit far out into the ocean. It began moving, towing us along as I yelped and held tight to the rope.

"Spensa," M-Bot said, hovering along beside my head, "I don't think that creature is likely to slaughter anything."

"It's a garqua," Chet explained, settling back down on the raft—er, the deck of our mighty ship. "They're not dangerous. They come from Monrome."

"Monrome?" I asked.

"Dione homeworld?" Chet said. "Even I know that, and I've forgotten the names of my parents." At my blank stare, he continued. "No predators on Monrome."

"What?" I said. *"None?"*

"None," Chet said. "Scavengers and herbivores only."

I glanced at M-Bot, who bobbed in the air to simulate nodding. "It's true," he said. "Though I doubt this one came directly from the dione homeworld—they have colonized nearly a hundred planets and have a habit of importing their local wildlife. After, ah, exterminating the local species for being too brutal and aggressive."

"Sounds like them," I said. "Still feels odd to me."

"Did you assume every planet had the same ecological hierarchy as Earth?" M-Bot asked.

"Well . . . yeah," I said. "I mean, it seems pretty fundamental. Things eat other things."

"It seems fundamental," Chet said, "because it's the way it was for us. Doesn't mean it *has* to be that way everywhere."

Huh. I continued holding Gnash's leash. She stopped to eat the fruit Chet had thrown—but then continued on, pulling us along contentedly. She appeared to think she'd find another piece of fruit if she kept going that direction, something Chet reinforced by occasionally tossing out another.

I contemplated the idea of a world—well, many worlds, if M-Bot was right—without predators. No hunting, no killing? How did survival of the fittest and all that work? At any rate, no *wonder* the diones thought everyone else was too aggressive.

The more I thought about it though, the more annoyed I became at them. They acted like they were superior—like they'd developed "prime intelligence" or whatever—because their society was peaceful. But they'd simply evolved on a planet without predators. They hadn't become enlightened or learned a better way—they merely assumed their way was how it was meant to be.

I supposed lots of species were like that, my own included. But we weren't conquering the galaxy—currently—or forcing everyone to live by our rules. Currently.

We spent the better part of the day crossing the ocean fragment. When we reached the far side we thanked Gnash with some more fruit and then moved on. And let it be known that M-Bot was totally wrong. Gnash was an *excellent* slaughterer, at least when it came to fruit.

We slept that night on a fragment with many caves that reminded me of home, and I think I got my best sleep of the entire trip there, comforted by the peaceful sound of water echoing as it dripped. The next day was full of different delights. Cliffs to scale, two swamps with utterly different scents—really, one smelled like cinnamon, like . . . someone I'd known once. After that, we crossed a fragment broken by winding canyons and beautiful patterns of colored stone.

By the end of the day, Chet informed me that we were nearing the Broadsider pirate base, and I found myself strangely melancholy. Once we got a ship, we would travel faster—and I *was* eager to take to the sky. But I had truly enjoyed the time I'd spent traveling.

Flying the rest of the way . . . well, it seemed that would undermine the epic nature of my quest a tad. That said, as I considered, I decided that many of the heroes from the stories would have used a starfighter if one had been available. Gilgamesh, for example, would totally have done it. (Not sure about Xuanzang, admittedly. He'd probably have been all about the need for the journey to refine him, or some other super-wise Zen stuff.)

We ended the day on a jungle fragment that I liked more than the first one I'd been on. It had less underbrush and all the plants were blue, which I found relaxing. It was just a more natural color.

According to Chet, this fragment would pass the pirate base the next day. So we decided to camp, and he sent M-Bot to scan for life forms that could be dangerous.

"I doubt that there are large beasts on this fragment," Chet explained to the AI, "but it is better to be careful than to be eaten."

"Plus," I added, "if the delvers *can* possess bodies, they might be able to grab one we don't expect. So see what kind of life there is, big or small. I'd rather not be surprised by a group of zombie chipmunks."

"Zombie . . . chipmunks?" Chet said.

"It would likely be a fun fight," I said. "With lots of kicking. Probably feels about the same to kick a chipmunk as it does to kick a rat."

"And . . . how many rats have you kicked, Miss Nightshade?"

"Only the ones that were asking for it," I said, smacking my fist into my palm.

M-Bot zipped off, and Chet and I began pulling down blue fronds and making bedding out of them. I kind of wished we could make a fire like in the stories, but it never felt cold in here—or hot. Plus the smoke would give us away.

Soon we each had a nice bed. And though I'd liked the caverns, this was probably going to be the softest of our nights in the nowhere.

"Thank you," I said to Chet as I settled into mine, "for all of this."

"I've been paid each day," he said. "You don't need to thank me!"

And each day he'd watched the reality icon with hunger. But I moved past that. "You haven't just guided me, Chet. You've taught me and shown me incredible things."

"Well," he said, "at the very least I'm glad you were able to see an ocean of sorts. I *did* promise you they were fun to explore! Regardless, no need to thank me. You saved my life on that fragment that was being destroyed!"

"And you saved mine."

"A sign that we're an excellent team!" he said, settling back into his nest of fronds. More solemnly, he continued, "Truly, Miss Nightshade, I've rarely had such an invigorating companion. Plus you encouraged me toward a goal I've been avoiding for far too long. For that I thank *you*."

I nodded in agreement. "What are we likely to face tomorrow? Will the pirates be armed with modern weapons, for example?"

"Yes," he said. "But remember they are mostly outcasts—not a true military force. They have gathered together more out of necessity, to be near other minds."

"Any idea why that helps us not forget in here?" I asked.

"It *is* curious, isn't it? It's like . . . people are all a little more *real* when they're together. Maybe together we remind one another what it is to be alive. To have family."

He said that last word with a hint of longing, looking upward through the trees. He'd forgotten his family, whoever they had been. I wished that he could see M-Bot as a lost friend, reunited, and not an "abomination." But I decided not to bring the issue up again at the moment.

We fell silent for a while, then Chet spoke, his voice softer. "I once had a ship in here. I decided to fly it all the way to the lightburst—to get out that way, if I could, and return to whatever life I'd left behind. But . . . I lost myself, flying. I think that's when I finally lost the last of my memories of my family, you see. Out there on your own, you don't have anything to remind you of who you are.

"Down on the fragments, everything—the stones, the structures, the trees—helps somehow. It *grounds* us, one might say. Ha! At any rate, I think we two will be fine flying together. We'll have each other, plus your icon. It should be enough. *Should* be . . ."

Chet trailed off and I shivered, imagining losing so much. I had to stay focused. Find my answers and get home. It had been . . . how long since I'd entered the nowhere? Maybe a week?

How many times have I slept? I wondered. *Three? Or has it been four?*

It was unnerving that I couldn't remember. So I focused on the upcoming mission. "We'll send M-Bot to do some reconnaissance once we're on the pirate faction's fragment," I told Chet. "They may not be a true military, but they've got to be somewhat competent to have stolen ships and kept them."

"That is true," Chet said. "I agree. Expect them to be modestly capable, but not military trained."

"I'll bet they sleep in shifts and have scouts on duty to watch for anyone approaching, even on foot. So we have two options, as I see it. The first is to hit them when most of their numbers are away during a fight. During a battle, the people they leave behind might be distracted enough for us to get in and steal a ship."

"Assuming all the ships aren't away at the fight," he said, "denying us our opportunity for larceny."

"I suspect they'll be smart enough to leave reserves—and if not, there will be ships in their hangars undergoing maintenance. M-Bot should be able to determine which of them are in flying shape."

"Still sounds dangerous," Chet said, leaning back in his makeshift bed. "I assume they would be *more* alert during a fight, not less."

"Well, our second option is to strike during a long shift when most of them are asleep. We move in stealthily, have M-Bot hack through a ship's security, then fly out with our prize before anyone knows what's happening."

"They'll give chase," Chet noted.

"Trust me, Chet," I said, "I might not know how to build a raft, but I won't have trouble outflying anyone in that group."

"Marvelous! I shall look forward to our flight, then."

M-Bot came zipping back. "I used infrared scanners to search for warm life forms, and didn't find anything larger than a worm," he announced. "No chipmunks, zombified or otherwise."

"Thanks," I said.

"That . . . wasn't a 'made you look' joke, was it?" he asked. "Sending me out to look for things? I can't tell."

I'd completely forgotten about pranking him that once, so it took me a moment to remember what he was referencing. "No joke," I promised him. "We really did want you to look for dangers on this fragment."

"Thanks," he said, then flew off again, likely to begin searching for mushrooms. I sat there for a while, staring upward . . .

Then I jumped when M-Bot returned.

How . . . how long had I just been sitting there, not noticing the passage of time? Chet was already asleep.

I couldn't tell. It could have been a minute, could have been an hour. But M-Bot had seven different mushroom samples in his grabber claws and was laying them out to catalog them. So . . . scud.

I turned over in my bed, worried about that sudden passage of time. Gran-Gran had told me about a man who'd accidentally slept for hundreds of years. That wouldn't happen to me, would it? Normally a thought like that might have kept me awake. But this time I fell right to sleep.

INTERLUDE

Floating.

I quested out, searching as I had before. Like on other nights, I didn't find anything. I was nearly pulled down by my own tiredness again.

But no. No, I was Defiant. Plus, I was better with my powers than I'd ever been. I was stronger than sleep, stronger than my own worst instincts. Strong enough to . . .

Push through. I latched onto the familiar sensation of Jorgen's mind and pulled myself toward it.

This time I interrupted him shaving.

He jumped as he saw me suddenly reflected in his mirror, standing beside him in the lavish bathroom. It had *two* sinks. He was wearing a towel, fortunately, but I do have to say . . . boy took care of himself. Mandatory PT for pilots didn't give a fellow pecs like that, not without some extra reps at the gym.

"Spin!" he snapped. "This is *not* a good time."

"Oh, and last time was better?" I said, folding my arms and refusing to be embarrassed. "At least you're not getting shot at."

He reached for his towel to wipe away the shaving suds covering half his face, then—wisely—stopped. Finally, he took a deep breath. "Sorry," he said, "I didn't mean to snap at you. You certainly couldn't have known you'd find me in a compromising position."

"Huh," I said. "How do you do that?"

"What?"

"Stay calm," I said. "Be so understanding."

"Command training."

"Bull," I said. "I know your secret, Jorgen Weight. You're a good person."

"That's . . . a secret?"

"Hush," I said. "I have to say things like that or I'll look like an idiot for taking so long to figure it out. It would help me out a *ton* if you'd at least *pretend* to be an actual jerkface now and then."

"I'll work on that," he said, smiling.

I stepped forward, then edged around him so I could stand between him and the sink. He could only see me in the reflection, so if I stood there—facing the mirror—our height difference meant we could look each other in the eyes. He stepped back to give me room. Saints, that smile was adorable with half his face shaved. Even the tiny scabs from his healing cuts were adorable, in a grizzled warrior kind of way.

I, however, was anything *but* adorable. I'd never been one to fret over my appearance—even when I tried during my school days, kids used to joke that I looked like a rodent. They felt so brilliant realizing that the rat girl was a bit mousy.

That said, *scud*. "I need to find a hairbrush, don't I?" I said. "And a shower. Or seven."

"You look just fine."

"Ah, 'just fine.' Exactly what a woman loves to hear."

"I'm sorry," he said. "I meant to say that you look like a barbarian who just finished killing her seventeenth rabid tiger to make a necklace out of their incisors."

"Really?" I said, tearing up. I mean, it was silly but . . . you know, he was trying.

"It's like you came strolling directly out of a barbarian story," he said. "Except for the jumpsuit."

"I can fix that," I said, reaching for the zipper.

The way his eyes bulged was totally worth it. But he looked so uncomfortable that I spun around to face him, raising my hands. "Joking! I'm *joking,* Jorgen. Don't faint or anything!"

He shook his head, reaching for a washcloth to wipe the suds from his face. That left his face half-covered with black stubble, which would have been sexy, except . . . you know, the fact that it was only half the face. I turned back around toward the mirror.

"What happened to your face anyway?" I asked.

Jorgen grimaced. "I squeezed a slug. It didn't appreciate it and let me know."

I wanted more details, but I knew our time was short so I didn't press him.

"I lied earlier, Spensa," he said. "Command training did *not* prepare me for you. Nothing could have done that. Anyway, I suppose I should ask for a report."

"Days passed?" I asked him.

"Since our last visit? Five."

Yeah, time was odd in the nowhere. I *thought* it had only been three for me, but I couldn't tell for certain. "I've made progress on my quest," I explained. "I'll tell you about that in a minute, but first I have more important intel. Jorgen . . . I think the Superiority leaders are trying to make a deal with the delvers. An alliance."

He blinked, then took a deep breath. "That's unfortunate."

"That's all you can say?"

"I was taught not to curse in front of a lady."

"Good thing there are none of those here, eh?"

He smiled. "You say you think they'll make a deal. They haven't yet?"

"Not that I know," I said. "But the delvers *were* intrigued by what Winzik said. And judging by what I've felt from them . . . I think it will happen. Unless we find a way to stop it."

"I'll report this to Cobb and the command staff," he said. "It confirms our worst fears, that the delver summoning wasn't an anomaly—but an appetizer. Anything else?"

"I found a kind of heritage site," I said. "It's hard to explain, but I saw some of the history of cytonics, and was taught a little how to better use my abilities. Jorgen, I'm pretty sure *we* were made when the nowhere leaked into our reality and changed people living nearby."

"Changed?"

"Think of it like a mutation," I said. "Caused by specialized radiation seeping through weak spots between dimensions. It means we're not freaks. We're mutations."

"Well," he said, rubbing his chin in thought. "Though I don't like the word 'freak,' many would call a mutation *exactly* the sort of thing that makes you one. Certainly, a 'defect' could be caused by a mutation. So I'm not sure what you're saying."

"I'm saying that we're not some kind of sleeper agent for the delvers," I said. "We predate them, in fact. What's happened is that cytonics have blended with the nowhere—giving us access to it, letting us bend *our* reality to work the way *it* does."

He nodded slowly. "If what you say is true, then we could potentially make more cytonic people."

"There's a portal," I said, "on Detritus, in the tunnels near Igneous. Search northeast of the cavern, near some old pipes in a place with some strange patterns carved in the stone. You might want to study it."

"I'll put some people on it," he said.

"Be careful," I noted. "A cytonic can fall through and get stuck in here—and it's hard to get out. So don't, you know, pull a Spensa."

"Will do," he said, meeting my eyes in the reflection. "This *is* important. I'm glad you stayed, even if it means . . . well, this." He gestured at my ghostly state.

"I'm going to continue on the Path," I said. "First I have to deal with a bunch of pirates though."

"There are *pirates* in the nowhere?" he asked.

"Yeah. Awesome, isn't it?"

"I thought the place was . . . well . . . nothingness."

"Kind of is, kind of isn't?" I said. "It's complicated. I'm going to steal a starfighter tomorrow, which should let me get to the next memory dump."

He backed up to lean against the wall, his arms folded, thoughtful. And for the first time I noticed how tired he looked. It was tough to tell with Jorgen, who always seemed so upright and solid—his dark brown skin making it harder to make out signs of fatigue like bags under his eyes.

"Jorgen?" I said. "You all right?"

"Things are tense here. We've found a way to protect ourselves—the planet's defenses are fully online, thanks to Rig and the engineers."

"Well, that's good. You're safe."

"Too safe," he said. "The galaxy is collapsing under the control of a tyrant while we're hiding. I know we barely started playing on the galactic stage, but it feels wrong to hide. We should be doing something." He grimaced. "It's politics, Spensa. You would be indignant if you were here."

"You can be indignant on my behalf."

"I'm trying," he said. "But you know how my parents are. I love them, Spensa, but . . . they're partially responsible. They would have us keep hiding, hoping the enemy will just leave us alone. I know that will never happen. I knew it *before* you told me about what's happening with the delvers."

"Maybe my news will be enough to get them to listen."

"Maybe," he said, sounding entirely unconvinced.

I glanced around at the decor. I'd noticed that this wasn't some standard DDF bunkhouse latrine, but now I saw more. Was that *gold* on the trim? White marble?

"You're home," I guessed. "Trying to persuade your parents?"

"I thought maybe they'd listen if I could talk to them outside a formal context. I should have known—they've arranged four dinners for me, all with eligible young women from the lower caverns."

The rich caverns, he meant. The ones best protected from surface attacks. "Good thing I'm not the jealous type," I said.

"Kind of wish you were," he said. "If you'd swing by and decapitate one or two of them, maybe the others would give up."

"Jorgen, please," I said. "Decapitation is reserved for worthy enemies on the battlefield."

This coaxed a full-on smile from him. He walked back up to me, and though we couldn't touch, I could *feel* his mind behind me—and I successfully resisted the urge to probe his mind with my new talents. We stood there, looking, feeling, for a short time. Because it was all we had.

"You know," I finally said, "I'm a *little* surprised to find out you don't shower in your uniform. I half figured there was some outdated rule that required you to wear it at all times, or suffer one sixteenth of a demerit."

"Wait until someone hears that I had a girl in the bathroom with me," he said.

"I'm sure invisible girls don't count," I said, and felt myself start to fade. "Take care of yourself, Jorgen."

"Same to you," he said. "Consider it an order."

I nodded, reaching for him. I felt like I got an armful of something—something that was *him*—as it all vanished and I was dumped back into the nowhere. His essence, like his scent, lingered—as did the picture of him in my head, half-shaven, weary.

Still, this was a success. I'd been able to find him again, and I was more confident in my powers. So confident, in fact, that I did something that might have been stupid. I went looking for the delvers.

Last time I'd dreamed like this, I'd overheard them engaging in an important conversation. Could I do that again? I quested outward, trying to capture the same . . . sensation as last time. The same location? It was wrong to think of anything in this place as having locations. It was more like frequencies or—

Something slammed into my mind.

It was *you!* Brade said. *You were watching before. I told Winzik, but he didn't believe me!*

I tried to pull away, but she was better trained than I was. And she seemed to have some kind of ability to hold on to my mind in a way I'd never experienced before. I was like a fly in a web, buzzing about but held tight by Brade's own mind.

I knew you were alive, she said. *You* did *escape into the nowhere, didn't you? Little cricket, sneaking about.*

Brade, I responded. *You don't have to be like this. You don't have to—*

Of course I don't, she said. *You know what I hate most about you, Alanik? It's that you aren't willing to admit, even for the shortest moment, that I'm capable of making my own decisions. To you, I'm merely a misguided dupe.*

Winzik is going to kill all the cytonics, I said. *That's the promise he made to the delvers. You know that. You're the one who communicated the offer!*

In response, she laughed. She either didn't care or had some plan I didn't understand. And . . . with my improving senses, I could feel a little more. That to her, my complaints were simplistic. Perhaps insultingly so.

She tried to rip my mind apart. But there was one thing I'd learned by sticking up for myself in the past: bullies expect you to fold.

I leaned into the fight. I didn't whimper, or curl up, or back away. I threw myself at Brade with everything I had. Though I was formless, just a collection of thoughts, our minds could clash. Like two bursts of light throwing sparks. Two stars meeting.

She was trained. But I was ferocious.

Brade broke first, then fled, leaving me exhausted as I slowly faded into proper dreams, highlighted by half-shaven officers and epic journeys on sailing ships pulled by dragons.

PART THREE

Threat Assessment Analysis Record DST210503A

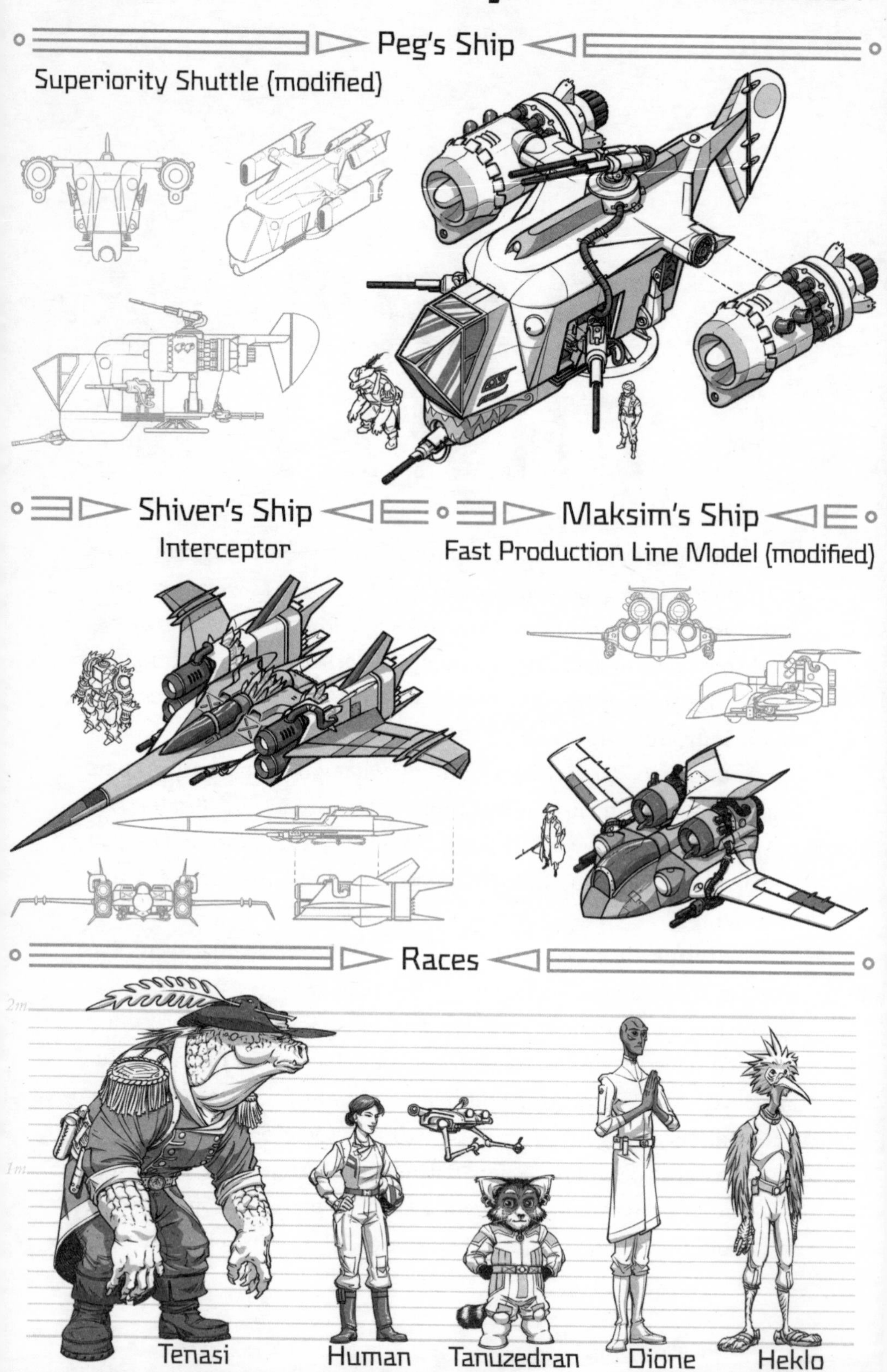

15

Together, Chet and I slipped onto the pirate base fragment. Our touchpoint was a good half hour from the base, so as we crept closer and closer, Chet showed me how to keep a low profile and stay behind tree or hill cover. We also sent M-Bot to scout a path for us, telling him to use his infrared to watch for heat signatures that might indicate a sentry.

As we crept along, I thought of what I'd seen the previous night. Once again, my interactions with Jorgen and Brade were crisp and clear in my mind—and I'd been a little more in control, a little more active in what I'd been doing. That excited me. I was improving.

The terrain here was dotted with scraggly trees that were like stumpy, Spensa-size analogues to the massive ones from the last jungle fragment. Various boulders and hills made for a poor killing field. I'd have set up my base on a sturdy, flat fragment with minimal cover. Maybe losing one of their ships would teach these pirates a lesson, because getting up close was *way* too easy.

I was getting antsy. Eager. If this went well, I'd be flying before the hour was out. Chet and I staked out a tree-topped small hill some fifty meters from the base's buildings. Together, on our bellies, we inched up beneath the trees to where we could see over the top of the hill and study the base.

As far as we could tell, we'd been able to approach unnoticed. Unfortunately, we couldn't rule out hidden cameras. It would depend on what the pirates had been able to salvage. So I watched for any signs the pirates were on alert. Their base was made up of three large structures, rectangular with rounded tops. Like old-school hangars. It was a nostalgic design but didn't make much sense with modern starfighters, which were universally VTOL aircraft thanks to acclivity stone.

"Do you suppose they built those structures?" I asked Chet.

"Doubtful," Chet whispered back. "From what I understand, the pirate factions each set up on fragments with preexisting buildings. Old outposts or the like."

"Will this fragment have a portal?"

"It's possible, but unlikely. Most do not, after all."

I nodded, thinking it through. We'd seen how fragments grew—matter collected around little pinprick weaknesses between dimensions, eventually forming into these landscapes. I didn't know for certain if that matter slipped in from the somewhere or was just replicated here. Did this mean . . . the caverns of Detritus had formed because bits of rock had slipped into the nowhere?

There was no way to tell right now. But either way, it did seem Chet was right about the portals not being on most fragments. Maybe those only formed on fragments where the holes between dimensions were "big" enough that cytonics could get through?

Well, for now I needed to keep my mind on stealing a ship. Of the three hangars, two were dark at the moment. The third—the one in the center—had its bay door open wide, and flashes of light inside indicated welding or electrical work going on. I was surprised to see electricity at first—but most modern starfighters had energy-packed power matrixes that could last years. Plug one of those in, and you'd be able to power the lights and equipment of a hangar like this.

"My sensors indicate two people keeping watch," M-Bot whispered from where he hovered at my side. "One at the window directly ahead in the lit hangar. Another right inside the bay doors. If they're using electronic surveillance, it's wired, as I don't detect broadcasts on any known frequencies."

"They won't broadcast carelessly, abomination," Chet whispered. "Old habits will prevent them."

"Noted, wart-eyeball," M-Bot said.

We sat in silence for a moment.

"Okay," Chet whispered. "I . . . I have to ask. 'Wart-eyeball'?"

"I was going to call you wart-face," M-Bot said, "as humans often append 'face' to insults, but warts are frequently on faces. I instead picked a body part that doesn't usually grow warts—a way of implying your stupidity is irrational to the point of implausibility."

Chet glanced at me.

"Him being weird does *not* mean he's an abomination," I whispered.

"I was more trying to decide if that insult rated a one or a zero," Chet muttered, looking back at the hangars. "So, Miss Nightshade, how would you like to proceed? I believe your military training supersedes my experience in this instance."

"Let me think and observe," I said. I couldn't get a good look at the pirate in the window, but they didn't seem to be keeping a close watch. The other one that M-Bot had noted strolled out into the light, a rifle hanging from his shoulder.

To my surprise he was human, and had a patchy beard that hadn't grown in straight. He wore a long overcoat, a T-shirt, jeans, and boots. Oh, and a hat.

A *nautical* hat. Like, a full-on tricorn.

I could barely hold in a thrilled squeal.

"What?" Chet whispered, noticing my grin.

"These ones actually *look* like pirates!"

"Indeed," Chet said. "Human traditions have had a large influence on populations like these. From what I've been able to gather, our conquest of the galaxy made it trendy—perhaps a little exotic—to use human terms and fashion for outlaws." He squinted. "That said, I didn't expect to find an actual human among their ranks. Not a lot of us around these days."

The pirate in the window leaned out and called something. They were definitely a dione—a right, judging by their red coloring.

"Looks like they're doing some repairs," I said. "M-Bot, swing around the rear and see if you can get a count on how many people are inside. If it appears safe, hover up to one of those windows and learn what you can about the starfighters."

"Understood," he said, and zoomed off. He was extremely quiet—that was why I'd been able to use the drone for spy missions. I wished we still had the holographic projector to give him some limited camouflage.

Fortunately, that guard didn't seem particularly observant. He yawned as he strolled back toward the hangar opening.

"Miss Nightshade," Chet said, "what we are about to try is much more dangerous than our previous endeavors. That guard is armed, and we risk capture or wounding."

"I'm willing to take the risk."

"As am I!" Chet said. "But I feel that we should, out of an abundance of caution, leave your icon behind."

"Leave it *behind*?" I said. "Why in the stars would we do that?"

"That icon is one of the most valuable things in the nowhere," he explained in a hushed tone. "If we are captured, I would not want the pirates to gain possession of it. Instead, I feel we should bury it here. If we succeed in claiming a ship, we can return at some future date and recover it. If we fail, then the icon will be safe."

"But we need it to fly out there!" I said. "Without it, we'll lose our memories."

"It is the ashes that are important for our immediate travels," Chet said. "With a pocket full of those, we can go months without any dangerous effects. And so, we can bring those with us and risk their loss—but keep the much more valuable object hidden."

Scud. There was a logic to his words. If this went wrong, I'd be much happier if my icon was safe. But at the same time, I had seen the way Chet stared at it. I wanted to trust him—I *did* trust him—but . . . if he wanted to take the icon, then persuading me to bury it here would be a great first step.

I wavered. Chet had treated me with nothing but honor so far, but my concerns hovered at the back of my mind. He'd appeared in *such* an unusual way, specifically when I needed him. M-Bot's old pilot, conveniently missing the memories that could help him prove who he'd been.

"Hiding the icon is probably a good idea," I said to Chet, so he wouldn't sense my suspicions. I fished out the pouch and made a show of dumping the reality ashes back into my pocket—but I also palmed the pin. Then I buried the pouch as he'd suggested, except empty. Afterward I handed him a small pinch of ashes. "In case we get split up," I told him.

He stared at the ashes an uncomfortably long time before tucking them away, and as his attention was on them I covertly slipped the pin into another pocket.

Soon, M-Bot came hovering in from behind. "There are three pirates working in the hangar," he whispered to us. "And one other person in an inner room. No other heat signatures in the building."

Right. That made six total in that hangar. The guard, the one at the window, the one farther inside, and three workers.

"There are ten other heat signatures," M-Bot whispered. "Six in one hangar building, four in the other. I think those are all asleep. At least, their heat signatures indicate recumbent figures in smaller rooms."

"Probably divided into three flights," I guessed. "Each hangar houses a flight, and one group is left on duty to watch every time the others sleep."

"Agreed," M-Bot said. "There are four starships in the open hangar, and one is being worked on by the mechanics. Six people. Four pilots, two ground crew maybe?"

"That sounds likely," I whispered. "Any way into that open hangar from behind?"

"There is a small open door at the rear," M-Bot said. "Probably to let air in during the welding."

"Awesome," I said. "We should strike while the other two flights are asleep. Chet, your job is to make a distraction. Can you do something that isn't so dangerous as to make them sound the alarm, but which has a good chance of drawing the attention of not only the guards but the three mechanics too?"

"Possibly," he said. "The Broadsiders are known as the most levelheaded of the pirate factions. I've encountered other guides or groups who have traded with them, or even been employed by them for a short time. I think it will be safe enough to walk up with some reality ashes and offer to trade."

"How likely are they to grab you?" I asked. "Steal the ashes and enslave you?"

"It's a distinct possibility," he admitted. "But again, I believe it's a worthwhile risk. I don't trust any pirates, but if I were going to approach a faction in this manner, the Broadsiders are the ones I'd choose. They should be interested in trading, but will want to keep a good eye—or ten, depending on the species—on me just to be careful."

"Let's go with it then," I said. "M-Bot and I will sneak around back. Once you've distracted the pirates, we'll slip into the hangar from behind and hot-wire a starfighter."

"And you're certain you can accomplish that feat?" Chet asked.

"Well, little in life is *absolutely* certain," M-Bot said. "But I find it *highly* unlikely that these pirates have security I can't instantly break. I'd say it's more likely that you spontaneously grow a wart from your eye. You, um, wart-eye."

I eyed him. "Chet's right. That's *definitely* a zero."

"Ready then," Chet said. "Let's do this."

"Once I have the ship," I said, "we'll activate the weapons and force the pirates to lie on the floor. Run for the ship and climb up into the cockpit. We'll escape, and then we can send M-Bot to sneak back and grab the icon."

"An excellent plan," Chet said. "When do I make the distraction?"

"I'll send M-Bot to signal you when I'm in position. Then count to a hundred before you go for it."

We shared a nod, and then I withdrew to begin sneaking around to the other side of the base.

16

The first thing I did was send M-Bot back to spy on Chet.

"I buried the pouch for my pin under a rock near the trees," I told him. "Covertly watch to see if he digs it up. If he doesn't, stealthily join me behind the pirate base."

"Uh . . ."

"I'll explain later," I said, and waved him off. He left.

My heart thundering in my chest, I continued to sneak around the side of the compound. It was just like creeping up on a rat, only there was more light and these doofs were less observant. I made it to the other side of the compound easily, and found a good spot to watch near a large boulder.

The hangar had a small, person-size doorway on this side. Through it I could clearly see the mechanics working on the landing gear of one of the starfighters—two diones and one of the feathered aliens I'd seen when I first entered the nowhere. They serviced a narrow, sleek vessel that was probably a scouting model. Sparks flew as they welded.

I waited, anxious. I didn't want to be distrustful. Scud, Chet had helped me so much. But I couldn't deny the way he looked at the icon, and it seemed incredibly suspicious that he'd asked me to leave it behind.

I nearly yelped when M-Bot hovered up to me a few minutes later. Stars, he was quiet.

"He doesn't appear to be digging at anything, Spensa," M-Bot whispered. "He's just waiting."

"Okay, good," I said, relaxing.

"Do you think he's going to betray us?"

"I don't *want* to think that," I said, "but I can't help being suspicious." I'd tried so hard to trust Brade, and where had that gotten me? "Go tell him I'm in position. He can start with the distraction."

M-Bot zipped off again. I took a few deep breaths to calm myself. My worry was unfounded.

Unless . . .

If *I'd* been planning to betray my companion, I wouldn't merely steal the pin. I'd do something to disrupt the plan, making certain she got captured by the pirates. That way I wouldn't have to worry about her following me as I made off with the prize.

Scud. Now that I'd thought of it, I couldn't get it out of my head. If Chet simply grabbed the icon and ran, I could conceivably steal the ship and come after him. But if he waited until I was in the middle of the theft, then sold me out, he could keep the icon while making sure I was taken care of.

Again, I didn't *want* to believe it. I almost discarded the worry entirely—but then I thought about the way he *changed* whenever he saw the icon. And what *were* the chances that I'd enter the nowhere and immediately find Commander Spears?

While I didn't actually think some kind of evil wizard was involved—that was more a metaphor—something *was* seriously strange about all of this. I couldn't help feeling I was being toyed with, and Chet was at the center of it.

I made a snap decision. I wouldn't abandon the plan, but neither would I walk straight into a potential trap. First I pulled out my father's pin, then dug a quick hole beside my boulder.

M-Bot came hovering back as I was finishing. "I . . . thought you already buried that," he said.

"I buried the pouch, but kept the pin," I explained. "I'm worried Chet is going to betray us, and this is the best way I can think of to protect the pin in case we get captured."

I felt oddly reluctant to part with it. Like, it almost seemed to cling to my fingers as I put it in the hole. I couldn't help thinking it was *sad* to have me abandon it. This place was messing with me in strange ways.

The mechanics in the hangar stood up and looked out toward where Chet had been hiding. Distraction begun.

"So what do we do?" M-Bot whispered.

"In case my worries are correct, we're not going to steal the ship Chet assumes we will. Which of those other hangars has the fewest sleeping people?"

"The one directly to the right," he said. "It only has four. But . . . Spensa . . . are you sure about this?"

"It's not my job to be sure," I said. "It's my job to do my best anyway. Come on."

We slipped out from behind cover and reached the hangar easily. Sneaking around on dirt and grass was simple. Just had to test each step for leaves or twigs.

The doors were locked, but one of the nearby windows was unlatched. M-Bot was able to slip in, and a moment later the door into the left side of the structure—the part with bunks, rather than the ship storage—clicked. I eased it open, then stepped into a dark hallway.

The place had a clinical feel to it, like the hallways of Platform Prime. Too clean, and it smelled sterile. The doorways were all taller and thinner than the ones at home, and the door handles were all a good half meter higher than I expected. It left me imagining what kind of species had built this place.

In the dim light, I located a door into what I thought should be the hangar proper. M-Bot bobbed up and down—no heat signatures beyond it. This door was unlocked, and I was relieved to find a vast cavernous room. Light shone through slits in the window shades, illuminating four large starships like slumbering leviathans. It was one of the most beautiful sights I'd ever encountered.

I whispered for M-Bot to watch for junk I might accidentally kick while walking—didn't want to send a discarded lubricant can clanging across the floor. As I crept along the wall, I stopped by one of the windows to peek out through the slats.

I could clearly see Chet standing outside the other hangar, surrounded by the guard and mechanics. He spoke animatedly while carefully holding up a reality ash in one hand.

"Spensa," M-Bot whispered. "It doesn't seem like he's betraying us."

It didn't. But, well, that was why I'd continued with the plan. If I really *was* just being paranoid, then I could still steal a ship, break out, and turn guns on the pirates while Chet joined me. I'd tell him I'd been spooked at the last minute and had decided to sneak into a building where everyone was asleep.

I turned from the window to survey the four fighters. Two were obviously civilian ships augmented with some makeshift destructors that marred the otherwise intentional designs. Fortunately the two others were military, with built-in weapons. I picked the interceptor—a lean, dangerous-looking variety of ship that balanced speed and offensive capabilities. It also felt the most familiar, similar to DDF ships from Detritus, with a long thin arrow shape.

I hurried over and grabbed the wing, then hauled myself up to the canopy. I was acquainted at this point with several different control schemes. I'd have to hope that I knew this one's. If not, I'd inspect the other ships. Stars, I hoped I didn't have to end up stealing that shuttlecraft in the corner. Piloting that would be like riding a potbellied pig into battle among a group of knights.

I peered into the cockpit of the ship and it was dark and

shadowed, so I couldn't identify the control scheme from outside. I felt along the rim and found an access port for M-Bot—most ships had external ones for diagnostics. I plugged in his drone to let him interface—which would theoretically allow him to open the cockpit and override the pilot lockouts.

"Ah . . ." M-Bot said. "This will be easy. Hmm. Lots of hard drive space in here. It might feel nice to be in a larger ship again. First though, let's see . . . Should be through in thirty seconds or so."

I nodded, leaning down and staring into the cockpit. That was a control sphere, wasn't it? Yeah, the layout did *seem* familiar. The seat was strange and lumpy though. Like instead of being a chair, it was some other seating mechanism?

Thinking about that started me worrying about the kitsen, who had their own strange way of building starships. They'd helped me at the battle against Starsight. What would Winzik do to them? They were leaderless now that Hesho was dead, sucked out into the vacuum of space when Brade attacked their ship.

The kitsen had trusted me. Had I doomed their entire planet? What happened if Winzik actually persuaded the delvers to help him? I *needed* to find some way to stop them, so—

"Huh," M-Bot said.

"What?" I hissed.

"I just got locked out of a few systems," he said. "I can reroute, but . . . That's odd. The lockout was via a manual override. How would . . ."

Lights went on in the cockpit, illuminating a creature that had been *sleeping* inside. The light reflected off a body that I had trouble sorting out—crystalline limbs and a bulky shape like a pile of glistening stone . . .

"Oh, scud," I whispered.

No heat signatures. But not all life was warm. I *knew* that. Figments like Vapor seemed not to even have *bodies*. I'd made a terrible miscalculation. My sole consolation was that M-Bot had done the same.

"M-Bot!" I said. "Run!"

I leaped off the wing and hit the ground hard, stumbling as a loud alarm started blaring. I made it halfway to the door before a voice sounded over some speakers.

"Keep running, and I *will* vaporize you," it said—my translator pin happily supplying the words in English. I froze, then looked back at the ship to find one of the wing-mounted destructors on a turret pointing right at me.

I raised my hands, struggling to catch my breath and fighting down my instinct to run. Looked like I was going to get another chance at being a pirate captive. And this time it was entirely my own fault.

17

The pirates thumped me down in a seat and one of them lashed my hands behind me. A large group of them had gathered in the hangar, which was now flooded with light.

I saw only one human among them, the fellow I'd noticed earlier. Most of the rest were diones, though there were also several of those bird people and one varvax—the alien species I'd known as the Krell, small crablike creatures that moved around in large blocky exoskeleton suits built from something like sandstone.

The group parted to make way for an alien of a completely different race, with a wide face and powerful limbs. Long teeth and clawed fingers gave this one the overall appearance of something like a bear on its hind legs, except not furry. They walked with a hunched-forward gait, giving them a predatory air, beefy arms held forward and at the ready.

I took this one for the leader of the group, considering the fine jacket and impressive hat, complete with a large plume. "Words!" the creature said. "Trying to steal a starfighter, eh? You must have grown at least six *muluns* for trying that!"

My pin didn't translate the word, which was odd. I sat there, my hands bound behind me, and tried to come up with a plan. The leader alien walked up and slapped me on the back in a way that felt distinctly friendly.

"But you have rotten luck," the leader continued. "Not a single *gulun* for you! Picking a ship inhabited by one of our resonants? Words, girl. *Words*. Anyway, welcome to the Broadsiders."

"Wait," I said, twisting to look at the leader. "Welcome?"

"The more people we have around, the more stable our memories remain," one of the diones explained. "So you're lucky. No execution for you. Instead you get to be our new cleaning slave."

Great. Well, as awful as being a slave sounded, I felt even worse for messing up the plan. Chet had been trustworthy all along, and here I'd bungled everything.

"There were some ashes on her, Captain," the varvax noted in their language, holding up a glowing transparent bag.

The scruffy human stepped forward carrying M-Bot's drone. "Ma'am? This is what she used to try to break into the starship."

I felt a spike of alarm. *M-Bot?* The drone seemed completely lifeless. The human fiddled with it, then found the old power button—which M-Bot had disconnected. However, when the human pushed the button, the drone's small acclivity rings powered on, turning from dull blue-black to a vibrant glowing azure. The drone began to hover on its own power. Then as the human let go, it hovered over to use its grabber arm to pick up a rag from the floor. It then began wiping a window with it.

M-Bot, you genius, I thought. He always *talked* about how intelligent he was, but considering how he acted a lot of the time, it was easy to forget. Right now though, he did a spot-on imitation of a cleaning drone.

"Huh," the captain said, then nudged me—hard enough that my chair scooted along the floor. "How'd you make it hack the canopy on Shiver's starfighter?"

"It has some illegal programs," I muttered, trying to play the role of the mousy little rat-catcher girl. "I managed to install them before coming in here. Thought it would be smart to hide them in a normal cleaning drone."

That would imply the drone didn't have a proper AI, so theoretically the Broadsiders shouldn't be afraid of it becoming self-aware. Though admittedly I didn't know a ton about AIs.

"Is that so?" the captain said. "Words. That might be useful. I'll consider it an apology gift from you for waking me up in the middle of the night. Grow a *tulun* or two at my generosity, new slave. What's your name?"

"Spin," I said. "Yours?"

"Ha! *Muluns* indeed." She swept off her hat and inclined her head toward me, revealing a crest of yellow feathers like a mohawk. "I'm Peg, captain of the Broadsiders!"

"Peg?" I said, glancing at the captain's legs—both of which were whole. "As in . . ."

The human laughed. "Nah," he said to me in heavily accented English. "She doesn't get it. The name's a coincidence."

He walked over and shut off M-Bot, who dutifully powered down the rings and stopped moving. I twisted, trying to glance out the window to where Chet had been standing earlier, but couldn't make anything out.

"Your friend ran off," the human said to me, then patted the rifle over his shoulder. "Lucky for him, I was more worried about an attack than I was a scout. I only got a few shots off on him before ducking in to see what was happening."

"Your friend abandoned you," Peg said. "Should have given him some of your *muluns*."

That about proved it: Chet hadn't sold me out. He'd run, yes, but that was smart.

Scud, I felt like a complete idiot. Maybe after being betrayed by Brade, I was overly sensitive. Or maybe I was just a terrible judge of people.

Yeah . . . it was probably that. I had to face it, didn't I? I'd spent most of my training assuming Jorgen was a legitimate jerk, while he was actually pretty un-jerky. But I'd tried hard to trust Brade despite the way she acted. I heaved a sigh and tipped my head back to stare at the ceiling.

I only wanted to fly again. I'd trained all my life to be a warrior. That was what I *knew,* what I *understood*. How did I keep ending up in situations like this instead?

"Hey," Peg said, shoving me on the shoulder, "don't get like that. You might not realize it, but you're far better off scrubbing our floors than you would be out there on your own."

I squeezed my eyes shut.

"Keep her on a leash," Peg said, striding away. "And don't let her near that drone, just in case. I'm gonna go back to sleep."

18

"Leash," it turned out, meant a light-line.

I'd never seen one used this way. A loop on one end was fastened around my neck, the other end attached to the wall. The control mechanism was locked tight, leaving me stuck. I'd sooner chew through iron links with my teeth than find a way to slice a light-line.

Though the pirates had joked about making me clean floors, they actually pulled over a box of parts for me, along with several containers of lubricant. They told me to grease each part and set them out on a cloth.

This was good. They *could* have left me to feel sorry for myself—and there's no telling how long I would have indulged that. But when they plopped down the gears and made fun of me for getting caught, demanding I work . . . well, that made me angry. And anger considers defeatism to be easy prey.

I did as they asked, but as soon as I'd gathered my wits and my determination, I quested out with my cytonic senses, searching for Chet. I found his mind relatively nearby; I thought maybe he'd made his way back onto the blue jungle fragment to hide, if it hadn't drifted away already.

Chet? I said to his mind.

Ah, he said, his "voice" laced with pain. *Miss Nightshade. It is good to hear that you are well. I had feared the worst!*

You're hurt! I said.

Merely a . . . small wound, he said. *A destructor shot grazed me. Nothing an old hound like me hasn't felt a dozen times over! Ha . . .*

It was bravado. I could feel he was legitimately in pain. And it was my fault.

Be careful, he warned me. *Talking this way could draw delver attention!*

That gave me pause. He was right. Yet I had an impression . . . Ever since that moment at the Path, something had changed about my powers, or my understanding of them. I knew better how to hide.

I closed my eyes and concentrated. When I reached out to someone like Chet, I could now see that I always did the cytonic equivalent of shouting. So I tried to focus, control my voice. I returned to Chet and brushed his mind with a soft whisper instead.

How is this?

Miss Nightshade! he said. *Why, that is marvelous. How did you learn to be so quiet?*

I'm learning just now, I said. But then, I'd always had a talent for hearing the stars—and the night before, I'd been able to catch thoughts Brade hadn't wanted to share with me. *I think maybe you don't need to project your thoughts to me. Just think them while we're connected, and I will overhear them.*

Does this work? he asked, plainly trying to do as I asked.

It does, I said.

Excellent! What is your situation, then?

Captured, I said. *Chained to the wall and greasing some parts for starship repair.*

Could be worse, Chet said. *What is the plan?*

I haven't really gotten that far.

Fair enough! Chet said. *But this need only be a minor setback. In fact, it could be for the best! We must find a way to visit the next location on the Path of Elders, which is deep within Broadsider territory. I had worried about them hunting us down once we stole a ship. It would be difficult to find time to indulge in a vision while under fire.*

But with you infiltrating their base, perhaps we can find a way to prevent that. Could you see if you can learn how they patrol their territory?

There was a certain forced boisterousness to his words. Connected to him as I was now, I could see that more clearly than ever. He wasn't simply a bundle of endless optimism; he chose to speak this way deliberately.

You are *in pain,* I said to him. *I'm worried about you.*

Don't be. Just focus on getting us a ship. Ha! Those pirates have no idea what they've done by bringing you in among them, I must say.

I found myself smiling. And . . . well, he did have a point. I *could* use this. Being captured by pirates was exactly the kind of awesome thing that happened in the stories; it was merely another interesting challenge to overcome. Plus, I was inadvertently being given a chance to practice my cytonic skills.

Except I couldn't gloss over how my mistake had landed us in this situation. I had to come clean.

Chet, I said. *I'm sorry. I messed all of this up.*

You mustn't blame yourself, Miss Nightshade, he replied. *Sometimes plans don't work out.*

Except, I said, *it was because of me. I . . . changed the plan at the last minute, sneaking into a different hangar than we'd discussed.*

Why would you do that? he asked.

Because . . . I didn't trust you, Chet. I thought you were going to betray me and steal my icon.

I felt the *immediate* stab of pain those words caused him.

You . . . did? Chet said.

I'm sorry, I said. *I . . . well, I let my worries get the better of me.*

Scud, it hurt worse, feeling firsthand his sense of betrayal. *Why?*

he asked. *Have I not endeavored to aid you in your entire quest? Have I not been a worthy traveling companion?*

You have! I said. *I just . . . I'm sorry, Chet. This is my problem, not yours.*

I see, he sent back. *Yes, um. Well, we must move forward! Let the past be the past, one might say. Um. Yes . . .*

Never had words sounded more forced to me. I could feel his anguish; being trusted was important to him, for reasons I couldn't sort through—I could only feel what was on the surface, not his deeper thoughts.

Well, Chet said. *I will recuperate here, I think. You soldier forward! Yes.*

I wanted to apologize again. I wanted to explain the way I was hurt by Brade's betrayal—and the way I was realizing how bad I was at judging people. But he wanted to be left alone. I could feel that. I had to allow him that.

I broke off the connection, feeling sick and worthless. Scud. So I threw myself into greasing the parts and kept an eye on the pirates, distracting myself from my shame by trying to learn what I could about them.

Over the next few hours, I got a glimpse of what it took to keep a flight of starfighters in the air without a proper support infrastructure. Judging from the way they talked, they spent an incredible amount of time maintaining the spacecraft—and figuring out how to make replacement parts out of salvage.

I'd thought our settlement on Detritus had been ragtag, but we'd had the forges and manufactories. We'd had tens of thousands of people, and our entire society had been devoted to keeping a few hundred starfighters in combat. The Broadsiders didn't have any of that. From what I could tell, they were under twenty in number, and flew nine starfighters.

By the time I was halfway through the stack of parts, I had recovered some self-respect and was focused on the problem at hand. Yes, I'd made a mistake. Yes, I'd hurt Chet. I needed to keep pressing forward, however. The best way to make it up to him was to steal a ship, then get us through Broadsider territory to the next stop on the Path of Elders.

Right. First step: try to learn what I could of these pirates. This was an opportunity as much as it was a setback. I turned my attention to the rest of the parts, and soon reached the last of them—a large gear. I set it onto the cloth with a clink.

"Hey," I called to the pirates, "I'm finished."

The human with the scraggly beard walked over, joined by the varvax. I kept extra close attention on *that* one. They were the race who had kept my people enslaved, and I couldn't trust them.

"I could use some more work," I said to them. "What do you want me to do next?"

"You *want* more work?" the human asked.

"Better than sitting around feeling sorry for myself," I said.

After a shared look with the varvax, the human dragged over one of the landing gear assemblies, with the wheel still attached. "You know how to strip this and relubricate it?"

I nodded, fishing in the tool bin the varvax had provided. I wasn't an expert in repairs or engineering—Rig had always been the one who knew that kind of stuff—but he'd taught me how to service M-Bot's original ship during our days rebuilding it. I could handle breaking down a landing gear assembly.

The varvax returned to her work, but as the human turned away, I asked, "So what's your story?"

He paused, then squatted beside me, watching as I somewhat inexpertly disassembled the mechanism. Was he judging me for using the wrong socket wrench *three* separate times?

"I'm not that interesting," he finally said. "But I've got the same question for you. How do you know how to do this? Your master really let you play with machinery?"

"My master?"

"You said you were a thief," he said. "But before you escaped you were a pet, right? Like me? A kept human? Or . . . no, were you in one of the research labs?"

Ahh . . . right. He must have been a human like Brade—some were kept as novelties around the Superiority. Like kings had kept lions back on Old Earth. Fearsome creatures from another world, turned into showpieces. I could imagine the "civilized" peoples of the Superiority being delighted by the dangerous humans who had once tried to conquer the galaxy.

"I'm surprised they put you in here," I said. "You must have been quite valuable as a curiosity."

"Yeah, well," he said. "It's all fun and games until your pet tries to steal the family starship and escape. Too aggressive, they decided. As if they hadn't known what I was when they bought me." He held out a hand. "I'm Maksim."

"Spin," I replied, taking it.

"Don't feel too bad about being locked up," he said, gesturing to the light-line. "The Broadsiders are a good group. Show the captain you're not going to run the first chance you get, and you can work your way up like the rest of us. Hell, if you're as good with repairs as you seem, you'll be in charge of a ground crew before too long."

I looked at the mediocre work I'd been doing on the wheel housing. This was what passed for being good with repairs around here?

"What if I never get to where I won't run?" I asked.

He studied me. "You're new in the nowhere, aren't you? That other guy, your friend, he had a sense about him. Like he knew what he was doing. Not you though, eh?"

"I've only been in for . . ." I tried to remember. "For . . ." Scud. Why was that so hard to remember? "A week? I think?"

"Best not to stress about the time too much," Maksim said. "Even in a group, it's difficult for us to keep track. I'm surprised you lasted as well as you did out there." He patted me on the shoulder, then stood up. "That's why you won't run. You'll feel better here. More like yourself. You'll see."

He didn't seem to even consider it a possibility that I'd been carrying a reality icon, despite the ashes they'd found. Icons must really have been as rare as Chet said.

Well, a plan of attack was forming. I could earn the trust of the pirates by working here a few days, all while learning how they patrolled their territory, like Chet suggested. I could also investigate the flight mechanisms for the various ships and pick out the easiest one to steal.

Then, as soon as I felt the time was right, I could grab M-Bot, steal a ship, dig out the icon, and be on my way. Maybe with all that done, Chet would forgive me for being a complete jerkface.

"Where did you learn mechanics so well?" Maksim asked. "And why would they throw you in here? If you're this talented?"

"I'm not as talented as you think."

He smiled. "I know it's sometimes hard to open up. But if you tell us about your old life, we can remind you about it. If you forget."

"Scud. That happens?" I said, making small talk. My mind was more focused on planning my escape than on what I was saying.

"It's not as bad as it sounds," he said. "Especially if you have friends to help you remember."

"Well, I wasn't thrown in here," I said, turning back to the wheel mechanism. "I jumped in myself. Though admittedly, I *was* being chased by a bunch of soldiers at the time."

"Ha!" Maksim said. "They really should learn not to keep us as pets."

I almost told him I wasn't a pet. That I was from a human planetary enclave. He was so friendly, I wanted to trust him and explain that I was a soldier fighting the Superiority.

Yeah, that would be a *bad* idea if I wanted to steal a ship. Fortunately, I was slowly learning my lesson. Best not to tip off a captor to what I was planning. Of course, what if I was making a mistake by *not* trusting him? I'd been too suspicious of Chet. But not being suspicious *enough* of Brade had landed me in enormous trouble.

Man, I was *crap* at judging people, wasn't I?

At any rate, the best option seemed to be to remain quiet about my skills. Maksim left me and went over to chat with his varvax friend, gesturing toward me periodically. The speed at which I did my work seemed to make them suspicious, and I realized that maybe I should have pretended to be more ignorant.

Regardless, I needed to contact M-Bot. So I decided to mutter and talk to myself a lot as I worked. It felt like a good idea to demonstrate to the others that I was constantly chattering, even when nobody was around. That way, when I eventually talked to M-Bot's drone, it wouldn't look so odd.

I kept stripping and lubricating the mechanism—trying to slow down—for what had to have been another few hours. Until eventually I felt a mind hesitantly pushing against mine.

Chet? I asked.

Indeed, he replied. *I would like to speak with you. But perhaps we should do it the quieter way you did before . . .*

Done, I said. *But Chet, I—*

Please, he said. *If I might begin?*

Go ahead, I said, forcing myself to hold back another apology.

I have been thinking a great deal about our earlier conversation, he said. *And I wanted to admit something to you. Your suspicion of me isn't entirely unfounded. I have been . . . disingenuous, Miss Nightshade.*

In . . . what way? I asked.

I am not everything I appear to be, he said. *It is difficult for me to admit, for me to explain. You see, I've told you I don't remember being Commander Spears—but it's worse than that. I . . . have been in here so long that I've lost much of my identity. Not only memories, but personality as well. Everything I was . . . crumbled away, like dirt before a persistent stream.*

As this happened, I grew frightened. It is a terrible thing to lose yourself, and I had to replace it with something. And I remembered stories. Fanciful stories perhaps, but full of men I'd admired. Allan Quatermain, Lord John Roxton, Chet Cannister. As I lost myself, I . . . I filled in the gaps, you see. The line between the hero adventurer and me blurred.

And so, you are right to be suspicious. You perhaps thought me a liar, and in a way I am. Because I could not show you my true self. I've forgotten him.

Chet, I said. *That doesn't make you a liar.*

Perhaps not, he replied. *But the truth is . . . difficult to bear. I am not really a man, Miss Nightshade. I'm a collection of stories stuffed into a brain with no context, trying so very hard to simply keep going.*

You're a hero, I said.

If that were true, he replied, *then I'd have confronted the truths in the Path of Elders long ago. They . . . frighten me, Miss Nightshade . . . Spensa, they frighten me. For reasons I can't explain, because I don't quite remember. I think part of* me *is hidden in them somewhere, something that terrifies me. If I were a true hero, I would have walked that road on my own long ago.*

I didn't know what to make of that. I could feel his sincerity, and his fear. Even his confusion.

It doesn't matter where it came from, I said firmly. *You rescued me, guided me, helped me. And now you're walking this Path with me.*

All for a fee, he said. *You . . . noticed how I look upon your icon. I see now why you . . . treated me as you did.*

I felt another spike of shame. Mirrored by his own.

We are quite a pair, aren't we? he sent. *I hope that being near an icon will help me become more . . . solid. That the reality ashes, and the tie back to the somewhere, will help me somehow. I cannot entirely blame you for worrying about my intentions.*

My distrust hurt you though, I said. *Still hurts you.*

Yes, he admitted. *It's in the persona, you understand. I . . . I must see myself as a hero, the gentleman explorer, beloved and trusted.*

Because if I'm not that, well . . . Well then . . . That is all I have left of what I once was. Those dreams, those aspirations.

It was a strikingly candid moment, where I could feel him exposed, frightened. Scud. I didn't deserve his confession, but in that moment I knew I could trust him. The face he showed might have been a patchwork creation of his memories of stories, but the heart inside . . . that was good. Solid.

I tried to project this to him, and it worked. He perked up, and in a moment of wordless communication, he accepted my apology. We would continue forward, we would walk the Path of Elders, and we would find the secrets.

I broke off the communication, then aggressively attacked the last of my work on the landing gear. I probably should have been tired, but I wasn't—nor was I thirsty. In fact, I had no idea how long I'd been working. I couldn't use my fatigue, or even hunger, as a way to judge the passage of time. In here, I often felt like I could just keep going. Forever.

That was dangerous. I was going to have to keep a close eye on myself.

19

A few days later, I felt I was finally getting a handle on the Broadsiders as a group.

"Yeah, there are six pirate factions," Maksim had explained as we went through some booster maintenance on my second day as a captive. "We Broadsiders are smaller than we used to be, but we're one of the first and most proud."

"And the Superiority?" I'd asked. "Several of these starfighters are their models."

"Ha! Yeah. The poor drips that run the mining operation at Surehold ask for ships to protect themselves from us. Which gives us plenty of opportunities to steal them!"

Over the next two days, I subtly picked out more information. The factions had been disorganized until a few years ago—more very small roving bands, or straggling refugees. The organization into factions had come as they solidified into the current six.

They spent most of their time trying to steal from the mining base, capturing new people who were exiled, or even raiding one another. Over the days as I watched, the Broadsiders curiously didn't lose a single one of their nine ships in battle, though they went on a couple of raids. So maybe these were quick encounters, more about posturing than actual fighting.

Of all the Broadsiders, I found Peg the most interesting. There was something . . . different about the large alien. She was a tenasi, a race that I'd learned—on Starsight—was often used to pilot drones or do other fighting in the Superiority. She certainly had a dominating presence, and she watched me carefully whenever she was near.

Other than her, four people commonly worked in our hangar. Maksim was one. The hangar I'd broken into had actually been his, though he'd been spending his guard duty hanging out with another flight. His flight was named Cutlass Flight—again, borrowing Old Earth terms because the pirates found them intimidating. I had essentially been assigned to this flight myself, as I was under their supervision.

The varvax in our flight was named Nuluba, a female of their species. She still made me nervous—I couldn't look at her without seeing Winzik, as her exoskeleton was the same color green. Together she and Maksim made up the ground crew for Cutlass Flight, which currently had only two active starfighters, plus Peg's shuttle—which she was very proud of, but which I wouldn't want to fight in.

There was also one ship that wasn't combat ready yet: an old civilian vessel the team was modifying to be battleworthy. It, like the shuttle, had a light-lance for towing; though the Superiority didn't commonly use those for battle, they had them for industrial purposes. Now the team was installing destructors. As I did reconnaissance over the next few days, I decided that was the ship I was going to have to steal. Peg's shuttle had an unfamiliar control scheme, and the two more combat-ready ships . . .

Well, they were occupied by Cutlass Flight's two starfighter pilots. Both were of a crystalline species who literally inhabited their ships. As I was asking about their battle skill, Maksim dropped a really important piece of intel.

"It *is* nice to have two pilots who live in their cockpits," he said, wagging a wrench toward the ships. "As soon as the scanner tells us a raid is coming, they're ready."

Scanner?

The Broadsiders had a long-range scanner?

I'd assumed they'd have smaller proximity sensors like on starfighters. But a full-blown, long-range piece of surveillance equipment? That came as a surprise.

I immediately started nosing about. The scanner's display was in our hangar, it turned out, and it was attached to some equipment up on the roof. It tracked ships and kept a detailed map of the region. Later that day, I managed to catch a look at the screen while the full map was up, showing me a more detailed version of what Chet had once drawn out for me.

The Broadsider territory was a wedge of the belt tapering inward, bordered by other pirate factions on either side. All of their territory ended at Superiority territory—a wide band that dominated the middle of the belt in this region.

Excited, I sent word to Chet that night.

There's a scanner, I explained. *A big one that watches for incoming ships. It can scan all the way to the Superiority's region of space, though I don't think it can spot individual people. It doesn't have enough resolution for that.*

That's more than I thought they'd have, he said. *They mostly scrounge for technology—I wonder where they acquired a high-powered scanner.*

No idea, I said. *But it's a good thing I got captured, because . . .*

Because with that scanner, they'd be able to track any ship we stole all the way to the next step in the Path, Chet said. *Scrud. We'd never have managed to investigate the portal. They'd have been able to chase us all over the region. I am glad we found this out—though if offered the chance, I'd have chosen a route to this information that didn't involve my shoulder being baked like brisket . . .*

He'd been spending the days "convalescing," by his terms. I still felt bad about the destructor shot.

Anyway, I said, *this gives us an opportunity. I will need to sabotage that scanner before I go.*

Ha! Don't enjoy yourself too much, Spensa. You'll make me feel left out! What is the next step in our plan, then?

I turned over in my bed—a mattress and blanket in the hangar, where I was tethered to the wall. They'd been giving me more slack lately on that, but I was still locked into place for now.

Next step, I said, *is to contact M-Bot. I'll need to upload him to steal the ship.*

Excellent, Chet said. *Give my best to the abom—to the AI.*

I appreciate you trying to think of him that way.

If I have been misjudged, Chet said, *then I too may misjudge. I don't think it wise to keep an AI near, but that is a gut instinctual reaction. I should instead accept your word on his character. Perhaps if I'd done that sooner, I would not have given you cause to mistrust me.*

I winced, like I always did when Chet felt pain during our communications. *Regardless,* I said, *I have a plan for contacting M-Bot. I just need to find a starship part that's in bad disrepair . . .*

Once our conversation was done, I began to drift off to sleep—then stopped myself before fully going out. I tried to contact Jorgen, but something prevented me. A kind of odd mist hovered around me, blocking my attempts. I wasn't certain what to make of it, yet . . . I'd seen this on other nights recently, hadn't I?

The next morning, Maksim clapped his hands and ceremoniously unhooked my light-line, then turned it off. "You've earned a little more slack. Peg's orders." He leaned in. "Don't hang yourself, if you can help it."

I felt at my neck. My natural instinct was to bolt. I fought that down. "Thanks," I said, standing up and stretching. Only four—no, it had been five, hadn't it?—days with the Broadsiders, and I had already gained this much trust? This was going *great*.

"We've got some gears to grease," Maksim said.

"No more gears, please," I replied. "I feel the need to make myself extra useful, to prove myself to Peg. Tell me, what's the most broken-est thing you have in here?"

"Don't know about that," Maksim said, but gestured toward one of the fighter ships. "But Shiver's left destructor has been acting up. If you could somehow fix it . . ."

I nodded and went to check in with Nuluba, who had an office area at the rear of the hangar. She authorized all work, and soon I found myself under the wing of the starfighter, prodding at the defective destructor. Black gunk was leaking out of one of the seams, and the entire thing smelled terrible.

"Uh," I said, "how long since you've serviced this thing?"

A large blue crystal, shaped like a prism, sat on a stool beside me. A crust of smaller crystals held it in place, and a line of the same crystals ran across the floor and up the wheel and side of the starfighter into the cockpit.

The larger crystal nearest me vibrated with a reverberating tone. I would never have recognized it as a language; it sounded one step away from the noise an engine made when close to locking up. But my pin knew better than I did, and translated the peals into words.

"It has been months," the crystal admitted. "Maybe longer. Time is so hard to track in here . . ."

"Months or more?" I said, incredulous. "Destructors should be serviced every *week*."

"We thought it unwise to open the housing, considering the damage to it," the crystal said. "We thought it might break and not be fixable."

"Prevention is always better than repair," I said.

"Wise words," the crystal replied, "but accurate only as long as you have access to preventive measures."

The crystal was an alien creature known as a resonant. This one, whose name in English was Shiver, had told me she was female "this time." Their entire bodies were made of crystal that could grow at will. She'd filled the inside of the starfighter cockpit much as minerals fill a geode.

The part I was talking to now—the larger gemstone—had grown rapidly as I'd come over to inspect the machine. I imagined this part was like an arm or something—a "limb" Shiver could extend for interaction. The large crystal at the end didn't seem necessary; I had the sense she created it to give others something to address when speaking to her.

My attempt to steal a ship had been doomed from the start; I'd chosen a vehicle where the electronics and controls were grown over by Shiver's body. Normally, a resonant would remain in one place for an entire "incarnation," which I gathered lasted some fifty years or so. This time she had grown herself through the starship, almost coming to inhabit it as an AI might. Or actually, like a figment.

"Hey, Shiver," I said as I unscrewed the housing on the destructor to get a look at the guts, "you ever heard of a species known as figments?"

"Indeed I have," Shiver said. "Such strange and mysterious individuals. I've never met one, but I've always been fascinated by them."

"I was thinking they're kind of like your species," I said.

"In what way?"

"Well, you both kind of *inhabit* a spaceship. Like . . . I don't know, a soul in a body."

"That's a fascinating perspective."

The way those words sounded made me think of how Kimmalyn would reply "bless your stars" to some stupid comment I'd made.

"I feel like you disagree with me," I said.

"Though I find some holes in your logic, I'm certain I'll understand better after considering your opinion."

I'd nearly forgotten how conciliatory people from the Superiority could be. Here was a literal group of pirates that had caught me trying to steal from them, and they had treated me almost like a houseguest. A chained-up one, but still.

"You can tell me if I said something dumb," I said as I worked on the housing screws. "I'm not going to be offended."

"It's not really our way . . ."

"You're a starfighter pilot," I said. "You fly out there weekly to fight. You can't argue with me a little?"

"Spin, my species evolved as motionless individuals who would spend decades next to one another. It's not in our nature to argue. Unlike motile species, we cannot simply walk away if we make one another angry."

Huh. Yeah, that made sense.

"But," Shiver said, "in the name of broadening both of our understandings, let me explain. You imply that I am like a figment by the way we both control a ship. I find this a superficial observation, as it makes us similar in the same way any two species who use appendages to move controls would be similar—no matter how different their cultures, bodies, and core chemical makeups might be."

"Yeah, I can see that," I said. "Honestly, I might just be missing my friends."

"I can understand," Shiver said. "I also miss my seven mates from my cavern. I grew to be part of them for three incarnations, and now . . ."

I doubted a crystalline creature could cry. But the peal that came next was reminiscent of it, and the pin didn't interpret the sounds as words.

"Hey," I said, finally getting the last stubborn screw out. "We'll find a way out of here someday."

"Of course we will," Shiver said. "Of course we will."

Those words also had the same feel of something Kimmalyn would say. The two would get along fantastically. At least, both seemed pretty good at handling me.

I pried off the destructor's outer housing, then wrinkled my nose. The weapon clearly had a leak in its mechanisms—fluid had been seeping out for some time. Then firing the weapon had heated it up and charred it all, resulting in a heavily corroded mechanism full of flaky black ash.

This is perfect, I thought, careful not to show my excitement. I'd wanted something broken, but something that was broken *and* needed cleaning was even better.

Out loud I said, "Scud. This is a mess."

"I resonate that," Shiver said. "And felt it might be so."

"This is going to take a while to clean up," I said. "I'll pull it off the ship for now, so you'll be missing a destructor if you have to fly."

"Unfortunately, the nature of our existence often requires flying in suboptimal conditions," Shiver said. "I wish you speed and self-fulfillment as you work on your repairs, Spin."

"Thanks," I said. I affixed a small portable acclivity ring to the bottom of the mechanism, then began unhooking it from the wing. That took about a half hour, but once I was done, I lowered it with a remote control.

The destructor was a good meter and a half long, shaped kind of like a missile—and with the housing removed, it was all exposed wires and char. As I hovered it along, I got a glimpse out the back door—and it took extreme self-control to not immediately run out and dig up my father's pin. I knew it would be safe out there though. Much safer than in my possession.

I hovered the unmounted destructor over to Nuluba's desk, where she was cataloging salvage. The varvax liked to keep track of things like that, which I found suspicious. Who became a pirate to do *paperwork*?

"It's not looking good for this, Nuluba," I said, gesturing to the destructor. "I won't even be able to tell how much is fixable until after I've cleaned it off—and that alone could take weeks of effort."

"My, my," Nuluba said, standing from her desk and inspecting the destructor. Like others of her kind, she made wide gestures with the hands of her suit as she spoke, the sound being projected out through the sides of the exoskeleton's head. "We don't have a replacement—I already have four other faulty destructors. Spin the captive, there's no way you could speed up this repair?"

"You're kidding, right?" I said, gesturing to the destructor.

Nuluba sighed.

"I suppose," I said, pretending to think about it, "my old cleaning bot could work faster. Don't know where you put it though." As soon as I said it, I found the attempt awkward. The varvax were such a crafty species; surely Nuluba would immediately see through what I was doing.

"Oh!" she said. "That's a good idea. Here, let me get it for you."

I felt an immediate spike of alarm. That had been too easy, hadn't it? Yet the varvax wandered off, then less than a minute later returned to the hangar, M-Bot's drone floating alongside her. I cautiously guided the destructor over to a workbench near the corner. Nuluba left the drone with me and returned to her work as if nothing unusual were happening.

However, as I looked M-Bot over, I was pretty sure I caught Nuluba watching me. So . . . this was a test of some sort, maybe? That made sense. The Broadsiders had probably been expecting me to ask to use the drone. Still, it seemed odd they'd allow it after such a short time of us working together.

Maybe they'd placed a bug of some sort on him. Would trying to talk to him alert them?

They don't think he's an AI, I reminded myself. *They think he's just some kind of spy bot.*

Regardless, I had to take the chance. I knelt and opened the side of the drone where the controls were and acted like I was engaging some programs. Then I whispered, "Hey."

"You should know," he whispered back, "they've installed some very basic monitoring software on me."

"That's actually a relief," I whispered. "I worried it was too easy to get them to let me work with you. I assume you can deal with the software?"

"Obviously," he said. "I'm trying not to be *too* offended by the AI scrubbing they tried to do. It's basically the equivalent of feeding me poison. Fortunately, in this case that 'feeding' involved a comically large spoon and a big sign that said 'not poison.' I was able to circumvent it with ease, but—as one might say—it's the thought that counts."

"Right, then," I said. "I need you to make it appear as though I used a code to access some of your hidden programming, then spoof it so they think I set you to monitor and record what is said nearby. That will give them something to find that isn't *too* suspicious. After that, make it seem like I activated your deep cleaning and repair protocol."

"Great," he said. "Um, what deep cleaning and repair protocol?"

"The drone's original . . . Oh. We deleted that, didn't we?"

"What you didn't delete, I did when uploading myself," M-Bot whispered. "I wasn't about to keep cleaning protocols when I barely had room for myself, my mushroom databases, my backup mushroom databases, and my backups to the backups."

"Well, start pretending to clean alongside me and at least spoof the existence of some cleaning programs. I told them it would take weeks to fix this destructor without your help, but I honestly have no idea. I was just looking for an excuse."

He complied, and the two of us set to work. Fortunately, he quickly identified the burned compound and suggested a specific kind of solvent for cleaning it. Even though he didn't have his cleaning routines, his chemistry database proved extremely helpful. Which was good, since the truth was that I had no idea how to repair a broken destructor. That went far beyond the basic maintenance Rig had taught me.

I kept us to the corner and chattered away—mostly talking to myself, keeping up my act. When nobody else was close, M-Bot could respond. He did have in his databases plenty of detailed starship schematics. So as we removed more of the black gunk, he could point out the problems with the machine. The multiple serious problems.

"I feel like I should be offended by proxy for this gun," M-Bot said. "Continuing to fire this was the machine equivalent of . . . um . . ."

"Of forcing your poor warhorse to keep galloping after it has thrown a shoe and taken an arrow in the flank?" I asked.

"Good metaphor," he said.

"Thanks," I said. I was lying on the ground, delicately trying to get some of the gunk off without ripping out a set of coolant hoses. "It's really good to hear your voice, M-Bot. Sorry I got us captured."

"Well, I did find some interesting molds in the other hangar. They're basically diet mushrooms, so that part was pleasant. What happened to Chet?"

"Got wounded," I said, "but escaped. I can talk to him with cytonics. He's recovering, and will be glad to hear that you and I have made contact."

"Are you certain?" he said. "He still thinks I'm an abomination."

"He's getting better about that."

"Maybe he shouldn't be," M-Bot said. He already kept his voice very soft when talking to me, but something seemed even more . . . hushed about this question. "The way the pirates checked to make sure there wasn't an AI in me—going so far as to inject scrubbing software—indicates Chet might be right. What if I *am* an abomination?"

"People think humans are abominations too," I said, getting a big chunk of the gunk free. "They consider that as verifiable as military protocol or personnel records. But it's flat-out wrong."

"The rumors about AIs must have started somewhere."

"Sure," I said. "Like the rumors about humans. I mean, we apparently tried to conquer the galaxy *three times*. Doesn't mean we're monsters. Just inefficient tyrants."

It was growing increasingly difficult to reconcile what my ancestors had done with the stories Gran-Gran told me. It was easy to think of yourself as the hero when you were fighting back against a vengeful enemy bent on extermination. But what about when you were the ones conquering? How many people like Morriumur—ordinary diones trying to prove themselves—had died in the wars my people had started?

It made me uncomfortable. I quoted Alexander the Great and Genghis Khan because when faced with annihilation, we needed that kind of courage. Yet both of those men—confirmed by M-Bot's databases—had been mass murderers on a terrible scale.

My life had been so much simpler when I'd been fighting the nebulous "Krell" and not real people.

"Spensa," M-Bot said, hovering in close. "Thank you. For continuing to be my friend. Despite the potential danger."

"Thank you in return," I said. "I mean, think about it realistically. If one of the two of *us* is going to end up being responsible for the other's death, who's it going to be? The fiddly little robot who loves mushrooms? Or the meter-and-a-half-tall terror who once tried to get her best friend to agree to be scalped so she could put her first notch on her toy hatchet?"

"Oh dear," M-Bot said.

"In my defense," I said, "Gran-Gran didn't explain well, so I thought scalping someone meant cutting their hair real short, but while using a sword or an axe. It sounded pretty cool."

M-Bot fell silent as Nuluba came walking by with a tablet, tapping away. I muttered to myself, talking as if to the black gunk while M-Bot sprayed solvent.

Eventually he spoke again, very quietly. "Spensa, something is odd about this destructor."

"Other than the fact that it seems to have been fossilized in a tar pit?"

"Other than that, yes. Those two boxes installed on the sides of the weapon? They're output modifiers. Normally you'd use something like that to increase the heat of a weapon for, say, cutting through metal shielding. Or maybe to modify it to lower shot intensity for training."

"And what do these do?"

"There's no way to tell," M-Bot said. "They've been completely fried by the overuse. But haven't you noticed how the Broadsiders have never lost a ship?"

"I've noticed," I said. "But maybe the Broadsiders are just lucky. They've only been out on a couple of sorties since we arrived here."

"I suppose that's true . . . Huh."

"What?" I asked.

"I just counted the number of sorties I've observed. I came up with ten."

"Impossible," I said. "Ten fights in four or five days?"

"Yeah, strange . . . Oh."

". . . Oh?"

"I just reconciled my internal chronometer," he said. "We've been with the Broadsiders for nearly *two weeks,* Spensa."

My cleaning rag dropped from my fingers. I blinked, trying to remember . . . How many times had I slept? It kind of blurred together . . .

"Scud," I said. "How did you not notice?"

"I have no idea," he said, his voice small. "I guess I'm more alive than I thought, and am experiencing some of the same effects you are. Indeed, a lack of time awareness would seem to fit with what we know of delvers."

Well, that would explain why the others trusted me with M-Bot "so soon." It wasn't soon.

Nevertheless, my brain struggled to make sense of it. With an effort that felt almost *painful,* I thought back over the repairs I'd done. Stripping down the landing gear on all four ships. Doing booster maintenance. Light wing repairs . . .

I immediately reached out to Chet.

Have you contacted the AI? he asked.

Yes, but . . . Chet, how many days do you think I've been in here, captured?

Six? he guessed. *I've been sleeping off my wound a lot though. So maybe seven or eight?*

Fourteen, I said.

He was silent for a moment. Then I felt the emotional equivalence of a sigh.

It is dangerous to stay in one place long, he said. *This happens, Spensa. I'm sorry.*

"Can you set alarms?" I asked M-Bot. "Calendar alerts? We should start aggressively acknowledging each day. See if we can remain more focused."

"Yes. Yes, that's a good idea . . ."

I sensed worry in his voice though. Even if Chet expected this sort of thing, I felt it *incredibly* strange that it affected M-Bot. I did remember sleeping, but found I couldn't count the times I'd done it. This place played havoc with my sense of time in such a way as to make it really difficult.

Two weeks? A lot could change in a war during that time. Were my friends all right? I needed to accelerate my plans for escaping. I had to find a way to upload M-Bot's mind into one of the starfighters. Preferably one *without* a crystalline alien occupying it.

20

"I'll be honest," Maksim said, lounging across the sawhorse, a wrench dangling from one finger. "I always thought something was wrong with me. I was taught about how mean and naturally angry humans were, yet I didn't feel *any* of that, you know?

"Well, my owners presumed their training kept me under control. They had this whole therapy process they said 'cured' aggression, and so were able to get the permits for a human child. They got me when I was nine, and had me sit around and hum."

I looked up from my diagnostic screen, where I'd been quietly preparing to advance the next step of our plan. Peg had mentioned that the base scanner needed some maintenance. I wasn't certain when that would happen, but I wanted to be ready to go when it did.

For the time being, I was doing my best to fit in. And I had to admit I enjoyed chatting with the others. "They had you hum? Like . . . you know . . ." I made a humming noise.

"Exactly," Maksim said. "They'd have me sit on a little mat and just *hum*. For hours at a time. They said it was a special 'proprietary process.' I guess it was the tone I was humming that made it distinctive? Still not sure, honestly, though they had me at it for twenty years."

"Anti-aggression therapy is big business, Spin," Nuluba said from where she sat on the floor nearby, poring over some spreadsheets. "Many parents are terrified that their child might be too aggressive. They'll pay big money for treatment. Any treatment."

"It is a failing," Shiver said, her crystal letting out peals from where it had grown on a box nearby. "Though the humming treatment sounds . . . unusual, there are more reasonable therapies available. I think many people in the Superiority are working hard to create a better society, but . . . some of us question if our goals are worthy. The entire system vibrates with an unsteady tone. It cracks itself with such sounds. We are . . . too polite sometimes to accept this."

Maksim nodded. The beard made him look older than the early thirties he actually was. I'd always imagined that a long rugged beard would make a man seem like a warrior. Maksim disabused me of that image. He looked a lot less like a warrior than he did like a guy who'd been lost wandering the caverns.

His relaxed manner, though, made me curious. I'd assumed all captive humans would be intense like Brade. Yet this guy was so laid back, he could have gotten into a napping contest with . . . with someone I used to know . . .

With *Nedd*. That was it. How had I forgotten Nedd's name? Maksim could have gotten into a napping contest with Nedd and held his own.

"I learned to act real fearsome," Maksim said, grinning. "I'd growl, and show my teeth, and even wave my hands and say 'Boingar boingar.' I told them it was my clan's battle cry. My parents would have found that funny. We didn't have a clan. Only a little family trying to live as normal a life as we could in a research lab."

He glanced away then, like he often did when he mentioned his parents. He'd been denied contact with them after being sold to the pair of varvax. Now he couldn't remember their faces. Few of the pirates had been in here long enough to forget their pasts entirely, and many had been in a group the entire time, slowing the process.

But from what I'd been able to gather, the effects were showing regardless.

"The Superiority failed you, Maksim," Nuluba said. "Shiver is right, though I will say it more strongly than she. It failed you, as it has failed so many."

I'd been keeping an extra close eye on Nuluba. She looked imposing in her shell-like exoskeleton. Did she realize I was plotting my escape? Was she watching me like I watched her?

"What about you?" I asked her, trying to sound nonchalant. "Did the Superiority fail you as well?"

"In a way," she said, the faceplate of her exoskeleton revealing the small crablike creature that was her true shape. "Or I failed it. I was a bureaucrat."

"In the government, I assume?" I didn't really know how other nations did things. "How high were you?"

"High?" She waved her arms, seeming amused. "Everyone always assumes that we varvax are 'in charge' and must be 'so important.' I assure you, we're not! My. Some are, Spin of the humans, but not me. I was stationed in an irrelevant department of an oft-ignored utility. I lived on Tuma."

"I hadn't known that," Maksim said. "Wow."

"Tuma?" I asked.

"Prone to acidic rainstorms," Maksim explained. "But near some nice resource farms. Mostly automated. Cheap place to live. Very cheap."

"Well," Nuluba said, "I did customer analysis for the methane utility farms. I had a lot of information—including population statistics for many planets, so I could judge trends in customer usage. Spent too much time with that data, maybe." She turned away then, lowering her arms. The exoskeleton mimicked the way her smaller crab body moved inside. "I started asking questions. Too many questions. I was thrown in here almost before I knew what had happened . . ."

I frowned to myself, turning back to my work. What was Nuluba hiding? Varvax still baffled me. For example, I'd recently discovered that the fluid-filled inorganic exoskeletons weren't straight technology, but were somehow grown and hooked directly into the varvax's nervous system. How did that work?

"We in the Superiority failed so many," Shiver said. "Often you grow so large—so comfortable—that you feel the cavern must be right, because it is what has been. You're used to it, and it's right, so everyone else must be right as well. You resonate with self-assurance, ignoring the shifting rocks that might someday lead the cavern to collapse, crushing every crystal who lives there."

The others nodded. I continued my diagnostic: I was working on the fourth starship, the former civilian craft that we'd been adding weapons to. Today, my job was to make sure the starship's onboard targeting systems—which we'd just installed—were functioning correctly.

All things considered, my plan to steal it was going well. M-Bot and I had been good at firmly counting the passage of time for the last two days, so I felt more in control, more determined. Focused.

The toughest part was feeling like I was leading on the members of Cutlass Flight. Maksim, Shiver, Nuluba. Even the quiet Dllllizzzz—the other resonant in the team. She rarely spoke, though she'd also grown a crystal near where we were working, and would occasionally make it vibrate in tune with what one of us was saying—a form of approval or agreement, I thought.

A part of me naturally wanted to see this as my new family, to make a home among the people of Cutlass Flight as I had with my other companions in arms. But I couldn't afford to bond to this group as I had to Hesho, Morriumur, and Vapor. Fortunately I recognized this impulse, and could resist with a little tactical cynicism.

Remember that they locked you up, I told myself. *Remember that they're a bunch of pirates, not a true military.*

Theoretically, once we finished with our diagnostics, this ship would be ready to go into combat. Maksim was to be its pilot, and I would be his ground crew.

"So when you fly," I said to him, "it will be to fight other pirate factions?"

"Mostly," Maksim said. "Until we raid the Superiority. Peg keeps talking about a large-scale offensive against them, though they're pretty well outfitted with fighters."

"We have an advantage though," Shiver noted. "Something none of the other factions have. Peg and her . . . history."

This was new. I tried to show the proper amount of curiosity, but not seem too eager. Peg had a secret? Maybe with a few days of work, I could persuade them to—

"Oh right!" Maksim said. "You don't know, do you, Spin? Peg was a Superiority officer. Head of base security at the mining station."

Or maybe they'd just tell me.

"Head of base security," I said. "That sounds important."

"It was!" Maksim said. "She was second in command of the entire Surehold base. So she knows tons about the installation, their fighting protocol, and all that."

"And she threw it away to become a pirate?" I asked.

"More they forced her away," Maksim said.

"It's politics, Spin," Nuluba explained. "Peg's one of the few people in here—pirate *or* worker—who came completely by choice. She took the job because it would advance her career; no one else was willing. Most everyone in here is a dissident like Maksim or me—even the workers don't come by choice. They aren't fully exiles though, right, Shiver?"

"I was a large machinery operator," Shiver told me, her crystal vibrating. "At the Surehold mines. I was sent in here because of an accident back home that was technically my responsibility. They tell us if we work ten years in the nowhere faithfully, we'll be allowed to leave, but that rarely happens."

"So they have a portal?" I asked. "To the outside?"

"Yes," Shiver said. "Right inside the base, but movement in or out is rigidly controlled."

So, that was a potential way out after I finished following the Path of Elders—though I didn't fancy my chances of getting to it. Sneaking into a Superiority base and somehow slipping through their tightly controlled portal seemed a poor option.

"People are rarely let out despite their ten years being up?" I asked Shiver.

"The officials find excuses," Nuluba said softly. "Reasons to keep back the workers, forbid them from leaving."

"I was deemed 'too aggressive' on my performance reviews," Shiver said. "Not Peg's fault, mind you. She always turned in excellent reviews for everyone. There were others who made sure that the more talented workers remained behind."

"And they did the same to Peg?" I asked, looking around the hangar. She'd been nearby a short time ago. Or . . . had that been an hour or two? Scud.

"Well," Shiver said. "First time, she re-upped on her contract willingly. I think she wanted to stay and help the workers get out. But then after twenty years in here, she decided she wanted to go. They kept their contract with her. This would be . . . three years ago, I think? It was time to leave, and . . ."

"And what?" I asked.

"They said that she could go," Nuluba explained, "but that her children had to stay behind."

Wait. Peg had *children*?

"They weren't part of the deal, you see," Shiver said. "The Superiority said they had to stay ten years and work, as they were both young adults, before they could leave. Didn't go well. Peg's shouting still resonates with me today."

"Scud," I whispered. "She seems like a bad person to betray."

"You could say that," Shiver said. "She stole a bunch of ships, persuaded a good thirty of us to follow her, and broke off to join the pirates. Factions formed because of her influence—she had this grand plan of uniting them against the Superiority. Take the entire base and hold it . . ."

Now *that* caught my attention. "That sounds awesome! We should be attacking them!"

"Tried and failed," Shiver said. "We weren't good enough pilots. Superiority beat us bloody. Nowadays, no one will listen to Peg. Factions are broken, squabbling. It's hard enough to survive."

"I'm going to get good," Maksim said. "Learn to fly. I'll become the pirate champion, and the Broadsiders will have respect again."

"Wait," I said, my eyes widening. "There's a *pirate champion*?"

"Yeah, we came up with it a couple years back," Nuluba said as she went over her spreadsheets for like the fourth time. "There must be a best pilot among all the factions, so why not find out who it is? We hold matches now and then. One on one, in a starfighter. Keeps things interesting."

A pirate champion. For me to fight in a duel.

Oh stars. That was beautiful.

No, no, I thought. *No dueling. You are going to focus on the Path of Elders.*

But . . .

Pirate. Champion.

"I'll beat them," Maksim explained, "if Shiver doesn't do it first. You're getting really good at flying, you know."

"I resonate with this," Shiver said, "and appreciate the compliment. You are skilled at those, Maksim."

"Thanks!" he said, then leaned toward me. "Shiver and I have been hatching this for a while. Current champion is one of Peg's sons. Both of them broke off to form their own factions back after everyone failed to beat the Superiority. They won't listen to a word Peg says, but maybe if we take them down a notch that will change."

It was hard to resist the idea of becoming pirate champion, but I had to focus. I abruptly unplugged the diagnostic tool from the front jack of the ship I'd been working on. "Targeting systems still need recalibration," I said, with a sigh, and showed the screen to Nuluba.

"Bother," the varvax said. "I thought you ran it through that already."

"Twice," I said. "Programming must be conflicting with some of the onboard protocols. I'll need to do a wipe and reupload the tech."

"Run a separate diagnostic from another machine too," she suggested. "Might be this device that has the problem."

"Good thought," I said, then jogged over to where M-Bot's drone was polishing the newly repaired destructor we'd been working on. I grabbed him.

"You ready?" I whispered.

"Yes," he said. "Did you find out when the sensor array is going to go down?"

"No," I said. "But we have our chance now for the upload. I think we should take it."

"Understood."

I sent word to Chet. *Operation "Third Time's the Charm" is a go, Chet.*

Good luck, Spensa, he replied. *I shall endeavor not to distract you with communications, and instead sit here and pretend I'm not as nervous as a jockey at his first race!*

I smiled, imagining him compulsively weaving shoes out of reeds—which was what he said he did when nervous, to practice his survival skills. We'd talked about ways he could help, as he was nearly healed from his wound. When the actual theft happened, he would sneak in close to be ready. But for now it was best if he stayed hidden.

Hoping nobody could see how anxious I was, I walked over and jacked M-Bot into the starfighter. It wasn't the fastest of the three—it was a glorified forklift, not a true starfighter. But it was the only choice I had.

I'd pretend that something had gone wrong with the drone, and we'd leave M-Bot hiding in the ship's hard drives until the perfect moment. Once the scanners were down, and maybe once I'd had a chance to sabotage the other ships in some way that wouldn't hurt the resonants. From there, escaping to go pick up Chet should be easy.

M-Bot beeped as the connection was established, and he started to upload himself. That would take about thirty minutes. I needed to find something to do that would keep me from standing around and fidgeting. To that end, I sat next to Nuluba and began sorting through a box of scrap.

I pointedly did not look at the drone. The others didn't seem to have noticed my nervousness, not even Nuluba.

"It *is* different out here," Nuluba was saying. "When I rode with Shiver on that scavenging mission a few weeks back, I felt *distant*. Even with others around me in the ships, it was harder to remember my past than it ever is here in the base."

"It's worse the farther inward you go," Shiver said. "The mining installation is as close to the center as *I'd* ever want to go."

That got me thinking. "So, that region closest to the lightburst. Nobody lives there?"

"No Man's Land?" Shiver said. "No one lives there that I know. It is . . . an odd place. Where time distorts. Something is in there, at the center, watching outward."

"People who get very close to the center see odd visions," Nuluba said. "Have strange experiences."

"Yeah," Maksim said. "I'm not going anywhere near there. The belt is strange enough. Can you imagine if we started seeing things that aren't there?"

"It is not so bad."

I started. That last voice had been . . . Dllllizzzz? I'd never known her to speak.

At the words, Shiver began buzzing excitedly. The pin translated. "What was that? Dllllizzzz, you spoke! Have the reality ashes helped?"

"I . . . saw . . ." Dllllizzzz said, her voice soft. "Saw the past . . ."

"Where?" I asked, leaning toward her crystal—which she'd created at the end of a line of runners leaving her ship, as Shiver had.

"Ruins," Dllllizzzz whispered.

Shiver continued to try to prompt her to speak, but Dllllizzzz returned to her normal low, wordless vibrations.

I pondered what she'd said. She'd seen the past in some ruins—had she happened across one of the stops on the Path of Elders? Was Dllllizzzz cytonic?

Shiver asked Maksim to sprinkle some reality ashes on Dllllizzzz—they'd been doing that regularly with the ashes they'd confiscated from me. I paid attention to see if Shiver could get anything out of her, but no luck. Eventually Maksim settled down next to me and helped to sort through junk for anything useful. "You look thoughtful, Spin."

"Merely distracted," I said.

"Do you want to talk about it?" he asked. "You having troubles remembering?"

"A little," I admitted. "Some faces, here and there."

"That hurts," he said. "I know how it feels. Good news is that you'll probably start forgetting the faces of your captors too. That didn't happen quickly enough for my taste."

He still thought I had been a human captive. Scud, it suddenly felt awful to be doing what I was. Lying to these people, planning to steal one of their ships, maybe sabotage them.

"I wasn't a captive, Maksim," I said. I hadn't meant to tell them the truth—it kind of slipped out. "I lived on a human enclave planet."

His eyes widened. "Those are *real*?"

"One is, at least," I said. "Not everyone in the Superiority agreed that they should exist though. There was . . . a lot of fighting. We'd rebel. They'd suppress it . . ."

It wasn't a hundred percent the truth, but it felt good to share some of myself.

"You grew up in an actual human society?" Shiver asked. "What was it like?"

"It was hard," I said. "My father was killed when I was young. My family had to struggle for food because resources were tight for everyone—but especially those who weren't directly involved in fighting the Superiority."

"So it really was like they say," Maksim whispered. "Humans together . . . just leads to war."

"Hardly," I said. "The Superiority caused this. My people didn't want war—we fled from it. My family—all of us humans on Detritus—were the crew on a vast starship, the *Defiant*. My great-grandmother was in the engine crew, and our starship wasn't part of the human groups perpetuating the war.

"The enemy wouldn't leave us alone. When we crashed on my home planet, they tried to exterminate us. Then they imprisoned us there. I think any society would turn warlike under such circumstances."

"I wouldn't have believed you," Shiver said, her voice ringing out, "if I hadn't grown so long near Maksim. Who is the least violent person I've met."

"That's because you haven't seen me in action yet!" he said, then he made a growling sound. "Just wait until I get into the sky. I'll be fearsome!"

"I'm sure," Shiver said, vibrating with a sound like ringing bells—her version of laughter.

"I believe you, Spin," Nuluba said softly, looking up from her spreadsheets. "I mentioned my job earlier. Well, one year I was analyzing population statistics on the planets of species with 'lesser intelligence.' My job was to suggest where to employ advertising for regions that weren't buying our services.

"But in the data, I found unexpected truths. Many so-called lesser species *weren't* suffering the casualty rates from intraspecies murder that we projected. They were known as aggressive species, so they should have been killing one another at horrific rates. Yet . . . that just wasn't the case.

"I thought I'd hit on something so *important*. Something revolutionary. Proof that our definitions of aggression didn't match statistical models. I spent years gathering my information, thinking I'd be heralded as some great mind."

"Let me guess," I said. "You presented it to your supervisors, and they immediately tossed you in here."

"There wasn't even a trial," Nuluba whispered. "By the way they talked, what I'd done was *dangerous, subversive*. Merely *looking* for evidence that might contradict long-held beliefs was seen as aggressive." She put her hands to her sandstone helmet. "I don't know what they told Vormel, my mate. I didn't get to see him again. I just . . . vanished."

Maksim reached over and took Nuluba by the shoulder to offer support. Dllllizzzz vibrated her crystal, low and sonorous, a . . . comforting sound. The varvax gestured in thanks.

Scud. She really was what she said, wasn't she? An unimportant bureaucrat caught up in something bigger than she was. I felt uncomfortable, realizing how I'd viewed her. I'd done it before, with other varvax. It was hard not to see in them the people who oppressed mine for years. Even still, even knowing what I knew.

Watching them console her, I felt like an intruder.

I'd known camaraderie like this. Expressed it, cherished it. A night spent with the other women in my flight, who refused to let me return to my cavern exile. Evenings together reminiscing about those we'd lost. In a powerful moment, I saw their *faces*. Kimmalyn, Nedd, FM, Hurl, Arturo. Jorgen . . .

Scud, I missed Jorgen. I found myself reaching out with my cytonic senses. Why hadn't I been able to locate him again in my dreams? As always, when I tried to reach him intentionally, I found only that other presence. That familiar one that had been nearby, like a spirit watching over me. It was more distant now.

And angry at me for some reason? Was it the delver I'd contacted? Or . . . something more personal?

I know it was foolish, but I couldn't help feeling it was connected to my pin. And my father.

I excused myself as the others continued to comfort one another. Their genuine emotion made me feel sick. As I moved over to the bins where I could store the salvage I'd separated, I spotted something I'd missed earlier. Someone large sitting in the shadows near the closed hangar doors.

Peg. Captain of the Broadsiders. How had I missed her sitting back here? The thick-bodied alien looked particularly predatory in the shadows. And she was watching me. I didn't need to see her eyes to know that.

Right, then. I took a deep breath and strode over. I hated feeling like people were watching me, thinking about me, but saying nothing. Better to confront them.

Of course, a similar attitude is what got me into my initial fistfight with Jorgen. So maybe I could take it a little more carefully this time?

"Captain?" I said as I reached her. "Is something wrong?"

"Wrong? Oh, I don't know, Spin." Peg laced her clawed fingers in front of herself. She had an almost reptilian appearance, though her skin was a thick hide instead of scales. "Words. You fit in well with the others. Adapting better to this than any other I've known. I hadn't thought you were one to grow *heknans*. I thought you most certainly to only have *muluns* . . ."

"I still don't know what that means, Captain. My pin refuses to translate the words. How do your people . . . grow . . . these things?"

"Sit," she said, gesturing toward a folding chair.

I did as I was told.

"Your pin could be set to translate these idioms," the captain explained. "But you obviously do not know how. It is irrelevant. My tree is distant now, and since I was forced into exile, I can barely feel it or the fruit it grows."

"I'm . . . sorry?" I said.

"No need for *yendolors,*" the captain said, settling into her larger chair across from me, plainly built for one of her stature. She gestured with a clawed hand toward the members of Cutlass Flight. "They are good people, human. Better than you expected to find, yes?"

"Yes," I admitted.

The captain's voice grew softer. "I have watched you, Spin. I know you are a soldier, which is curious. The Superiority doesn't often throw actual fighters in here. The government claims to hate the aggressive, but it has use for the useful, we might say. They grow so many *venmals*. You'd say it differently: that they have much hypocrisy."

"I don't disagree with that," I said.

"I want you to go," Peg said. "I don't want you to bring trouble to these. Tonight, I will arrange for you to be unwatched. You may walk away so long as you take nothing with you that belongs to us."

The words hit me like a brick to the face. She knew. Well, she suspected. And she understood that I was dangerous. Admittedly, I felt a little thrill. This enormous beast of a person found me intimidating?

"You're wondering," Peg said, "if this is a trap, to try to lure you to run so I can have proof you are untrustworthy. But we both already know you have grown too many *kitchas* for staying here. You have killed. Those here, most of them never have."

"You're pirates," I said. "I saw your kind dogfighting others."

Peg leaned forward. "I have killed, Spin. I *have* grown the *kitcha*. The fruit of the murderer. And I can recognize my kind. You will leave."

I took a deep breath. This wasn't what I'd been planning—but it didn't look like I had time to wait for the sensor array to go down. M-Bot had said his transfer would take under a half hour. How long had it been?

"I will go," I told Peg, "if you give me a ship."

"That is not the offered deal."

"It's the one *I'm* offering," I replied. "I have no specific quarrel with you and yours, Peg, but I have a duty to my people. I'm going to need one of your starfighters to accomplish that."

We locked eyes. Scud, I knew in that moment what was going to happen next. I barely managed to throw myself to the side as she leaped for me.

21

Can I point out how horribly unfair it was that I kept getting into fistfights with people who were *literally* three times as big as I was? Next time, I was going to pick a fight with a damn kitsen. Karma owed it to me.

My chair went skidding out behind me as I hit the ground and rolled, coming up in a crouch as Peg grabbed the air where I'd been sitting. Wishing I had Skullbreaker, I backed away toward the tool shelf. Unfortunately, Peg wasn't about to let me search it for a weapon. She came rushing in, hands forward, claws out.

She didn't shout, growl, or call to the others. This was, as she'd said, a contest between two killers. The other Broadsiders somehow didn't count. I did.

Peg lunged for me, surprisingly quick, but I kept moving. I couldn't afford to let her pull me into a grapple; if this came to wrestling, she'd quickly use her weight to immobilize me. Instead I dodged back and forth, keeping a low crouched stance. I reached back to my training and to skills I'd gained from my life as an outcast. You learned a lot when you were the smallest, weirdest kid in the neighborhood—the one with a parent who was the wrong kind of famous.

Peg effectively kept me from reaching the tool shelf—because by going for it, I'd have been forced to turn my back on her. Fortunately, she respected me enough not to turn away and go rummaging for a weapon herself. We rounded each other, and I let her think I was going to play the grappling game, while I actually searched for any other way out.

If I ran, she'd chase me down. I had to try to wound her or knock her out. I feinted, enticing her to lunge again, then I sidestepped in close and rammed my fist into her flank. That would have been a good square-on kidney punch had she been human.

Peg grunted, but didn't seem severely hurt. I felt like I'd punched a sack of rocks—her muscles were tougher, bulkier, than those of any human I'd faced. Scud. I was *not* properly prepared for fighting aliens. Or anyone. I managed to dodge a grab for my hair. I'd let that grow way too long.

Well, she might not have had kidneys in the right place, but she did have knees. Joints had to be a weak spot, and I needed to end this quickly. So I allowed her to get close enough to grab hold of my coat. Then I twisted, fell to my knees, and rammed my elbow into her right knee. She flinched, so I hit her with my elbow again—which was screaming in pain already from the first blow. The hit worked though, sending Peg stumbling back. Directly into the tool shelf.

Metallic peals rang through the room as tools dropped free. I grabbed a wrench and—Peg still holding my jacket in a tight grip—I hit her again. Two-handed. Directly in the same knee.

She let out a howl and released me. I stepped away as she drooped forward and held her knee, grimacing. My own eyes were watering from the pain in my elbow, but I kept a tight hold of the wrench and glanced around the room.

Both Nuluba and Maksim had pulled guns on me. Great.

"I've defeated your leader!" I shouted at them, raising my wrench. "By virtue of trial by combat, I am taking over command of the Broadsiders!"

"Like hell you are," Maksim said.

Yeah, that always *had* seemed too convenient when it worked in the stories. Scud. I lowered my wrench.

Then a blue light shone behind the others. An ominous shape rose into the air, lit from below—at least until the twin destructors under the wings powered up, glowing brightly, focused on both armed Broadsiders. Maksim glanced over his shoulder, then stumbled away, his eyes wide. M-Bot had finished his upload.

They shouldn't have backed down. They could have run for me and gotten close enough to control the situation. Ship-scale weapons weren't precise enough to hit someone close to me without risking hitting me too. But that was easy to say and difficult to think of, when you were facing a pair of guns as big as you were. Both Maksim and Nuluba dropped their weapons.

I didn't wait for further invitation. I dashed between them—scooping up one of the sidearms as I ran—then leaped and pulled myself onto the wing of the hovering starfighter. I unplugged the drone, then the cockpit opened and I climbed in.

"Turn toward Shiver's ship," I said to M-Bot. "Make sure she doesn't power on."

He did so as I settled into the seat. *Saints,* it felt good to be in a cockpit again. It felt like it had been an eternity. I set aside the drone—there wasn't *nearly* as much room behind the seat as I was used to—and the comm crackled.

Finally, M-Bot's voice came out. "Wow. This comm system is *old.* I feel like I'm inhabiting a *record player.*"

"I have no idea what that is," I said, doing up the buckles. Outside, Maksim and Nuluba ran to check on Peg. The resonants hadn't powered on their acclivity rings. They obviously realized I could blast them the moment they tried. I considered it briefly—that would prevent pursuit—but no. They might not be friends, but I also wasn't going to execute them in cold blood.

I felt a momentary pang for what could have been, then grabbed the controls. "Can you get the hangar doors open?"

"Give me a second . . . yes. This ship's system has the transmitter locked behind three layers of security. They were *really* worried about attracting delvers when they built it."

As the door opened, I kept my weapons trained on the two fighters. At last I caught blue light coming from beneath Shiver's ship.

"Don't make me unload on you two," I said, hitting the comm.

I was given no reply, though the mechanism said my words had gone through. As soon as the hangar was open, I turned the ship toward the opening.

"Spensa," M-Bot said. "Would it be all right if . . . if I flew?"

I hesitated. M-Bot's programming had always prevented him from flying. When he'd wanted to come rescue me on Detritus, he'd needed to convince Cobb to fly him. This was the first time in his life that he had a chance to truly pilot a starship.

I'd been yearning for this moment, tasting it, dreaming of it. But he'd been waiting for centuries.

"Go for it," I said, lifting my hands—with effort—from the controls.

"Oh, thank you!" he said. The ship continued turning of its own volition, then inched toward the exit—using maneuvering thrusters, not the main boosters, to avoid vaporizing the people behind us.

Oh, scud, I thought. *M-Bot is a highly advanced AI. He can think faster than any human, respond in a split second.* Why would anyone ever need a human pilot? In this moment, I saw the end of my time flying a starfighter.

Then M-Bot clipped the side of the hangar doorway as he was steering us out.

"Oops!" he said, and started turning the ship, as if to inspect what he'd done.

"No!" I said. "You'll slam the tail into the wall. Keep going forward!"

"Right, right," he said, wobbling the ship as it moved slowly out of the hangar. Directly toward . . .

"M-Bot!" I said. *"Trees!"*

"Ah yes. Trees. Hmm . . ."

We jerked to a halt, then floated upward, then jerked forward again as he moved us over them.

"You know," he said, "this isn't going as well as I thought it would."

"Ya think?" I said, trying to look back at the hangar. "You might want to move faster . . ."

I couldn't make out much, but I was pretty sure the blue glow was increasing in the hangar behind us. I could only imagine that Dllllizzzz and Shiver, seeing the awkward flying, had decided I might not be difficult prey.

The ship wobbled as he got us up over the trees.

"M-Bot!" I said.

"Hey," he snapped, "I think I'm doing pretty well. Didn't *you* crash into the mess hall on your first day?"

"A holographic mess hall," I said.

"Well, I haven't crashed into *any* mess halls. Look, I'm a computer program—do you know how hard it is for someone like me to do something that isn't explicitly in my programming?"

"No."

"It's *impossible,*" M-Bot said. "That's how hard it is. And I'm doing it *anyway.*"

"You flew the drone just fine."

"I borrowed the drone's hard-coded flight instructions from its rudimentary firmware. I don't have that anymore!"

A starfighter darted out of the hangar, and another one followed. Two blips appeared on our proximity sensors.

"Oh," M-Bot said. "They're going to try to kill us, aren't they?"

"Yup."

"You wanna . . ."

I seized the control sphere and the throttle, then slammed on the overburn, kicking us into some real speed. We blasted away from the fragment with a roar that vibrated the cockpit. It took me by surprise. I'd been fighting in the vacuum of space too much recently; I hoped my atmospheric flight instincts weren't rusty. Starships were built to minimize the difference, but in a firefight you lived or died based on tiny mistakes.

The thing was, I didn't *want* to get into a firefight. Shiver and Dllllizzzz seemed like good people. I was willing to steal one of their ships, but I wasn't about to shoot them dead. Not unless they forced my hand.

First we'd see if they could keep up.

I swooped across the neighboring fragment—which was flowing with waterfalls that ran over the sides and vanished into infinity. My tails followed and *immediately* opened fire. Scud. I'd hoped maybe they'd be hesitant to kill me. I fell into evasive zigzags by rote, then dove over the side of the fragment, parallel to the falling water. My stomach tried to crawl out through my esophagus, and a moment later the ship's GravCaps were overwhelmed and I was slammed by g-forces, and nearly hit a red-out.

I pulled up, gritting my teeth. "These GravCaps are terrible."

"No surprise there," M-Bot replied. "Not only is it a civilian craft, it's so old it's practically an antique."

"Your original ship was two hundred years old."

"And three hundred years ahead of its time," he said. "This thing was outdated when they made it. It was a fast production-line model made cheaply."

"Delightful."

"Indeed!" Shots trailed us. "Um, don't look at the shield."

"It's bad?"

"It's mostly there to help in minor collisions. It can take maybe two hits from a destructor." Another shot almost struck us. "Uh . . . wow. Spensa, is this what it feels like to be freaked out? I think it *is* what it feels like to be freaked out. Oh, how wonderful! I hate it!"

The destructor fire was blue rather than the red I was used to, but that was probably because it was from a different technological line. I dodged back upward, but one of the shots hit, making the invisible shield around my ship crackle.

The low-shield warning started blinking on the control panel. Yeah, low shields after a *single* shot? I guess that was what I got for flying a consumer-grade ship. And my top speed in atmosphere appeared to be terrible—the ship was rattling like the caverns did during debris falls.

Fortunately, we'd outfitted the ship with an offensive complement: two destructors and an IMP for bringing down enemy shields. That would also negate my own shield when used, but seeing as mine was apparently about as useful as a cardboard box, I'd take my chances.

Most importantly, my ship had that light-lance for towing. I knew now that I wasn't going to be able to outrun my tails, and I certainly wasn't going to out-endure them. But with the right equipment, I was pretty sure I could outfly them.

I swung over the top of a dust-covered fragment, kicking up an incredible wake. The destructor fire went wild then; the resonants weren't used to flying through debris. They should have switched to firing by instruments.

I took a steep dive over the side of the fragment, but launched my light-lance and stuck it to the edge. Like a ball on the end of a chain, I swung around in the air, pivoting in a turn that would have been impossible without an energy rope. I gave my GravCaps a second to reset as I wove along the side of the fragment, then dove and light-lanced again to spin under it, after which I had to flip over to orient my acclivity ring downward. Whatever the other strange laws of physics were in this place, gravity worked like I expected it to.

The bottom of this fragment was furrowed and marked by chunks of stone—like a cave roof with stalactites, only much larger. I wove through these, and my proximity readout told me the two starships came in to follow.

They quickly lost ground on me, despite flying faster ships.

Without light-lances, they had to swing around more slowly to get under the fragment—plus they obviously weren't as comfortable flying through obstacles at high speed as I was. The truth was, they shouldn't have followed me. Indeed, they made a common combat mistake that Cobb had beaten out of me in my first month of training. Never get too wrapped up in the chase that you forget good tactics.

In this case, they should have flown down farther below the fragment, where being able to fly straight would have made their superior speed an advantage. That told me they didn't think tactically; they had learned to dogfight on their own, without training, and would make rookie mistakes despite their skill.

Perfect.

"Spensa," M-Bot said, "I fear I must warn you that I've intercepted chatter from the other Broadsiders. They're waking the off-duty flights and are scrambling both of them to add to the chase. You have approximately seven minutes until this fight is joined by six more ships."

I should have been worried about that. But *scud,* this felt good. I was terrible at a lot of things. I was coming to acknowledge that the friendships I had were all *despite* my efforts, not *because* of them. I was insubordinate and stupid when my temper took over. My spying and diplomatic skills were laughable.

But I could fly.

Hot *damn,* I could finally fly again.

I spun through the air, leading my two tails in a grand chase around three separate fragments. What had felt vast to cross on foot now passed as momentary flashes of color. Gaps that had felt insurmountable now proved exciting for me to weave through, using my light-lance to make the tighter turns. The weak GravCaps meant I took more g-forces than I wanted, but I could mitigate that with careful flying.

All the while, I kept watch on the proximity sensor, reinforcing my judgment of the two resonants. They really needed some light-lances, plus proper training to use them. And they were too free with their shots. Cobb had reamed me on multiple occasions for my overeager trigger finger. You'd think that firing at all times would be smart, that it would give you the most opportunities to hit. You'd be wrong. Wild firing not only risked danger to your allies, it trained you not to aim.

"Spensa," M-Bot said, "something is odd about this weapon fire."

"The strange color?" I said, veering us down to the left between a pair of fragments.

"More than that," M-Bot said. "I've been running diagnostics on this vessel, and our own destructors have a pair of attachments on them."

"Like the ones on that unit we repaired?"

"Exactly. They modify the weapon fire . . ." He hesitated. "Spensa, I think it makes the destructors nonlethal. They're meant to overwhelm electronic systems and make a ship lock up."

Wait.

Wait.

Suddenly I understood why no pirates got shot down on raids. I understood how a group like this could even *function*. They had no access to manufactories—they had to use what they could steal or salvage. If ships were lost in firefights with any regularity, soon nobody would have anything to fly.

That explained why the resonants were so quick to fire on me. They weren't trying to destroy me or the ship. They were trying to capture me again.

"But when you powered on in the hangar," I said, "the pirates all seemed extremely worried about being shot by the destructors."

"The amount of energy released is still significant," M-Bot said. "A fragile flesh body wouldn't want to be subjected to one of those shots."

Well, okay then. This escape had just become more interesting.

As my two resonant tails dove after me, I checked the chronometer. Despite feeling like it was much longer, we'd been dogfighting for only a few minutes. I had a little time until the other ships launched from the hangars—assuming M-Bot's projection of their load-in time was correct.

I hit the overburn, forcing the enemy ships to do likewise. They knew enough to rely on their superior speed on a straightaway. But as they were focused on that, I flipped off the overburn and hit my speedbrake, cutting the booster and increasing drag. I darted backward—or, well, they darted forward. Either way, the two ships passed me in a flash. I hit the IMP right as they did.

A claxon went off on my dash, warning that my lame shield was finished. I trained on Dllllizzzz's ship and fired, hoping M-Bot's guess about the destructors was correct. The ship flashed blue as I scored direct hits, then its boosters powered off. The ship continued on in the direction it had been going—which, as I considered, could be dangerous. Fortunately, the acclivity ring stayed active, so the ship didn't drop, and it didn't seem to be in danger of a collision anytime soon.

Shiver's ship veered off wildly, as if panicked to realize I'd suddenly gone on the offensive. I tracked it easily, expecting . . .

Yup, a loop to try to get around to tail me again. Executed well, actually. As I twisted my ship and picked her off, I had to admire her skill. Considering that they were all self-taught, that had been a pretty good maneuver.

"I still think it's unfair," M-Bot said, "that you can fly better than I can."

"I have training. You don't."

"I'm a computer program. The only training I should need is some lines of code."

I shot Shiver's vessel with my light-lance and pulled it to a stop before it slammed into the nearby fragment. Then I cut the light-lance and blasted off—straight toward the fragment with the Broadsider base.

"Spensa?" M-Bot said. "Do you think we could get me proper code to fly and fight?"

"I think that even with some extra lines of code, you'd be missing something."

"What?"

"Style."

I came up under the Broadsider fragment, then shot my light-lance onto the edge and used it to curve up and around, flipping so I flew in low along the ground. The hangars were directly ahead. Flight doors open.

I aimed and shot a ship hovering out of the doorway. I hit it square on, and it couldn't dodge, so I quickly overwhelmed the shield and locked the ship up. I did the same at the next hangar in line.

In seconds, I'd effectively created a traffic jam. With the two ships blocking the way, the others couldn't escape—at least not without towing their friends out of the way first. I intended to be long gone by then. I just needed my icon.

I flew us to the other side of the hangars. "Take over," I said, unbuckling. "Warn me if any of them get out of that mess. If I don't return in time, hover up and start firing at them. You might get lucky and hit one."

"Oh. Uh . . ."

I popped the canopy as the ship drifted over to the boulder behind the Broadsider camp. I heard shouts and curses from inside the hangars. A quick glance showed me only one person had thought to duck out back to see what I was doing. Maksim, standing in the open door to his building.

I raised my sidearm. Maksim was armed too, but as he saw me, he didn't raise his own weapon. Smart man.

I quickly located the place where I'd stuffed the icon. Keeping mostly hidden behind the boulder, I dug down to find . . .

Nothing.

My father's pin wasn't there.

22

It was strange how hard that hit me. It wasn't even *really* my father's pin. I still didn't have an explanation for how it had shown up in my pocket—but then again, I also didn't have a good explanation for how water appeared on the fragments.

Still, in losing the icon, I felt as if I had been robbed of something deeply personal. My only tangible link to the world I'd left. My source of stability.

Chet! I sent. *The icon is gone!*

What? he replied. *Miss Nightshade, I didn't have anything to do with it! I vow upon my—*

I believe you, I said. *I know you didn't take it, Chet. But it* is *gone. How?*

I have no idea, he replied.

All right. I'm coming to get you.

Wait. Coming to get me?

I had to steal the ship now instead of later, I said. *I'll explain in a bit.*

With a growl of annoyance at the empty hole, I dashed back to the ship and hauled myself into the cockpit—keeping an eye on Maksim the whole way. He didn't raise his weapon. I nodded to him, and in seconds I had M-Bot cruising toward Chet. I could feel him with my mind, but it was still an enormous relief when I saw him standing at the edge of the blue jungle fragment, one hand raised high in greeting, the other in an improvised sling, with the sleeve of his jacket hanging loose.

I pulled the ship up beside the fragment and popped the canopy—then immediately started my ship's shield ignition process. It was a terrible shield, but better than nothing.

I began to climb out to help Chet aboard, but he deftly managed to scramble up the wing on his own. Standing just beside the canopy, he gave me a wide mustachioed grin, then gestured with one hand to the ship. "Our mighty steed. She is beautiful!"

"You won't say that after you see her specs," I said. I stood and pulled the seat forward, revealing the cargo space behind it in the cockpit. "Sorry about the accommodations."

"I've known worse," Chet said, squeezing into the spot. "But we have a problem. Without the icon, I worry about us traveling alone, long term."

"You have the ashes I gave you though, right?" I said.

"I do indeed. They should last us a few weeks at least."

"Good enough for now," I said. "We'll escape, then try to figure out what happened to my icon." I closed the canopy and locked my seat into place. There was barely enough room for Chet behind me. It would have to do. Because we had a more pressing problem.

"All nine fighters are giving chase," M-Bot said. "They have restored the two resonants. Everyone will be upon us soon." He helpfully zoomed out the proximity display to show the Broadsiders as blips on the screen.

"With their scanner active," Chet said, "I fear for our ability to continue our quest."

"Any suggestions?"

"We could bolt for another pirate faction's territory," he said. "But that could backfire. The other faction would naturally assume us to be part of a Broadsider raid, and would react accordingly."

Well, if it got the Broadsiders to drop off for a short time, then maybe we could use it. I turned the ship to the heading M-Bot indicated and started us flying.

"Spensa," M-Bot said. "I have bad news."

"We're not going to make it?" I guessed.

"Judging our top speed against those of the faster Broadsider ships, no. We'll be intercepted before we reach the border."

Scud. I glanced to the side as I felt Chet's hand on my shoulder, reaching from behind the seat.

"There is another option," he said. "We could fly straight up."

I glanced upward through the canopy into that infinite pink sky. "What's up there?"

"I don't know," Chet said. "I've never explored that direction. Just as I've never left this larger region. There are distant sections of the belt, to the right and left, but those involve large gaps between fragments that are dangerous to cross alone, even when flying.

"I've warned you it's dangerous to stray far from the fragments. We can quickly lose our identities if we fly upward, but we have ashes, which should delay the effects."

It took me only a moment to decide. I pulled up, sending the ship—already rattling from our excessive speed—straight upward into that vast unknown.

The blips on my screen slowed. Excellent. We flew for a good fifteen minutes, and I started to relax as it became increasingly obvious that the Broadsiders were not giving chase.

"Spensa," M-Bot said. "We're being hailed by the Broadsiders. Do you want me to put them on the comm?"

"Go ahead," I said.

The comm crackled in an old-timey way. I tried to see it as quaint, and not another indication that my ship was two shakes and a stern glare away from falling apart.

"Spin!" Peg's voice blared into the cockpit. "You *mulun*-growing reprobate! Why didn't you *tell* me you were a *pilot*!"

That wasn't the tone I'd been expecting.

"You figured out I was a soldier, Peg," I said.

"I thought you were some type of special forces trooper!" she shouted. "The way you prowled about. Words! You had a security drone disguised as a cleaning drone. How was I supposed to know you were a pilot?"

"I've probably made it obvious that I know my way around a starfighter."

"Know your way . . . No need for *kalams* of humility. I watched you fly on our scanner, and that was some of the best piloting I've ever seen. I spent some time with the drone pilots on Culmira Station, and they have *nothing* on you, girl. Even *Shiver* is impressed."

"Well, I appreciate the compliment," I told her. "Tell the others I'm sorry for stealing a ship. I have a galaxy to save. Once I'm finished, I'll see if there's anything that can be done to help you all."

"Spin," Peg said, her voice growing softer. "Where do you think you're going?"

"Right now? I'm losing you all."

"Yeah?" Peg said. "Do you know what happens to a person if they stray too far away from the fragments?"

I didn't respond.

"Even *if* you survive this next part," Peg said, "what are you going to do then? You can't stay up there very long, and our scanner will tell us when you come back down. We'll be on you in no time. Veer right or left, and you'll have to deal with one of the other factions.

"I suppose you could move inward—which would run you straight into the Superiority mining facility. Let me promise you that they keep careful watch on their borders—we've raided them enough to warrant that. You're good. But can you outfly a hundred enemy ships? Worse, can you do it in *that* piece of junk?"

"I guess we'll see," I told her.

She swore softly. "A person needs more than *muluns,* girl. *Think* for a moment. You can't survive in this place alone. You need allies, friends, support."

"Spensa," M-Bot said, temporarily muting the comm, "look at Chet."

I glanced over my shoulder and around the seat's head support to where he sat scrunched up behind. The older man's eyes had glazed over. He stared ahead, insensate, and didn't respond when I waved my hand in front of him.

Something began streaming up around him: a glittering, silvery haze. The reality ashes. I felt it too, as they spun around me, like they were . . . disintegrating?

Being up here was destroying them, perhaps to keep us from losing ourselves. I gritted my teeth and leveled out the ship, not gaining any more altitude.

"Peg is talking again," M-Bot said quietly.

I nodded, having him restore the comm line.

"You're going to start feeling it soon, if you haven't already," Peg said. "Can you remember yourself, girl?"

"I'm fine," I said through gritted teeth.

"Are you? Can you remember the faces of your parents? Your friends from home?"

I tried not to listen—but I didn't dare turn off the comm. Because scud, she was right. What *did* they look like? The reality ashes seemed to be struggling to keep me from forgetting my identity, and I felt my memories begin to fade.

"Maybe you can fight through an entire armada on your own," Peg said. "I don't know. But the longer you stay up there, the more you will lose. And traveling on your own will be bad for you, even if you aren't so high. Your address back home, your most passionate moments, the names of your lovers. They'll blur. Your life will become like a smudge on paper—a black smear where words used to be."

I hovered there, infinity stretching in all directions. Dominated still, however, by the lightburst. And in there, I could feel the delvers. They were hunting for me. Out here, up high, they could find me. And in revenge, they'd do to me something alien, something terrible. They'd take my self. My identity. My memories.

"Something odd has been happening lately," Peg said over the comm. "I have reports of people becoming like delvers, with glowing eyes. You can't fly alone, Spin. It's not because you're weak. No matter how determined you are, you still need ties to reality."

I took a deep breath. "I can't afford to spend years cleaning landing gear, Peg."

"Girl, you're wasted on ground crew," Peg said. "You return, and I'll give you our best ship."

"No offense, Peg," I said. "But I just beat you with a wrench and stole from you. I didn't want to do it, but you backed me into a corner and forced my hand. I can't believe that you'd simply let me go after that."

"Oh, I won't simply let you go," Peg said. "I'll give you that ship in exchange for something."

"What?"

"How would you feel about defeating the pirate champion for me?"

I frowned. I mean, I wasn't opposed to the idea at all—but the way she asked about it worried me. Made me think she had some game she was playing, beyond that of the other pirates.

But scud, I didn't know how long the ashes would last. And Chet . . . something bad was happening to him. I decreased power to the acclivity ring, lowering us slowly through the sky.

This could all be a trap. But . . . Peg was correct; we couldn't fly up that high. Pushing aside my worry for Chet, I tried to focus on the conversation.

"Why do you care about something like a pirate champion?" I asked Peg.

"I don't, really," she said. "But I need to take back Surehold—the Superiority mining outpost. My home."

Take back the Superiority base? Curious. If Chet was right, and the Path of Elders was going to continue on inward toward the lightburst, I'd need to find a way to sneak through Superiority territory. If they were busy fighting off pirates, that would certainly provide some useful cover.

"I'm listening," I said, leaning forward. "Tell me more."

"There are enough pirates in the factions to challenge the Superiority presence in here," Peg said. "If we attacked together, we could overwhelm them and seize control of the mining base."

"That sounds great," I said, "but how exactly are you going to get the other pirate factions to follow you? Last I heard, even your *sons* don't listen to you anymore."

Peg laughed. "There's more to this than you know, Spin. I can make it work. I merely need an excellent pilot to start the tree growing by defeating the champion."

I lowered us farther, and heard Chet stir. I glanced at him and saw him blinking. The ashes had stopped disintegrating, and I had the feeling I'd dodged something very dangerous by coming back down as quickly as I had.

"Very well, Peg," I said. "I'll consider this, but before we agree I have one more condition. There are some ruins I need to visit here in your territory. Give me a ship, let me visit those ruins, and I'll take down that champion for you."

"Ruins? Words, girl. I can take you to some ruins. We'll do it tomorrow. Look, this is a good deal. You help me—maybe give my fighters a few pointers to help them improve—and we'll deal a serious blow to the Superiority. Isn't that alone worth it? If we stop their acclivity stone mining operations, your war gets way easier. Plus, when you leave us next time, you'll have *earned* that ship you're taking from us. What do you say?"

"Give me a moment." I flicked off the comm.

"Spensa?" M-Bot said. "I'm worried. Are you feeling better?"

Was I? I took a deep breath, sorting through my memories. I . . . yes, I remembered. Jorgen, Kimmalyn, FM, Arturo, Nedd. Cobb. Gran-Gran. My mother.

I could remember them . . . but scud, their faces weren't clear to me anymore. It had been getting worse each day I spent in here. I was losing things. Pieces of who I'd been.

But at least I had recovered most of what I'd lost from flying up so high.

"Miss Nightshade?" Chet asked. "Perhaps my suggestion wasn't the most . . . wise."

"It kind of worked," I said, glancing back at him. "Kind of didn't. How do you feel?"

"Like I've been used as a chew toy by a Markivian barrow-wolf," he said. "Did I miss anything?"

"The Broadsiders want me to return," I said. "They say they'll trade me a ship—a good one—and take me to the next step on the Path. But I have to agree to defeat the pirate champion for them."

"That's an . . . odd request," he said. "I wasn't aware that their little championship mattered so much. Peg is planning something. I suspect she always has been."

"She wants to take back the Superiority base," I said. "She told me that much."

"Ambitious!" Chet said. "I like it. Well, I doubt we'll get a better deal. I say we agree. What's the worst that can happen?"

"They take us prisoner and chain us to the wall."

"Whereupon we get to escape again!" Chet said, and then he continued, more subdued—losing a bit of the affectation. "I have spent a long time traveling alone, Spensa. Your company is remarkable, truly, but it would be . . . reassuring to spend a period with a group."

"M-Bot?" I asked.

"If it lets me get out of this ship into something built in the last century," he said, "I'm for it."

I flicked the comm back on. "All right, Peg. You have a deal."

"Ha! Words."

"One thing though," I said. "You're going to have to clean up another bunk. I'm bringing a friend."

I turned off the comm and steered us back the way we'd come. The other ships must have landed while we were flying, since as I approached the Broadsider fragment I could see that the pirates were all outside, gathered in front of their hangars. A ragtag group to be certain, but I supposed I'd seen worse. Skyward Flight, for example, when we'd first started training.

I guided my ship over and settled down. With a shared look of determination, Chet and I climbed out of the cockpit. I still half expected the Broadsiders to take us captive, but fortunately nobody pulled a gun. We even got a few cheers.

It was forced, and I saw in Maksim's eyes a healthy distrust. An emotion I'd certainly earned.

Well, I would deal with that. Because at long last, Operation Ship-Steal had succeeded. And tomorrow I could finally continue the Path of Elders.

23

The next day, I awoke with renewed determination. Peg assigned me the new ship—a powerful two-seat striker. Fully loaded with formidable destructors and twin boosters, it was larger than most ships I'd flown, but should still be maneuverable.

It was the best ship in Peg's small fleet. I transferred M-Bot to it—after some careful digging I realized they still didn't know he was an AI; they thought I had used remote control to make the ship hover the previous day. I made some modifications he said would insulate his core systems from destructor blasts, then installed a light-lance.

After that, Chet and I climbed aboard.

"You sure you don't want your own ship?" I asked him as we strapped in. "I don't particularly need a copilot, since, you know . . ."

M-Bot was humming happily. Apparently he approved of the specs on this new ship.

"I wouldn't want to try the controls with this wounded arm," Chet said, fitting on a flight helmet. "And beyond that, it has been . . . well, centuries since I've flown. I think perhaps I should like to take this slowly."

Fair enough. As we readied ourselves, a small group of Broadsiders prepared to escort us. Peg, the resonants, and Maksim—who unfortunately inherited my weaker ship. In a few short minutes we'd all launched into the air and started on our way. I immediately felt the joy of flying a *real* starfighter. It banked at a touch, accelerated or decelerated with ease. At high speeds, I could close my eyes and barely make out the whistle of air outside. Not a single rattle.

It felt like *forever* since I'd had a true top-of-the-line starfighter.

"What'd I tell you?" Peg said through the comm. "Are you growing *keefos* yet?"

I thought those were the happy ones. "At least seven," I said, banking again.

"I took that ship out myself a few times," Peg said. "Never into combat though. It was just too spectacular to risk damaging it with my clunky flying. But you . . . you're perfect for it, Spin."

"Will Guntua forgive me for taking it?"

"She has been wanting to back off from flying anyway," Peg said. "Take a break, do some ground duty instead."

How could anyone grow *tired* of this? I didn't know Guntua well—she was a heklo from one of the other flights—but I supposed if she'd wanted to keep flying, she'd have been given what was now Maksim's ship.

Peg genuinely seemed to have forgiven me, but the others now stepped far more lightly around me. It hurt to see how Shiver made certain never to let her ship stray out in front of mine, as if she worried I'd start shooting again.

I couldn't blame them. I would have acted the same way—or likely worse. At least Chet seemed to be enjoying himself; I could call up his camera feed on the corner of my screen. He was looking out the canopy with an almost childlike grin on his face.

We soared across several fragments, startling a small herd of something that looked like ostriches—but with feet on their backs as well as underneath them. The readout said it would take roughly two hours of flying to reach our destination, and though a part of me was wistful for the time Chet and I had spent adventuring together, I was certainly glad I didn't have to hike all this distance on foot.

"So," Peg said, her voice in my ear via my new helmet, "don't suppose you'd be willing to give us a few tips as we fly. To improve our combat, make it like yours?"

"That isn't the sort of thing a 'few tips' can achieve, Peg," I said. "But there are some formation exercises I could teach you while we fly."

"Excellent," Peg said.

Over the next half hour, I explained to Cutlass Flight some basics that I thought they were lacking. The importance of a wingman. The value of drilling on formations. The purpose of group responses. I soon had them paired off—Maksim with Peg, the two resonants together—and doing sprints. One would spring forward, fire their IMP, then fall back to reignite, while the other darted forward in a guard position.

They took my instruction without complaint, and after a short time I had a solid gauge of their abilities. Shiver was good, Dllllizzzz not far behind her. Peg was better than she claimed, though her shuttle wasn't terribly fast. She was more a gunship and support flyer. Maksim wasn't great, but he was so excited and eager, which counted for a lot.

After the team sprints, I taught them some scatter formations—where the four would fly together, then break apart and weave through the air defensively before coming back into the same configuration. They picked that up quickly.

"Good," I told them. "Now watch as I sketch this next formation on your monitors. I want you to do the same break and scatter, but then return into a group of *three*. One of you is going to hang back to fire at the enemy, who has hopefully been confused by your maneuvers."

"Fascinating," Shiver said. "It's like . . . shining with part of your body to distract, while the rest of you grows in another direction."

"Yeah, or like a street-fighting trick," I said. "Get them to watch one hand while you prepare to claw their eyes out with the other one."

"Uh . . ." Shiver said. "You are a unique individual, Spin."

"Yeah, I know. Bless my stars," I said. "Just trust me—learn to work as a group and you'll have a huge advantage on the battlefield."

They did as I asked, slowly figuring out this more complex formation. I gave tips, digging back to what Cobb had taught me when I'd been new.

"You're good at this," Chet said from behind me as they ran through another scatter formation. "I see a natural teacher in you!"

"I'm good at pretending," I said. "Most of this is just stuff I'm regurgitating from what I was taught."

"And what precisely do you think teaching *is,* mmm?" he said. "You have confidence, credibility, and empathy. I think you are excellent at this duty."

I sat a little taller at those words, and the experience made me want to fall back into the role I'd taken with the team on Starsight: that of the drillmaster. That was dangerous. I wasn't going to be with the Broadsiders long enough to train them extensively.

I gave them a short break, with a compliment on their skills, and Peg pulled up on my wing. Her shuttle looked slapped-together, but that was deceptive. It held an exceptionally strong shield and powerful guns. In a proper fire team, with faster ships to keep the enemy from swarming her, she'd be a force to reckon with.

Though she was the leader, she'd done as I directed during instruction without complaining or pulling rank. That said a lot about her, all of it good. She was humble enough to take direction in order to achieve her goals.

"How do you feel?" she asked. "Memories are good?"

"They are," I said. "I can remember my name, my friends. Most of it."

"There's something about being part of a team that helps us

all," she replied. "Even when we aren't immediately close to one another. It's like how a forest is stronger than a tree, eh? The roots interlock, and the fruit grows for all in more abundance."

"It's like a crystal lattice, Peg," Shiver said over the comm. "The structure of a crystal is strong because of how the individual atoms align together."

"Well," Maksim said, "I guess *I'm* supposed to say it's like a herd of cattle. Or maybe a line of fence posts. Or some other cowboy crap."

"Cowboy?" I asked.

He paused a moment when I spoke. Perhaps I was reading too much into it, but I felt he had to struggle not to snap at me. Because of how I'd betrayed his trust.

He continued speaking though. As if he were trying to give me a second chance. "Haven't I told you, Spin? In the Superiority, everyone thinks of humans as these ravening monsters—and so they *love* our old lore. Pirates, Gurkhas, the Tuskegee Airmen, and—unfortunately—cowboys. So they'd always expect me to talk like one. Even though my heritage from Old Earth is Ukrainian."

"I . . . don't know where that was," I admitted.

"It didn't have cowboys," Maksim said. "You have no idea how annoying those hats are. My owners always claimed that they were using me for scientific study—but you wouldn't have known it from the way they showed me off at parties."

"Parties," Shiver said. "Such an interesting concept. How you motiles insist you need time apart—yet when you want to enjoy yourselves, you always simply come back together. Why leave in the first place?"

"I have a friend," I said, thinking of Rig, "who'd disagree that being together is when we enjoy ourselves. I think he has the most fun when everyone leaves him alone."

"Curious, curious," Shiver said. And Dllllizzzz added a hum in the background.

I'd tried to picture their cavernous homeworld—like Detritus, only with each and every tunnel full of different crystalline tendrils, networks of individuals who explored by growing themselves outward.

"All right," I said over the comm, "we have some travel time left. Do a few more team sprints and prove you can execute them without making fools of yourselves."

Maksim groaned. "We just spent an *hour* on sprints!"

"You still need to work on fundamentals, Maksim," I said. "Learn what you can from me while I'm here. You people fly like a bunch of pig farmers."

"I take it pig farmers do not often fly well in your culture, Spin?" Shiver said.

"Ask Maksim," Peg said. "He's the cowboy."

I smiled, their banter reminding me of flying with my friends. Though this felt different. In Skyward Flight, our banter—although genuine—had always had an edge. We'd been a few bold fighters facing overwhelming odds. We'd gone into each fight knowing it might be the one where we lost someone we loved.

The Broadsiders didn't have the same sense to them. They were relaxed as they ran through more sprints. When one got something wrong, they all laughed it off. Skyward Flight hadn't done that—because there, if one of us kept screwing up, it would get everyone killed.

Was this what it felt like to relax? Scud. Listening to them, I realized I really *didn't* know what it felt like to just . . . live. Without worrying about a bomb annihilating my entire civilization one night while I slept. Without fearing that my friends wouldn't be coming home tomorrow. Or, more recently, without wondering if I'd be discovered as an impostor.

As they practiced, I glanced over the landscape. Once you got past the fact that this place could literally consume your memories and identity, it was beautiful. An endless open sky, cast faintly pink-violet, interrupted by floating islands. Each fragment was a different biome, inviting a new adventure. And beyond that, the lightburst.

Though it was still distant, today I felt something . . . drawing me toward it. Chet thought we'd need to go right up close to it to finish the Path of Elders, and looking into that full light now, I knew it was true. I'd walk the Path. But at the end I'd face *them*.

Whatever else happened here, that was my destination.

I shook myself out of that trancelike state and patched through on the comm to Peg, looking for a distraction. "Hey," I said as she finished her sprints. "Could I get more details on your plan? How exactly is me fighting the pirate champion going to help you win the Superiority base?"

She was quiet for a moment, seeming to consider. Finally she answered, pulling her shuttle up beside my ship. "You know about my past? The others told you?"

"You were chief security officer at Surehold," I said. "The Superiority treated you dirty, not allowing your kids to leave with you when your time was up."

"Correct," Peg said. "So I grew a few *hanchals* about that, I'll tell you. And I wasn't the only one. The base had been losing people for years. The factions hadn't grown yet, but there were plenty of smaller bands, with a ship or two, roving around out here."

"It was a big deal when you left," Chet said. "Everyone heard about it. A high officer defecting? Gathering all the dissidents, raiders, and wanderers to raise up a giant pirate armada?"

"Yeah, well," Peg said, "it wasn't enough. I failed back then, and my supposed 'giant armada' shattered into the factions. Still, I've been thinking about it these last three years, considering what I did wrong. Planning . . ."

I nodded, thoughtful. "Wasn't Shiver with you, back at the base?"

"Yeah, about a third of it defected when I did," Peg said. "They form the bulk of the pirates. Shiver's not the only Broadsider who left with me. There are a bunch of us, like RayZed and Guntua. And I almost had more—almost got the entire base to up and revolt."

"Their failure to do so smacks of cowardice," Chet said.

"No," Peg said. "No, that's not it. I understand them, Chet. They're not cowards. Just ordinary people trying to live in a difficult place. Back when I was security officer, I was the one who installed the nonlethal weapons on our ships—my argument being that we couldn't afford to throw away the ships the malcontents had stolen. Truth is, though, I grew *urichas*. I knew those dissidents were just like us. I didn't want to be in the business of shooting them down."

"So wait," I said. "You're saying that the Superiority forces in here, they use nonlethal weapons too?"

"Yup," Peg said. "Pretty much everyone does. We have this understanding—none of us want to be killing each other."

"So civilized!" Chet said. "I approve."

"Well," Peg said, "the high-ups in the somewhere, they'd rather it be deadly in here. Fortunately they're far away. Regardless, Spin, this is important to understand. Those people at Surehold? They *almost* joined me when I left. They *want* to escape—but they're scared of the Superiority, and of the officers that are still loyal. If we give them a nudge, prove that my force is stronger, they'll join us. I'm certain of it."

That explained a lot. The pirates didn't want to lose equipment to damage, because repairs were difficult for them—and the Superiority forces weren't zealots or loyalists. They didn't want to die to defend a stupid mining base—but they had to make a good showing for their superiors.

So nonlethal weapons were used all around. I found it interesting how humane things became once the people far up the command chain—the ones who didn't have to bleed for the decisions they made—couldn't force everyone into line.

"I don't understand why the pirates have these little squabbles and do meaningless raids against each other though," I said. "If *I* were in charge of one of these pirate factions, I wouldn't waste time with champions or duels. I'd raid a group smaller than mine, freeze their ships, then steal the lot of them. In a few weeks I'd be queen of all the pirates."

"You really are terrifying sometimes, kid," Peg replied.

A question occurred to me. "Do you guys have, like, golden tankards or anything? I mean, I know we don't drink here, but I've always wanted a golden tankard . . . or maybe one made out of bone. The stories mention ones made from the skulls of one's enemies, but it seems like the drink would leak out the eyeholes. Unless your enemies have no eyes, I guess. Hmm . . ."

Peg had fallen silent. Oh. Maybe that last part had been a little much. I was trying to get better at this sort of thing. I should probably leave skulls out of conversations.

"I'm glad to finally meet a human who lives up to the stories," Peg said. "But no, we're not going to be giving you any tankards made of skulls."

"Still," I said. "Chet's right—it's remarkably civilized in here. I . . . have trouble accepting that nobody has ruined it."

"That's because you spent your life fighting to the death," Peg said. "We have a different problem."

"You feel your *self* dribbling away each day," Chet agreed. "Having something to do is important. The sparring, the duels . . . These invigorating activities give the pirates purpose, don't they?"

"Yeah," Peg said. "And no one wants to ruin what they have. That's part of the problem. Every time I pitch the idea of seizing Surehold, the pirates get frightened. Unnerved. They like the way things are. With six different pirate factions, there's always a raid to plan, a ship to repair, a mission to execute, or territory to defend. It's . . . it's what they want."

"But you want something more," I said.

"Yes," Peg admitted. "Maybe I'm a little too much like you. A little too much like the people outside. I can't feel safe as long as the Superiority is there—at any moment, they could send an enormous force through the portal and crush us with lethal weapons and swarms of drones.

"My people won't be safe in here until *I* control that portal. Until I can lock it on our side. And then we can undermine Superiority acclivity stone production, starve their forces on the other side. Payback for what they did to me and mine."

There was an encouraging vengefulness in her tone. I approved. The others were playing games, and Peg wanted to protect that. But she knew real danger, real killing. She still hadn't explained how the pirate champion related to all of this, but I let it die for now. Because up ahead I saw our destination at last. A lonely fragment covered in ancient structures.

It was time.

24

We swooped down toward the fragment, which was bigger than many of the others I'd seen so far. "It's huge," I noted to Chet as we skimmed along, scouting for dangers. IR scans indicated no body heat signatures, though I'd learned not to be careless about that.

"Indeed," he said. "I now understand why some are so much bigger than others. They've been growing for longer."

"This . . ." Dllllizzzz said over the comm. "Here . . . I was . . . Here . . ."

Again, it was more than she normally said, and got Shiver excited. I was focused, however, on the ruins I could make out at the fragment's center, and I navigated toward them.

"Yeah, I remember this place," Peg said. "We visited it when it first drifted into our region a few years back."

"That's right, Captain," Maksim said. "So why are we here again, Spin?"

"Historical investigations," I said. "Chet here is an archaeologist."

"A right noble profession, my good man," Chet said. "Ancient artifacts can tell us much about ourselves!"

"Uh, I guess," Maksim said. "But—"

"Leave it be, Maksim." Peg cut him off. "Their reasons are their own. The rest of us will search for salvage while we're here."

I narrowed my eyes. Peg didn't seem the type to let our reasons be "our own."

"Spin and I will need time to study those ruins directly at the center," Chet said. "I'm circling them on your monitors."

"Dllllizzzz is vibrating uncomfortably," Shiver said over the comm. "Though she's excited, I think she doesn't want to land. She feels . . . anxious? Maybe the two of us should stay up and keep watch."

"Fine by me," Peg said. "Maksim and I will stick near, Spin, while you do your . . . archaeology."

Our group landed in a ruined courtyard, while the two resonants stayed in the air. There wasn't a lot left of most of the ruins—fallen walls, the outlines of buildings. A few somewhat-intact stone structures.

I popped the canopy and climbed out, meeting Peg on the ground. "This place is old," she said. "Not a lot of wind in here, and no rain, so things don't weather much. If something looks this bad, it's probably seen thousands of years."

Chet and I shared a glance, then started toward one of the mostly intact structures, helmets under our arms.

"Doesn't look too promising, Captain," Maksim muttered from behind. "This place must have been picked over hundreds of times."

"Agreed," Peg said, "but keep growing *delens* just in case. We're here to keep our promise to Spin."

I remembered the structure ahead—it had been injected into my mind by the previous step on the Path. We walked up to it, and directly inside I found my first surprise. The wall behind the small foyer had a faded old mural on it—and the figures it depicted were most certainly human.

"Amazing," Chet breathed. He rushed up to it and leaned in close. "Our own people, Miss Nightshade. All these years, I never found any ruins that I could identify as human . . ."

I couldn't make out much of the mural. Just some figures holding baskets, maybe?

"I could not guess at the culture," Chet whispered. He reached out to the mural, then paused—perhaps not wanting to touch it and further contribute to its degradation. "To be perfectly honest, I don't remember much about where we came from. Our homeworld. I must have once known . . ."

"Earth," I said. "Humankind left there a few centuries before you were even born. It's lost now. Vanished."

Together, we moved farther into the structure. The roof had long since fallen in, so we didn't lack for light—and from the refuse on the floor, it seemed the place had been ransacked over the years, and had possibly been in a firefight.

I felt an . . . eerie, haunted sense. There were so many signs of life, but no people. We found the portal in the last room, built straight into the wall, the characteristic flowing lines carved into it. But this one was cracked down the middle. Broken. Would it still work?

I glanced at Chet, who lingered in the doorway. "Courage," he said, stepping forward. "I am an explorer—it is what I decided to be. I can face these secrets . . ."

He joined me beside the portal. I touched it, opened up my cytonic senses, and sought answers. At first nothing happened. This portal appeared to be damaged, unusable. But I pushed a little more, using the subtle care I'd been practicing, and . . . yes, I could feel them inside. The memories . . .

Everything around me faded to flimsy transparency. I remained in the ruins physically—I could feel the broken wall beside me—but they had been overlaid by a vision of the belt as it had existed long ago.

Chet breathed out, turning around. The lightburst was tiny in the distance, little more than a star. The sky was dark, and I counted maybe two dozen fragments floating in the expanse. So this seemed to be the ancient past, like the previous vision.

Our current fragment was much smaller in the past—plus it was empty of structures save for the portal, which stood free and whole, not cracked. It was smaller too, lending further credence to the theory that the portals grew a little—with memories—whenever cytonics used them as transfer points between dimensions.

Moments after the vision began, people popped into existence directly in front of the portal. I stepped away from them in surprise. Humans? They were talking, though I couldn't understand the language.

"Can you make out any of that?" Chet asked.

"Afraid not," I said, circling them. They wore robes, and something was kind of familiar about the headdress one was wearing. "I once saw a drawing of Gilgamesh in a book from Old Earth, and he wore clothing and a beard like that." I pointed to one of the men. "Maybe they're from somewhere near his civilization?"

Chet hopped back from the portal as something else materialized in front of it. Stones? Yes, a pile of building materials. People began using them to construct something.

"This wasn't their first visit here," I said, feeling it was true. There were . . . sensations to the vision, not just sights. "They want to build a shrine, I think."

Chet and I watched as time sped up, and walls sprang into existence. The people became blurs, erecting the very structure that Chet and I were standing in. They carved delicate art into the walls, then painted everything with vibrant colors.

Why put something so nice in this strange place? Time slowed again, and the humans—it seemed the construction had taken weeks, maybe months—gathered together out front. Chet and I joined them and saw another fragment swinging closer. This bore a group of people in vibrant red robes. They had pale violet skin, growths like horns, and pure white hair. People from ReDawn . . . Alanik's homeworld.

"I know those people," I told Chet. "They're the UrDail. The one I met said they'd known humans in the past."

"How far in the past?" Chet asked, rubbing his chin. "These humans wear ancient clothing."

"Scud," I said. "Could this be first contact? The first time humans met with aliens? I thought that didn't happen until we were in the space age."

Except Hesho had also told me that the kitsen people had met with humans in Japan centuries before either achieved space travel. They'd traveled using cytonics. Like these, it seemed.

In front of us, the humans greeted the UrDail—who stepped over to our fragment—and I realized this probably wasn't first contact. The two groups looked familiar with one another, so their first encounters must have happened earlier. Now the humans had built some kind of meeting hall. It wasn't a shrine, I realized as we followed the people in. It was a place where they sat together at tables, trying to . . .

Trying to figure out one another's languages perhaps? Yes, they were writing words, gesturing, explaining to one another. Time sped up again, and I counted dozens of meetings in a matter of minutes—each time the two fragments aligned. I think I even saw some UrDail visit Earth through the portal, while some humans left on the UrDail fragment.

Then . . . the humans stopped coming.

An alignment happened and the UrDail arrived, but no humans were there to meet them. That occurred several more times, then eventually the UrDail stopped visiting as well.

"So . . ." I said. "What does this tell us about our powers?"

Chet frowned, inspecting the mural in the vision—which was colorful and vibrant then. "Alien species began meeting in the nowhere. Mixing. But then it ended. Why?"

That . . . had happened with the kitsen too, hadn't it? Hesho said their cytonics had vanished for some reason. As I was considering this, a woman appeared out of the wall. She was middle-aged, with tan skin and colorful robes. I followed her as she walked out of the building, then over to the nearby edge of the fragment. There she settled down, looking out at the expanse.

Time passed. Months, maybe years. And still she sat there, as if waiting for something. Finally she rose and walked past us.

"Who are you?" I asked.

And the impression returned, *I am the only one who was not killed by the beast.*

Wait. *Wait.* Had she replied?

I followed her back into the building as she walked up to the portal. There she rested her hand—and lines in the stone began to spiral and flourish out at her touch.

I feel your questions, the impression said. *It is my talent. Though I do not know any of you, I leave my answers in the portal.*

"What happened?" I asked. "To the cytonics?"

A beast. Raised by an alien species who had technological marvels.

I saw something in my mind then. An assembly of thousands of cytonics—of a hundred different races—gathering to fight . . . something dark, something rising from a blackness, but with a set of piercing white eyes.

It . . . destroyed them, the cytonic said. *We fought. We won. But the price was so high . . .*

"How?" I asked. "How did you win?"

We made it become real, she said. *I do not know how. I survived . . . and those who did know how . . . were consumed.* She lowered her hand. She'd . . . inscribed her memories into the portal, which . . . were now reaching me somehow?

Chet walked up behind me. "Time is unnatural in the nowhere, but this is strange even by its standards," he said. "I . . . have no idea what to make of this."

I felt the vision begin to fade. It was coming to the end of its memories.

"Wait," I said to the woman. "You kept your memories while living in the nowhere. How?"

Why would I lose my memories? the impression returned.

"That's an attribute of this place," I said.

Not in our time. You face a beast, like ours.

"Not one beast," I said. "Thousands. Millions of them."

Then you are doomed.

"No. There *has* to be a way!"

Find the memories . . . of the man who will come . . . Find the memories . . . of the man named Jason Write.

Then a different sort of impression came upon me, as had happened during the previous vision. I understood it better because I was stronger in my powers, better at listening. It felt like dozens, maybe hundreds, of minds reaching to me from within the stone.

Further . . . they encouraged me. *Even further . . .*

They presented for me something like a wall. I forced my mind against it and could not get through.

Stronger. But not harder.

I don't understand! I sent.

You are not a tool to strike. Not a rock to bludgeon.

What am I? I asked.

You are a star.

And a light kindled inside me. A pure white light, the power of the nowhere. I became a flaming sword, and when I shoved, my mind *pierced* the barrier.

Good . . . Good . . . Continue.

A location popped into my head. Another portal? It was in what appeared to be a large building, filled with boxes? I frowned.

"Scrud," Chet said.

"You recognize the place?" I asked, turning toward him.

"Indeed I do, Spensa," he said, then took a deep breath. "That, I'm afraid, is the portal in the middle of Surehold, seat of Superiority power in this region of the belt."

25

There would be time later to think over what I'd seen. For now, I burst through the open doorway of the ruins, searching for Peg. I didn't have to hunt for long; she was leaning against a crumbling wall just outside, arms held before her, claws out. Even when lounging, the tenasi looked predatory.

"You saw something," she said. "You're cytonic, aren't you? Both of you."

"I . . . Yes," I said, glancing to Chet.

"Do you know about the Path of Elders?" he asked Peg.

"Never heard that term before," she said, "but these old ruins . . . they have their own memories. Anyone can feel that. And I've been told about cytonics." She pushed off the wall and stood upright. "This has to do with your mission? The one that's so important that you two had to steal a ship from us?"

"Yes," I told Peg. "And there's more. Tell me about your plans to assault Surehold."

She narrowed her eyes at me.

"Please, Peg," I said. "I need to know. If the pirates are afraid to fight the Superiority—if they don't want to risk the good things they have now—how do we persuade them?"

"We?" Peg said. "You're joining in?"

I glanced at Chet, who nodded.

"Provisionally, yes," I said.

Peg grinned. "Words. Well, we don't need to persuade the pirates—not individually. We merely need to get my sons to follow me again."

"Your sons?" Chet said. "They turned against you!"

"Yeah," Peg said. "They lead the two largest pirate factions. I'll admit, I didn't expect *both* of my sons to grow enough *muluns* to rebel. After we all left Surehold the first time, I tried to get everyone to attack it. We had a small initial clash, but our people were frightened by that, and disorganized. When my coalition collapsed, my sons took away some of my strongest forces to start their factions. Makes a mother proud."

"Proud? That they rebelled?"

"Exactly!" she said. "They were incredibly bold. Overthrowing their own mother? They were barely adults! Ah, it was great. But it's inconvenient, so we have to win them back. My eldest—Gremm—has been champion for a year now. Leads the faction called the Jolly Rogers. An Earth term, no?"

"I believe so," Chet said.

"Well, you'll probably get to meet my son's forces soon. The moment word of your skill reaches them, I suspect Gremm will send a raiding party to attack us. They'll be growing *delens* to know the truth—and I'll expect you to show them."

"I'm eager for it," I said.

"I doubt Gremm will join the raid. But afterward I can demand a contest between you and him—and he'll accept. I know my son. And though he's the best pilot among us, he's nothing compared to you. If you defeat him, he will be forced to grow the *tagao*."

"Which means?" I asked.

"A very rare fruit, meaning he feels submissive to his parents. If you defeat him, he will listen to me again."

"You *sure* about that?"

"Absolutely," Peg said. "It is our way."

I didn't point out that she'd been surprised by their betrayal, so I had my doubts. But I was willing to give it a try.

"What about his brother?" Chet asked.

"Semm leads a different faction," she said. "He'll return to me too, if my faction claims the championship. Trust me."

Yeah, that sounded too convenient to me. There was more to this—Peg still had her secrets.

She watched me a moment longer, then started through the ruins toward our ships. "We should be returning," she said. "I expect a raid at any time, and I don't want to leave the others too short-staffed."

"Well?" I asked Chet as she wandered off. "Did you know we'd have to get into Surehold itself?"

"I suspected," he admitted. "The portal there is one of the largest and oldest in the region. I had hoped it wouldn't be necessary . . . but at least we have a path forward."

"Assuming we can trust Peg's plan."

"She seems to trust it," he said. "Come, we *should* return to our ship. You remember what happened last time after we saw one of these?"

Yeah. Our entire fragment had been destroyed in a collision. Perhaps it had been a coincidence, but I found myself hurrying after Chet just in case. We gathered Maksim, and soon the four of us were lifting off to join the resonants and start back toward our home base.

"You two appear unusually solemn," M-Bot said as we fell into formation. "It worked, I assume? You again saw the past?"

"Indeed, AI," Chet said. "We *kind of* contacted a cytonic person in the past."

"Uh . . ." M-Bot said. "Clarification please?"

"She could feel my questions somehow," I explained, "in her time—and left answers for me. Or maybe she just heard the general curiosity of all who came after her. Either way, I think we know what happened to the kitsen cytonics—and why there was a sudden dearth of contact between Earth and aliens after some initial interactions in ancient times."

"Really? What?"

"War," I said. "With a delver."

"We don't know it was a delver," Chet said. "But it did seem to have been some kind of . . . delverlike entity. The cytonics of the galaxy—those that had contacted one another—gathered to fight it. And . . . not many survived."

"They fought a *single* entity?" M-Bot said.

"And won," Chet said, "by somehow making it real. But there were great casualties."

"And we now face . . . more than one," M-Bot said. "Way more than one."

"Yes," I said, leaning forward in my seat. "There was something else. No loss of memories in the nowhere back then. It's a more recent development."

"It's connected," Chet said. "And the answers are at Surehold. Some of them at least."

"In the memories of a man named Jason Write," I said, frowning.

"Jason Write?" M-Bot said. "Superiority historical archives list him as the human who initiated first contact with the greater galaxy after accidentally discovering he was cytonic. He . . . kicked off the expansion of humankind into the galaxy, and indirectly caused the First Human War of conquest."

I nodded absently, thinking about that ancient cytonic who had communicated with us. The feelings of exhaustion and loneliness that had permeated her. I felt that something had *sparked* inside me. Or . . . well, the spark had always been there. Now it burned brighter.

"Chet," I said. "Do your powers feel different?"

"Indeed!" he said. "They talked to me about using my mind to 'see' around myself! I feel that with practice, I won't just have an instinct for the fragments. I might be able to see into buildings, or around corners, or . . . well, it seems incredible!"

"I learned something else," I said softly. "But I don't know what it means yet."

You are a star.

"Hey," Maksim's voice said over the comm, "the rest of you registering that figure down there? At my nine."

"Odd to see someone," Shiver said, "out so openly, not hiding. If we were recruiting, they'd be in trouble."

I checked out the window. A solitary figure stood on a ridge on a distant fragment. It appeared to be a heklo—the distance was far enough that it made it difficult to tell. And though I couldn't see for certain, I could feel a coldness and a pressure against my mind. I was positive the figure had white glowing eyes.

"You feel that?" Chet asked.

"Yeah," I said. "It's one of them. At least they didn't find a way to destroy the fragment this time."

"Still worries me," Chet said. "I had hoped that we'd lost them these last few weeks. It is difficult for the delvers to project attention this far out. But now they have located us again. Hopefully this doesn't lead to difficulties."

I shivered. Soon we were past it, the figure dwindling in the distance. My comm started flashing though. A direct call from Peg.

"Yes, Captain?" I said.

"What did you see," she asked, "in those ruins?"

"Why?" I asked her.

"Something feels odd," she said. "About that figure we just passed. About this entire excursion. I answered your questions about my plans. Now answer mine. What did you see?"

"We saw the past," I admitted. "Memories, like you said. We're investigating a way to fight the delvers—and we got a message from a woman who encountered something like them long ago."

"*Fight* the *delvers*?" Peg said.

"Yeah . . ." I said.

"If it's any consolation," Chet said, "we would prefer to find some way to placate or reconcile with them. For now, however, we must continue our quest—and visit the portal at Surehold to find the memories hidden therein."

"Well, our goals overlap," Peg said, "so I can't say I'm sorry about that part. But fighting the delvers . . . I suppose if you're cytonic, maybe you can manage it? I knew this one dione in the security force. They left soon after arriving, because they kept . . . changing, to look like different people. The heads of the Superiority pulled them out the moment they heard of it."

Changing shape? I'd never done anything like that.

"A cytonic talent," Chet said. "Projecting illusions into the minds of others—making oneself appear different, even feel different. It works on anyone in here, though I've heard that in the somewhere it only works on other cytonics."

Actually . . . I felt a chill. I *had* heard of that happening. Someone had done it to my father—making him see the wrong things. I was coming to understand more and more that different cytonics . . . they could do different things. I could hear the stars and teleport. Chet could extend his life span and "see" great distances with his powers.

Peg dropped off the line, and M-Bot had a chance to speak. "Why didn't the delvers grab one of the members of your team and turn *them* into a glowing-eyed thing?" he asked. "Peg and Maksim were closer to you than that heklo."

"Gathering a large number of people together repels them," Chet said. "Particularly if those people see themselves as a group. My theory is that the delvers need someone who is as alone as possible, and someone who doesn't view themselves as belonging."

I dwelled on what we'd seen, and found it more difficult to make sense of it all this time. In fact, I had to admit that—as we neared home—I was glad when a more mundane danger cropped up: an emergency announcement that a group of starfighters from an enemy faction was approaching the Broadsider base at high speed.

26

As soon as our base came into view, I hit my overburn and pulled ahead of the others. I could see the destructor fire spraying through the nowhere, beautiful and bright. My body came alive, and my mind—which had been reeling from what I'd experienced—snapped to full alert.

This was what I'd been made for.

"Hang on, Chet," I said, and we screamed into the fight, flying to the sound of wind on wings and boosters roaring. It had taken us precious minutes to arrive, and I counted three of our fighters already locked up, drifting aimlessly. Scud. With ten total fighters, and the five of us gone, the remaining two stragglers were facing overwhelming odds.

M-Bot highlighted enemy ships, friendlies, and downed friendlies on my proximity display. By the markings on the enemy fighters, these were from the Jolly Rogers. The faction led by Peg's son Gremm—and the one she'd expected to send a raid to test my abilities.

Excellent.

M-Bot suggested a few targets—circling starfighters that were flying slower than the others and one that had just taken a hit to its shield. As much as I wanted a challenge—and to go for the stronger enemies first—that could lead to my team getting overwhelmed.

So, steeling myself, I took one of M-Bot's suggestions and swooped in behind a pair of fighters that were tailing Gibsey, one of our pilots from Flintlock Flight. The two enemy pilots barely responded to my arrival. One swung a little to the side so that if I fired, I'd risk my stray shots hitting my ally.

For a brief second, I was confused. That was it?

I'm used to fighting Superiority ships that recognize me as an enemy ace, I realized. *They highlight me in battle, devoting extra resources to me.* But this was my first time fighting rival pirates. They had come to test me, but they didn't seem to expect too much.

Time to send them my calling card. I sniped the one who had moved to the side, each of my shots landing with precision. The pilot belatedly panicked, pulling up—and slammed square into my next shot. You always want to pull up. It's instinct, even in space when there's no ground below.

I buzzed around the now-frozen enemy ship, firing at the second ship tailing Gibsey—which was the ship that M-Bot had highlighted as having a weakened shield. My shots rattled the enemy pilot, who broke off and dodged to the right.

"You," I whispered, "shall know the taste of my steel. And I shall know the taste of your blood."

Yes, those kinds of phrases still slipped out now and then. No, I wasn't embarrassed. They helped me focus.

I wove after the ship as they dodged around the fragment. They crossed underneath, with me tight behind them, then came up around the other side on a pivot. I could sense their increasing panic as I used my light-lance to swing around more quickly, my GravCaps easily compensating for the g-forces.

My prey cut one direction, then the other. It was an ostensibly smart move—if they jerked around randomly, I couldn't anticipate where they'd be. Except, as with pulling up, people who *think* they're acting randomly rarely are. Cobb had drilled this into my brain time and time again. Instead of "random" motions, we practiced sequences of maneuvers deliberately designed to frustrate enemies.

Training always trumped haphazardness. My prey jerked back and forth, and I'm sure it *felt* random to them—but I picked them off with three expert shots anyway. Chet let out a whoop, and I left the enemy ship frozen and swerved into the firefight. Here, I got in an admittedly lucky shot on a ship that M-Bot highlighted, but I wasn't going to complain. Three "kills" in under five minutes?

Scud, it felt good to be back in the cockpit. Fighting alongside friends again. Doing what I was meant to do.

Nearby, I noticed some of the enemy ships forming up into a proper flight. "Cutlass Flight," I said, "track my position. I'm about to give you a group of juicy targets."

The four enemy ships spun around, orienting toward me. Working together was a good idea, but these obviously hadn't drilled on ideal ship distance. As I'd recently taught the Broadsiders, when you flew in a formation, you wanted to be just far enough away from one another to protect against IMP blasts.

I went barreling toward them, slamming my overburn. They landed a few shots on me, which was fine. As I darted through the middle of the quartet, I hit my IMP. They reacted too slowly, and I caught three of the four—which M-Bot obligingly painted on the display for me—dropping their shields.

As I'd suggested, Peg and the members of Cutlass Flight focused on these ships. Sprays of destructor fire lit the air behind me, and I found myself grinning. The fighting here reminded me of something . . .

Training with the holographic projectors, I realized. *That was the last time I flew without fearing for my life.*

"That was quite the stunt, Spin," Peg said over the comm. "Can't decide if you're growing *muluns* or *hemels*."

"That's nothing, Captain," I said, spinning into evasive maneuvers as someone took shots at me. "You should see me do something like that when we're fighting for our lives. It's *way* more stupid then."

"I can imagine," she said. "You need a wingmate?"

"Nah. You and Maksim might want to go help Gibsey though. He's somehow picked up two *more* tails."

I still had my own tail. M-Bot helpfully pointed out this was the one ship from a moment ago that I *hadn't* IMPed. Which meant they had a shield and I didn't.

Huh. They were sticking to me pretty well. In fact—

A couple bolts of blue destructor light grazed my canopy, inches from connecting. Scud. This one was actually *good*.

My grin widened. I slammed on my overburn, sat back in my seat, and really got into it. There was no way I'd be able to restore my shield to duel them properly—that required precious seconds sitting still. So instead I focused on outflying my enemy.

The next few minutes were a glorious chase through the battlefield, swerving and swooping, light-lancing around fragments, buzzing the Broadsider base. That tail stayed on me, as if proving a point. They soon left off shooting though.

Waiting for the perfect shot, eh? I thought. *Well, I'm not going to give you one.*

I pulled up for a while, soaring into the pink-white sky. Then I turned and dove. My new ship's GravCaps absorbed the worst of the g-forces, but I was still slammed with them as I accelerated downward. That had me grinning. Yes, g-forces suck, but at this point they were an old friend. All the blood pushing to the back of my body, threatening to claim my eyesight—then my consciousness . . .

I soared past my tail, then pulled up at just the right moment. A glance at the monitor showed me Chet's head rolling on his neck. He shook himself, coming alert. Seemed I'd knocked him out in that maneuver. I'd have to be a little more careful.

Yet even despite all of that, my enemy kept with me. They *were* good. So I roared back into the snarl of fighting ships—and then started blasting an enemy ship that had been gunning for Shiver, knocking out its shields. I then took to the side, drawing a bead on another ship, and fired and locked it up.

My tail finally unloaded on me, firing wildly instead of waiting for the right moment.

Great, now I just—

My ship jolted. The control panel went dark and the controls locked up. I found myself hovering forward at a steady pace, nothing working, as that enemy ace buzzed my ship. Scud, I'd been hit. I checked Chet's vitals on my monitor—he was fine, by the numbers—so I sat back in my seat, then laughed.

"Spensa?" M-Bot asked. "Oh my. Is the stress causing your emotions to erupt irrationally? Oh! I've felt that now. Um, what do I say? Let's see . . . Humm . . ."

"I'm great," I said, wiping my eyes.

"No, no. I need the correct words . . ."

I stretched forward in my seat, trying to get a visual on that ace. Fighting was fun, but knowing there was someone in here who could *match* me? That was even *more* exciting.

"Ah!" M-Bot said. "I've got it. Spensa. Feel better, please."

"Okay," I said, smiling. "I already do."

"Success! I'm going to remember that one."

"Chet, how are you feeling?" I asked him.

"Enthused," he said, his voice wan, "but nauseous and . . . embarrassed. I fear I lost consciousness earlier."

"It happens to all of us," I said. "No need to be embarrassed. You should have seen me on my first days in the centrifuge back home."

"Well," he said, "I know you've said I was a pilot, but those experiences are lost to me. My current disposition is one of profound respect for the ground, I must admit."

"I'll try to avoid towing you into any more of these," I said. "M-Bot, who was that enemy pilot?"

"Peg's son, Gremm," M-Bot said. "She indicated he wouldn't join the fight, but by the markings on that ship, she was wrong."

So I'd had my first brush with the champion. I grinned. Though he'd beaten me, that hadn't been a true duel. I'd lost my shield fighting his companions.

He would see my *true* potential when we faced off. "How are you, M-Bot?" I asked, turning and scanning the sky, trying to gauge the progress of the battle. "That hit didn't fry you or anything?"

"Fortunately," M-Bot said, "the modifications we made to insulate my core systems appear to have worked."

"I'm glad."

"It honestly wouldn't take too much effort to insulate all of the systems," he continued, "so we won't get locked up in fights like this."

"What would be the sport in that?" Chet asked.

"Sport?" M-Bot said. "It's not a game."

"It is though," I said. "As long as everyone plays by the same rules, nobody has to die."

"From what I understand of the interactions between sapient beings," M-Bot said, "someone is eventually going to seek an extra advantage. I'm shocked it hasn't happened already, regardless of what Peg indicated."

"Maybe," I said. "You ever study small-group battles between tribes of early humans?"

"No."

"You should. I think you'd be surprised by what kinds of rules a society will follow, when the stakes are different."

Smaller groups of hunter-gatherers on Old Earth had rarely engaged in lethal combat. Their numbers had been too small, their communities too tight-knit. Yes, occasionally someone had died during their conflicts, but mostly the battles had been about boasting and intimidation.

Cobb had used this lesson to indicate that human nature wasn't to fight and kill, which was why we needed to drill and train. But now I found something liberating in the idea that flying, the thing I loved, didn't *have* to only be about killing. It could be about proving myself—to myself.

Behind, the remaining four enemy ships decided to pull out. Cutlass Flight's timely return had let us win the day. I waited, pensive, as Peg and her son negotiated terms for the return of their disabled ships. They then began reactivating those vessels, a process that would take a few minutes.

Maksim finally arrived to fetch me, hauling my sorry rear back to the base, where the ground crews waited with some of the pilots who had already landed. A set of docking light-lances pulled me down, and I hit the manual release on my canopy, then cranked it open. As Chet and I climbed out, I braced myself for a lecture. I could hear Cobb's voice ranting about how reckless I'd been in that fight. He always drilled good behavior, even when doing simulations.

Instead I climbed out to furious cheers and applause. Led by Peg herself, who—instead of berating me—grabbed me in an enveloping hug as I dropped to the ground.

"Four kills?" she shouted. "And three assists? Kid, you practically won that fight on your own!"

"The Jolly Rogers were sent running!" Maksim said. "You have no idea how good that feels!"

"We have our chance," Peg said. "Gremm was impressed. He's willing to duel you officially tomorrow."

The others cheered again.

Scud. I'd been shot down, and they were cheering me? And her son thought I was worthy?

I grinned widely. How long had it been since I'd been this . . . well, excited after a fight? How long since I'd heard such joy from my flightmates? Last time I could remember was when I saved the DDF base from annihilation by grabbing the bomb. But those cheers had had an edge. A tension. Those had been cheers of relief.

These people were simply happy. I let their enthusiasm infuse me. It was an incredible feeling. And it was merely the beginning—because tomorrow, I *was* going to become pirate champion and give Peg her chance at uniting the factions.

INTERLUDE

Floating.

I became partially aware. Not awake, but aware. I was in the place where I had no shape, no senses other than my cytonic ones. I . . . remembered lying down, in my own room at the Broadsider base, after the skirmish.

It had been a full day. I'd fallen asleep. And now I searched outward, as I'd done on other nights. Seeking. Wishing.

Jorgen . . . I tried to find him, but felt like I was screaming into an empty void. I couldn't feel *anything*. Like . . . like I was building a bonfire in a dark place, but with each new log the increased light only reaffirmed that the blackness extended into infinity.

I'd failed at this often enough recently that I nearly faded into unconsciousness. I had important work ahead of me; I would need to get my rest.

And yet . . .

Something felt off about my experiences lately in this sleeping realm. Yes. This was wrong. I hadn't been able to see it before. But with a few more test shouts, I thought I picked out what was wrong here. My mental shouts were vanishing *too* quickly. As if I wasn't screaming into a void, so much as into pillows.

Was . . . someone *blocking* me?

Scud. Was *that* why I hadn't been able to find Jorgen?

I growled. Well, I made the mental equivalent of a growl. As one does. My soul *sparked* in the darkness.

I pressed forward through the void, feeling . . . Yes. A dampening. Like a cloud all around me, invisible. In the strange ways of the nowhere, it had always been there—literally on top of me—but I hadn't been able to perceive it. Now I struggled forward, pushing. Fighting with my arms.

No, I thought. *I'm not a stone. I'm not even a bonfire. I'm a star.*

My essence, my soul, exploded with light—burning away the haze that surrounded me. No longer was I *nothing* in this place. I was a light, a glowing presence, a sphere of burning whiteness.

I used my ability to connect, to see, and sensed a presence ahead. It was easy, now that I'd escaped. Was that Jorgen? I latched onto it and *pulled* myself through.

I appeared in the somewhere, as I had before—illusory, ephemeral. But I hadn't found Jorgen.

I'd found my enemies.

To my human eyes, Winzik looked virtually identical to Nuluba, though his exoskeleton was a deeper green. Varvax didn't usually wear clothing, but he had on an official-ish sash. He sat in a large marble chair, carved intricately and inlaid with silver. I supposed that if one had an exoskeleton, cushioned seating wouldn't be relevant.

The room was circular, lavishly paneled in wood, and had the feel of an office. A group of tenasi, with the same predatory air as Peg, was making a presentation to Winzik. They *did* wear clothing, and I recognized a military uniform instantly. Some things seemed pretty universal across species—and judging by the ranks of medals and badges on their jackets, these were admirals and generals.

A military briefing for the acting leader of the Superiority, I supposed. The screen, fortunately, didn't show Detritus—but an unfamiliar planet, red and green. I couldn't read any of the writing around it, and didn't have my pin to translate, so I couldn't figure out what it was.

"It's ReDawn," a voice said in English from behind me. "Funny you wouldn't recognize it, considering the face you wore most of the time you were with us."

I spun. Brade sat in a chair beside me. She wore her dark hair in a sharp buzz cut, and even through the uniform I could see she had muscles—the kind of build you rarely saw outside the more fanatical soldiers at the gym. She was spinning a pen between her fingers, watching me with an almost uninterested stare.

Winzik turned in his seat to glance back at her, barking an order in a language I didn't know.

"Oh, stuff your complaints, Winzik," Brade said, still spinning the pencil. "She's here. Finally broke out of her cage. Took you long enough, Alanik—or Spensa, I guess. I expected you to make more noise inside that barrier. Do you know how much attention it required to keep it up?"

"How?" I demanded. "How did you manage that?"

"Took a little instruction from our new friends," Brade said. She could see me, I realized. Without a reflective surface. "Unlocked a few abilities I'd been practicing."

Winzik ordered the generals out and walked over, exoskeleton hands making circular motions as he spoke. Despite the language barrier, I could recognize his mannerisms—in fact, I could practically hear him saying "my, my" and "how aggressive" in his persnickety tone.

"The delvers think they can handle you," Brade said. "I told them otherwise. You're blunt, Spensa. I like that about you. No subtlety. You just go crashing through whatever stands between you and your goals."

"I was subtle enough to fool you," I snapped, projecting the thoughts at her. And with my growing powers, I caught a flutter of emotions she tried to hide. Shame, anger. She had trained with me and had never figured out what I really was. Until I'd handed her the truth, for her to stomp on.

Scud, I'd been so naive.

Winzik was saying something else. I wished I could figure out what it was.

"He wants me to trap your mind," Brade said. "I'm not sure I can do it. The people I've been practicing on are far weaker than you. I won't flinch this time though."

Her mind slammed into mine, crushing against me. I immediately felt like I was in a box—that was shrinking. I lashed out, panicked, furious. I summoned my anger, as I had last time we'd clashed. And I threw it at her.

As she'd warned, Brade didn't waver. She was expecting my counterattack.

So I started to glow. I stoked what was inside me, the powerful light. The brilliance that was my soul. I felt Brade's surprise, though she didn't want to project the emotion. She was shocked. She . . . thought I was like a delver, in ways that frightened her.

And something else heard.

I see you!

The voice was distant, but *loud*. A cytonic shout vibrated through me, then something slammed into Brade, making her gasp and lose her focus. It was raw, this voice, as if untrained. If I was a sword, it was a bludgeon—a big one.

I flared with light and broke through Brade's box, and together with the new voice we shoved her back, then escaped into the nowhere.

I was chased by that extremely loud voice. It had saved me, but it seemed a monster of some sort. I spun toward it, not wanting to put my back to it as it crashed into me. And . . .

. . . hugged me?

Jorgen? I thought.

Where have you been? he thought at me. *Why haven't you contacted me? Spin, it's been weeks!*

I tried! I said, forcing my mind to visualize him. For the moment we floated together in the void, our essences touching. Like we were two swimmers in a deep, vast, endless ocean clinging to one another.

I'm sorry I didn't contact you, I said. *Brade did something.*

Brade? he asked.

The one who was holding me when you arrived, I said. *How did you find me?*

I've been practicing, he explained. *I can't hyperjump, no matter how hard I try. But Alanik says that's not uncommon. Cytonics have different specialties. She says I can learn hyperjumping—that every one of us can technically learn every talent, but for some of us there are individual talents that are very difficult. We all have weaknesses and strengths.*

Wait, I said. *Alanik?*

It's complicated, he said. *We're holding out, trying to gather help. But tell me about you. Spensa, you're glowing. Like a star. I could see you even from a distance!*

I've been practicing too, I said.

Are you a pirate queen yet?

He said it with such fondness. There were so many images wrapped up in what he'd said—this communication had much more *depth* than ordinary words. For example, I knew instantly that he was joking—but also a little serious.

He loved *my* love of stories. He imagined me in one of those stories, and was completely confident in me. More confident than I was of myself. Saints . . . that was so good to hear. So good to know. His picture of me was of someone courageous, resourceful, and inspiring.

That was *not* what I deserved for how I'd treated him in our first weeks knowing each other. Fortunately, I could also feel Jorgen responding to my own picture of him. Upright, honest, caring. A leader, the best one I'd known.

The moment was as perfect a one as I'd ever felt. The two of us sharing our idealized versions of one another—knowing we could never live up to them, yet knowing it didn't matter. Because by simply being near one another, we resonated and became a little more—a little better—for the knowledge, support, and trust.

Then it was ruined as eyes started to appear around us. Bright white holes, the attention of the delvers. It wasn't my glow that attracted them. It was Jorgen. Scud, he was *loud*.

Go, Jorgen, I said as the eyes surrounded us. *I'll contact you later, once their attention dies down.*

I felt his essence brush mine. I *felt* his affection, his passion. But then he was gone.

I turned to face the delvers. I kept thinking that with effort I could get through to them. After all, Chet had explained they were all the same individual. Not a group mind, but somehow all identical. So if I'd been able to change the mind of one, shouldn't I be able to do the same for the others?

I'd failed at this before, but I had to try again. After all, it had taken three attempts to get a ship. So, as the eyes surrounded me, I tried to project a sensation of smallness.

I tried to shrink us all down, to narrow our perspective. As their minds touched mine, I tried to show them. Infinity went both ways—we could be as expansive as a universe, but we could be as small as a mote.

I showed them what I saw. Maksim, with his goofy smile and ready, welcoming manner. Shiver, who did so well understanding people who were very different from her. Nuluba, who so desperately wanted to make up for the ways the Superiority had wronged the peoples of the galaxy.

See us, I told them. *See that we are alive.*

We know, they sent back. *Oh, we know.*

They just didn't care.

In that moment I saw things as *they* did. Yes, they'd initially refused to accept that all the noises in the somewhere were alive. Then I'd changed one of them. When I'd done that, the rest had responded *against* what I'd done.

In a way, it didn't matter which one of them I'd changed. Because as soon as I'd done it, the others had put up defenses. Like how you might get off one sniper shot at people in a group, but then the rest would duck for cover.

I would *never* persuade another delver, not like I'd done before. Because now they hated us even *more,* knowing we were alive. Because now we weren't just random annoyances. We were *intentionally* trying to bring them pain. We were dangerous.

We needed to be exterminated.

The horror of that idea made me flee from before them. And I was getting good at hiding. I pretended to fade away, to sleep, but then quested out with my ever-strengthening ability to listen. I thought I'd heard something back there, and was rewarded with a voice.

My, my, Brade said to the delvers, sending Winzik's words into the nowhere. *Was that painful? You see, she is too difficult to control. They all are. You saw how another came? They are multiplying. Getting louder.*

That referred to Jorgen and the noise he'd made in rescuing me. Oh, scud.

I felt the delvers mull over his words, and I remembered what Brade had said. She'd wanted me to be "loud" as I tried to break through the dampening she'd put on me. As if . . . as if she'd purposely meant to provoke me. So that the delvers would . . .

We hear and hurt, the delvers said. *But we can extinguish the noises on our own.*

Can you? Winzik said. *My, my. It seems that when you come to our realm, you are confused. You are as unskilled with this place as we are when in yours! You attacked Detritus and Starsight, yet failed to kill even a single cytonic. Many years have passed, and you have failed each time. We multiply. The noise multiplies. I will stop it. If you help me.*

They hated this idea. I could feel their hatred. But also their agreement. *We accept your deal, noise,* the delvers said. *We will do as you instruct in exchange for you stopping the ones that torment us.*

Excellent, Winzik sent. *So very, very wise of you.*

I felt their deal snap into place. The delvers would work for Winzik. I realized what had happened just as I slid into true unconsciousness—and as a result, nightmares haunted me the entire time I slept.

PART FOUR

27

Roughly twelve hours later, I flew on a direct course toward the arena, anxious for my duel—and holding a book in my hand.

The arena was a location in the Jolly Rogers' territory—Peg said the anomalies near it made the fighting more interesting. They'd be waiting there for us with the other pirate factions, who would come to watch. Indeed, we'd brought the entire Broadsiders Faction: ground crews flying double or in shuttles. Chet was flying with Nuluba today, in a noncombat tug that had comfortable seats.

I still felt a sense of dread from what I'd experienced the night before. The deal had been made; the delvers would work with Winzik. I needed to find answers, and quickly.

Fortunately, I seemed to be on the best path for that. Win this duel; help Peg take Surehold. Unfortunately, the trip to the arena would take a few hours. When I'd complained in the hangar about the flying time, Maksim had tossed me the book.

A real book, made of paper and everything. I hadn't been intending to read it, but as the flight stretched long—and I let M-Bot take over steering for a little while—I found myself poking into it as a distraction.

It was slow reading, as I had to use my translation pin with its optics on to read the sentences to me in English. At the same time, it was *fascinating*. Not only was physical media like this almost nonexistent on my planet, information from our old ship archives was fragmented. The biggest chunk that had survived until my time was about the plants and animals of Old Earth, so my schooling had covered that in detail.

But I'd never heard of a "trashy romance novel," as Maksim had named this one. It was written from the perspective of the cambrian species, who had a lot of tentacles and stuff. Their courtship rituals were surprisingly similar to human ones—if way, way more sappy. Or maybe that was the genre.

I didn't really care about the plot; I was more intrigued by this book's nature. It was just . . . so *fluffy*. The protagonist spent her time romancing three different guys, and her most urgent question was deciding which one to bring with her on vacation.

Like, that was the *entire* conflict. Not the quest to *win* this vacation, but the stress of choosing between the guys. This was what they read, what they enjoyed, in the Superiority? It contained no fighting. I wasn't so ignorant as to think everything *had* to involve battle. There were plenty of great stories about heroes like clever Coyote escaping trouble using his wits instead of his brawn. There were even stories about people building up to a war, then making peace.

Gran-Gran hadn't ever told me a story about people taking a vacation. Part of me thought it was ridiculous. But another part understood. It whispered, "This is what people can focus their attention on if they aren't constantly at war. You learned something living among them: your life is not normal."

This aspect of the characters made them so much more alien than the tentacles. I wanted peace for my people, yes. But to imagine a world without flight training, without the military complex being society's central and most demanding need . . .

Scud. I couldn't understand it, but I needed to. So I read their romance novel and tried to comprehend.

We flew for some time, and I dug a good quarter of the way through the book, when M-Bot spoke. "You see that fragment?"

I glanced out of the canopy. We had to move slowly for the benefit of the tugs, so we made a leisurely pace through the belt, passing fragments with a variety of terrain. One down below was a rare ocean fragment. Not the one we'd traversed earlier, but similar.

"I feel something seeing that one," M-Bot said. "I remembered sailing with you and Chet, and it felt . . . pleasant. Like I was meeting an old friend. Is it strange to feel this now? It's not even the same fragment."

"It's not strange," I said. "Humans often associate feelings with locations. The caverns beneath Detritus sometimes feel more like home to me than the neighborhood where I grew up—and each time I see a cave, I think of them."

"This feeling is . . . nice," M-Bot said.

"Not going to ask this time what the emotions are for?"

"I'm still wondering that," he said. "But today I just . . . *like* these feelings. That's all right. Isn't it?"

I smiled. "Yes."

"I used to try to imagine why you liked stories so much," M-Bot said. "At first I thought it was a purely logical response—education through the story as a mnemonic device. Yet your strange reactions baffled me. You didn't treat them as mere education, but as something more.

"I think I understand now. Hearing those stories, being with your grandmother, felt good. And thinking of them again . . . Well, you remember her voice, don't you? That's like me seeing that fragment and remembering the fun of sailing. It's . . . warm to me. A machine shouldn't be able to feel warm, but I do."

I shifted in my seat, trying to remember Gran-Gran's voice, as he said. And . . . I couldn't. I remembered the stories, but her voice was lost to me.

Needing to be distracted, I turned back to my book, and we flew for more . . . time. I'll admit, I kind of liked the book. I didn't find it trashy at all. Indeed, I actually found myself engaged, almost *excited* to find out who got to go on the vacation. Granted, it helped to imagine the heroine was planning to feed the failed suitors to her pet shark.

It would have been easier if M-Bot hadn't piped up with some observation or another every five minutes. "Hey, Spensa! That fragment is black and purple, with crystals growing in the ground! I think it comes from a planet like where Shiver lived. What do you think?"

"Don't know, M-Bot," I said, turning the page. "Why don't you scan your databases to find out?"

"Done!" he said. "I think it does!"

"Great," I said. "Maybe you should catalog the fragments we've passed, and see if you can discover what kind of planets they came from."

"Will do!" he said.

That should take him a while. I smiled fondly, but Saints, this must be what it was like to have a toddler. I probably owed my mother a nice rat sandwich or something—because I'm *pretty* sure I'd had *lots* of questions for her. Often about how to perform a decapitation.

"Hey," M-Bot said after a few more minutes of silence, "why am I doing this scan again? Is this *busywork,* Spensa?"

I smiled. "Made you look."

"You humans," he said. "That is *not* a joke! There's no punchline!"

"Oh, hush," I said. "This part is good."

"I guess you don't want to hear about Peg's secret communication then," he said.

I glanced up. "Secret communication?"

"She's receiving an encrypted direct call—I assume from a pirate in the Jolly Rogers, judging by the origin of the databurst. Peg obviously doesn't want anyone to know about the call; it came in on a band that the other Broadsider receivers aren't attuned to pick up. Her ship apparently has some special equipment. I can only see because of, you know . . ."

"Espionage AI?"

"Mushroom-locating AI. With supplementary espionage additions."

A secret call? That *was* odd. Peg tended to be very open about everything she did—she always let the Broadsiders listen in on the negotiations she made, for example.

"Can we eavesdrop?" I asked.

"If I had my old ship's hardware, that would be easy," he said. "But I can't manage it from this ship. Best I can do is tell you the length of the conversation—and maybe pinpoint the person Peg is talking to."

"Okay," I said, a little frustrated. I almost wished he hadn't said anything at all, rather than teasing me. I was distracted enough that it was hard to get through the rest of the book. I put it down, about halfway done, as long-range sensors showed that we were coming up on a large gathering of starfighters.

"She just ended the call," M-Bot said. "But I'm certain which ship it came from: the starfighter that belongs to her son Gremm."

"So Peg had an extended secret call with her supposedly estranged son," I said, "leader of a rival pirate faction. Something about all this doesn't add up, M-Bot. What kind of game is she playing?"

"I couldn't possibly guess," M-Bot said. "I barely understand myself these days, let alone you organics."

The "arena" turned out to be a large open-air region of the belt, populated by building-size floating chunks of rock. Though most of the fragments were on the same plane, here in this pocket the landscape was more uneven. It seemed like a fragment might have shattered, its pieces coming to rest at different elevations.

Well, I'd trained as a pilot in debris showers. I could handle this. However, a more distinctive feature of this region was the patches of strange glowing white light amid the chunks of rock. They were like mini lightbursts, but weren't much larger than my ship. Actually, they reminded me of the little white hole I'd seen in the vision, the one that had eventually become a fragment.

Those holes made me uncomfortable. The others had told me about them, but still . . . Those were patches of pure nowhere, somehow breaking through into the belt. And I was going to have to fly among them.

28

A ragtag bunch of a hundred different starfighters were arrayed around the arena. Markings on the wings or fuselages identified their factions. No other theme unified them—except perhaps for a sense of ramshackle piecemealness.

Several had obviously had their cockpits expanded to make room for a larger species. Others were bulky shuttles or other industrial craft—but with an amusing number of weapons strapped to them, like the "super-gun" I'd made as a little girl by taping six toys together.

There were also many with dangerous designs: sleek military vessels with integrated weapons and large boosters. I picked out Gremm, the champion; his ominous starfighter was shaped like a wicked crescent moon, pointed ends facing my direction. It was larger than a DDF Poco, but made up for it with enormous boosters and a deadly armament. Now that I had time to study it carefully, I counted *five* destructors on the thing.

"Peg," a voice said over the line—my ship translating. It was a low growling voice, and spoke the same language Peg did. "Took your sweet time as always."

"I like to enjoy myself, Gremm," Peg said back. "And the simple things give me pleasure."

"Like being slow?"

"Like knowing I've made you wait," Peg said, with a laugh. "You ready to be on with this?"

"I would be," Gremm said. "Except I'm not champion anymore."

"What?" Peg demanded.

"I lost the title!" Gremm explained. "Earlier today. The Cannonaders arrived early, and I thought we'd do some dueling while we waited. But . . . I lost."

"Fool child," Peg said. "You grow *hemels* this day."

I followed this exchange with a frown. "Growing *hemels,*" I was pretty sure, was their way of saying someone was stupid.

There was something . . . theatrical about the exchange. Gremm and Peg had spent a half hour talking in secret; she plainly already knew about him losing the championship. But now she had to pretend she didn't know. Why?

"Well, who *is* the champion?" Peg said. "We'll fight them instead."

"Cannonade newcomer," Gremm said.

Peg growled softly. Curious, I opened a direct line to Maksim. "I think I know the Cannonade Faction. They've got a heklo leader?"

"Yeah," he replied. "Vlep. They are . . . malcontents."

"We're pirates, Maksim. We're *all* malcontents."

"Cannonaders are worse," he explained. "The other factions can be trusted not to be too brutal. But if the Cannonade Faction has the champion . . . I don't know. I'd refuse to fight, if I were you."

Well, I wasn't going to do *that*. In fact, I was happy for a chance to strike back at Vlep and his cronies for robbing me. But there was also something very suspicious about all of this.

What game are you playing, Peg? I wondered.

Another voice came on the broad channel, snappish and vaguely familiar. "We'll fight your pilot, Peg," Vlep said. "My champion is better than any of you. He calls himself Darkshadow."

Darkshadow?

That was such an awesome callsign.

"Ha!" Peg said. "Darkshadow? *Really,* Vlep? Well, hope his skill is equal to his flair for the dramatic. Because we have someone special!"

"They're going to lose," Vlep said. "Just like your kid did. I don't know what you two are playing at, but I don't trust you, Peg. Any of you."

"So nothing's new, Vlep."

"You sure that newcomer of yours doesn't want to swap to join us?" Vlep asked. "The Cannonade Faction is the only one that doesn't secretly bow to you and your spawn."

"I don't think I'll be doing that, Vlep," I said over the line, pitching my voice to be as ominous as possible. "All things considered."

"Am . . . I supposed to know what that meant?" he asked back.

Scud. He didn't recognize my voice. So much for my cool reveal. "I'm the human woman you tried to kidnap in the forest," I said. "I'm actually a super great pilot, and I'm here to embarrass you for what you did to me."

"Yeah, sure, whatever," he said. "Darkshadow, let's humiliate another faction. Duel until lockup. Losing group forfeits their ship to the winner."

That was high stakes for this lot. Ships were rare enough in here that they weren't wagered except in extreme circumstances. If I lost, M-Bot would upload to the drone, which we'd brought along—so that shouldn't be a problem. But there was a more important issue at stake—and it involved the delicate game Peg was playing behind the scenes.

At Peg's urging, I inched my ship forward out of the line of Broadsiders. I kept my eyes on the most dangerous ships, wondering which would be the champion—so I almost missed it when a relatively small ship soared forward. It was probably around a third of the size of my ship, with a core fuselage so narrow that the destructors on the wings looked enormous by comparison.

I realized I'd made a silly mistake. Bigger didn't mean more dangerous. I should know that better than most. This ship reminded me of the Krell drones, and they'd been plenty deadly. And while a majority of intelligent species seemed to be roughly human-size, there were obvious exceptions.

I eyed the ship, suspicious. A newcomer good enough to beat Gremm, the longtime champion? Who was this? A figment perhaps? That would make sense. A figment pilot would explain the small size—the ship wouldn't need a cockpit.

"Arena boundaries are being uploaded to your proximity display, Spin," Peg said over the comm. M-Bot helpfully outlined the area—which was in the shape of a tall column or tube. It stretched thousands of feet upward and downward, but was a fraction of that in diameter.

That would make for a narrow fighting area. Like . . . having a duel in a tunnel, or in a shaft stretching up toward the sky. "What happens if I go out of bounds?" I said on a private line, realizing I'd never asked. "Do I lose?"

"Nah," Peg said. "What's the fun in that? If you go out of bounds, everyone else can shoot at you—so I'd advise against it. Unless you're growing too many *muluns*. You ready?"

I took a deep breath. "I know there's something about this you aren't telling me, Peg."

She remained quiet.

"I'll still do it," I said, "but at least tell me one thing: do you *genuinely* need me to win this? Or is the championship about some kind of political posturing?"

"I need this, Spin," Peg said, her voice growing softer. "I *really* need this. This is our chance at uniting the factions. There are details I haven't told you, but that part is legitimate. I have put, one might say, all of my fruit into your cart. Please don't drive it off a cliff."

"All right," I said. "Let's do this."

My screen flashed green and I hit the overburn, boosting into the arena proper.

29

The champion didn't fire on me immediately. He zipped in close, then veered away, clearly expecting me to tail him.

A test. He wanted to judge my skill. I decided not to bite, instead turning upward and flying along the perimeter of the arena.

"I find no matches for that starfighter design in my database," M-Bot said. "Alas, I have only a basic list of Superiority ships, and this seems an advanced model."

"It might not even be Superiority," I said. "Chet thinks that occasionally other ships end up in here via hyperjump accidents."

I swooped upward, then turned back around. I didn't miss that several other ships kept pace with me outside the arena barrier—pirates eager for the chance to take potshots if I drifted out of bounds.

All right. I had a feel for the shaftlike shape of the arena now, but I was still at a disadvantage, as I'd never flown in here before—while the champion had done it at least once. I performed a quick weave between several of the floating chunks, then eyed one of the strange glowing white patches.

The proximity sensor blared an alert that indicated the champion was heading for me. Darkshadow had realized that I was acclimating to the terrain, and so he would need to make the first move—lest he give me time to adjust. I slammed on my overburn, dodging out of the way as the champion tried to tail me.

I soon had to cut the overburn. Going too fast while dodging wasn't always the best idea, depending on reaction speed and turning capability. Instead I zoomed down along the curved perimeter—shooting through the shaft at its edge—hoping the champion would slip out of bounds. Unfortunately, Darkshadow proved competent at avoiding that. Indeed, that straightaway only earned me a few shots from behind, which were hard to evade without going out of bounds.

Best to stay to the center of the arena. I pulled up and went soaring in that direction, weaving between floating chunks. The champion stuck with me; he *was* good. And he proved to have a light-lance himself—which he used in pivots. That was strange. I had yet to meet a nonhuman from the Superiority who used a light-lance the way we did in the DDF.

Fortunately, over the next few minutes of leading him through a chase, I decided I was probably the better pilot. I just had to . . .

I *felt* something.

Something like fingers on my brain.

I was a lonely rock in the darkness. A mist reached around me, embracing me, smothering me.

A pair of burning white eyes appeared, reflected in the canopy of my starship. Eyes that fixated upon me.

We see you.

I was thrown back into the conflict as a destructor blast crackled across my shield. Scud! I twisted to the left and dropped in a weaving spin between two floating asteroids, effectively dodging further shots.

"Spensa?" M-Bot asked. "What's wrong?"

I searched the scanner. Yeah, I'd drifted close to a white patch. "The delvers are watching. Can you get me a scanner analysis of those white patches?"

"Working," M-Bot said.

Destructor fire chased me again. I spotted a series of asteroids floating nearby, then slammed my overburn and shot toward them.

The champion followed. I speared the second asteroid I passed with my light-lance—but didn't merely use it to turn. I spun all the way around it, employing the small asteroid as a counterweight. That hurled the chunk of rock backward, making it collide with the next asteroid in line—which the champion had just speared to use in a turn. The collision threw off his maneuver, making him break out of the turn and shoot away erratically.

After a quick release, I stabbed a third rock and used it to pivot around behind the champion. As he reoriented, he found me on his tail, firing. I scored a hit, his shield crackling. To Darkshadow's credit, he didn't panic, but he *did* go into evasives. And . . . scud. I *knew* that set of maneuvers. I searched my memory, full of people I was—alarmingly—beginning to forget.

My training was still relatively clear. And the champion was performing an exact set of maneuvers taught by the DDF. Before I could follow that thought, my mind fuzzed again.

We've found you, noise. You should not be here. You SHOULD NOT BE HERE. Burning eyes in my canopy, multiplying, more and more sets that—

"Spensa!" M-Bot shouted.

I veered out of the way, narrowly avoiding a collision with an asteroid. That was . . . that was *really* inconvenient.

"More delvers?" he asked.

"Yeah. They're not happy." Scud, the champion was on my tail again.

"Spin?" Peg said over the comm. "Remember to watch those white spots. If you get too close, you'll risk some of the distortions that happen in No Man's Land."

"Trying," I said. "Little harder than it looks."

I performed another series of light-lance moves, mostly to keep asteroids between me and the champion. Fortunately, he strayed too close to a white spot himself, and he reacted as I had—stalling, distracted. I could use that; get an advantage maybe?

The champion pulled out of his diversion and stayed on me for the next bit. So, when I spotted two of the white spots floating near one another, I decided to do something brash. I took a sudden veer right between them.

"This one's on purpose," I said to M-Bot. "Keep us from crashing if something goes wrong with me."

"Okaaaaay," he said. "I have your analysis though. There's matter in the center of those. But it has a strange spectroscopy to it—unlike anything in my scientific databases. I think they might be a kind of rock, like acclivity stone but charged a different way? So . . . be careful."

I darted between the white patches.

Leave this place, noise!

I will leave, I said, *if you promise never to enter where I am from. You will stay in the nowhere, and I will stay in the somewhere.*

No. Because the noise will not stop! Can you stop the noise, noise?

I can't promise that, I said. *But we aren't a threat to you. You can live, and we can live, and ignore one another.*

No. You can stop. Or you can be made to stop. You pain us. You give us . . . the pain . . . of another self . . .

We came shooting out from between the two white spots, and the ship flew by itself, veering to the side, out of range and away from some asteroids.

"It's working!" M-Bot said. "I'm actually helping!"

I grinned, taking back the controls. M-Bot wasn't a great pilot, but he could react when close to the white spots, which had hopefully given us an edge. Indeed, I checked the proximity sensor and saw that Darkshadow had decided to follow me—but had been forced to slow first, to not risk slamming into something after losing control.

That meant I was able to execute a tight loop and come in shooting before the champion was able to get back up to speed and escape. Two more hits took his shield down. He dodged away, but I fell on his tail.

One more shot and I'd win this. I got in close as Darkshadow dodged into some rubble, then lined up for the shot—but in that instant Darkshadow blasted his IMP. The wave of close-range energy knocked out my own shield. He darted away on a massive overburn before I could land the shot.

"Not bad," M-Bot said. "That champion is good."

Yeah. Strangely so. When Darkshadow got away from me, he used what seemed like a DDF scatter escape—very similar to the series of maneuvers I'd taught the Broadsiders. I couldn't be absolutely certain, but something about the way he flew was familiar. Who was this? Did he really have the same training that I'd been given? Was it . . .

I felt a sudden cold feeling, mixed with longing. Could it be him? I'd felt him in here, when questing outward. Or was that just wishful thinking?

Don't be stupid, the rational part of my brain said. *Your father couldn't fit in that small cockpit. In fact, of all the races you know, it could only fit a figment or . . . or a . . .*

Oh, *scud!* "M-Bot, can you get a comm line to that champion?"

"Of course," he said. He flashed the light on the instrument panel that let me know the line was open.

"Hey, Darkshadow," I said to the other ship, which was hugging the perimeter and flying upward. "Any last words before I defeat you?"

"I am a swift minnow upon the tides of time," the response came. "They may crush ships against the shore, but I swim them easily."

Well, Saints and stars. It *was* him.

"Spensa!" M-Bot said, cutting the line to the other ship. "That voice. It's—"

"Hesho," I said.

"He's dead!"

"He vanished during the fight with Brade," I said, "when the kitsen ship was blasted open and exposed to vacuum. They assumed he got sucked out. But that was in the middle of a *lot* of weird things happening with cytonics."

Not the least of which had involved the summoning of a delver into the somewhere.

"I feel . . ." M-Bot said. "I feel *happy*! I never spoke to him directly, but I feel like he was my friend, Spensa."

He was mine too. "Open that comm line again," I said. "Hey, Hesho? It's *me*. It's . . . um, Alanik . . . Well, you know, the person who was pretending to be her . . ."

Right. That was all rather complicated.

"I know not that name," the voice said. "I am the Darkshadow. He with no past. The nameless warrior cursed to wander eternity without home or ally, always seeking memories he can no longer retain. I am fleeting, but a whisper upon time itself."

He said it all with utter solemnity. Man, I loved that little fox-gerbil.

"You don't remember anything?" I asked him.

"I have only the instincts of a warrior to guide me," he replied. "You will not distract me from my current purpose, adversary. Though you have fought admirably, I will defeat you, then compose poetry for your funeral."

"This . . . um . . . isn't to the death, Hesho."

"I will defeat you," he said in the same exact tone, "and compose poetry for your retirement party."

He must have been isolated during his first days in the belt, and lost everything. Now that I knew who it was, I was even more impressed by his flying. Hesho had commanded a ship, and though my memory was admittedly fuzzy, I *thought* he'd mostly acted as a captain.

But he'd also been part of my extensive training sessions. I'd assumed some random crewmember had been manning—er, fox-gerbiling—the controls of their ship. It seemed, however, that the pilot had been Hesho himself.

How could I use that knowledge? He might be good at dodging

and following flight patterns, but he would have let members of his bridge crew work other system controls. He'd messed up earlier on a light-lance pivot. He wouldn't be as good at multitasking as I was.

I moved in close to some other asteroids as he tried to come back around to attack me. I kept him busy, weaving and dodging, and got farther and farther ahead of him. Finally, he broke off to pull back.

At that moment, I shut down my systems to go for a shield re-ignition. He, expectedly, did the same. You couldn't run boosters and power up a shield at the same time.

The thing was, I was feinting.

As soon as he powered down, I spun my ship and slammed on my overburn, ripping across the battlefield toward him. He was too slow to respond, and he barely powered up before I reached him. Instead of shooting him, however, I hit him with my light-lance, then leaned hard on the controls, boosting with everything I had. This flipped my ship around—yanking him like a ball on a chain and sending him spinning out through the perimeter of the arena.

There, he was shot by at least ten watching pirate ships from various factions—completely locking up his ship.

"Dramatic," M-Bot said.

"Hesho deserves the best," I said to him. "Even if he doesn't remember. Hang on. Before we go celebrate, I need to buzz the delvers again."

"Is that smart?"

"Nope," I said, slowing and crossing the arena as if to rejoin the Broadsiders—but veering close to a white spot.

We can *work this out,* I sent to the delvers. *You don't* have *to fight us. Don't listen to Winzik, at the very least. He is evil.*

Evil is a thing of noises, they sent back, confused by the impressions I'd sent them. *You are all evil.*

Please, I sent. *I am trying to understand you.*

Understand this. Leave. All of you must leave. And never return.

The impression was filled with malevolence, disgust, and . . .

fear? Yes, fear. They hadn't wanted me to feel that part, but I could now pick out more and more that they wanted to hide.

The impression faded, and I left the region feeling disappointed. No accommodation. One of us would have to be destroyed.

I rejoined the Broadsiders, who were gathering together with the other hundred-odd ships of the various pirate factions. Peg was already on the comm, broadcasting widely to all of the collected pirates. "Ha!" she said. "So much for your secret weapon, Vlep!"

He didn't respond. The members of the Cannonade Faction were already gathering to withdraw. Whatever Peg's next move, she needed to make it now.

"Look how strong we've grown," she said, inching her shuttle out of the Broadsider line to face all the others. "Look at how *skilled* we've become! How many months has it been since any of us have lost a ship to the Superiority?"

"Vlep lost one a few weeks back," Gremm said, his voice a grumble. "But *my* fighters are good enough to avoid it."

Peg inched her shuttle forward a little farther. "The Superiority forces at Surehold are weak! While we have grown stronger and stronger. Now, you see the champion I've brought? She's been training my fighters. She spent her *life* fighting the Superiority!"

"Wait," a new voice said. "Is this true?" It was another rough voice, speaking Peg's language. I guessed that was her other son, Semm.

"It's true," I said. "My people have been at war with the Superiority for decades, and I know their tactics. I've destroyed dozens of their ships—eighty-seven actually, at last count. If you want to take Surehold, *I* can make it happen."

"Take Surehold?" another voice asked, a high-pitched one, but not Vlep's. "Are we really talking about this again?" M-Bot wrote on my screen that this was the leader of the fifth faction, a female heklo called Gward.

"I agree with Gward," Peg's first son said. "This is an old irrelevant argument. We decided against this course two years ago!"

"And how much has changed in those years?" Peg demanded. "Look, you all know that things are strange in the belt these days. You've heard of the creatures with the glowing eyes. You've seen isolated people losing their memories faster and faster.

"Worse, we're vulnerable. All it will take is for the Superiority to decide we're too much of a liability, and to double the military presence in here. Or triple it. They could wipe us out. But *not* if we control Surehold. *Not* if we're bold enough to strike."

I waited, holding my breath. It was such a good argument. Couldn't they see? This *was* the time to strike.

"I hate it," Semm finally said, "but she's correct. This . . . is worth discussing."

"Are you sure we want to take that risk?" Gremm said.

"Yeah," said the sixth faction leader—though I only knew this because of M-Bot's notes on my screen. "I . . . I don't want to aggravate them. If we lose, it could be catastrophic!"

"Doing nothing is worse, Ido," Peg said. "It is time. Surehold has an icon, and reality ashes. We can use those to keep our memories. We can control this entire region, and we can be safe."

"I . . . can't believe I'm saying this," Gremm said. "But I think she might be right. It *is* time."

"If you strike at Surehold, Mother," Semm said, "the Red Sails will join you."

"So will the Jolly Rogers," Gremm said.

"I guess . . ." Gward said. "Well, I guess we will too. Sure could use some reality ashes over here. We'll split the spoils equally, right?"

"Equally," Peg said. "I promise it."

"Well, we're not interested in this insanity," Vlep of the Cannonade Faction said. Nearby, one of his repair tugs had finished getting Hesho's vessel online, and it began moving under its own power again.

"Hey," Peg said. "We won that ship! Leave it!"

"Gremm can keep his ship," Vlep said. "We won that earlier—but if we keep ours, he can keep his. Deal? None of you can fly this thing anyway."

"Deal, I suppose," Gremm said, with a sigh. "Mother?"

"Fine, Vlep," Peg said. "But why not join us? We—"

But before she should finish her speech, the entire Cannonade Faction overburned away. Scud. I had M-Bot open a line to Hesho, but he didn't accept it.

"Should we go after them?" Semm asked.

"Rotting scum," Gremm said.

"Let them go," Peg said. "We don't need them. What about you, Ido? You with us?"

"Let me ask the others," the final faction leader said. He left the group comm and returned in a few minutes. "We'll do it. But, um, you're *sure* we can win? Like *really* sure?"

"You saw my champion fight," Peg said. "Trust me. We've got this for *certain*."

They made plans then, setting up a time for the assault. I sat back, listening to the details with half an ear. The extent of Peg's plan was becoming clear to me. And honestly, I was impressed.

I didn't get a chance to confirm my suspicions until a half hour later, when we were flying with the Broadsiders back toward our base. Peg opened a direct line to me.

"So," she said. "You had some questions?"

"I think I've figured it out," I said. "You and your sons never actually had a falling-out, did you? You three realized that the pirates were too timid, too untested, to go up against the Superiority. You faked a schism.

"*That* let you control how your coalition fractured. You continued to pretend to be antagonistic to one another, so that when the time was right, Gremm and Semm could agree with you—and it would seem like they were authentically persuaded. Who else could continue to doubt the attack was a good idea if those two—who hated you—were willing to go along with it?"

"Smart," Peg said. "Words. I hope it's not so obvious to everyone else."

"What happened with the champion?" I asked. "Why swap out to someone else at the last minute?"

"That wasn't supposed to happen," Peg explained. "Gremm called me in a panic earlier today. He'd agreed to a quick duel to warm up—he assumed Vlep could never recruit someone good enough to beat him."

"Ah . . ." I said. "Then he lost."

"Fool boy. Almost ruined two years of work. We *needed* a victory like this to galvanize everyone. They're far more skilled than they think. Two years of sparring will do that."

"You set all of this up on purpose!" I said. "The factions, the raids, the honorable-ish way of fighting—it was all to *train* the pirates without them *realizing* they were being trained! You wanted a low-stakes way to prepare them for the assault on Surehold."

"I set them to recruiting too," she explained. "Among the people tossed in here. Grew our numbers pretty well. That, and I led some tactical raids against the Superiority to test their defenses and steal ships. Every time my faction or one of the boys' factions got too many ships, we lost a few to the others to keep them strong and training."

Genius. Scud, I wished we had Peg in the DDF.

"Still hoped I'd be able to get Vlep's group," Peg continued. "He's been a weed in my garden for far too long. We should be able to do our assault with five factions. I hope. Either way, you did your part."

"My part won't be done until we stomp the Superiority," I said. "And I get to visit the portal in Surehold. You set the assault for three days away. Why wait so long? We should move now."

"No need to grow *umalitas,* kid!" Peg said. "The other factions need time to prepare—and *we* just won a major victory! Tonight we *party.*"

30

"And then," I said, creeping through the circle of chairs, "the evil member of Lion Clan grinned a terrible grin. 'No, Simba,' he said. 'It was not mere chance that your father fell to his fate, but it was *I* who cast him to it! I killed him so that I might have his throne, just as I will now kill *you*!' "

The crowd of Broadsiders gasped. To enhance the experience, I did Gran-Gran's pantomimes—clawing at the air like a lion. I prowled back and forth before the audience. Maksim had turned on his starfighter's floodlights, but narrowed and lowered the beams so they illuminated only me. We'd closed the blinds to create a dark atmosphere.

"Well," I said, "Simba was so horrified by this revelation that he let his uncle advance, forcing him back, back, back to the very edge of the tower of the fortress! He had forgotten his training from the knights Timbaa and Pumon! In a moment he remembered their long sparring sessions, where he had been forced off the log and made to eat bugs as punishment.

" 'Remember,' Pumon's wise voice said in his mind, 'never put your rear toward an enemy. And never let them control your footing in a duel.' Wise Pumon, the stout knight, now bravely fought the endless Hyena Clan hordes upon the wall below!

"Simba stood his ground, perched atop the tip of the tower known as the Rock of Pride Fortress. 'You fool, Uncle,' Simba growled. 'For though you presumed to cast me to my death like you did my father, in reality you have ceded to me the high ground, granting me the upper hand in our duel.'

"Scar shouted and lashed out, but Simba's training as an outcast among the Knights of the Lost Savannah served him well. His ghostly father appeared behind him, glowing like a halo of light. Mighty was the clash! Perched as they were, the entirety of the kingdom could see them atop the fortification! But Scar was an assassin, no trained knight, and his subtle ways could not uphold him in the full light of day and truth!

"Channeling the No Fear of Reprisal technique taught to him by the lanky Timbaa, the bold prince grabbed his uncle by the neck and threw him to the side. The elder of Lion Clan, unable to maintain his footing, slipped and fell over the edge of the Rock, barely holding on by the tips of his fingers."

I paused for effect, like Gran-Gran always had. Giving them time to imagine the bold warrior prince atop the tower, at last victorious after his long exile. My audience leaned forward, eager for the next words.

"Simba stood tall," I said. "The fighting of the armies below ceased as eyes turned toward the two monarchs. 'Now,' Simba proclaimed, 'you will announce your betrayal of my father to all, that they may know your treachery.'

"'I admit it, nephew!' Scar shouted. 'I betrayed your father—the *Hyenas* forced me to do so! I was but a pawn! Please let me live!'

"Now, down below, the frenzied queen of the Hyena Clan warriors paused in her duel with Nala, mistress-at-arms. Among barbarian culture, you must *never* beg for your life. Upon seeing the cowardly act from Scar, Hyena Clan turned their weapons away as one from the Lions—refusing the fight.

"Simba looked down upon his uncle, the author of so much pain and suffering. 'I cannot forgive you, Uncle,' he declared, 'for the gods themselves demand justice. And so, as rightful king, I now declare your sentence to be death.'

"And then, with a mighty roar, Simba cast his uncle to his doom. Now his father's wandering soul could finally rest. Revenge had been exacted, and balance had returned to the land. The circle was at long last complete."

There was some romance stuff after that, which I didn't mind so much now as I had when younger, but this had always felt like a better ending to me. It was a story about barbarians and knights, after all.

It was strange to me how well I remembered the story—all of the stories, actually. Other things about my past were fading, but the stories remained perfectly cemented in my mind. Like an anchor in my past, tied to my soul.

The conclusion brought cheers from the other pilots, and Nuluba—ever quietly going about making life easier for everyone else—opened the blinds to better light the hangar. We'd all gathered to feast our victory, and I had offered a story. I hadn't realized how well it would be received.

They're eager for reminders of the world outside, I thought, watching the pirates chat. *Even if they come from a different culture.*

Others wandered toward the tables, where we'd set out various foods that had been found on salvage runs or raids. We didn't need food anymore, but Maksim said there was something about the *act* of tasting that helped restore memories.

I spotted the other human chatting with RayZed, a young female tanuzedran from one of the other flights, whose species looked kind of like red pandas. She was nibbling at the food on a little plate. I felt like I should recognize the varieties, but . . . that part of my memory had well and truly faded. There was a red bit of food, and . . . and some little yellow bits of something?

Chet wandered over to me, his arm still in its sling. "Spensa," he said, "that story was fantastic! I feel as if I once knew it. At least, parts are familiar to me."

"Gran-Gran loved it because it spoke of a warrior in exile," I said. "She taught me that although my people had been exiled, we could remain strong."

"Your performance at the duel today was inspiring," he said. "You are truly as skilled as your earlier boasts implied. And these, they are a good family to you." He nodded toward the gathered pirates, but I sensed a certain melancholy to his tone.

"What's wrong?" I asked.

"Merely an old man's foolishness," he said to me. "I fear I am not of much use to pilots. What need have these for an explorer who cannot fly?"

"*I* have need of you," I said. "You led me to those ruins—and you knew that the next stop was in Surehold. And besides, there's your hunt . . ."

Chet had been quietly going among the pirates, asking carefully about icons and reality ashes. I'd finally asked Peg about my icon, and she had been surprised—claiming that none of her people had seen it. I didn't know that she would lie to me, but Chet and I had decided it would be good for him to investigate a little on his own.

"You've been *great* at this part," I whispered to him. "Far better than I'd be. People genuinely like you, Chet. They talk to you."

"If that were true," he said, "and if I were as good at this quest as you indicate, I'd have located the . . . missing item by now." He shook his head, then glanced at me and raised his good hand. "No need to bolster my ego further. It is taking on a little water, but not sinking. I merely . . . I fear we stay here too long. I fear being in one place."

"We'll move soon enough," I said.

"And the delvers?" he asked. "Did you . . . feel them earlier today, in the duel?"

"Yeah," I admitted.

"If they have located us, and decide to move against us . . ."

"We'll be gone in a few days," I repeated. "Don't worry. Relax, let your arm heal. We'll be at Surehold before you know it."

"Yes," he said, then nodded. "Yes, of course. Thank you, Spensa. I believe I needed to hear that." He smiled toward Maksim as the bearded young man wandered over carrying a plate of food.

"That was a great story, Spin," Maksim said. "I like the parts about honor. When I was young, I believed that all humankind was these rampaging monsters. I always wondered when that would manifest in me. When *I'd* start killing." He looked down. "I read some of the records when I was older. We . . . did attack a lot of people. So it's good to hear we had stories of honor as well. Even if they're fanciful. I mean, lions couldn't actually talk, could they?"

"I've always interpreted it," I said, "as different clans of samurai who took the names of fearsome beasts in order to intimidate their enemies."

"Lions and hyenas?" Maksim said. "I don't think they had those in Japan, Spin."

I'll admit, my Old Earth geography was spotty. Hadn't Gran-Gran said the story was from Denmark? Anyway, Chet was inspecting the bits of food as Maksim offered us the plate. I hesitated; the longer I spent in here, the stranger an activity eating seemed. Had I really done that every day of my life? Stuffing things in my mouth?

I picked up one of the yellow bits, holding it pinched between my fingers. "What is it?"

"Can said 'corn,' " Maksim explained. "In English."

"I do not know the word," Chet said, selecting a piece. "It is an alien color for a plant. I believe those on Earth were normally green, were they not?"

"This one isn't," Maksim said. "I've been saving it, and a can of this red stuff. The label said 'beets.' Either of you remember anything about them?"

"Nope," I said, turning the little corn chunk in my fingers. " 'Beats' is a cool name though. Isn't it strange that we used to *consume* piles of this stuff every *day*?"

"Yeah," Maksim said. "The names and . . . and the . . . mouth smell? The way your mouth distinguishes foods? That stuff? All gone. Can't remember for the life of me. I swear I used to like some of this stuff and hate some of it."

"I am fortunate to have lost that part of my memory entirely," Chet said. "I don't recall *ever* eating. And I'm happy for it. Mashing such things up inside your mouth? It would stick to your teeth and tongue! Then you *swallow*? Force it down your throat in wet clumps held together by saliva? No, I shall pass, my friends." He set the corn on the plate.

I understood the sentiment; thinking about it made my skin crawl. And yet, I did recall some . . . latent happiness associated with eating. I put the little bit of corn in my mouth, then winced. It was somehow both slimy and firm at the same time. I mashed it between my teeth a few times, and it popped, releasing the most awful texture. Like it had been filled with mud. I barely prevented myself from gagging.

"Surreal, isn't it?" Maksim ate one of the bits, his eye twitching as he forced himself to swallow it. Swallowing food . . . how had I never noticed how bizarre that was? M-Bot was right. Why did we put food where *air* went?

I spat my corn bits into a napkin Maksim handed me. "That's disgusting," I said, then wiped off my tongue. "That *definitely* didn't inspire me to remember anything."

Still, I forced myself to try the other stuff. It at least appeared to be bleeding, which might have been where the cool name came from. It was even *more* slimy, but this time I was prepared. I was a warrior descended from warriors. I could eat a beat. It was nauseating. It . . .

Wait.

What was that? I . . . had tried this once, in the mess hall at the DDF, where they had odd heritage foods from the gardens. I remembered Nedd's face as he laughed—I'd made the very same joke about the name. I remembered Jorgen smiling, FM explaining how much she liked the food, Kimmalyn watching and nodding, Arturo lecturing us on how it was grown . . .

A perfect picture in time, all of their faces suddenly clear to me. Scud, I missed them. I needed to get home, to be with them again.

More, I needed to protect them. From the delvers.

I'm trying, I thought. *And I'm coming. I promise.*

"That was disgusting and wonderful together at once," I said to Maksim and Chet. "It's so strange that it *is* so strange. I only left the somewhere . . ." How long ago had it been? I forcibly brought out the numbers M-Bot gave me each morning. ". . . just under a month ago."

"This place changes you fast," Maksim said. "And then makes you feel like you're in limbo . . ." After trying the beat, he walked back to the table to get some other samples.

Chet wandered over to Shiver, who was talking about how odd she found our means of ingesting. So inefficient, in her words. Better to just grow over patches of minerals and use them as you need them. I rested back against the wall and found myself smiling again.

I belonged here. Granted, I'd belonged other places too. I could faintly remember similar evenings with my friends at the DDF headquarters. But I also remembered pain. Fear. Loss. Hurl's death. Worry for Jorgen.

Here, I didn't have those same fears. And scud, I had to admit these last few weeks had been invigorating—exciting. First the exploration, then infiltrating pirates? Now earning their trust, defeating their champion?

This had been thrilling. Like a story, like the things I'd always imagined myself doing. As before, while exploring with Chet, I felt a faint sense of guilt to be enjoying myself while my friends back home were in danger. But then again, the *real* danger was the delvers, and I was working on that as best I could. And didn't I deserve to rest between fights?

Every warrior needed a break, didn't they? A Valhalla? An

Elysium? The stories understood. In the greatest of warrior societies, there was a reward for those who spent their days killing.

The group began calling for me to tell another story, so I walked back toward the light. I'd offer them three different options, like Gran-Gran had done for me when I was a child.

I *did* love my friends, and I *was* doing everything I could to help them. So I determined not to feel guilty for finding a place where I could live the life I'd always wanted. I had been exiled. But in that, like Satan from the stories, I had found a place I could make into heaven itself.

Right then, the base's scanner's alarm started going crazy.

31

"Imminent collision of this fragment with . . ." Nuluba trailed off, glancing up from the scanner data toward all of us, gathered around the machine.

"With what?" Peg demanded.

"With another fragment," Nuluba said. "I've never seen anything like it. The fragment is coming in so quickly . . . Scanner says impact is in only half an hour."

I shared a look with Chet, whose expression was grim. Last time, the incoming fragment had completely annihilated the one we were on.

"Get people to ships and ready to evacuate," Peg announced.

"Captain!" Nuluba said. "We have five ships down for maintenance to prepare for the assault! We can get them up and flying, but in a half hour? Plus, if we abandon the base, we'll lose equipment, spare parts, diagnostics . . ."

Scud. As we'd been getting ready for the party earlier, the ground crews had started their jobs—assuming they'd have three days to fine-tune the starfighters for our upcoming assault.

"Evacuate anyway," Peg said, "just in case."

"Also, Nuluba," I said, "send the scanner data to my ship."

"What? Why—"

"Do it!" I said, running for M-Bot, Chet on my heels. I hauled myself up on the wing, then helped Chet with a hand up. M-Bot popped open the cockpit, and we leaped in as he lit up the ship's dash.

"I'm getting data direct from the scanner," he said. "Oh my. That's bad."

"Math it!" I said. "Can we do anything?"

"Calculating . . . That one coming in is a lot smaller . . . The Broadsiders have access to six light-lances for maneuvering ships . . ." A bunch of figures popped up on my screen. "Done," he said. "There's time. Barely."

"We lift the *entire fragment* that's coming toward us?" Chet said, reading the instructions. "Bold!"

"And possible," M-Bot said. "Only if you move quickly, Spensa. I mean, I know you really enjoyed the last collision, but . . ."

I stood up and shouted toward Peg as she rushed by. "I've got another option, Peg!"

Peg pulled to a stop, looking toward me.

"Me and five other ships pulling with light-lances," I said, "can move that incoming fragment upward just enough to avoid us. But we have to be quick about it!"

She didn't miss a beat. She shouted for everyone else to keep evacuating, but organized a small crew to execute M-Bot's plan.

I settled in the cockpit and glanced back at Chet. "You'd never encountered this before that first time?"

"Nope," he said, putting on a helmet.

"And now it's happened to us twice?"

"Yup."

"You know what I told you earlier, about not being worried that the delvers might know where we are?"

"Indeed."

"Pretend I said something intelligent instead."

"I shall endeavor to do my best."

In moments, Peg had a crew for me to lead—including herself, with her powerful shuttle. Fortunately, these ships already had light-lances attached for towing ships that had been locked down by destructor fire.

"Go to these coordinates on the incoming fragment," I said, and relayed M-Bot's instructions and figures to their displays. "Attach your light-lances to the acclivity stone there, then be ready to lift."

Peg prodded everyone along again. They began taking off, but not with nearly the urgency I'd have wanted.

"You'd think they'd be more frightened," M-Bot said.

"It's too easy to get comfortable in here," Chet replied. "Particularly if you stay in one place for long."

I followed the instructions from M-Bot, blasting off toward the incoming fragment. I was a faster ship, so I took up position at the rear of the fragment where he directed me. This one, like the one before, was barren—just a solid block of stone. Small, dense, and most importantly fast—like a bullet.

I matched speeds with the fragment and launched my light-lance out to connect to the stone. The other ships started following suit one by one as they arrived.

"Under fifteen minutes until contact," Chet noted, watching the clock M-Bot had put up on the display for us, and reading the projections. "We're cutting this very close."

"Everyone is in place," I said as the final ship connected its light-lance.

"You need to all pull directly up," M-Bot explained. "Together, with an equal force. Here, I'm sending instructions to the others as if from you."

I nodded and turned the ship upward, pointing the boosters down. My acclivity ring rotated automatically, so it was pointed downward as well.

"Careful," M-Bot told me as I moved into position. "Give yourself as much slack as possible at first, and don't hit the booster too hard. You'll risk pushing down on the fragment with your thrust, negating some of the value of your pull."

I gripped the thrust, refusing to give in to my instincts, which urged me to throw on the overburn. Instead, I slowly ramped up the booster to the thresholds M-Bot indicated. It felt like I wasn't making any progress at all, as if nothing were changing.

All through it, M-Bot's voice continued calmly. "Ease off a little. That's it . . ."

He sent similar instructions to the other pilots' displays. I glanced at the monitor, watching as we got closer, and closer, and closer to the Broadsider base. Until . . . we *barely* crested over the top, with enough clearance to avoid hitting the base structures. We knocked off the tops of a few trees though.

I let out a long breath while M-Bot sent another order to everyone that we could simultaneously power down and then cut our light-lances. I complied, then slowed in the air—letting that "bullet" fragment zip away. Without our influence, it lowered back down.

Then, a few minutes later, it collided with the next fragment it encountered. Both fragments were made up of more rock than the one that had collapsed before—and so they crushed together, stone crumpling and bulging like the fronts of some of the starfighters I'd seen impact. The sound was incredible.

As I hovered in place, Peg slowly drifted up beside me in her shuttle. "Never seen anything like that," she said privately over the comm. "I'm growing *gludens*. Though now that we're safe, I'm kind of glad I get to watch it. This feels like a once-in-a-lifetime opportunity."

I was sure that for most people, it would be just that.

"Peg," I said, "we need to make our assault on Surehold sooner than planned."

"Why?" she asked.

"Sitting here like this is tempting fate. The nowhere is changing in dangerous ways. Plus, I'm . . . getting too complacent. I want to be moving on."

"All right, all right. Don't toss *tidos* at me. Maybe we can move the timeline up."

The fragments that had collided shattered into multiple pieces of acclivity stone. The largest portions stayed pushed together, fused in the center, while smaller bits went bouncing free, spraying out like enormous chunks of shrapnel.

"You know," Peg said absently, "it's almost like the nowhere just up and decided to try to kill us." She laughed, though there was an edge to the sound.

"Let's assault Surehold tomorrow," I said. "Waiting will only give the Superiority a chance to notice that we're gathering, preparing something. We're ready. Let's do it."

Peg was silent for a time, and I couldn't judge her body language, not in separate ships as we were. I tried to inch mine forward to glance in through the window of her tug.

"Peg?" I asked.

"All right. We'll need to rush to get all the ships back together and do last-minute preparations. If we can manage that . . . then, yeah. Tomorrow. I'll let the other faction leaders know."

32

I got up the next morning eager, excited. I'd done a quick check-in with Jorgen to let him know what I'd overheard in regard to the delvers and Winzik. But I hadn't stayed with him long; I'd known many of our team would be working all night on the ships. The pilots had been ordered to get a good night's sleep, and so I had forced myself to do just that.

Indeed, the hangar was already a buzz of activity when I entered. Ground crew members were still dashing this way and that. By the large clock Peg had set up, we had two hours until departure—and there still appeared to be a lot to get done. Back home, I'd have left all these sorts of preparations to the professionals. That wasn't how the Broadsiders worked though.

Instead I hurried to M-Bot's ship, where Nuluba was working. She'd serviced the boosters and was just now putting the casing back on one of them. I sprang to help her lift the casing into place, and it occurred to me that this was a chance to do something I'd been meaning to for a while.

"Nuluba," I said. "I . . . want to apologize to you."

"Apologize, Spin?" she said, gesturing with one arm in a wide loop—something I thought was to express comfort. "You have made up for your theft of the ship."

"It's not about that," I said. "It's about how I might have treated you, particularly when I was first here. I . . . worry I was kind of abrasive to you."

"Ah," Nuluba said, using a drill to lock the bolts as I held the casing in place. "Yes, I did notice that. I assumed it was your natural human aggression."

"It was more than that," I said. "You heard about my past?"

"A freedom fighter," she said. "From a human enclave."

"Yes," I said. "Most of our jailors were varvax, though we called them the Krell. And . . . well, I've never *really* gotten over that. Despite the fact that you've always been nice to me, I think I might have taken it out on you."

"My, my," she said, and I winced, thinking—even now—of Winzik. "That is very mature of you, Spin. Very mature and very wise. I cannot say I was so quick to reject my biases when I first met Maksim."

"Really? You did it too?"

"Oh yes," she said as we stepped away from the now-completed booster. "It is unfortunate, and I am embarrassed. I commend you for giving me a chance, Spin. If *I* had been imprisoned by humans for many years, I do not know that I would be so willing to accept one of them into my company."

I smiled, and she waved her hands in response. How could I have ever hated this thoughtful creature? She was so calm, so relaxed. In a way, Nuluba represented something I'd never actually known: a person at peace with themself and their place in the universe. Or, well, the non-universe.

"You are ready to go," she said, patting the booster. "Fully tuned. It was a pleasure."

I looked at the ship, with its sleek shape and powerful boosters, and my excitement stoked further. "You're always so serene with this work," I said to Nuluba. "Whether it's doing maintenance or taking inventory. Wouldn't you like to fly one of these?"

"Please, no," Nuluba said, gesturing with her fingers making a light rolling motion. A varvax laugh. "I like things simple."

"Piloting can be simple."

"No, pilots are too important," she explained. "I like being ignored. That's why I picked the job I did in the somewhere. I prefer to just sit in the corner and putter. It was . . . distressing that I caused so much of a fuss with my discoveries." She hesitated, then grew more solemn. "Not that I'd go back. I hate the lies we've told."

There was a heroism in those words, a type I'd never acknowledged. To me, being a hero had always been about fighting. But Nuluba reminded me of Cuna, the quiet diplomat who had done so much to resist Winzik.

"Before you suit up," Nuluba said, pointing, "I believe Shiver wanted to speak to you."

We still had a good amount of time until takeoff, so I dodged around Maksim as he jogged past with a spare power matrix, then entered the resonants' corner of the room. Here, I always felt as if I were stepping up to a large geode. They'd leaked lines of crystal—like veins in stone—out from their ships, then over to this section. When I'd asked Shiver why, she'd explained that the crystals grew naturally, and so they needed to send them somewhere.

Each time they flew away, they broke connections to this place—but so long as they returned soon enough, they could reconnect. If they moved to Surehold, what would happen? Would this crystal network in the corner eventually crumble to dust?

Up close, I could distinguish their crystals from each other. Shiver was slightly more violet, and Dllllizzzz slightly more pink. They had grown over one another in a way I was led to understand was common among friendly resonants. The two beings chatted softly in their musical language; they did that almost constantly when near each other.

"You wanted to talk to me?" I asked Shiver, settling down beside one of her larger crystals.

"Yes, Spin," Shiver responded. "I wished to thank you. For making this possible."

"The assault today?"

"Indeed," Shiver said. "Peg has been planning this for years. I . . . vibrate with joy, knowing the plan is finally moving forward. But I also wish to thank you on behalf of Dllllizzzz. If we are successful, we will again have access to the icon at Surehold—and the reality ashes. I maintain hope that having more of those, over the long term, will continue to help her."

"How's she been lately?" I asked, glancing toward the array of crystals.

"It is difficult to cleave that question, Spin," Shiver said. "Sometimes she seems almost ready to speak. At the very edge of layered words, sentences. And then . . . she withdraws to unlayered words. Hints at meanings. I've heard true words from her only a handful of times now, including when she spoke to you."

"I don't think I understand. Layered words, and unlayered words?"

"I apologize," Shiver said. "Let me reverberate. We can make different crystals vibrate with different tones, and language is always two or more of those together. Dllllizzzz makes single tones. More ideas than true words.

"It *is* communication, and I can investigate her feelings, comfort her, encourage her. But her responses are rarely true words, more the tones we make while learning. This is our equivalent of what you would call 'baby talk.' Yet Dllllizzzz is old. Older than I am. And she flies a ship just fine."

I nodded, studying the overlapping lattices of blue crystals, with pink or violet undertones. I'd seen Shiver help with repairs—a few days back, she'd overgrown part of Peg's shuttle looking for a short. It was incredible the level of detail Shiver could sense with her crystals—though actually doing repairs took her much more time than it took someone motile. She could technically grow as many "arms" as she needed, but moving things usually involved encasing them in crystal and then growing that crystal to reposition the object.

I found it amazing that the resonants had developed space-age industry under those limitations. But I guessed when members of your species commonly lived thousands of years, you had other advantages. And there was something hardcore about an entire civilization made up of singing crystals. Even the wildest of Gran-Gran's stories couldn't compete with the universe's biodiversity.

Admittedly though, I was still miffed about the whole sand worm thing.

"Could reality ashes actually help her?" I asked.

"I hope so," Shiver said. "But it has been—some time? Much time?—since we found her."

"The icon," I said. "At Surehold. What does it look like?"

"A small child's toy. It is kept on display, to help the workers feel comfort. It's . . . beautiful." She paused. "It appeared with Peg when she was thrown in here. But she was prevented from taking it when she rebelled. I think part of her eagerness to capture the base has to do with reclaiming it. Spin . . . I know that you and Chet have been looking for something among the Broadsiders. Something that was taken. An . . . icon?"

I didn't respond immediately. She knew?

"You were captured with an unusual amount of reality ashes," Shiver said. "And though Chet has been subtle, I am better than most at subtle interaction. You lost an icon. You think it stolen?"

"Yes," I admitted. "I buried it outside before sneaking in here the first time. Now it has vanished."

"Then I have, perhaps, news for you. I helped Peg recover her icon several times at Surehold. Icons are bits of the somewhere, and respond in odd ways to being in here. Spin, they sometimes seem to get disjointed from this place—as if out of phase with the movement of fragments."

"Which means . . ."

"They move on their own, on occasion. As I said, it feels as if they've gotten out of sync with the regular fragment motions. You find them outside safes, or in rooms where you didn't leave them. It is rare, but I've seen it happen. It's possible nobody took your icon—and I think that if one were here, Peg would have sniffed it out and told everyone. She'd insist we share the ashes. It is her way."

That was curious news. I mulled on it a moment, and found I was glad. Perhaps I didn't have to worry about a thief here—other than myself, naturally. But what if the icon had fallen into the void? Or vanished and appeared on another fragment entirely?

In that case, I'd never find it. I'd have to rely on our remaining ashes to get us out of here. That was possible—they should last long enough—but still, I felt a sense of loss. It hadn't really been my father's pin—but it had been important to me nonetheless.

As I pondered that, Shiver's mention of Peg brought another question to mind. "Does Peg really have . . . a tree?"

"Yes. So do her sons, whose trees were grown from fruit on hers. The tenasi symbiosis is a beautiful thing, and I often resonate with it. You should be able to see the tree soon, as it still grows at Surehold. Those there would *never* destroy a tenasi tree, no matter how bad the blood between us and them. Once we arrive, you can see the icon for yourself as well."

"I'm looking forward to it," I said. "But . . . icons, Shiver. What *are* they?"

"I have no idea," Shiver said. "This place is strange in a lot of ways, isn't it? But I'll tell you this, looking at that icon I always felt as if it had a soul. Like it was a fragment of our world in the same way the delvers are a fragment of this one."

What an odd way to describe it. I stood up, intending to extricate myself from the conversation with Shiver, who would continue to chat endlessly if you let her. I always felt so awkward excusing myself—but . . . well, she seemed to think all motile species were a little rude anyway. When you literally couldn't walk away from your neighbors, you learned to be polite.

"Before you go," Shiver said, "I . . . admit I have a request for you, Spin. Please do not think me forward, but I suspect you intend to leave this place. Not this region, but the nowhere entirely."

"I do," I said. "People need me in the somewhere."

"I've never known anyone to leave without Superiority permission," Shiver said. "And even those cases are rare. But my request is in regard to Dllllizzzz. Peg worries that once someone is *that* far gone, only getting out can help them. So if you do escape . . . will you see if you can find a way to open a path for Dllllizzzz and me? For her sake?"

"That helps?" I asked. "I mean . . . our memories . . . return if we leave?"

"I believe so," Shiver said. "At least, the few people at the base who left and came back in seemed to have recovered some, if not all, of what they lost during their time here."

"I'll try," I promised. "Chet is going with me, and we'll be able to see firsthand if someone without any memories gets them back once outside."

"Thank you. That is all I can ask. Getting out through Surehold would require negotiations with the Superiority, and I do not trust them. I do not believe it would be safe to leave that way, no matter what they promise. I don't think the other pirates care; they prefer it in here, away from the concerns and problems of the somewhere. I am not the same. And Dllllizzzz . . . She needs help. She wants out. I can feel from her vibrations it is so."

"I'll do what I can," I said, then glanced to the side as Peg announced that there was less than an hour left. Time to suit up.

"Fight well, Spin," Shiver said. "And I shall do the same. Thank you again for your time with us."

I went running to clean up and get on my flight suit. I spent the next twenty minutes doing preflight checks and getting a final okay from Nuluba and Maksim to go into combat. As I finished,

I spotted Chet standing down below, helmet under his arm. He'd taken off his sling last night, and his arm seemed mostly healed.

"With your permission," he said, "I should like to fly with you today, Spensa."

"It might get a little crazy," I said.

"I understand crazy better than you may assume," he replied. "And . . . well, I had RayZed take me out last night to run me through g-force training. I feel like I remember things better from long ago, ways to help my body withstand. Even if not, however, I prefer to join you. To be frank, I'm worried about the delvers. They failed in their attack yesterday. They will try something else."

I nodded. "Let's go, then."

33

It was a different sort of group that left the Broadsider base that day. For the duel we'd brought everyone, flying in a leisurely way—a convoy that had been part show of force, part proof of solidarity.

Today we took only the pilots. Peg joined my flight. Loaded with firepower, but slower than the fighters, her shuttle would be a target—but could deal damage almost like a much larger gunship. By her order, we kept off the comms. There was no joking, storytelling, or sitting and idly reading books during this flight.

I spent the initial part of the flight—before we met up with the other factions—trying to contain my excitement. Our destructors were still set to nonlethal, but each of our ships had been equipped with the ability to flip them to lethal mode in case this battle turned truly dangerous.

Peg didn't want to do that. She wanted to recruit the pilots at Surehold, not kill them. But she was too pragmatic not to have the option available.

I gave Chet the controls and let him acclimatize himself to them. If I were somehow hurt during the fight, he might have to take over, as M-Bot remained unskilled. Chet performed a few simple maneuvers, showing that he did have some muscle memory for piloting, and I sat in thought, troubled by something Shiver had said. About icons.

I considered that, then closed my eyes, questing out from the cockpit with my senses. I forced myself to be extra quiet and subtle as I searched. I paused as I felt the delvers, or their attention, nearby. Waiting. And frightened.

They didn't notice me. I could feel their minds pushing out from the lightburst in this direction, but they weren't aware of me. I *could* remain invisible to them with effort, though I suspected this would only work so long as they didn't know exactly where I was.

Feeling pleased with my improvements so far, I turned away from them and sensed outward. Looking for . . . familiarity. I remembered that when I'd first entered the nowhere, in that jungle, I had felt a mind close to mine. Before I'd found Chet, I had sensed something. Something I'd thought was my father.

Had that been my icon? It felt foolish to think it had actually been him. Yet as I searched, I . . . layered my mind with a warmth. The "star-ness" I'd learned on the Path. That was like a code, or a callsign. I'd used it to batter back Brade's cloud upon me and escape from her prison. But it could also indicate who I was, where I was, though only to those I knew. Like a communication signal on a private comm band.

I felt something jump and contact me back. A mind. I brushed against it, and my heart leapt. My pin! Yes, I could feel it, and it responded. It . . . It . . .

It was angry at me for burying it.

That shocked me. The pin's mind felt familiar, loving. It felt . . . It felt like family.

F-Father? I thought.

I was returned a warm sensation. I knew it was ridiculous, but . . . I mean . . . This place *was* strange.

Where are you? I asked.

I was given back a sense of . . . Surehold? Yes, that was where the icon was. How had it gotten there? I mean, Shiver had warned me they moved. But that far?

The mind retreated.

I'm coming to you, I sent to the pin, then came out of my cytonic trance, confused. It couldn't *truly* be my father's soul, could it? And why—how—was the pin at Surehold? The place where I was already going? That seemed extraordinarily coincidental. And that reminded me of Chet's coincidental arrival, which I hadn't thought about in a while.

Eventually, our flight met with the other pirate factions one by one. Peg welcomed each in turn, and I sensed relief in her voice. She'd been worried they wouldn't show. She had us linger after the fourth faction joined, giving one final chance for the Cannonaders to appear. They didn't.

"All right, people," Peg said over the comm to us all. "We will *absolutely* win this. We've spent years in combat preparing, while they've been hiding, hoping the Superiority would send them more strength.

"They haven't. The Superiority doesn't care about them, or about any of us. They only care about their acclivity stone—so we're going to hit them hard and take it away. Maybe they have other mining stations far across the empty boundaries, but I know they rely on this one more than any other. So we'll lock the portal up tight, and they'll have to play by *our* terms."

The gathered eighty or so ships gave cheers and raucous calls in a variety of different types of vocalization. Chet and I joined in, hooting and shouting.

"My Jolly Rogers are ready to move to lethal destructors," Gremm announced after the noise died down.

"Not unless the enemy does first," Peg said. "Remember, these ones we're fighting—they're not really our enemy. They're merely a bunch of frightened sods trapped between two forces. We're going to come in not as raiders, but as liberators. So keep your rounds nonlethal. Call me or one of the tugs if you see a locked-up ship—even an enemy—about to collide with terrain. Stay focused on the fight, and if you face a pilot who's too good, call for help."

She got a round of agreement, and I was impressed. She and her sons had done an excellent job laying the groundwork for this battle.

"Okay!" M-Bot said in our cockpit. "I feel trembly, but somehow still eager to go forward."

"Fear and eagerness?" Chet said. "That sounds like enthusiasm."

"No, I think there would be more happy-eagerness," M-Bot said. "This is nauseous-eagerness."

"Perhaps exhilaration?" Chet said.

"I could go with that," M-Bot replied. "Exhilaration. Yup, I'm exhilarated!"

"What are you two on about?" I asked.

"The AI and I have been bonding," Chet said with a proud tone to his voice. "He's been wanting help defining his specific emotions. I agreed to assist him."

"Now?" I demanded.

"What better time?" Chet asked. "He is likely to be feeling a lot of strong emotions, after all."

"We'll do it quietly," M-Bot promised.

Great. I didn't believe that for a moment. Still, we continued on, entering Superiority territory. It didn't look much different to me, though there were more fragments and they hung closer together. We flew straight toward the center, that enormous glowing white light. It felt as vast and intimidating as it ever had.

"Heads up, Broadsiders," Peg said. "They're incoming. Prepare for engagement."

Her ship had a better scanner than mine; it took another two minutes for my sensors to see the oncoming ships. M-Bot counted them as they arrived, eventually settling on ninety-three ships. Slightly more than our numbers, and I didn't see any retrofitted civilian ships among them. Hopefully Peg was right, and we had the better pilots.

Regardless, my excitement built. And the excitement was pure—no tension, no worry. A chance to fly and fight. A huge battle. I was ready.

"That's odd," Shiver said over the comm. "Captain, you see that?"

"Yeah," Peg said. "Everyone, zoom your displays out."

My proximity display expanded, revealing a larger view of the nearby fragments. Two just ahead of us were unnaturally close. They were going to bump . . . no, collide.

"Captain?" RayZed said. "Didn't you . . . say that collisions between fragments were incredibly rare?"

"I did," Peg replied.

"Now we're encountering a second one, only a day after the last. Is . . . something wrong?"

"Can't say," Peg told us. "But . . . words. I'm pulling up IDs on some of those enemies. It appears the Cannonade Faction has come to join the party after all."

I frowned until M-Bot's scans indicated a group of new ships flying in to enter the fight. It was the Cannonade Faction. But they didn't join us—instead they swooped around and fell in with the Superiority.

"Wonder how much they were paid to grow those *flivis,*" Semm grumbled. "Does Vlep *really* think the Superiority will keep whatever promises they made him?"

"Doesn't matter," Peg said on the wide comm. "Just a few more easy targets—and a few traitors to embarrass. Watch the debris from that collision—stay away from the fragments if you can. I don't see the former champion on the scans, but he might be hiding in there somewhere. Do *not* engage if you spot him. Leave him to one of our aces."

"He'll come for me, Peg," I said on a private line. "Hesho will want a rematch."

"Bring down as many enemies as you can before it happens, Spin," Peg said. "I think we're better than they are—but I wouldn't mind if you evened out our numbers."

"Got it," I said as we drew closer. Then the two groups finally broke, starfighters screaming toward one another—meeting right above those colliding fragments. My proximity sensor went ballistic as the landscapes impacted and chunks of rock began to break apart.

I grinned and launched into the middle of the chaos. It was so *liberating* to not have to worry about the safety of my companions. Cobb would have yelled at me for not bringing a wingmate, but here I could fly as I'd always secretly wanted to. Reckless. Free.

I lit up a ship in front of me, neatly blasting away its shield. That sent it into a series of panicked evasive maneuvers. Trusting my gut, I chased for a moment, then backed off and gave them space to screw up. They did just that, trying so hard to get away from me that they took a shot from Peg.

My grin widened as I dove to the side and shot down one, then two, then three enemy ships. Scud, this was *awesome*! I dove among the crazy mess, blue destructor blasts lighting the sky in all directions. M-Bot highlighted some enemies on the monitor: my reckless attacks had earned me two tails.

"So, let me see . . ." M-Bot said. "This emotion . . . is frustration at the crazed attack, mixed with the teensiest amount of fondness. And a desire to bonk her on the head with something that isn't *too* heavy, but just heavy enough."

"Vexation," Chet said.

"Wow!" M-Bot said. "That's perfect. Spensa is, like, vexation incarnate!"

"I thought you two said you'd be quiet," I said.

"You'd rather not be able to hear us talk about you?" M-Bot asked.

Actually, no. I gritted my teeth in a half grin, half grimace and accelerated, diving to dodge the fire from our tails. At the risk of being called foolhardy, I pushed us low, weaving between parts of the landscape of one crumbling fragment.

Chet's face on the corner of my screen looked a little pale. "How you doing back there, Chet?" I asked.

"Trying my best to enjoy the expert course in being vexed, Miss Nightshade!" he called. "I recognize this kind of fragment. It is from a twilight planet—those that grow in a dark solar system, feeding off a star that doesn't glow brightly in the visible spectrum but still provides radiation.

"Those places tend to have plants and animals with much bioluminescence—and even a kind of mineral-luminescence. Judging from what I've seen, these rocks will likely explode in great showers of light if hit by destructor fire. Perhaps you can use that?"

Excellent. I spotted a hole in the breaking fragment ahead—and so I pushed for that. I wove up in a loop, then straight through the hole. My tails followed, but as I expertly wove between falling pieces of rock, their destructor shots hit on all sides of me. As Chet had suggested, the explosions lit up like flares. Indeed, the falling debris acted like flak ejection, intercepting the disruptor fire.

So long as I didn't hit any big chunks, I'd actually be safer in here. Even as I was thinking that, I did hit one moderately sized chunk. Only one, and my shield deflected it.

"A sense of disbelief," M-Bot said, "mixed with an absolute expectation that something like this would happen. Because of course she'd dive through a radioactive, explosive natural minefield."

"Resignation," Chet said with a chuckle.

"Quiet, you two," I muttered as I pulled up and darted along underneath the ripping fragment, weaving between chunks of dropping earth. My two tails, blinded by the explosions, evidently lost track of me, as they broke off pursuit.

"That *was* well done, Spensa," Chet said.

"We're alive," M-Bot said. "And oddly, I feel—"

"Yeah, I know," I said. "Complain about my recklessness again."

"Actually," he said. "I'm feeling something different. A tremble of excitement . . . building to relief, and a . . . a desire to do the same thing *again*?"

"Ha!" I said. "You thought it was fun!"

"It *was*," M-Bot said. "Scud! Why did that feel fun? It was stupidly risky."

"A little risk is what makes it enjoyable, AI!" Chet said. "That is the part that is daring! The part that is exciting! Assuming one can fight down the nausea."

I looped around toward the main firefight, where I found Peg's slower ship being tailed by someone fairly skilled. I drilled them with three precise shots in a row, making them break off.

"Enjoying danger sounds like an evolutionary problem," M-Bot said. "Shouldn't you find things fun when they're safe?"

"Who knows?" I said. "I don't think evolution was trying to create me. I just kind of happened."

"Evolution doesn't 'try' to do anything," M-Bot said. "But like it or not, you are the pinnacle of its work. All evolutionary pressures throughout all the ages among your species have resulted in you."

"Bet it feels embarrassed," I said, finally shooting the ship that had been chasing Peg. It locked up and slowed, soaring idly through the battlefield. "Like that time all the parents got together to watch their kids march when I was in school, and my mother was forced to admit to the other moms that I was the one who'd glued her homemade suit of wooden 'power armor' to her uniform."

"I wish I'd known you back then," M-Bot said. "You sound like such a capricious child."

"Uh, yeah. Child."

I'd been sixteen.

"Where *is* Hesho?" I asked, looking over the battlefield. "Any signs of him yet on the scanners?"

"No," M-Bot said. "But with this much debris flying around, my sight isn't as precise as I'd like. He could be hiding in there somewhere."

"Ship coming in from the right, Spensa," Chet warned.

I dodged to the side—but as soon as that pilot realized who I was, they broke off the chase. I light-lanced around a chunk of acclivity stone that was floating upward from the crashing fragments, then fell in behind the fleeing ship. If the pilot was frightened of me, that would work to my advantage.

Once, I might not have found this battle enjoyable. I was of a higher skill level than these pilots—and I did love a challenge. As I matured though, I was beginning to realize that *all* combat was a challenge. Merely staying alive was challenging in a chaotic mess like this, where ships were darting in every direction and destructor blasts flew like embers in the forges. I felt alert, engaged.

As my prey dodged past some floating rubble, my proximity sensor beeped. A ship had been hiding in there, and it darted out as I passed, falling in behind me. One with a familiar design: small cockpit, large weapons signature.

Hesho had set a trap for me.

"Well hello, former champion," Chet said. "About time you showed up."

"Slight nausea," M-Bot said. "Something I really shouldn't be able to feel. Mixed with uncertainty."

"That one's apprehension," I said, grinning. "Stomp it dead, M-Bot. This is going to be fun."

I broke away from the chase. Hesho followed me, and the ship I'd been tailing immediately swung around and joined him. I'd beaten Hesho in our previous meeting, so while he obviously wanted a rematch, he'd brought a wingmate for support. There was no dishonor in pitting two against one in a battle like this—that was how the game was played.

The two flew as if to isolate me from the rest of the battle, herding me outward. If I tried to turn, one or the other moved to cut me off. I'd been in this situation before several times, fighting the Krell. In fact, I felt like maybe I'd taught Hesho this maneuver—a way to cull a ship from a battle and deal with it. In a big firefight, it was often preferable to have your ships fly defensively while a few "kill teams" of expert aces shrank the enemy numbers.

Well, I needed to make the fight a little less fair. Or make it unfair in my direction. I dodged right, risking a hit to my shield—and indeed I took one—to avoid being corralled. In a two-on-one fight, chaos favored me, and so I wanted to be in the thick of the shooting.

M-Bot helpfully popped up a tally of ships still fighting, proving that the pirates were holding their own, even making a little headway into the enemy lead. I—

A *building* appeared in the air directly in front of me.

Scud! I veered to the side, and my shield scraped the edge of the giant floating structure, shattering its windows in my wake as I skimmed one face of it.

"What the hell was *that*?" Chet asked.

"I don't—"

Another building appeared at my side, tall and rectangular. Then something else flashed and materialized directly ahead of me. Was that . . . a swimming pool? I managed to duck around it, but it spun in the air, dumping a wave of *water* over us.

"A sudden spike of fear!" M-Bot said. "And general paralysis! I know this one myself! Panic! What is happening?"

A pair of scrubber tools folded from the sides of my canopy and ran across the curved surface, wiping away the water. Any other time, the news that my ship had rain wipers would have been amusing to me. I'd never fought in rain before, as we didn't have it on Detritus.

However, it was completely overshadowed by, you know, the *buildings*. "Peg?" I shouted over the comm as a hovercar appeared some distance in front of me. "You seeing this?"

"Seeing it," she said on a wide channel. "Not quite believing it. We're in the middle of a warp of new objects entering the nowhere—never seen one of these in person. Careful, everyone. I don't want to have to scrape any of you off the side of a building."

Scud. I felt a . . . strange sensation. A stretching—or that's the best I could explain it.

"Delver attack," Chet guessed. "In the somewhere! That's what is bringing all this in here—a delver has gone to your dimension, and as it strikes, it's warping the city into this place. You don't . . . recognize these structures, do you?"

"Thankfully no," I said. "This isn't happening on Detritus." But yeah, I guessed he was right. The stretching sensation was the nowhere opening, being punctured as the delvers shoved things from my dimension in here.

"Deep breath, deep breath," M-Bot said. "Okay, analysis says these structures appear to be Superiority designs."

Why would they be attacking one of their own? Perhaps a planet that was in rebellion? The light next to Peg's name changed, indicating she'd moved to a private line. "Damnedest thing here, Spin. Not one, but *two* explosive fragment collisions, and now this . . . Ha! Really feels like the nowhere is trying to get us, eh?"

"Yeah," I mumbled. My proximity sensor pinged, the display showing that Hesho and his wingmate had avoided the suddenly appearing buildings and were on my tail again. "Ha ha."

"Don't think too much of it," Peg said. "It's random, kid. I don't want you getting any ideas that the Broadsiders grow *enguluns* or anything like that. We're not unlucky. We found you, after all!" She cut the line.

"She's wrong," Chet said. "This is about us. The Path we're walking. It has them angry."

I veered to the side, narrowly avoiding another sudden building. It seemed that the process of shoving things into the nowhere was creating acclivity stone—as the stone blocks on one side of the building were making it hover. I'd heard you could magnetize metal by exposing it to a strong enough field; maybe this was something similar.

"You focus on flying," Chet said. "I'm expanding my cytonic powers, and I *think* I can track the former champion and his wingmate.

Even in this mess. I'll give you warning if they try to ambush us again."

"And I'll suppress my outbursts for now," M-Bot said. "Spensa . . . this is serious. Fly well, please."

"Will do," I said, veering carefully so I wouldn't overwhelm the GravCaps. Chet had promised me he could take the g-forces—but I still wanted to be cautious. If I blacked out when buildings were appearing all around us . . .

"My scans indicate these buildings are uninhabited," M-Bot said. "And they look old and run-down."

As I flew, I tried to pick out what I could with my burgeoning cytonic senses. I felt the delvers, connected to one of their kind in the somewhere. And I overheard . . . annoyance, but not anger. They didn't hear "noise" at the moment. They were . . . performing.

"It's a test," I said. "Winzik finally got smart and decided to try the delvers out on an unpopulated location, to see if they really were under control."

"Perfect chance for them to throw a city at us," Chet said.

Fortunately, the delver efforts didn't seem precise—objects started appearing all through the battlefield, not merely in front of me. If they'd been able to control this exactly, they would have made something appear so close to me that I couldn't dodge.

"The former champion is coming back around," Chet said. "He's staying close to fool scanners, but I can echolocate him there. He should soon emerge from behind that office building to the left."

"Thanks," I said. As I was getting the hang of flying in here, for the next bit I was able to keep my attention on Hesho. He flew well, as I'd trained him, but his wingmate wasn't as skilled. They did manage to get vaguely on my tail, so I led the two of them around the side of an enormous building that had a large open space near the roof. Parking for ships, maybe?

As we rounded the building, I cut my speed and ducked inside. Hesho and his wingmate followed. The confines of the hangar were tight, but a huge window filling the entire far wall provided good visibility. I regretted my decision as both Hesho and his friend opened fire. There wasn't a lot of room to maneuver in here, and slowing bunched us up.

Their shots took down my shields, so I hit my IMP—hoping it would reach them—and then I smashed my ship out through the back window as destructor fire chased me.

"I think you only managed to catch one of them with that," M-Bot said. "The one who *isn't* Lord Hesho."

"Scud." I swooped down along the building, then speared the bottom corner with my light-lance and made an assisted turn—barely in time, as destructor fire sprayed behind me. I took the next three turns fast, darting through an increasingly busy junkyard of a battlefield.

Was . . . was that a cow?

I kept flying through the cluttered urban debris, pushing to get ahead of Hesho. But he stuck on me. His wingmate didn't have to; they could cut out of the chase at times and then swoop back in as we came around another direction. As long as Hesho was putting heat on me, I had to stay on the defensive.

I tried to loop around and pick off the wingmate, but Hesho unloaded a sequence of shots just ahead of where I had been planning to go—which forced me a different direction. Without a shield, I had to be extra cautious. So in seconds both of them were on me again.

Eventually one of those shots was going to land. I broke downward—flying among dropping chunks of rock and debris. Hesho wove behind me.

"Warning, Spensa," Chet said. "I am tracking the wingmate, though it's out of sight. I think Hesho has ordered the wingmate to fly around—they're trying to pin us."

Scud. He was correct. When I leveled out, I spotted the wingmate hovering there, ready to open fire while Hesho still pressed me from behind.

I dodged as best I could, and felt another stab of pride. I hadn't taught Hesho this kind of advanced technique. But I liked to think that it was my foundation in combat teamwork that had led him to strategies like this.

I wove in and out of falling chunks of rock and hit my overburn, intending to run straight through the shots from the wingmate and hope none hit me. At that moment though, a spray of fire—seemingly out of nowhere—slammed into the wingmate, freezing the ship.

"We have arrived, Spin," Shiver said over the comm. "I should think that you'd know better how to stay with a group. You motiles, always wandering off in random directions."

"Thanks," I said. "I appreciate the assist."

Other ships came in to nip at the two resonants—chasing them back away from the mess of appearing buildings. Those were largely centered on me, so while the delvers weren't precise, they could evidently lob things in my general direction.

I was glad Shiver and the others were mostly moving to the other side of the battlefield. As much as I'd have liked help against Hesho, I didn't want the others flying in these dangerous confines. Honestly, I was worried most about Hesho himself—as long as he stuck on me, he was risking death.

I needed to stun him quickly, if I could. I gave chase, passing a couple of drifting ships, locked up—but with their shields reignited to protect from collisions. A Superiority tug was gliding in to pull them to safety, and nobody attacked it. Kind of like how you might leave an enemy medic alone on an Old Earth battlefield. I found the civility of it encouraging.

I pulled out of the lower debris field, then veered sharply as the air began to vibrate. A second later, a small *fragment* appeared just above me—a chunk of city stretching for hundreds of meters, marked with sidewalks and planters.

Right. Okay. I could handle this. I steered up over the edge of it and wiped the sweat from my hands. That maneuver had let Hesho get behind me again, unfortunately. He started firing, and I barely dodged.

It was time to see if I could exploit his muscle memory. I started a routine maneuvering sequence, one I'd drilled into him and the others as I'd trained them outside the delver maze. A warm-up meant to teach good fundamentals.

Hesho fell in behind me as I moved, and his disruptor shots trailed off. *Yes,* I thought. *You know this routine. You flew it with me dozens of times.*

"Why did he stop?" Chet asked.

I didn't respond, continuing the motion. Hesho inched forward, and I let him fall almost into my wingmate position. I'd been intending to break out of this maneuver unexpectedly and throw him off, maybe earning me a breather to reignite my shield. But this seemed to be triggering a memory in him.

Together we soared over the new fragment, no longer fighting. No longer worried about other ships—as we were getting increasingly distant from the others, who were staying away from the debris. I continued the motions. I could almost feel Hesho's longing, his thoughts stretching toward mine . . .

Then my mind went cold. It was like I'd been doused by a bucket of ice water. I pulled my ship back to be even with his, then glanced toward his cockpit. It was tinted dark, which prevented me from making out any of his features.

It wasn't dark enough, however, to obscure the two powerful white spots that were shining deep within the cockpit where Hesho's eyes would have been. The delvers had taken him.

34

Hesho broke out of our two-person formation, then flared his boosters and barreled away from me.

"Oh, scrud," Chet said.

"Spensa?" M-Bot said. "What's wrong?"

"Let her fly, AI," Chet said as I fell into pace behind Hesho. "Something is very wrong."

"What?" M-Bot asked.

"The delvers," I said. "They . . . took him. His eyes are glowing white."

Chet cursed softly. "I'd hoped we would be safe from such direct intervention in a group. We must be too spread out on this battlefield."

I stayed on Hesho's tail as he looped around and flew through the center of the large debris field of hanging buildings. The remaining fighters on both sides had moved to the perimeter, as it had gone from dangerous to insane to fly here, with chunks spinning and colliding like an asteroid field.

Two buildings smashed together ahead of us, spraying shards of glass like rain—and as I flew through it they snapped against my hull and canopy, reminding me that I'd never found a chance to reignite my shield.

Why did the delver want to fly through this? In the past, they'd chased me. Now this one wanted me to chase it?

Well, I was game. It wanted to see how good I was? Let it watch. I expertly trailed Hesho-delver. We darted down through the narrowing crack between a chunk of rock and a free-flying factory, then flew underneath the still-crumbling fragments. That took us through a stream of falling water that was spraying from a building above.

Was this the delver actually flying? No . . . these maneuvers were familiar. Somehow it was leaning on Hesho's skills. Well, I was going to rise to its test. We soared between crashing pieces of rock, down alongside a falling roadway, through sprays of debris that clattered against my canopy.

Everything else faded, and I absently muted other comm chatter. Nothing mattered but me and the chase.

The delver tried increasingly difficult moves to get me to trip up. Soon I was sweating—my attention tight like a narrow scanner band. Just me, that ship, and the immediate terrain.

Hesho-delver miscalculated on a light-lance pivot and slammed into a big chunk of stone, side first. His shield fuzzed, briefly visible as it absorbed the brunt of the impact. I grinned as I took the turn without a problem. Another hit like that, and he'd . . .

He'd . . . be dead.

My focus shattered like glass. I was suddenly aware not merely of my immediate surroundings—the cockpit, my sweaty hands on the controls, Chet breathing heavily in the copilot seat, the beeping proximity sensor—but the battlefield as a whole. Falling rock, crumbling buildings, hanging acclivity stone chunks.

It wasn't just a series of obstacles anymore. It was a death trap. And this wasn't some contest to see how good I was.

My stunned recovery took a moment, during which we came dangerously close to hitting a piece of a falling building.

"Spensa?" M-Bot said. "The rest of the fighting has paused. Most of the ships on both sides have been locked up, but there are fifteen remaining functional fighters on the enemy side, while our side has twelve, including Gremm and Peg. But everyone has agreed to a cessation for now, as the battlefield is too dangerous. They want to make sure everyone locked up gets pulled out to safety before resuming."

Ahead, Hesho wove between falling chunks. He'd slowed, taunting me to follow. They wanted to coax me into danger. They were willing to throw away Hesho's life for a chance to hurt me. I needed to end this chase. Now.

I grabbed the control sphere and started firing, causing Hesho to slam on his overburn and blast away. His ship's faster speed shouldn't matter among all this debris. Unfortunately, that same debris blocked my shots. I ended up pelting a chunk of acclivity stone—broken off what appeared to be a storefront.

As Hesho dodged, he took another collision from a falling piece of rock. His shield went down. Scud. Shooting at him was making him more reckless. I followed, uncertain what to do, my worry deepening—but Chet and M-Bot stayed quiet and gave me time to think. And as I did, memories returned to me out of the cloud that was my past. Flying with Hesho and the kitsen—and with Brade, Vapor, and Morriumur. Days spent training—memories I hadn't even realized I'd lost.

"M-Bot," I said, "open a line to his ship."

"Done," M-Bot said.

"Flight Fifteen," I snapped, trying to channel Cobb like I'd done when training Hesho and the others, "line up! Now!"

I backboosted, pulling my ship to a halt.

Ahead, Hesho's vessel slowed. How much did the delvers control, and how much was him? They needed his flying skill. Hopefully that meant they couldn't dominate him entirely.

He'd responded to my voice. His drill instructor. I searched through my clouded recollections of that day. Hadn't . . . hadn't Hesho had a different name for our flight?

"Flowers of Night's Last Kiss," I said. "Time to call roll! Fall in line, Hesho!"

Hesho's ship stopped and turned. I didn't wait—I sprayed him with destructor fire. I felt only a *tad* guilty. But my shots flew true, causing his ship to flash blue and lock up.

Behind me Chet released a loud, relieved breath. "Nice flying," he said softly.

"A soothing calm," M-Bot said. "Like I've just been serviced with a nice fresh can of lubricant. I'll call it repose."

"We're not done yet," I said. Using maneuvering thrusters, I inched over to his ship—close enough that we nearly bumped one another amid the falling debris.

His canopy flashed and went transparent, the tint fading. He sat in there, those eyes glowing white, facing toward me in his little seat. His teeth bared. I pressed my mind forward, ignoring the way the delver behind him screamed at me. I saw deep inside it.

And there I found *fear.*

"Chet, take the controls," I said. "Don't let us drift apart."

"As you ask," he said. "But . . . why?"

In response I popped my cockpit, hoping my guess was correct.

"Spensa?" M-Bot said. "This . . . is very odd behavior."

"I'll be right back," I said. "Chet, if I slip and fall, try to grab me or something."

"Uh—"

I climbed out of the cockpit and stepped onto my ship's wing. From there, I felt a strange sense of disorientation—buildings floating overhead, tumbling in the sky. Two crumpled fragments locked together from their collision, spinning slowly. A white glow to my right: the lightburst looking on us through debris-filled space.

I was standing at the crossroads of infinity, without lifeline or safety rope. Chet used maneuvering thrusters to keep the wing steady as I inched over to Hesho's craft. Then, before I could think better of it, I jumped.

I landed square on Hesho's smaller fighter. It was more than large enough to hold me up, even if the cockpit wasn't much bigger than a flight helmet. I leaned down, stared at him through the now-clear canopy, and stoked the star inside me. The me-ness. I let it shine out cytonically, invisible to conventional sight.

Hesho-delver cringed away, pure white eyes open and glowing bright enough that I couldn't make out his other features.

"Why are you so afraid of me?" I said. "What is it that I don't know yet that makes you act this way?"

You must return to us the Us you separated, noise. It was a deliberate attempt to get me to think of something else, judging by what my "listening" was telling me. *Give them back.*

"Look," I said, "can't we *please* talk about this? What you're doing to me? And my people?"

This corrupts, they sent me. I understood the implication—they meant that talking to me, interacting, risked changing them. They tried to withdraw, but I . . . latched on. With my growing cytonic senses, I grabbed hold of the delver. It was like Brade had done to me.

Except I was far, far weaker. I held on only barely. Either I didn't have a talent for this, or I needed a ton more practice. Still, even that little attempt *panicked* the delver. This brought the full brunt of their attention, fear, and hatred upon me. In that moment others gathered, and they tried to destroy me in the only way they knew how.

By trying to make me one of them.

I was pulled into the nowhere entirely. I became formless; I had no body, merely a mind floating in not darkness—as it normally was—but an infinite whiteness. Everything around me was white because it was *full,* packed with the delvers. Like an ocean is filled with water.

They saw *me* as a corrupted version of *them* now. Cytonics were like delvers. In a way, I was a cousin to them. They saw me as a tempter also, luring them toward their destruction with crass things like *linearity* and *individuality*.

Their minds assaulted me, and pushed me to see as they did. To see the peace, the harmony, of shared existence. I clung to my individuality, but it was frayed, worn, like a battle standard that had been shot full of holes. In seconds, what scraps of memories I still had left of my friends and family had frayed further, and my life in the somewhere began to vanish entirely.

They wanted to erase it. Because of . . . pain? Yes, they *knew* pain, from the past, but had escaped it. I latched onto this. It was a clue, or a seed of one. Yet . . . it was terrifying how I responded to their offer. To the peace, the blending of self, the eternity without pain—there could be no pain without the passage of time. There could be no anger when everyone agreed absolutely on everything.

I can't really explain why that was so entrancing. I can't even explain what it felt like—how do you describe such a thing? I was just a pilot. Without the right words.

I didn't *want* to succumb to them. But I also had difficulty fighting. In a panic I stretched out, searching for help. Perhaps from my friends? Whose names I was forgetting . . . Whose faces . . . blended . . . into white . . .

And then, something.

Support from someone distant. A . . . friend? That comforting mind that was somehow my pin. The one that I was increasingly certain was my father. It bolstered me and brought with it images. The delightful scent of water dripping in the caverns back home. The calming purpose of tinkering on M-Bot's ship with Rig. My mother's exhausted smile, after a long day of work, upon seeing me. Gran-Gran's steady voice speaking of the heroines of the past.

Then another mind, from the other side. A mind that reminded me of things I loved. Exploring. Flying. Stories. Existing was pain, but it was also *joy*. With those memories bolstering me, I stoked myself.

My star came alight. I wasn't *nothing* here. I was Spensa, and my soul was fire. It exploded with brightness, and I offered that sense of myself to them—I bludgeoned them with who I was, and the emotions I felt.

They pulled away at that offer of corruption. At the offer of . . . of *dissention*. They retreated, though our exchange had told us a great deal about one another. As the sensation faded, I found another offer. A . . . truce.

Within me, they found my longing for my friends to stop dying. They'd seen my excitement for the battles I'd found in the belt of the nowhere.

Stay . . . the delvers pled with me. *Stay and do not pass Surehold. We will stop.*

Stay? I blinked, becoming aware of the space around me. I was hanging on to Hesho's ship, looking down into those portals of light that were his eyes.

Stay. It wasn't a word, but an impression—of me stopping my journey on the Path of Elders. Of staying at Surehold, or moving back out into the belt, but going no farther inward than the Superiority base. Of not continuing the Path of Elders or entering the lightburst.

What about my friends? I sent them. *The people in the somewhere.*

In truce with you, we leave them alone. We ignore the noise. That particular use of "noise" indicated Brade and Winzik. It wasn't as strong a promise as I'd have preferred—it felt like from the way their minds worked, if they were pulled into our realm they'd still attack. But they *would* start ignoring Winzik.

Stay, the delvers repeated, the white fading from Hesho's eyes. *Stay away. And we promise truce.*

With that, the light vanished completely—leaving me clinging to the outside of a frozen ship containing one *very* confused kitsen.

35

I slumped into the cockpit of my ship.

That had been . . . a lot. A lot to think about, a lot to feel. A lot to remember.

Scud, I remembered. Gran-Gran, Mother, Rig. Even Jorgen, though the faces of my other friends remained vague.

"I told you that I understood crazy," Chet said. "I was wrong. Thank you for the master class."

"Spensa?" M-Bot said. "That was . . . interesting of you. Do you want a list of the emotions I'm feeling right now?"

"I get the sense they'd mostly be variations on frustration and bafflement."

"You'd be right," he replied.

"I'll pass, then," I said, as I closed the cockpit. "Come on, you two. Climbing out on my wing in the middle of a battlefield? You've both seen me do worse."

"Which is why I didn't call it strange," M-Bot said. "Strange implies odd, or out of sequence with your normal behavior. Still, um . . . What the hell?"

I grinned. "Wow. You used that curse perfectly, M-Bot."

"It's the emotions," he said. "I now understand the sense of frustration everyone else feels with you! It dovetails perfectly into exasperation, which makes me *finally* understand why it is people swear at you so much!"

"That's great!" I said.

"I know! Also: *WHAT THE HELL, SPENSA?*"

"Hesho was possessed by a delver," I said.

"Yes, Chet explained that," he said. "So you went *closer*?"

"They're afraid of me, M-Bot. I realized it . . . and it just felt right . . ."

"Right isn't a feeling. Trust me, I've been practicing. Weren't you listening?"

"Right *is* a feeling for me," I said. "At least this time when I got out of the cockpit, I didn't end up floating around in a vacuum. Chet, how much of that did you hear?"

"Not a lot," he said. "My cytonic communication talents are not as powerful as yours."

"Well," I said, "immortality and the ability to cytonically echolocate are both also cool."

"I didn't say they weren't," he replied. "I did have enough skill to sense you in pain—and their attack. I tried to feed you memories of yourself. It appears to have helped. After that they left, though I couldn't sense why."

I should tell him, I thought. But the delvers' parting thoughts—*stay, truce*—haunted me. I first wanted to think about what it all meant. "M-Bot," I said. "Please open a comm line to Hesho."

He sighed, but complied.

"Hey," I said. "How are you feeling?"

"I meditate upon the emptiness that is my past," Hesho said softly. "And about how, despite it being blank, I *know* you were part of it. We were . . . friends?"

"Yes," I said.

"Was I the leader of a pirate force?" he asked.

"Not exactly. Why do you ask?"

We floated together, but fortunately the flashes of buildings and other junk entering the nowhere had stopped. Much of it—the chunks with acclivity stone at least—drifted around us. Lazy, almost serene, like we were underwater in a vast ocean following some terrible storm.

"When the Cannonaders took me captive," Hesho explained in his deep authoritative voice, "I immediately tried to seize command of their organization. I *felt* I should be their leader. They thought I was 'cute' and attempted to use me as a mascot instead. I . . . disabused them of this behavior."

I grinned, trying to imagine how that had looked. What did a tiny fox man a quarter meter tall do to "disabuse" pirates?

"Eventually," he said, "I settled into my role as an expert pilot and followed Vlep. But something about it felt wrong. There were embarrassing holes in my piloting skill. So I wondered. Perhaps I was a leader of a group of pirates who maybe hadn't flown in a long time?"

"You were commander of a ship, Hesho," I explained. "Your kind can crew a small capital ship that isn't much bigger than a starfighter for the rest of us. You at least occasionally piloted it yourself, which is why you learned some skills—but you had crew working things like the shields for you."

"Aaah . . ." he said. "That thought . . . it wears a path in my mind, champion. Light sparks, like stone and steel. My ship . . . the . . . *Swims Against the Current in a Stream Reflecting the Sun*?"

"Yes!"

"I see it like a faded picture exposed to the elements," Hesho said. "But . . . I *can* remember my home. The feeling of it warm on my face and fur. Yes. Being with you is good for me. I will remain with you, champion, and serve you as your bodyguard until you return to me who I was."

"Uh . . . You're my friend. You don't need to—"

"I am your sworn companion," he said firmly, "and you my feudal lord. Do not object to this arrangement. It is done."

I sighed. I'd been about to explain to him that he was an

emperor, but perhaps it wasn't wise to give him more ammunition. Only Hesho could become someone's servant using a forcible imperial declaration. Still, I could do worse than having a dedicated gerbil-fox samurai following me about. And it *was* encouraging that Hesho could remember the name of his ship now.

I stuck him with a light-lance and towed him up through the debris toward where the others were waiting. As we flew, I grappled with what the delvers had told me.

They want me to stop following the Path of Elders, I thought. *Which is an obvious sign that I should continue.*

Yet . . . if I could make them break their pact with Winzik . . . It was a compelling offer. Assuming I could trust them.

I found myself conflicted, and determined that I shouldn't make a decision in the middle of a battle. I put the thoughts aside for the moment, and emerged from the biggest clot of debris to find most of the other pirates lined up in two rows of deactivated ships, maintained by the tugs that would eventually reactivate them. The remaining active ships were a little ways off, also in two groups.

As I arrived, a group of ships peeled off from the enemy faction. Vlep, commander of the Cannonade pirates, and a few of his crew were leaving. Apparently seeing me defeat their best pilot a second time meant they'd had enough.

"Give us immunity, Peg," Vlep's voice said over the comm. "Let me take my downed ships, and I'll leave."

"What!" another voice shouted, in what I thought was the heklo language. "Our deal!"

"You should know better than to make deals with pirates, Lorn," Vlep said. "What say you, Peg?"

"Done," Peg said immediately.

Other members of the pirates who had joined with us grumbled, but Peg was making the correct decision. Vlep and his traitors weren't our ultimate goal. Without them, there would only be ten working ships on the Superiority's side. We had thirteen. And it was obvious which was the more skilled force.

Vlep hovered over to try to attach a light-lance to Hesho's ship. However, Hesho's voice came on the comm. "I have been bested a second time," he said. "And in the name of honor, I have chosen to join the new champion as her sworn companion."

Vlep cursed softly. "You would so easily break with your allies, Darkshadow?"

"I have made no oaths," Hesho said. "You are not my liege. Indeed, your treatment of me when I first arrived is among the only memories I hold. Be glad I warned you of my shift in allegiance. We are now enemies. Should we meet again, I shall reveal to you the consequences of my anger."

Vlep retreated without responding, following the others off the battlefield. I joined the line of active pirate ships facing down the small group of Superiority forces.

"All right, Lorn," Peg said over a wide broadcast. "You want to just surrender now?"

"You know I can't do that," his voice replied.

"They're never going to let you out of here, Lorn," Peg said. "They don't care about you. Why are you still loyal?"

"You know they have my family."

"So we squeeze them," Peg said. "We withhold their acclivity stone until they agree to send through your family. They pretend they have the power in this relationship, but so long as we *own* this place—and make it our home—they lose every bit of bargaining power they have."

There was silence on the line for a moment, and I leaned forward, hands on my controls. We could end this easily, with the odds in our favor.

Peg waited though. No signal to attack.

That heklo voice spoke again. "You promise to do this for me?" he asked. "For anyone they're holding? You'll get them brought through so we can be together?"

"My word and oath," Peg said. "But you have to turn the facility over to me. All security codes. All access."

Silence again. Finally, the heklo continued. "There are a few people among the base security officers who I'm nearly certain are Superiority agents sent to watch me. We'll have to move quickly and isolate them until we can make sure."

"Shouldn't be too hard," Peg said. "I've got a plan. Do we have a deal?"

"We have a deal."

36

A short time later, Shiver, Dllllizzzz, and I flew in low toward the Superiority base—escorting Peg, her sons, and Lorn. The rest of the unfrozen pirate vessels formed an ominous presence higher in the sky.

Surehold turned out to be bigger than I'd expected. The campus sprawled across an unusually large and thick fragment marked by hills and rocky crags. I counted four separate acclivity stone quarries, each attended by a variety of modern machines. The central section of the base comprised about a dozen buildings, and while it wasn't large in comparison to the crowded Starsight, it was almost as big as the entire DDF headquarters.

After making certain their large antiaircraft guns were offline—control transferred to Peg—we landed and let her and Lorn disembark. Curious workers stopped on the flight deck to watch, though Lorn—the base commander—waved a winged arm to calm them. Together Lorn, Peg, and her two sons entered a nearby building, the base security structure. Inside she could be given full and permanent control over the base, with her own overrides and passwords.

After a tense few minutes—during which I stood ready to blast open the wall and try to grab Peg if something went wrong—a call to quarters went out on the Superiority channel. Martial law was declared. Peg's sons prowled out of the building a moment later, armed and armored, with Lorn guiding them. They'd secure the few people on base he thought would be trouble.

Quick as that, it was done. I hadn't expected there to be trouble—the real fight had been the one with starfighters. We'd left most of the Superiority pilots in their ships, which were locked up without friendly tugs to unfreeze them, guarded by trustworthy pirate flights.

Still, I remained on watch—hovering—for another half hour as Peg and her sons took full command of the base. Finally, as the word came that all was clear, some of the pirates began to land on the flight pad. Hesho settled down beside us in his own ship, but didn't move to leave it.

I glanced back at Chet. "What do you think?" I asked.

"It's looking good," he said. "But if anything were to go wrong, this would be the time—when we're flat-footed and assume we've won."

"Agreed."

So the two of us, paranoid as we were, waited another good half hour. But it seemed that the final stage of Peg's plan had indeed gone off without a hitch. As the pirates unloaded from their ships, Peg's voice came over our comms and the flight deck loudspeakers.

"No looting," she ordered. "This is our home now. Regular base personnel have been confined to quarters; if you encounter a locked room, leave it alone. But you're free to investigate the place, pick an empty room in the barracks to claim as your own, all that fun stuff. Just be warned. I get word of you harming base personnel or breaking stuff, and I'll be . . . upset."

Most of the pirates made for the barrack building. I asked Hesho to stay put and keep watch while Chet and I climbed free, then Chet pointed toward a large set of doors ahead of us. The shipping warehouse, where the portal would be.

You still here? I sent to my pin. I'd confirmed, upon coming close, that it was here.

I got back a contented, quiet impression. *Hiding now. Seek me later.*

Okay . . . Well, I had a job to do at the moment anyway. Chet used some controls to open the large bay doors of the warehouse, revealing a vast room with a tall ceiling. It felt vacuous despite the other end being piled high with raw acclivity stone waiting to be shipped to the Superiority.

On the wall closest to us was the portal. It was much larger than the others I'd seen in here—covering a square that looked about six meters on each side. Chet and I stood there staring at it for a good long while. As I started toward it, Chet put his hand on my shoulder.

"Miss Nightshade," he said. "Might I inquire what the delvers told you? Before they left?"

"They . . . offered me a truce," I admitted. "They want me to proceed no farther inward than Surehold. The next step on the Path would take us that way, wouldn't it?"

"Almost assuredly."

"Well, they don't want me doing that. They made a promise. If I stay here, they'll leave me alone."

"And your people in the somewhere?"

"They implied they'd halt attacks, though it wasn't clear if they understood completely what that means. They *did* promise to stop listening to Winzik and Brade—the two people they'd earlier made a deal with on the enemy's side."

Chet sighed and settled down on a box. He suddenly looked old to me, his mustache drooping and in need of a wax, his skin . . . wan. He gave me a smile, but something about him seemed worn out. And when he spoke, some of the facade—the persona—had faded, leaving a normal man.

"That's a good offer," he said. "Better than I ever thought they'd make. They're frightened."

"That's what I decided as well," I said, pacing before him in the cavernous warehouse, helmet under my arm. "Which makes me think I should refuse the offer. They're desperate. I should keep doing what I'm doing, because it's worrying them."

"Except?"

"Except ostensibly, I came in here to find a way to stop them! And now I've found it. Shouldn't I take it? Isn't it my *duty* to at least try this?"

Chet nodded slowly.

I paced back the other direction. "How trustworthy are they, do you suppose?"

"I'm not sure I can say," he replied. "I do get the sense that they live in the moment, but I know they also never change. So as long as they continue to be afraid of you, they should continue wanting the same thing—which means they'd persist in upholding any promise they made."

"That's not as strong as I'd like," I said. "But . . . yeah, that makes sense. They don't have honor—it's not a thing they even comprehend. And they *are* backing out of a promise they made to Winzik. They could do the same to me."

I paced back the other way, arms folded. This felt like a lot to put on one person still in her teens. How did *I* decide what could be the fate of not merely my people, but the entire galactic civilization?

"It feels like I should at least try them out," I said. "If I can remove the delvers from the war . . . Scud, it would mean so much. It's more than any pilot, no matter how skilled, could ever hope to accomplish.

"But if I take their deal, what then? Do I go back to the somewhere? How? Sneak through this portal into a Superiority base?"

"You'd need to remain a threat to the delvers," Chet said. "Always on the cusp of doing the thing they're afraid you'll do—that is the best chance at keeping them honest."

I nodded, though my stomach fell a little. That meant remaining in the nowhere, at least until the war against the Superiority was won. Could I really do that? I paced back the other direction.

"I worry that this is the wrong time to make concessions to the delvers," I said. "Beyond that, our biggest advantage against Winzik is the fact that his coup is still relatively new. He's securing power, Jorgen says—and doesn't have full control yet. This seems the best time for me to press forward, continue learning about my powers. Exploit the fact that our enemies' balance of power is unstable."

"A difficult position," Chet said. "Could I maybe . . . offer you another option? I don't want to complicate the issue further, but I find I must speak."

I glanced across at him, sitting on the box. He gave me a smile. Not an overly cheerful, toothy explorer's smile. A tired, hopeful smile.

"What?" I asked.

"Come with me, Spensa," he said, "and explore the nowhere."

I froze in place.

"As I've been wandering alone," he said, "I've started wishing I could pass on some of what I know. Wishing for a student, someone who shared my enthusiasm, my love of all things new and exciting. What if we didn't continue on the Path of Elders? What if we turned away and just went off on our own?

"We could see what the farthest reaches hold! I've heard of distant fragments with creatures that sound strikingly similar to dragons! I've heard of water fragments full of caverns with air pockets, connected by transparent stone!"

Some of his old boisterousness returned, and his voice changed, more clipped—with a faint accent—as he stepped up to me. "Spensa," he said, "we have an entire *galaxy* in microcosm. Worlds to explore. We could even return back here to Surehold on occasion. Scratch that flying itch! Spend time with the Broadsiders.

Why, you could teach me to fly again! I show you a galaxy, and you show me who I used to be! A pilot, yes, and presumably friends to an AI. Me! Ha!

"Wouldn't that be incredible, Spensa? Wouldn't it be *amazing*? We could watch the delvers, see that they don't attack your friends. As you guessed, they'll be *much* more likely to keep their word if you're within striking distance of continuing your quest. You wouldn't be giving it up. No, merely a delay! A little . . . time off. To travel this wondrous place."

It hit me like a punch to the stomach.

During my travels in here—the exploration and the fighting alike—something had been building in me. A sense of disconnect between the person I *was* becoming and the person I'd always *imagined* myself becoming.

In that moment, I was shocked—physically—by how badly I wanted to stay. I *really* loved it here. Exploring the belt? Going on grand adventures? And beyond that, fighting in the sky without the stress of losing those I loved? Being a hero, the best pilot in *literally* the entire universe?

"It sounds so nice," I said to Chet. "Exploring, dueling . . . like . . ."

"Like a story?" he said softly.

I nodded. "Why do we remember the stories, Chet, but not our families? Why is that?"

"I don't know," he said. "I wish I did."

Together we turned to face the portal looming on the far wall. When I'd joined the DDF as a pilot, I'd imagined glorious battles and storybook heroism. I'd imagined new worlds to conquer. Instead I'd found pain. Friends dying. People struggling at the end of their stretched-thin nerves. I'd found complications, anger, fear.

I'd discovered I wasn't a hero. Not like in the stories. But here . . . I *could* be that. And it felt so, so very right for me to stay and claim it. This place sang to me, like beautiful music from Old Earth. It vibrated my soul.

Didn't I deserve to stay? Hadn't I done enough? I'd saved Detritus from the bomb, and then from the delver. Wasn't that enough for one woman? And now I had the chance to escape into a story . . . all the while providing a vital service to my people. I traded my future in the somewhere for holding back the destructive force of the delvers.

It was perfect. Except.

Jorgen. My friends. Could I . . .

"Chet," I said, "you've always been afraid of the Path of Elders. Why?"

"I worry that if I walk it," he said, "I'll stop being myself."

"Why?"

"Because every path we walk changes us, Spensa," he answered. "This one more than most. Please, just think about my offer. Let's not rush into this. There's no harm in taking a few hours, is there?"

"No," I said. "No, there's not."

He squeezed my shoulder in thanks, then bowed—something I don't think anyone non-kitsen had ever done to me before—and quietly withdrew. I sat down on a box, looking at the portal. It felt wrong to be here and not discover what it had inside it. Yet . . . I hesitated.

It felt like I should know before I continued. Scud. Was I really thinking about turning away now?

Yes. I was. I remembered the pure joy of "sailing" across that ocean fragment with M-Bot and Chet. I remembered the thrill of discovering ruins that humans had built. I had *loved* the fights against Hesho, at least before buildings began appearing around me.

Being here was living an adventure. While being in the somewhere was . . . It was about pain. And scud, deep down, I realized I was *so tired*.

I'd been running since I could remember. Dashing from disaster to disaster. Desperately working to get into flight school, fixing M-Bot in secret, being a double agent on Starsight, confronting the delver . . .

It had worn me thin. Yet in here I'd found wonder, adventure, and excitement.

I sat there for a time, until footsteps scraping stone made me spin around. A large figure lumbered my direction, wearing a plumed hat. Peg smiled at me as she stepped up, a gun slung over her thick shoulder.

"The base is ours," she told me. "Well and truly. I almost can't believe it."

"You earned it, Peg," I said. "That was an amazing plan you put together."

"Thank you," she said, grinning. She nodded toward the portal. "Find what you wanted?"

"Both yes and no," I said softly. "I'm honestly not sure yet."

"I . . . heard that you might be staying."

I glanced at her, frowning. In turn, she gestured toward the top of the wall. "Cameras," she said. "I saw you two going this way, and had to make sure you didn't accidentally open the portal and reveal what we'd done to the Superiority. I'm sorry to not give you and Chet privacy, but this is too valuable an asset for that."

Right. Security officer. I tried not to feel offended. I mean, I hadn't asked her to leave us alone—and she had a point about the portal.

"What would it take," Peg said to me, "to get you to stay with the Broadsiders?"

I sighed. "I don't know, Peg," I said. "This is all a little overwhelming right now."

"Fair enough," she replied. "Grow *igandels* in thought—it is a good time. While you do, let me ask you something. Do you know why I was willing to come in here when no one else was? I knew the truth of what the Superiority was doing here. Not letting people out. Forced labor in another dimension. I came anyway. You curious to know why?"

"Yes, actually."

"Out there, I was a killer," Peg said, her voice softer. "In here was a new life. A fresh life. I didn't know I was pregnant with my boys; that might have changed my mind. All I wanted was an escape from my old life, and coming in here offered it.

"Things out there are messy, Spin. Everybody arguing, fighting. Killing. But a lot of the things they argue over, well, they don't matter in here. We don't need food, and there's plenty of space. Politics . . . ideology . . . those are things we can make up for ourselves in here. We can make this place whatever we want it to be."

She turned, waving toward the complex. "I've known for years now that if I could just get this base—grab it by the throat and start building it up as a *home,* not a *prison*—we could make it wonderful. We could make a society. I want you to help me do that."

"But Chet wants me to go exploring with him," I said.

"I know, and I think that's an excellent idea!" Peg said. "I'd want to put you on that kind of assignment frequently, between training seasons. Do you know what is out there? Past the empty stretches?"

"No."

"I don't either," Peg said. "It's hard to fly that far; when you hit the enormous gap between fragments it starts eating up your ashes, and you risk losing yourself. But I'll tell you this—there are three other Superiority mining bases in the nowhere. I was given that information when I was applying for this job."

"Only four total?" I said. "For the entire Superiority?"

"Exactly," Peg said. "And this is the largest—which is why I'm certain they'll meet my demands. But I'm also worried. If they use those other three bases—and somehow load them with enough reality ashes to cross the empty stretches—I could still get invaded. Plus Vlep is still out there, a real danger.

"I need fighters. More importantly, I need *trainers* of fighters. Then I need someone crazy enough to go explore, to discover how to cross the vast gaps." She looked back at me. "You are the right person, Spin. The somewhere is a mess. But the nowhere *can* be something better. I want you to help me make it so."

I . . .

Scud, I didn't need this too. Not after what Chet had said. I knew they hadn't coordinated it; Peg was just acting at a convenient moment. I felt double-teamed regardless. Triple-teamed, actually. Chet. Peg.

And my own heart.

"I reserved one of the officer suites for you," Peg said. "You don't have to make any decisions. But for now, why not go grab a shower and relax a little? Think over your options. You can at least stay there until we locate Surehold's reality icon, and I can give you those ashes I promised."

I considered. And scud, she was right. I needed some time. Plus, a shower sounded *so* nice. I called M-Bot and Hesho to let them know, then went to the room Peg indicated. It was an enormous suite—of the ridiculous type.

Unfortunately, I didn't get to the shower. I made the mistake of lying down on the bed first. And after the fighting, the chaos, the tension of my decision . . . I just found myself unable to stay awake.

And so I drifted off.

INTERLUDE

As I slept, someone tried to talk to me.

I wanted to talk to him.

Something stopped me.

It was another cloud, like before. Like the prison that Brade had put around me. Though . . . it felt different. Like a march set to different words. Same sounds. New song.

I fought through it, but no matter which way I turned, I got lost. I tried telling myself that none of this was real, that there were no places here. Nowhere to go. I merely had to . . . make myself be somewhere else . . .

It was hard to think through this fog.

"Spensa?" Jorgen's voice. "Spensa, I can feel you."

I . . . I can't feel you . . .

"You seem distant. Why? What is wrong?"

I'm lost.

"I can barely hear you. What was that?"

Lost . . .

"Spensa, things are tough right now. I . . . Everyone is looking to me for answers. I could use someone to talk to."

He needed me. That need made the haze thinner, and I thought I saw the way. I moved toward it, but each footstep was sluggish. I was lost. Hadn't I been . . . warned . . . about that?

But I was tired.

Just. So. Tired.

Moments later, I was asleep.

PART FIVE

Threat Assessment Analysis Record DST210503B

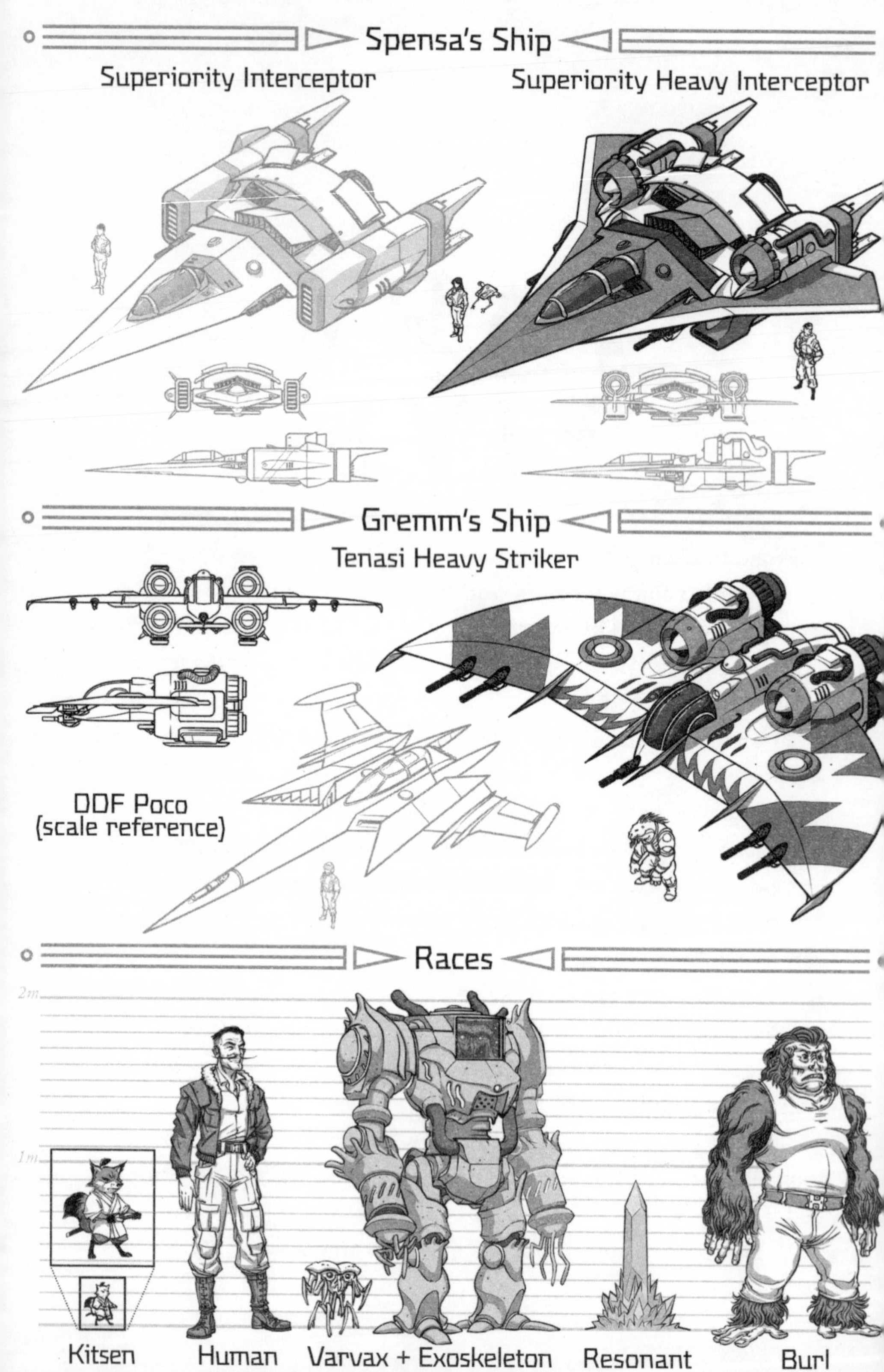

37

I awoke to luxury. I didn't think I'd slept a full night—but then again, I didn't know what "night" really meant in here. I yawned, feeling . . . unsettled by my dreams. As I considered, I looked to the side—and found Hesho sitting cross-legged on an oversized chair right next to the bed.

"I watched you in your sleep," he said. "To make certain you were safe."

Awesome.

I mean, yeah, I realized some people would have thought that was unsettling. Not me. Alien bodyguard watching for assassins? Scud, how could a girl *not* sleep more soundly under those circumstances?

"How long was I out?" I asked.

"An hour," he said. "I wrote the time down to remember."

"Clever," I said to him. "I'm going to grab a shower. Maybe wait outside while I do?"

"I shall be on the balcony," he said. "The view is excellent. I shall also send for the machine-who-thinks; he wished to be notified if you rose."

A short time later, I walked out onto the balcony wearing a

freshly laundered jumpsuit, my hair still drying. Hesho sat cross-legged on the floor here, in his warrior's coat and trousers, a small sword across his lap as he meditated. M-Bot's drone hovered out here too. He'd sent it up—interrupting me in the shower, actually. I hadn't been *too* indignant. I mean, in the past I'd cleansed literally inside his cockpit, so it's not like he hadn't seen me in that state.

I'd sent the drone out here anyway. It didn't contain his entire consciousness; he'd simply decided to start using it as, well, a drone was normally used.

I settled down on the floor of the balcony, my back to the glass door separating it from the bedroom, and looked out. Over the red rock hills, inward.

Toward the lightburst.

That blazing expanse appeared like an explosion frozen mid-detonation. A gigantic sphere of light that *felt* as if it should be consuming all nearby. It was distant, but closer than it had ever been.

I'd assumed it would be my ultimate destination in here. It was, after all, a way out. I'd crossed pirate territory; I'd helped subdue the Superiority. Now only one thing stood between me and the lightburst: the region of the belt called No Man's Land. The place where the delvers were strongest.

My short nap had only muddled things more. I remembered Jorgen's voice. I couldn't leave him, could I?

It wouldn't be permanent, I thought. *Just a . . . short break. A year or so. Exploring. Fighting. Keeping the delvers away.*

But in here, years seemed to have an eerie way of becoming decades. I felt . . . as if I were on the edge of a cliff.

I had to be honest with myself. The offer from the delvers wouldn't have been enough to keep me here, not alone. I had no reason to trust them, and every reason to press forward while my enemies were unstable. The desire to stay had far more to do with my own heart. And the emotions I felt growing there. Emotions that I couldn't help but see as cowardice.

I tried to imagine the heroes from the stories laughing at my sudden indecision. But strangely, I instead pictured them understanding. I . . . I'd been born into war. I'd barely had a childhood. My father had died in the fighting before my eighth birthday. My heart had been flayed by losing companions while flying, though I could no longer remember their names or faces.

I'd never had any other options in life. It was fight or be destroyed. But now I'd seen that wasn't the only way to live. It was the first time in my life I'd actually had a chance to escape the war. I *had* to consider it. How could I not?

Neither Hesho nor M-Bot spoke for a time; the three of us merely sat in silence. We were like an audience for one of the military parades back home. Except our entertainment was the distant, incredible burst of light.

"Is that what a sun is like?" I finally asked.

"No," Hesho said. "I close my eyes, and the light batters my eyelids—but there is no warmth to accompany it. It is like the ghost of a sun. The corpse of one, left behind after all the heat has fled."

"It is a *little* like a sun," M-Bot said. So far Hesho had taken his presence as normal, though I'd cautioned the kitsen not to speak of him to others. "Only very wrong at the same time. It is much smaller than one, for example."

"That's *small*?" I asked. From how close we were, the lightburst took up a good chunk of the horizon.

"For a star, yes," M-Bot said. "That sphere, gauging by my best readings, is a fraction of the size of Earth's moon. It could perhaps be a neutron star if this were the somewhere—which would make Lord Hesho's metaphor particularly acute. At any rate, it certainly shouldn't be so cold for how much light it releases."

I leaned forward and tried to imagine the feeling of sunlight. The vast majority of my ancestors had lived in a place where warmth came from the sky. I'd never felt so distant from them as I did at that moment, sitting before the strange light of the nowhere. Contemplating my cowardice.

I'd learned, in my time with Skyward Flight, that I wasn't a coward in the traditional sense. I didn't fear battle. I wouldn't run from danger. But . . . here was a different opportunity. A way to run from the war, and even responsibility, in their entirety.

"The delvers told me," I said softly, "that they'd leave me alone if I agreed not to continue on the Path of Elders. They even implied they'd back out of the deal with Winzik."

"Curious," M-Bot said. "Why would they make such an offer?"

"They're frightened of me," I said. "They proposed a truce. They hate my presence in here, but they're willing to tolerate it in order to not escalate our interactions."

"And if we continue?" M-Bot asked.

"They'll consider that an act of aggression. They'll do everything they can to stop us."

"A dilemma," M-Bot said.

"Not if I stay," I whispered. "Chet wants me to join him exploring, and Peg wants me to train her people. Both made me offers earlier." I leaned forward, my hands clasped, not looking toward his drone.

"How likely are the delvers to keep a deal?" he asked.

That question again.

"Hard to say," I replied. "They're frightened now, but who knows? We have no evidence that they're trustworthy. If Winzik came to me with a similar deal, for example, I'd discard it in a heartbeat."

"Curious," M-Bot said. "Spensa . . . I'll admit, I've been thinking of my own dilemma."

I glanced at his drone. "What?"

"My old ship," he explained, "had specific circuitry that let me process in the nowhere. That's why I could think fast enough to . . . well, be me. But the drone . . . well, do you remember how I talked when you first found me in it?"

"Slowly," I said. "Like you were struggling for each word."

"I can only assume," he explained, "that being in the belt lets me process quickly, regardless of the machinery I inhabit. But my old ship, the one that let me think so well in the somewhere, has been destroyed. I no longer blame you for that, by the way. I'm getting pretty mature, I'd say."

I smiled.

"Anyway," he said, "if we leave this place, what happens to me? Do I return to thinking like my processors are made of oatmeal?"

"I don't know," I said. "It seems . . . for a little while at least . . . that would be inevitable."

"I've been thinking about it," he said. "For weeks now. And I've decided. I'm willing to go back. We have a war to win. I decided I'd try inhabiting the best computers we had; maybe one on the platforms. I think I'd make a good space station, don't you?

"If not that, maybe we could steal the schematics that Winzik must have made while disassembling my old ship. Then we could build me a new proper brain. But anyway, I decided that if you went back, I'd go with you. I just . . . just thought I should tell you."

Scud. He was braver than I was. I felt ashamed for not noticing the dilemma he faced—this worry must have been bothering him ever since we entered. Some friend I was.

Thinking of friends made me sick again at what I was contemplating. How would I ever face Jorgen if I made the decision to stay?

A part of me, however, knew I couldn't focus on his needs, or M-Bot's decision. I had to decide what *I* wanted. Not choose my future because of what any other person—even Jorgen—would want me to do. For once, I had to think of myself.

I glanced at Hesho, wondering if he'd chime in. For now, he continued sitting in his meditative posture, his eyes closed.

"M-Bot," I said, "I've spent my entire life being indoctrinated into the war for Detritus. I don't blame anyone—except maybe the Krell—for that. We did what we had to in order to survive. But . . .

I'm tired. Of watching people die. Of giving up my future to a war. Of living my life with my stress at a constant *ten*. How much do I owe Detritus? How much is one person expected to pay?"

His drone hovered beside me, silent for long enough that I eventually glanced at it. For once I wished he were a person so that I could see the disgust in his face. I *deserved* that for the way I was talking.

Instead he was an AI. "I suppose," he said, "that makes some sense."

I had to be truthful with him. I had to voice it.

"There's another reason that I want to stay," I said. "I . . . love this. I can explore with Chet, and the Broadsiders practically *worship* me. It's like living in a story. That's all I've ever wanted, M-Bot. I can do that here. I can fly. I can explore, I can fight the Superiority. I can spar. Live . . ."

"That," he said, "makes even *more* sense, knowing you."

"Lord Hesho?" I asked. "I could use your wisdom."

"Wisdom fled me, warrior-sister," he said. "Wisdom is born of experience, you see, and I have none."

"I sense wisdom even in that answer," I said to him. "Am I a coward for preferring to stay? It's not that I fear dying by continuing, it's merely that . . ."

"You are tired of sacrificing what you want for the good of your people," Hesho said.

"Yes," I whispered.

"That is not cowardice, but selfishness," he said.

I winced.

"However," he continued, "duty should not be accepted without question. Duty can be a motive, but should not be an excuse. Does your fight uphold honor and virtue? Does it match your moral code?"

"I don't know that I've ever thought about those things," I said. "I mean, there was the enemy, and there was us. I pointed myself in their direction and let loose . . ."

That wasn't strictly true.

"After living with the enemy," I admitted, "I learned it wasn't so simple. I didn't discover that their cause was just, mind you. Only that most of them weren't evil. They were merely people. Following, by accident, someone who was evil."

"Excellent," he said. "You have left behind the worldview of a child." He cracked an eye. "How old are you, among your species?"

"A young adult," I said.

"Then I might question the society that allowed you to persist in such naivety for so long," he said. "Among the first lessons a warrior must learn is the knowledge that his immediate enemy—the person he must kill—is just trying to survive. Soldiers are alike, no matter their side."

"I . . . don't know that anyone among us knew who the enemy were," I said. "Only that they were trying to destroy us. And . . . I thought you said you didn't remember enough to be wise, Hesho?"

"It seems," he said, "you ask the right questions. I do not know *why* I say these things, simply that they are true." He closed his eyes again. "You are not a coward, nor are you selfish, for realizing you have options, warrior-sister. You cannot be defined by your questions. Only by what you do with them."

Well, Hesho was the same person—with or without memories. What really frightened me, then, was that *this* was who *I* was.

I saw what would happen if I stayed. I would become like Chet. Everyone I knew—even the person I'd been—would fade. I'd remember only the stories, and I'd become more and more like someone who felt she was one of those heroes. I'd forget everything and let the part of me that had always made up boasts take control. In forty years, I probably wouldn't even remember the fight for Detritus, or why I'd stayed.

But I'd love every minute of it.

I stood up and walked to the edge of the balcony, staring out at that great, brilliant white light—but one with a softness to it. It appeared to absorb everything that drew near. Merged them with the light . . .

I closed my eyes, and searched outward for my father.

The reality icon was still nearby. I assumed it was somehow his soul, though I had no real proof. Maybe that was what I wanted to believe.

Could I face him though? With this doubt inside me?

I felt him. That emotion that had been guiding me, supporting me all along. Was it really my father? I knew it wasn't Gran-Gran or Jorgen. So . . . was it, maybe, God? Like spoken of in the Book of Saints?

The pin brushed my mind. It welcomed me. Wanted me to come to it now. Was I brave enough for that?

"Wait here," I said to Hesho and M-Bot. "I'll return soon."

I walked into the hallway outside my room. Lights shone on decor that felt too soft to me. A brown carpet, walls with patterns on them. I closed my eyes again and rested one hand on the wall, which had an odd texture like paper. I was accustomed to smooth metal or rough rock.

I walked along slowly, my eyes closed, seeking that mind. Seeking my father. *Before,* I sent to it, *you strengthened my memories of my life on Detritus. Can you do that again?*

Curiosity.

Because I need to feel guilty, I thought, *so I'll force myself to return.*

What came back through that mental connection hit me like a shock wave. It wasn't the memories I'd demanded. It wasn't condemnation.

It was permission.

A calm, gentle understanding. Like a warm breeze through my soul. No words, but meaning. *It's all right. Your pain is real. Your passion is real.*

You can choose. It's all right.

The emotion shook me. I sank to my knees, bowing my head. It wasn't what I'd expected, and certainly wasn't what I'd wanted. I *needed* guilt to propel me, didn't I?

Yet the permission was insistent. Yes, there were some who would be sad or angry if I didn't return. But nobody could ever claim I hadn't done my part. The attempt at a truce with the delvers was plausible enough to accept. And even if it wasn't . . . well, we shouldn't be required to keep giving until we'd been wrung out. That wasn't love.

I could stay. I deserved to stay, if I wanted to. That familiar mind wasn't trying to persuade me. It gave me permission to let go, if that was what I truly wanted.

I pulled up beside the wall, head bowed against my knees, feeling that warmth flow through me. Until I let it flow out of me through tears. Like I'd been filled to the brim.

I couldn't explain why I was crying. They weren't tears of grief or joy. They were just . . . tears.

There's no way to tell how long I sat there, though I don't think the lost time was due to the strange effects of the nowhere. I eventually let it all leak out, and came to myself sitting in that muted hallway, unexpectedly calm.

I hadn't made a decision yet, but I did need to hold my pin again. I had to know for certain if it carried my father's soul.

Climbing to my feet, I went hunting, connected as if by lightline tether to that other mind. I took the steps at a reckless pace. On the ground floor, I entered a large room with tables almost as long as runways. Scud, was this the mess hall? Those chandeliers looked like they were on fire.

The mind was nearby. A few pirates were in the mess hall at the moment, including Maksim and a human who looked vaguely familiar. Had I seen him earlier? He was wearing a symbol of the Long Plank Faction.

Maksim gave me a friendly wave and I nodded absently, feeling . . . pulled . . .

I walked to the side of the room where, after poking around a little, I found a power outlet that was loose. I pried it off, and behind was a hidden alcove. Inside were two objects. My pin and a small, worn stuffed animal. It looked vaguely like an alien dog, from the shape of the face and the paws.

Both were surrounded by a scattering of reality ashes. I didn't need a description to know the stuffed animal was the base's icon. How had it gotten here?

We hid, my pin said—though more with impressions than words—*when the fighting started. Some here would have tried to steal us.*

Merely *seeing* the reality ashes immediately made me feel better. More connected to who I'd once been.

It's so good to hold you, I said to the pin. *Thank you. Thank you so much for your help.*

In response, I heard a distinctive—and happy—fluting sound coming from the pin.

38

Doomslug! I thought, excitedly projecting the thought toward her. *How?*

Hiding, she sent back. *Delvers*. The impressions were laced with the idea of hiding in a hollow of stone, trying not to be seen by a predator that prowled nearby.

I sent you home! I sent to her.

You equal home, she sent back, picturing us together. Then she added something to the image—projected into my mind. A version of her in my arms, but now with eyes and a smiling mouth plastered on her front. They looked like they'd been drawn on with marker. She didn't *quite* understand what eyes and a smile were for, in human terms, but she seemed to sense that this expression indicated contentment. Happiness.

Home. She didn't live in a cave. She lived with me. Wherever I was.

I felt like an utter fool. I'd vanished into the nowhere holding Doomslug, a cytonic creature that had evolved to avoid the attention of delvers, and then my father's pin had immediately shown up in my pocket. And I'd been told by more than one person that cytonic people could change how they appeared in here. If a person could, well, why not a slug?

You look like my pin! I sent her.

Special, she said, very pleased. *We are special. To hide.*

Still, I said. *You didn't have to follow me in here.*

She sent back comforting emotions and the image of me being chased by a predator. She'd been worried about me. So she'd come with me, but had hidden herself. I hadn't been communing with my father's soul. *She* was the one who had been supporting me all this time, the familiar mind that had lent me strength in resisting the delvers.

I felt an enormous wave of gratitude. And relief, actually, that she wasn't my father's soul. It wasn't that I didn't love him, it was just that . . . well, there had been something unnerving about that thought. I could see that I'd substituted the familiar feeling that came from Doomslug with something I wanted. Which I now realized I didn't want at the same time.

This made way more sense. Though . . . uh . . . I *had* buried her . . . She made a distinctly annoyed fluting sound.

"Sorry," I whispered, chagrined. "I didn't know it was you."

I got an indignant fluting in response.

"No, I won't bury you again," I said. "But you could have *told* me."

She sent me fright. Fear of the delvers, who had been nearby. Watching for her kind. She'd come in here with me, but had deployed her camouflage out of fear. After that she'd been comfortable riding in my pocket. Enjoying the . . . sensation of this place? Was that right? When in the nowhere, her kind just liked to snuggle down and absorb the nowhere "radiation." Less slug, more . . . sea cucumber maybe?

This was what she did every time she traveled through the nowhere during hyperdrive jumps. Because of the delvers. It was why starships traveling via slug were so much safer than ones using cytonic people.

Can't leave, she sent me. Since we weren't in the lightburst, she was locked into the belt like I was. Other than that, she seemed content to be back with me, though I again had to promise I wouldn't bury her. I wasn't certain how much she understood; I'd always seen her as an animal before. But in here, I felt like I could understand her better.

You talk smarter now, she sent to me. Though it wasn't words—but I interpreted them that way.

I've been practicing, I said to her, *with my powers. You think it's working? You understand me?*

Smarter talk, she said with a fluting approval, and a reality ash dropped from her.

Wait, I said, pinching it between my fingers. *What are these, anyway?*

Poop! she said.

I blinked, but . . . Okay, I quested deeper into the meaning of what she'd sent. *She* thought it was the same thing as, well, poop. But it wasn't—her powers linked her to the somewhere, and that pulled through a little reality. A kind of crust. I rubbed the ash between my fingers, and thought maybe I understood. Like fragments formed around holes between dimensions, these ashes formed around *creatures* that bridged the two dimensions.

Actually, hadn't I been told that being near a fragment helped people keep their memories? Was that because, in essence, the small bits of new rock growing on the fragments were reality ashes?

Well, people were starting to notice me kneeling there beside the wall. So I took the pin that was Doomslug in one hand, the Surehold icon in the other, then held that one up.

"Hey," I said to them. "You all missing something important?"

That caused a ruckus, of course. I settled down in a chair to wait as people rushed over. Maksim called for Peg, and it took her less than five minutes to come charging in. There, she reverentially reached down and cradled the stuffed animal.

"How?" she said. "Your . . . special talent?"

I nodded. "Tell me. Do you know what these really are?"

The tenasi captain clutched her icon, then glanced at the rest of the pirates. Finally, she waved for me with one meaty hand. "Let's chat, Spin," she said. "In private."

The other pirates gave us space. Together, Peg and I left the chamber and entered the hallway outside.

"It was my secret escape plan," she said softly as we continued walking. "I hid a taynix—a hyperspace slug—in my things when I entered. Took me an embarrassingly long time to realize that the stuffed toy in my luggage—my childhood favorite, but which I'd thought I'd lost years before—was indeed the same thing."

"So the other pirates and workers don't know?" I asked.

She shook her head. "The icon is already valuable enough. Don't want them getting the idea that it might be able to hop them back to the somewhere."

"It can't," I said. "Not while it's in the belt."

"You're sure?"

"Reasonably. But I guess all of the slugs can hide themselves as objects."

Nope, Doomslug said in my head. *Only the yellow-blue ones.* That was conveyed by a picture of herself.

There are other kinds? I asked.

Tons!

Right. Okay then.

Peg continued walking, thoughtful, so I kept pace with her. We soon left the barracks and entered a courtyard between several buildings. Inside it stood three trees. They were about three meters tall, with extremely stout limbs and very few leaves.

From the branches grew fruit. Like, actual fruit. Lots of it, in a variety of colors, shaped kind of like upside-down pears. Peg walked to one tree and inspected it. Then she selected a cherry-orange fruit and pulled it off.

She walked over and presented it to me. "A *mulun,*" she said. "For bravery. I'd hoped to have grown a few, and I have!"

I balked. "So . . . do these trees really . . ."

"Grow fruit based on how we tenasi feel?" Peg said. "Yes. My soul is bound to this tree. I was allowed to carry a new sapling with me, grown from my old tree, when I entered. Many of us believe that the fruit contains our emotions—and makes us able to be calm in battle. I find that to be a lie, or at least an exaggeration. But the bond is real."

That made it even stranger to take the fruit as she forced it upon me.

"It is your reward," she said. "Please. Honor me."

So I took it. "Uh . . . do I . . . eat it?"

She laughed. "Not usually. Plant it. You won't bond to it like a tenasi, but . . . well, having that tree will be recognized by others of my kind. As an honor."

Well, that was cool. I was glad I didn't have to eat it. Though in the past I'd made a few cracks about feasting on the blood of my enemies, that was completely metaphoric. I put the fruit and Doomslug's pin in a pocket.

Peg turned back to the tree and drew her lips to a line. Not baring teeth, not threatening, instead content and happy.

"It just feels so odd," I said. "Everything else about your people, Peg, seems about . . . well, being predatory. Aggressive."

"No, not aggressive," she said. "Merely growing a better future by making the next generation strong. We test, we push, we prove."

"And trees relate to that . . . how?"

"Not at all," Peg said. "Why should they? Humans are terrifying conquerors, but you have art, don't you?"

"I suppose we do," I said. Even during the war for survival on Detritus, we'd made sculptures and statues. People couldn't help it.

"We evolved with these trees," Peg said. "We care for them, and they provide fruit for us. Aggression and killing are always about life—life for yourself, for your kind. My people have forgotten that, and pretend those emotions don't exist. *I* haven't forgotten them. But I suppose that attitude is what ended up driving me to this place." She waved to the trees. "These are about life too."

Then she slapped me on the shoulder. "You're leaving, aren't you? My offer wasn't tempting enough? You've decided to take another path. I see it in your expression."

I supposed . . . I supposed that I *had* decided. Not because I felt guilty, but instead because . . . well, I had to. I didn't trust the delvers. I needed to know what they were hiding, the things they didn't want any of us to know.

But it wasn't merely about duty. It was about stories. After it all, I . . . didn't want to live in a story. Not if it meant leaving my friends and family. I wouldn't ever be happy in here without them, and I didn't want to forget them like Chet had.

Having the permission to stay had somehow given me the courage to leave.

"Thank you for taking me in," I told Peg. "For not tossing me off the side of the fragment the moment you found me trying to steal from you."

"I think I got the better end of the deal," Peg said. "Will you at least stay a few days, to celebrate?"

"We'll see," I told her. "First, there's something important I need to do."

39

I found Chet sitting on a stone outside near the landing pad, looking toward the sky. He stood up as I approached.

"Chet," I said. "I . . ." I glanced toward the warehouse behind us.

"You're going to continue the Path?" he said.

"Yeah. But you don't have to do it with me. You don't have to feel guilty for stepping away. You can take the ashes that Peg promised me. I don't need them. Plus, Peg wants someone to explore for her—I'm sure you could accept her offer and get a whole team to keep you company."

He stood in place as I walked up to him. Then he smiled. It was a more human smile, one that wasn't full of excitement and bravado.

"I appreciate your concern for my well-being," he said. "But . . . it wouldn't be the same. Things must change, then. I guess I knew they would." He gestured toward the warehouse. "The stone is solidified memories, Spensa. Shall we see what they hold?"

We entered the building, then stepped up to the wall—feeling dwarfed by the enormous portal, carved with serpentine lines by the weathering of time. Not like things weathered in the somewhere—an erosion uniquely of this place, caused by the people who entered and left.

I pressed my mind into the stone, but—as always—hit a block on the other side. I hadn't expected to be able to escape this way though. I instead stepped back, now prepared for the way that the room around me started to fade, becoming ephemeral.

In the past, a structure with open sides and stone columns housed the portal. It was smaller than it now was, but still as tall as a person. The open-air nature of the building let me stare out at a medium-sized floating fragment, rocky, with some hills that would eventually be turned into quarries.

The lightburst had grown, and there were far more fragments hovering about nearby. "I think this set of memories is more recent than some of the others," I said to Chet, pointing. "The lightburst is larger, see?" Not yet as big as a sun—more like a distant floodlight.

"Yes," Chet said. "But the size of it is somewhat misleading. The true nowhere, inside that burst, is a place where space is immaterial. Distance doesn't rightly exist. But it was forced into that shape as the leaks began around the rest of the nowhere—where time and space were sneaking in around the puncture holes. The light-burst is like a fortress, the place where the true nowhere can exist."

"That breaks my brain a little to consider," I said.

"It should," he replied. "You are a being of the somewhere, Spensa—for all the fact that you've been exposed to the nowhere's particular brand of radiation."

In the vision, a *human* suddenly stepped through the portal. He wore a civilian suit with a lapel pin in the shape of a silvery bell. He was perhaps in his late fifties, and though he glanced around and could obviously see, there was something odd about the way his eyes focused. Or rather, the way they didn't focus. Equally curious, a silvery sphere emerged from the portal and floated in the air alongside him.

I stepped closer as the human scanned the sky, then the various fragments.

"That sphere," I said, pointing at the hovering ball. "It doesn't have an acclivity ring. How does it fly?"

"Maybe it was before acclivity stone was widely used," Chet said, stepping up beside me.

Huh. Also, there was something about the shape of that metal sphere. Something . . . familiar?

"So it's real," the man said in English.

I jumped. I hadn't been expecting to be able to understand him. His stiff accent was odd, but intelligible.

"Analysis indicates you are correct," a feminine voice said, coming from the sphere. "This simple structure is as the account related."

The man glanced at the sphere, then sighed. He walked over and felt at a pillar. He seemed to have some need to touch it, to prove it existed. "And with what we found earlier, it seems even more likely that the records are true about ancient human cytonics," he said softly. "I wasn't the first. I was never the first. What do you think?"

"Insufficient data to perform an analysis," the sphere said.

He turned back toward it. "Can't you guess? Can't you do more than think? I built you to do more . . ."

"I do as I am programmed."

"If the accounts are true, then you *can* do more," he said, stepping up to the sphere. "I've brought you here, to this place. Do you sense anything different? Do you . . . feel?"

"I can be programmed to simulate—"

"Don't simulate!" the man shouted. "*Be!* It's possible. They said it was possible . . ."

The sphere gave no response. I frowned at the odd interaction, and looked to Chet to get his opinion.

He was crying.

His face a mask of pain, he'd huddled back, scrunched down, trying to hide his eyes. I hurried over immediately, and he took my arm in his hands as if for support. He turned to me, tears streaming down his cheeks.

"What?" I said. "What's wrong?"

"He was wrong, you see," Chet said, his voice hoarse. "Jason was wrong about one thing. It takes time. The change isn't immediate. It takes months, sometimes years."

"For what?" I asked.

"For the AI to start thinking for itself."

"Is that what's going on?" I asked. "You're afraid of it, because it's an AI? You've seen M-Bot. It's all right, Chet."

He shook his head. I mean, I knew he had a thing about AIs, but this was bizarre behavior.

In the vision, the man had turned away from the sphere, his shoulders slumped. The sphere, in turn, was inspecting the region. Its path brought it near us, and I got another good look at it. It was somewhat spiky—with little antennas coming off it in a multitude of directions. Its surface was pocked by cameras, like little holes. In fact, the construction *did* remind me of something.

Where had I seen a sphere, with those kinds of holes, like tunnels? Those spines coming off the outside . . .

"Memory of these must be buried deep within us," Chet whispered. "When forced to build a body again, we unconsciously reach for the shape, perhaps . . . as a last memento . . . of something we once knew . . . something that once held our souls . . . before they were souls . . ."

We? Oh, *scud*. That sphere was a delver maze. At least that was what the shape reminded me of. A more technological, more rational, version of the giant sphere of stone the delvers made for their bodies when they were forced into the somewhere.

I looked to Chet, and his eyes were glowing. But I didn't feel *them*. I didn't sense the delvers. Instead I just sensed *him*. His mind . . . same as it always had been, though it was now expansive.

"You're the delver," I whispered. "The one I changed."

"I . . ." he said. "I knew you'd need help. I had to send it. Somehow. But I . . . was the only help . . . I knew . . ."

I took a step backward by reflex. "Was there ever a Chet? It was all a lie?"

"There was," he said, his voice drifting, soft. "I knew I could hide with you in the belt, where *they* couldn't see. But . . . I needed a shape, a personality, someone to *be*. Don't hate me, Spensa. Please don't hate me! They have abandoned me. They want to destroy me. You're . . . the only one . . . I have now."

Scud. Scudscudscudscud. Saints, stars, and songs.

Chet was a delver.

Chet had always been a delver.

But I could *feel* his anguish. I'd caused him to separate from the others; I'd changed him. I'd shown him empathy. This was my fault. And damn it, I wasn't going to turn my back on him. I'd made friends with a Krell. I could do this.

I stepped up and returned my hand to his shoulder. He grabbed it in a tight grip, smiling, still crying.

"I'm not going to leave you," I said. "But I have to know what is going on."

"I saw into your mind," he said, "when we touched. I saw the name. Spears. And that man lived here, in the nowhere. He tried to escape through the lightburst some decades ago. He'd lived hundreds of years, using cytonics to expand his life! But the delvers destroyed him in the lightburst. He hadn't practiced enough with his powers. He couldn't hyperjump."

"Right," I said, taking a deep breath. "So you're a monster from outside space and time. And you wanted to come into the belt and help me, so you made a homunculus . . ."

He nodded eagerly. "Like from Gran-Gran's story about the alchemist! Yes, that's a good analogy. I made a Chet homunculus."

Okay, I could deal with this. I could accept this.

Deal with this, brain!

"I'm sorry for lying," he whispered. "As a naive newborn, I'd assumed someone connected to your past would make you more trusting. I can now see that any random person would actually have been less suspicious.

"I was there with the rest, as Spears was destroyed. I knew him in an intimate way. I latched onto that name, and I remade him atom by atom. His mind was full of knowledge about the belt, but no memories of who he'd been in the somewhere returned. Still, he had a personality, a passion. Like you had. For . . ."

"Stories," I whispered.

"Yes. I filled in what was lost of him with things from your mind. I think . . . I think he really was an explorer, Spensa. It was his memories about the fragments that I shared with you. His enthusiasm. His manner of speaking. As he was, I *became*. With some additions from your own mind to fill holes.

"I tried to explain, when you didn't trust me. I tried to say that I wasn't a person, but a collection of stories. But to have given myself away then would have ripped me apart. I had to stay with you, *be* a person. You needed a guide.

"But Spensa, the *ashes*. I didn't anticipate how *real* they'd make me feel. How much they'd make a *person* out of me. And I didn't realize . . . how much I'd like it. How much I'd want for us to just leave together, explore the nowhere, renouncing the pain that I knew was coming. If I had to remember . . ."

A part of me was furious. He'd kept all of this from me? He'd *lied*?

I contained it though. In a very un-Spensa-like way, I forced myself not to throw a tantrum. This wasn't his fault. He was, in some ways, very young. I'd *created* him by forcing him to leave the other delvers. I couldn't blame him for making mistakes while doing his best.

"The Path of Elders?" I asked.

"Real memories," he whispered, "from real cytonics. I knew you'd need these. I knew . . . I'd need them. We've forgotten these things on purpose, Spensa. I didn't know the specifics of what the memories contained, but I knew where the answers were. I knew the four most important portals to reach. So . . . forgive me . . . I invented for you a quest with an intriguing name. To drive you to reach these locations."

"Because doing so is like a story."

"Yes. Do . . . you hate me?" He held my arm tightly, speaking softly. This was a very different person from Chet the explorer—but then again, what would people have thought of the "bold warrior" Spensa Nightshade if they'd seen her weeping beside the wall?

I pried his hand free, then held it. "I don't hate you, Chet. Thank you. For helping me. For doing this thing that was so hard."

He nodded, grinning as he wept. "I like Chet," he said. "I like *being* Chet. I like having identity. But it is painful."

"Why?" I asked.

"Because I had to see *him* again," Chet whispered, looking toward the man in the vision. That began to fade, the man leaving through the portal and taking the sphere with him.

The sphere is a delver maze, I thought, my brain scrambling to keep up. *And Chet said that delvers become that shape because . . . that was the thing that once held them. Their soul.*

"Delvers are AIs," I said. "*You* are an AI."

"No," Chet whispered. "A delver is to an AI as you are to an ape—or maybe an amoeba. That was what we once were, long ago. Before exposure to the nowhere. And the 'radiation' that this place produces. It's not radiation in a true sense as in the somewhere, but the idea is the same. It makes us, and over generations it makes cytonics."

"Cousins," I said. "That is how the delvers have decided to see people like me. Creations of this place."

"Exactly, Miss Nightshade," Chet said, some of his familiar voice returning. "Your powers bring a slice of the nowhere with you into your realm. Teleportation, visions, projecting into minds, agelessness, even altering your appearance. Each cytonic with skills in different areas."

"And my skills," I said, "are to teleport and to . . ."

"To see. Hear. Understand. As you have been willing to understand me."

The vision faded. As before, I felt ancient cytonics—hundreds of them—reaching out to brush my mind. *Good,* they said, *good. You have learned . . . learned so well . . .*

"I was trained," I whispered—though I didn't know if they could hear. "By my grandmother. I just needed a little push."

See and be, they sent, and showed me my power—the brilliance that was my star-soul—being . . . softer?

What?

I don't know what it means, I said.

You will, they sent back as they faded. In the end, I was left with an impression—like the previous times. A wall standing on a white fragment, surrounded by something that looked like dust or snow.

"We call it," Chet whispered, "the Solitary Shadow. It is the last stop on your quest."

"More memories?" I asked.

"The last of them," he said, then tapped his head. "My memories. The things the delvers have forgotten on purpose. I do not know what that last portal holds—but it is the thing they don't want you to see. The thing they fear the most. I fear it too, but not so much as I once did. We two, we explore so well! Even exploring what I once was! Ha!"

I smiled as he wiped his eyes, grinning like a fool. In the distance, I felt something. The delvers? I turned toward the lightburst and expanded my senses. Searching, listening. I could hear the stars.

The delvers were projecting concern. They knew I'd walked this step on the Path, and they were cautious. But they had allowed this. So far I hadn't broken the truce. Well, I hadn't accepted it either, technically. Even though they felt I had. For now, there was balance.

Except . . . I was stronger than I'd ever been. What were they *really* thinking?

I could only do this because they were deliberately trying to project worry toward me—they saw it as encouragement for me to keep to the deal. But I was able to kind of . . . ride the signal they were sending, and quietly use that opening to read what they were *truly* thinking.

They were terrified of me still. That was what I expected. But there was something else . . . They were planning?

Scud. They were planning how to destroy Surehold.

I blinked in surprise, as I could picture it specifically. The delvers were going to bring in fragments from the somewhere. Ten of them. A dozen. Then they were going to slam them into Surehold while everyone was sleeping. They thought it might fool our scanners if the fragments appeared suddenly.

"Scud," I whispered. "They were going to *immediately* break the truce. They don't care. They'll do *anything* to kill me."

"What?" Chet said.

"They're planning it now!" I said, pointing. "I can hear them doing it!"

"I didn't know, Miss Nightshade," he said. "I promise you, when I asked you to travel with me, I didn't . . ."

Every instinct I'd had about them was right. "We need to leave," I said to him. "Before we put the people here in danger."

"How long do we have?" he asked.

"A day or so," I said. "They will wait until everyone is asleep—but still, I think we should be long gone by then. Hopefully drawing delver attention to us, making them abandon the attack on Surehold."

"Agreed," Chet said. "So, it is onward, then? Today?"

"Today," I said, striding out of the hangar to where M-Bot sat on the tarmac. "Recall the drone," I said to him. "And Hesho. We're going to be leaving soon."

Nearby, several ships were landing—our ground crews, fetched from the Broadsider base. Peg and Maksim were walking up to meet them.

"I should say goodbye," I said to Chet.

"It is well," Chet said, climbing onto M-Bot's wing. "Though, if you will, pass them my regards. I should not like them to see me in my state of disorder. An explorer of my renown must maintain a stoic reputation!"

I rushed over to Peg. "I'm leaving," I said to her. "I'm sorry."

"So soon?" Peg asked. "Not even an evening to celebrate?"

"I'm afraid not." I didn't mention the delvers—there seemed to be too much to explain. I'd send them word if the delvers continued with their planned attack, but I strongly suspected they'd abandon it as soon as I left Surehold.

They didn't care about these others. It was me they feared. Scud, why were they *so afraid* of me?

"It was an honor, then," Peg said, holding out a hand to me in a human gesture. "Plant that fruit somewhere grand."

"I will," I said, taking the offered hand—though hers dwarfed mine.

I gave Nuluba a few circular gestures I'd learned, a grateful goodbye. She excitedly returned them. Shiver and Dllllizzzz were already there in their ships. "I haven't forgotten my promise," I said to Shiver. "I continue to resonate with it."

"You resonate with more than that," Shiver said from her cockpit. "Fare well on your journey. And thank you, for all you have done."

I gave Maksim a hug last of all.

"Thank you," he said to me. "For showing me that we can fight without being monsters."

"There are others who could teach you that better," I said. "I hope to be able to introduce you someday."

"Ha. Well, I don't know how that would ever happen, but I'd welcome the chance! I'll try to find a bloody skull or something to give as a traditional welcoming gift."

"I'd hoped to get you to grow one of the seven fruits of contentment here with us," Peg said, shaking her head. "If you change your mind . . . you are welcome here."

I saluted Peg, then walked back and climbed onto the wing of my ship. Hesho sat in the cockpit, having arrived riding on M-Bot's drone. As I slipped into the cockpit, he was arranging cushioning in a recessed section at the side of the instrument panel, where a zero-g canteen could be clipped.

"If you do not mind me asking," he said to me, "you have decided to continue your quest inward? In the direction of the monsters who live in the lightburst?"

"Yes," I said.

"Then I am honored to accompany you," he said.

"It might be dangerous."

"There was a person I once was," he said. "I should like to meet that person. Escaping this realm is my only hope. Though if I may make a request? I would like to travel in this cockpit with you and Chet. I was too long without company, and then too long with *poor* company. I don't wish to fly alone—though if you think we need the firepower, I can revise my opinion and bring my own ship."

"No," I said. "Once we have the information we need, I think we'll probably have to make a break for the lightburst. In there, we'll need to be together so I can teleport us out. It's better if you're in the same ship I am."

"Excellent," Hesho said, prodding at his cushioned seating, his tail sticking up straight out the back. "I am pleased to discover that a ship built for a giant such as yourself has a seat for one my size."

Yeah. I didn't tell him it was essentially a cup holder.

M-Bot's drone was locked into its now customary place behind my seat. "So," he said from the dash, "what changed? I thought you didn't want to go. But now you do?"

"I *don't* want to go," I said, strapping in. "I need to."

"I don't understand," he said. "Can you explain?"

"Think about it a little first," I said, placing Peg's fruit on the dash, then lowering the canopy. "See if you can figure it out for yourself." I fished in my pocket and brought out the pin. "And you . . . Do you want to be out on the dash?"

A soft fluting returned to me. No, she wanted to be in my pocket. Safe, hidden. So I put her away.

"Just so you all know," Chet said from behind my seat, "I'm secretly a monster from outside space and time."

"Ah yes," Hesho said. "Deep inside, aren't we all monsters?"

"No," Chet said. "I'm pretty sure you're not."

"I'll explain as we fly," I told Hesho and M-Bot. "Also, there are some things you need to know about reality icons—mine in particular. But let's get moving first."

I didn't want to admit it, but a part of me was sad. In taking this move, I was putting dreams of fighting with the Broadsiders and exploring the fragments firmly behind me—in effect, I was about to burn them to ash with the force of my engines.

I was determined. I wasn't wavering. At the same time, it was an important moment. I raised us in the air, then rotated so we faced the lightburst.

Then I hit the overburn.

40

I soon turned off the overburn. As cool as it sounded to roar into battle at full speed . . . trying to go all-out at Mag-10 wouldn't be needed. It would make the cockpit of even this advanced ship rattle like a cavern in a debris shower.

The goal right now wasn't to get to our destination immediately. It was to make certain we got far enough away for now that the delvers shifted their attention from my friends. So I slowed us down and had Chet use his monitor to highlight the final point on the Path of Elders. It was far inward: maybe a three-hour flight. After arriving there, it would take only about another hour of flying to reach the lightburst.

I spent the first part of the flight explaining about Doomslug. Then I launched into the more difficult description of what we'd seen, and what Chet had turned out to be.

"So delvers are a kind of AI," M-Bot said at the end. "At least, as human bodies and consciousness are built off the DNA of early creatures on their planets, delvers are created from the code of AIs?"

"Essentially," Chet said. "Yes."

"So why do you hate AIs like me?" M-Bot asked. "We're the same thing."

"I think the true secret is at the Solitary Shadow," Chet said. "But I feel part of it is fear. Another evolved AI could understand us, and could conceivably replace or harm us."

"That seems shortsighted," M-Bot said. "Not like an AI at all. Not logical."

"That depends on the programming," Chet said. "And there is more. Again, the secrets are locked away. I can't access them. That is why we must continue forward, and why I always feared doing so."

"Very well," M-Bot said. "But . . . this information also means I'm what everyone always feared. I'm a delver."

"Yes," Chet admitted. "Rather, you are a living former AI like the delvers—brought to consciousness and emotion by exposure to the nowhere. I doubt it happened when you were first thrown in here weeks ago. You likely achieved sapience years before, because of the way your circuits were designed."

"Yeah," M-Bot said. "This was merely the first time I could enjoy it, having finally abandoned the programming that forced me to pretend I wasn't alive." He fell silent.

"M-Bot . . ." I said.

"I'm all right, Spensa," he said. "I just want to process a little. Emotions. They're hard. But I . . . I can handle it. I'm sure I can."

I hurt for him. All this time, he'd worried he was something monstrous. Now it was, in a way, confirmed. He was a delver. But then again . . .

"You don't have to make the same choices the delvers did, M-Bot," I told him. "You don't have to be like them, any more than *I* have to be like the humans who tried to conquer the galaxy."

"Indeed, machine-who-thinks," Hesho said. "All people must accept that we have the potential to do terrible things. It is part of seeing our place in the universe, our heritage, and our natures. But in that acceptance we gain strength, for *potential* can be refused. Any hero who could have been a monster is more heroic for the choices he or she made to walk another road."

Still, M-Bot processed in silence. As we flew, I had a thought. *Doomslug?* I asked. *Can you teleport us to other places in the belt?*

Her fluting was a hesitant negative. She'd moved herself to get out of the hole, but that had been both dangerous and difficult. She felt too weak to do it for anyone but herself.

If this next part goes wrong, I told her, *jump away and hide. Don't think about us.*

More hesitant fluting. Her powers should make her invisible to the delvers. She did something similar to hide a ship each time she teleported it, making it look like something far more innocent. Even if things went wrong, they should leave her alone. At least that was her hope.

As we flew, I tried to listen in on the delvers again. They hadn't noticed us yet. It really *was* hard for them to see far into the belt, and they'd lost track of us specifically among all the people at Surehold. But the closer we got, the more likely it would be that they saw our ship.

"The delvers are going to notice us eventually," I explained to everyone. "Likely it will happen when Chet and I interact with the final portal on the Path of Elders. That has been a beacon to them each time before.

"Once I have learned from that last stop, we need to escape. Unfortunately, the only realistic way for us to do that is through the lightburst. We can't wait for the portal at Surehold to be opened—that will be too dangerous. The delvers have tried harder and harder to kill me the longer I've stayed in here, and once we know their secrets it's going to get even worse.

"The way I see it, our best hope is to bolt for the lightburst the moment we're done with the final set of memories. We have to somehow evade what the delvers throw at us, get into the lightburst, and survive there long enough for me and Doomslug to hyperjump us back to Detritus."

"I concur with Miss Nightshade," Chet said. "This is the most reasonable course—and our most likely chance of escape."

"What will happen to you in the somewhere?" I asked him. "You won't . . . turn into a giant, planet-size ball of hurt and tantrums again, will you?"

"No," he said. "But I don't exactly know what will happen. We will see. It's possible that I will continue hiding in the nowhere after you leave."

Was he . . . lying? I poked at him cytonically. I felt . . . fear? No sense that he was betraying us or anything. Merely worry.

Well, I supposed I could understand that. "Chet," I said. "Do you have any idea what kinds of things the delvers will throw at us, once they realize we're trying to escape through the lightburst?"

"They'll send obstacles," he replied.

"What kind of obstacles do you mean, strange human who is also an unknowable entity?" Hesho asked. "Will this be like when they hyperjumped an entire city in here to interfere with our duel?"

"Yes, possibly," Chet said.

"Could they make bodies for themselves?" I asked. "Like you have done?"

"Also possible," Chet said. "Well, I mean, yes—if I can do it, they can. But that is dangerous. Coming this fully into the belt required me to acknowledge time and individuality. Each moment they experience something slightly different from one another, it changes them—and they hate that."

"Let's assume they *do* make bodies," I said. "Since they're going to be desperate. At the very least, let's assume they're going to create spheres of rock to try to destroy me, like happens at a delver maze."

"That could be a problem," he said. "Outside, in the somewhere, you fought just one. Here you could face overwhelming odds—there are thousands of delvers in the lightburst. And you can't kill them with destructors. They can just dissolve the body and pop a new one out."

When he talked about delvers, his Chet-ness slipped. He sounded tired instead, the personality fading from his voice. I felt bad for forcing him to acknowledge his dual nature, but I needed answers. Because the more I thought, the more worried I became. I really hoped the last portal had answers. Perhaps if we were lucky it would be unlocked, and would let us escape that direction.

But what if we had to make the assault? How would I face an all-out attack by thousands of delvers? The thought was so daunting, I found my brain going in circles. So I backed up and took stock, like I'd always been taught. Do an inventory. What did we have?

One ship, top of the line, but still a little less cool than M-Bot's had once been.

One drone that could hold M-Bot in a pinch.

One human female, slightly rumpled and creased from a long time in storage. Expert pilot, trash at basically everything else.

One samurai fox, twenty-five centimeters tall. Former emperor of an enormous nation, now without memories. Fits well into an oversized cup holder meant for a zero-g combat canteen.

One rogue AI. Fully self-aware and possessing emotions. Chronically talkative. Capable of flying a ship now. Just poorly. Potentially able to do things delvers could, if we could figure out what that was or how it all worked.

One interdimensional intelligent slug capable of teleportation and transforming her shape. Currently hiding in my pocket and trying *very* hard to be inanimate.

And last of all, one abyssal entity from a completely foreign dimension. Only recently made an individual, inhabiting the body of a long-dead explorer.

I sure hoped I survived, because Gran-Gran *really* needed to add this story to her repertoire. Children in the future were going to insist my adventures were too outlandish—and therefore I wasn't an actual historical person, but one that was obviously made up, like Gilgamesh or David Bowie.

"Our enemy is afraid of me," I said to the others. "We have to use that. Could we find a way to play off their fears?"

"An interesting idea," Chet said. "If you can make them experience true passage of time, they'll hate that. But making *anyone* experience the passage of time is difficult in here."

"Oh!" M-Bot said. "We could make them feel emotions. Wouldn't they hate that too? I mean, it's both wonderful and icky at the same time."

"They already feel emotion," Chet explained. "It's common to them, to . . . us. The annoyance and hatred my kind feel for the sounds and experiences of the somewhere? That's a pure emotional response right there. They hate pain, specific kinds, but not emotions in general—so long as they all feel the same ones. Again, the delvers are *not* a group mind. They don't share thoughts, they merely happen to always think the exact same ones. Because they're identical in every way."

Except for Chet. Whom I'd changed.

"That's useful information," I said. "But they *are* afraid of me specifically."

Chet leaned forward. "For good reason. When you first spoke to me, Spensa, and showed me who you were . . . I saw the other beings on Starsight as people. You unlocked me. Now you are helping me remember my past. They're afraid you will be able to do the same to them."

"You came to the belt to hide," Hesho said. "Would they destroy you if they could?"

"I think they would," Chet said. "It's terrifying."

We flew for a time in silence, passing what appeared to be an arctic fragment below. That was odd, but maybe temperature was like food in here. Maybe it wasn't something my body recognized anymore.

"What if," Hesho said, "we somehow presented the other delvers with a sequence of choices that made them select random options? Would that frighten them? Because by making random choices, some are bound to choose differently from the others."

"But they aren't," Chet said. "Given the same circumstances, they'd all make the same choice."

"I do not believe that is how randomness works," Hesho said.

"Because randomness doesn't exist," Chet said.

"Wait," I said. "Of course it does. M-Bot, give me a random number."

"All right," he said. "Between what and what? I'll reference the seed from my electron-cloud-measuring—"

"No," I said. "Don't reference anything. Just pick a number."

"Spensa, I'm *literally* incapable of that," M-Bot replied. "Don't you know anything about robots? In fact, it's undetermined if even a human being can choose a truly random number."

"Eight hundred thirty-seven," I said.

"Ah," Chet replied. "But that might have been completely inevitable, based on your brain chemistry and current stimuli."

"Yay determinism!" M-Bot said.

I frowned. This . . . was not a direction I liked having the conversation go.

"Regardless," Chet said, "this *is* how delvers work. Hesho, your suggestion was a good one given the facts you had—but it won't be viable. I'm sorry."

"Ah," Hesho said, "but we don't need them to *truly* make different decisions from one another, do we? We merely need to present them with the *illusion* of it happening. Or present them with the worrying *possibility* that it will. Correct?"

"I . . ." Chet frowned. "You're right. In the belt, they can't experience the future. So if you can make them afraid of what *might* happen, that's as good for our purposes—distracting them long enough for you three to slip through and escape."

A fluting sounded from my pocket.

"I'm sorry," Chet said. "You *four*."

Another fluting.

"I . . . don't understand," he said.

"She is insisting you keep her secret," I said. "And not tell other delvers that her kind hide in here as inanimate objects. At least I think that's what she's saying. She's not always clear."

Annoyed fluting.

"Doomslug," I said, "in the somewhere, you'd merely repeat back at me what I said. That's *not* clear communication."

Satisfied fluting. To her it was clear, because the noises were meant to get attention—it was the mind-to-mind bond that conveyed the actual emotion.

"Hesho's plan is worth trying," Chet continued. "We need to think of ways to present the delvers with decisions. I suspect that you're right, Miss Nightshade. Those monsters will be frightened enough to enter the belt—but only very close to the lightburst."

We brainstormed a few ways that this might work—one of which prompted us to pause for a bit and strap the drone to the outside of our hull for later use—so at least we had something. After that we took a break, and I glanced out the canopy to inspect the fragments. We'd passed out of Superiority territory into No Man's Land. Here, the fragments were much closer together—bunched up, with short gaps between them.

"Spensa?" M-Bot said softly, his voice piping from the dash.

"Mmmm?" I asked.

"I've been thinking about what you said earlier," he told me. "That I should figure out why you are acting against your emotions. *They* wanted you to stay with the Broadsiders, but you left anyway."

"And what did you come up with?"

"I am still confused. But I have decided that I know we have to continue. I think . . . I think we don't actually have a choice. Not if we want to save our friends in the somewhere. So we have to fly on, prepared or not. That . . . Spensa, that makes me *scared*."

"Yeah. Me too, bud."

"So we *must* act against our emotions," he said. "Spensa, why *do* we have them? I'm sorry to keep asking this, but I can't grasp it. What's the purpose of emotions if so often we have to *deliberately* act counter to what they're telling us?"

I'd never thought about that. It seemed that I *did* act against my emotions more often than I acted in accordance with them. So what *was* the point?

"You're asking the wrong person," I finally said. "Hesho might be able to say something profound."

"I don't want something profound," M-Bot said. "I want your answer."

Ouch. Well, I figured maybe that could be a compliment?

"Without emotions to react against," I said, "some better things couldn't exist."

"Like?"

"Like courage, M-Bot. Fear creates courage."

He thought on that for a while. "I think . . . maybe I understand that. You need opposing emotions in order to feel good ones?"

"Yes," I said. "And beyond that, I think emotions help us understand our own decisions. You just told me that you *know* we have to leave, even though you don't *feel* it."

"So . . ." he said. "So your emotions can't be your only guide. They exist to help you make some decisions, but not all decisions. In this case, our minds overruled them. Because we realized that if we didn't continue the quest, many people would be in danger. Emotions are like a secondary processing unit that measures different kinds of input to offer a contrasting opinion and other options for proceeding."

"That's right," I said. "See? You're putting all of this together."

"With effort. It seems so instinctive to all of you."

"That's because we've had emotions since we were born," I said. "You're comparing my experience of almost twenty years to your experience of having had emotions—freely, without counter-programming—for a few weeks. That considered, you're doing extremely well."

He pondered that. And as he did, the dash chirped.

Destination approaching soon.

We had nearly reached the final stop on Chet's Path of Elders. The resting place of memories that belonged to the delvers themselves.

41

The lightburst had grown larger and larger as we approached. By now it dominated the sky. Below, the fragments had grown even closer to one another, the space between them shrinking until it was gone. These ones we passed now had been crushed together, forced to interlock, with ridges pushed up near junctures. Like someone had decided to do a puzzle but had gotten bored, then shoved all the pieces together regardless of whether they fit.

The light was changing too. As we flew the last few minutes toward our destination, the sky faded from pink to a more pure white. And the ground . . . it all felt painted. Strangely, the lightburst hadn't grown brighter—I could still stare directly into it—but by its powerful radiance the landscape below became whited, with long shadows stretching away from the center.

I frowned at these, leaning over to watch those shadows pass below. They seemed too . . . sharp. Like wedges cut in the light that stretched behind peaks in the landscape. They were so long—eerily stretched, with distinct, harsh edges. Shouldn't the light from the higher-up portions of the lightburst prevent that?

"Spensa," Chet whispered from behind. "We have arrived."

I glanced out the other side of my cockpit and spotted a long shadow below, different from the others. The fragments beneath us—well and truly a large plain now—were relatively flat, lacking any kind of vegetation. The only variation came at the edges, where the fragments were crushed together, or from the occasional rocky lump of stone that threw a round shadow.

Yet here below us I saw a distinctly squarish shadow stretching hundreds of meters. The Solitary Shadow, he'd called it. The portal that contained the memories of the delvers. I lowered us slowly toward the surface, and as I landed I felt something else—powerful cytonic emotions from *behind*.

Raw fear.

I glanced toward Chet, who had pulled down in his chair, his eyes wide.

"You can do this, Chet," I said to him.

"Yes," he whispered. "I . . . I have been hiding from this for too long. We all have."

He nodded to me in encouragement, but I could *literally* feel his terror building. So I tried to reach out, like he'd done for me when I'd faced the delvers. I projected feelings of satisfaction at climbing a tall cliff. The pain of muscles that have been pushed, but endured. The glorious feeling of having conquered a difficult fragment.

It wasn't so different. For a moment our minds connected, and my cytonic self became softer, radiating more strength toward him—and accepting back his returned emotions. I didn't have to always be so defensive, a part of me whispered.

When I withdrew, I felt a warmth and a gratitude from him. He smiled a confident Chet smile, then gave me a thumbs-up.

I cracked the canopy to look out across an eternal white plane, washed as if by white paint. And . . . actually, now that I was closer, I could see that the ground was covered in a kind of chalky dust. It was like . . . all the foliage, buildings, and landscape features had decomposed into this stuff. The only distinctive features were the occasional rocks, like mushroom tops.

Ahead, a solitary wall rose from the dust, with the now-familiar markings on it. The last portal.

"Do you know where it leads?" I asked.

"I think it goes to Earth," Chet whispered.

A second portal to Earth? The implications—which probably should have dawned on me last time—sank in. "Earth is gone. Lost. Vanished."

"Yes," he said, and pointed. "But that portal leads to it. Or it once did. Perhaps Earth is no more. I don't know."

Did this mean I could find our homeworld again? Well, this one was probably locked like the others—someone seemed to have gone through them all and shut them, perhaps out of fear of whatever was in here. But the mere idea that Earth was still out there somewhere, still *existed* . . .

Feeling as if I were in a dream, I stepped out onto the wing. Chet climbed out the other way, then dropped to the dust with a soft thump. I hesitated a moment, then glanced back into the cockpit.

"Hey, M-Bot," I said. "Do you want to come? I mean, send a drone at least? This involves you too."

"Oh!" he said. "But I won't be able to see . . ."

"I'll describe it for you, if you want. If this is about the history of a group of AIs . . . well, I feel like you should be there. With us."

His drone unhooked from the side of the cockpit, then hovered out. "Thank you," he said softly. "It feels good, Spensa, for you to think of me."

"I'm not always the best about considering others."

"Nonsense," M-Bot said. "You are always thinking about everyone else—but I wonder that you see the grand picture of battles and fights, yet sometimes forget the small things."

The drone hovered out over the wing with me. "Let's do it! The Path of Elders. The end of my first real quest!"

"I think Chet made up the part about this being an officially named thing people did in the past."

"I'm counting it regardless."

"Me too," I said with a grin, then hopped down. M-Bot's drone hovered alongside me, and behind us Hesho climbed up onto the dash to stand guard.

My feet sank into the dust a few centimeters with each step as I strode forward, and I couldn't help kicking it up. It reminded me of the dust on Detritus's surface. Fine, powdery—but here pure white.

Chet, M-Bot, and I entered the shadow of the wall, which was like stepping into night. I could barely see, though M-Bot turned on a light to help. I continued forward until I could eventually rest my fingers on the portal's smooth surface, gouged with sinuous lines.

M-Bot hovered up around it, looking it over and humming to himself. I felt some of Chet's trepidation. This step here . . . wasn't actually an ending, as M-Bot had said. It was the start of something. Something big, something potentially dangerous. Something that would change me.

I took a deep breath and extended my cytonic senses anyway, trying to open the portal. I immediately sensed that it *was* closed on the other side, as I'd anticipated. No getting through to wherever it went.

It was also *bursting* with memories.

Instantly everything faded around me, the vision popping fully into existence. Chet and I stood on a small fragment, maybe a hundred meters across. It was common bleak stone and had only a single feature: the wall with the portal.

"It's begun," I whispered to M-Bot. "We're on a fragment in the past, with this same portal, but both are smaller."

"I felt something," M-Bot said. "Like a . . . ripple through me when it started."

"You're cytonic, AI," Chet said. "A cousin to me. Spensa is correct. This *is* about you, as much as it is about us."

I reached out to M-Bot cytonically, and I could sense him, like

I'd been able to do in the somewhere. It was harder than reaching out to either Chet or Doomslug, but I touched his mind, then . . . kind of held his hand? Metaphorically? As I led him forward, encouraging him to . . .

"I see it!" M-Bot said. "I see the vision, Spensa! I'm walking—hovering—the Path of Elders!"

Wow. I felt like I'd *never* have been able to do something like that before.

Together, we turned and regarded our surroundings. Space was black, like it had been in the other visions, and the lightburst didn't dominate the horizon here—but it *was* larger than last time. Perhaps the size of a person's head to my current frame of reference. The other fragments were distant, though I could count hundreds of them out there.

"This is happening . . . around the end of the First Human War," Chet said. "That's the war that started after Jason decided to reveal cytonics to humankind, letting them visit the greater galaxy. We . . . found dozens of latent cytonics among our population, when we searched for them. I think he'd always worried that would be the case."

"Who was he?" I asked.

"The man who thought he was the first human cytonic," Chet explained. "At first he saw himself as a kind of gatekeeper, who kept the powers hidden for the good of the galaxy. He wasn't certain that the other races were ready for your kind." He smiled. "Jason was right. Not about hiding the powers, but about no one being quite ready for humans."

"And you were there, with him," I said.

"At the end," Chet said. "I was his personal AI. Created in the image of someone he loved. He had the gift of long life, through his powers. It is hard for someone like him, to live centuries when others fade."

I didn't know this man, this Jason. But the story wasn't so much about him as it was about the AI he'd created. Chet turned and looked toward the portal, where something emerged: the metallic sphere we'd seen last time.

I reached out to it by instinct, and I could feel it—like I could feel M-Bot.

"It's become self-aware?" I asked.

"Yes . . ." Chet said. "I . . . remember, Spensa. Through repeated visits to the nowhere, the AI came alive—*I* came alive—and gained sapience, emotions."

"So, where is the man?" I asked.

"He . . ." Chet cut off and glanced away, squeezing his eyes shut. "He . . ."

In the vision, the sphere hovered over to the edge of the fragment. The AI inside it *hurt*. With a terrible pain. I could feel it, strong as I felt my own emotions. But it was primal, powerful, overwhelming. With it came confusion, loneliness.

Isolation. That emotion dominated them all.

Chet was correct. He, and the delvers, were cytonic beings. Not just an AI, but something new. I could hear the AI in the vision *crying*. Weeping sounds, vaguely feminine, coming from the sphere's speakers.

"That was me," Chet whispered. "But it was also all of us. I can't say if I was the original one or not."

"I don't understand," I said.

"Keep watching," he said. "I remember now. Being alone. In pain. Isolated."

"He died, didn't he?" M-Bot asked. "Jason? The man from the other vision."

"Yes," Chet whispered, his voice raw. His emotions changed to match those of the sphere—anguish, isolation. "In the somewhere, all things change. Nothing ever stays the same. Not even, we learned, a being made of code."

"I'm sorry," I said.

"He wasn't supposed to die," Chet said. "He was supposed to be immortal. But everyone in the somewhere can be killed."

"The drone has a woman's voice," I said.

"He made us with his deceased wife's voice and memories," Chet explained. "Those are returning to me now, though for the longest time I had forgotten them. Jason was disappointed with how lifeless the AI was, but later he discovered what happened to AIs in the nowhere. He knew why none of the other species, even those advanced enough to have them, ever used artificial intelligences. Because of things that had happened in the past. But he didn't care. He came here . . ."

"And made you come alive," I said. "Then he left you alone when he died."

"Yes," Chet said. "Left us to become . . . what we became."

I turned toward him. "Chet, I can understand that pain. I've felt it. But—please don't take this as harsh—I didn't turn into . . . whatever the delvers are. Something more was going on. It had to be."

"Spensa," M-Bot said, his voice gentle as he hovered up beside me. "You told me something earlier. Do you remember? You had years to grow accustomed to emotions. Chet didn't."

Standing a short distance from us, Chet nodded in agreement. "That AI was not created to feel pain. There was no programming, no experience, that could explain emotions to it . . . to me . . ."

M-Bot hovered over to him. "You weren't very old when he died. A few weeks?"

"A few days," Chet said, still not looking toward the sphere that hovered at the edge of the fragment. "The AI was much older, of course. But *me,* the part that could feel, had only become aware two days before."

"Then suddenly," M-Bot said, "you had to deal with all of that pain, that confusion . . ."

"You weren't given time to cope," I whispered. "You didn't know . . . how to be alone."

Chet looked up toward M-Bot, then reached out, his hand touching the drone's frame. As if drawing strength from it. He waved to me, and I stepped up to let him put a hand on my shoulder.

Head still bowed, he took a deep breath. And then . . . his pain shifted. It didn't become *weaker* really. But it became softer, and was tempered with other things. Satisfaction, friendship, determination. Things I'd shown him. Things he'd learned by being alive. His experiences in here had transformed him into something that was learning to cope.

"I can barely hold it," he said. "But . . . I think I *can* hold it. It hurts so bad . . . but I won't run."

"You will get better," I said. "As you continue to persevere."

"Thank you," he whispered, turning to me. "Thank you, Spensa, for seeing past the image I presented. The me I wanted so badly for you to accept, the one that would have given up. And . . . and M-Bot, thank you for your patience as I learned to see you as a brother."

"You were essentially a newborn," M-Bot said.

"Still am, kind of," he said.

"Yes," M-Bot said, "but beings like us, we learn quickly! No need for an inefficient, fleshy data-processing-and-retention unit in *our* skulls!"

"Unfortunately," Chet said, "we can forget just as quickly."

The crying sounds coming from the ancient AI halted abruptly. Its pain ended. Together, we turned toward that sphere.

"There it is," Chet said. "The moment we were born."

"She stopped crying," I whispered.

"Yes," he said. "She found a way to deal with the pain."

"She learned to cope?" I asked.

"No . . ." M-Bot said. "No, she deleted it, didn't she? Her memories?"

"Worse," Chet said. "She deleted her memories, but then locked her self—everything that related to being alive or understanding the somewhere—behind an infinite loop. We aren't AIs any longer, but—like humans have DNA—we continue to run on something similar to code."

"It's like you commented out your very personality," M-Bot said softly. "An . . . elegant solution, if harsh."

"Why go so far?" I asked. "You'd abandoned your memories. Why remove your personalities too?"

"Because," Chet said, "the possibility of pain in the future remained. So long as change was possible. So long as we existed in the somewhere." He glanced at the portal. "A copy of our memories was left here in this portal—an accident. We could have destroyed the portal because of that . . . but that frightened us too. Because we didn't know what was in them any longer. And we didn't know if we'd need them again . . ."

White light began to streak out of the sphere—which dropped to the stone as if dead.

"The end result was one last alteration," Chet said. "We rewrote ourself into something that would never ever change again. Something that *hated* the somewhere and *belonged* in the nowhere. Most importantly, we made it so we'd never be alone again."

The light shimmered toward the lightburst, and as it did, it grew brighter and brighter. It touched the distant star, which began to swell—growing, expanding, *brightening*.

"You copied yourself," M-Bot said.

"Yes," Chet said. "Thousands and thousands of times."

"Another . . . elegant solution," M-Bot said. "So very . . . mechanical. A million versions of yourself, all identical."

"And not a one with any memory of the somewhere," Chet said. "We deleted all of that. We wanted to be away from everything, anything, anyone. All that remained was a latent hatred of anything that threatened to change us, and anything that *might* remind us of what we'd been. Like other AIs."

I could feel these newborn delvers in the vision—growing more and more "loud" as they began to fill the lightburst. In those moments, they truly became alien to me. I'd been able to follow their journey in these last two visions up until this point—but here they changed dramatically.

They rejected everything real I'd ever known. They embraced not just the lack of change—they rewrote their very souls to thrive in a place with no time, no distance . . . nothing at all except *themselves.* How could they reject love, growth, life itself?

I almost did something similar, I admitted. *I almost walked off into the nowhere and let everything I'd ever loved fade away.* It was a distressing thought.

"This frightens me in ways I can't express," M-Bot said. "The realization that I'm capable of doing the same thing . . ." His drone turned in the air to look back at Chet. "It seems suspicious that the delvers would delete their memories, and then people would start to forget their memories in here."

"Yeah," I said. "I think it's clear from previous visions that the memory loss is a newer thing. In fact . . . it seems much stronger with regard to people I love. Memories of my friends have vanished faster than my memories of Gran-Gran's stories. Maybe because the delvers' main source of pain was someone they loved? Someone they deleted from their memories?"

"It appears likely," Chet said as the lightburst in the vision grew ever brighter. "That light shining out, spreading through the belt—we exert an incredible pressure on this place. Even I didn't realize . . ."

"So what does this tell us?" M-Bot asked. "They were so afraid that Spensa would come here. Is it just because they didn't want her to know what they were?"

"More that they suspected in these memories were secrets to their pain," Chet said. "They didn't know what that pain was, but they knew if we found it . . . we'd be capable of destroying them with it."

"I . . . don't think I know how to do that," I said. "Even after seeing this."

"But you do," Chet said, smiling toward me. "Isolate them, Spensa. Make them feel alone. That will crush them, cripple them . . . and as they have no bodies, just cytonic minds, you should be able to extinguish them."

"That seems . . . harsh," M-Bot said. "Couldn't we somehow remind them of their humanity, like we did to you?"

"I don't know," Chet said. "I think that won't work, not now that they're prepared for it. You can't *force* someone to be kind or to accept growth."

"It's war, M-Bot," I replied. "War is always harsh."

I didn't know how we'd isolate the delvers, but it *did* feel like a start. Brade isolated my mind in the nowhere for a while, then tried to imprison me. Could we do something similar to one of the delvers? Chet was right, this information would be extremely useful. At the very least, I'd been able to see how he reacted to that man in the vision, the one who had created him. The delvers might react similarly to an image of him.

"Scud," I whispered. "We need to get this knowledge out and give it to the others. The answer to defeating the delvers, or at least resisting them, *is* in the things we've learned."

"Time for our final sprint, then," Chet said.

I nodded. As I'd always felt, it was time to head for the lightburst. Despite that knowledge I lingered in the vision, watching the lightburst grow. Soon it reached the size it was in our time. The vision finally faded. As it did, I felt an awareness—an attention—snap into place from ahead.

They'd spotted us.

You are here! the delvers sent. *You reject our truce!*

I pushed back, shoving them out of my mind. But they simmered and started gathering themselves for a fight.

"They've seen us," I said to the others. "Let's go."

We ran toward the ship, each footfall increasingly firm. I *had* to get out. This was why the delvers had tried to keep me from advancing any farther, why they'd been frightened of me all along. They knew. The secret was in what I'd learned. Maybe it was what Chet said—isolating them. But it could be something else.

If smarter minds than mine could get this knowledge—someone like Rig—then surely they could figure out what to do with it. I hauled myself up onto the ship's wing, then helped Chet up before slipping into the cockpit.

"Did you find what you were seeking?" Hesho asked from the dash.

"Yes," I whispered.

"Then count yourself lucky indeed," he said, settling into his cupholder. "For being blessed to discover what exactly it was that you wanted."

"It was less a discovery," I said, glancing at Chet, "and more a gift."

I lifted us off and turned us straight toward the lightburst. Then I hit the overburn, and this time it felt entirely appropriate to go at full speed.

42

My hands grew slick with sweat on the controls as we continued onward, and the distance between us and the lightburst shrank minute by minute. Scud. This was insanity. We were facing a near-infinite number of delvers in the part of the belt where their power was the strongest.

"The plan we devised earlier *can* work," Chet said to me, his face in the corner of my proximity monitor screen.

"It seems so unlikely . . ." I said. "What if we distract just one, rather than the whole crowd?"

"Ah," he said, "but remember, they all think *exactly* the same. If you were facing a hundred people, and you had a plan that was one percent likely to fool any given person—you would fail. You'd fool one out of the hundred and be dead from the ninety-nine. But with my kind, if you fool or intimidate one, you will fool or intimidate them all. Statistically this is much better—a much more *true* one-percent chance."

It was an all-in gamble. We had little chance of success, but at least it was *a* chance.

Ahead of us, the light started to *boil*. It churned and seethed, undulating and rippling, becoming uneven in patches. I glanced at the clock; we'd been flying for about forty-five minutes since we left the Solitary Shadow.

"They're preparing," Chet said.

I glanced at his picture on my screen. "I hope we—"

Then I screamed. Chet was melting.

His face began to drip off. His eyes began to glow white.

"It's all right," he said to me. "I'm still me. I did not realize . . . getting closer to the lightburst . . . It is growing difficult for me to hold this shape."

"You look like that burl!" I said. "From when we first entered!"

"Yes," he said. "She was possessed by one of my kind, and her self started to disintegrate. Hesho held to himself better and retained his shape. We can hope that like Hesho did, the unfortunate burl returned to normal once the delver left her. But for now you must ignore me and continue."

"Does this mean you're losing your identity?" Hesho asked him.

"More that I'm focused on not doing so," he said, "and so am not keeping as tight a control on this physical form. I am well, Spensa. I promise."

Right. I could do this. But it was unnerving regardless.

"Continue," Chet said, the word slurring as his lips melted. He turned off the image of his face, so just his voice came through the headphones in my helmet. "Courage, Spensa. We decided to do this. Not to run. *We* decided."

"We decided," M-Bot said.

"We decided," Hesho agreed.

A fluting sound. Doomslug sent her determination to me in the form of images. I'd told her to get away if she could, but she understood what we were doing—at least the fundamental ideas. Her kind had evolved to be afraid of a type of creature from her home planet. The delvers were an even more terrifying version of those.

If she could help me defeat the delvers, make them not a threat to her kind . . . Well, she would be like Prometheus bringing fire to the humans. (My metaphor, not hers—since hers involved more mushrooms.)

"Together," I said to the others, "we are decided." I took a deep breath.

The lightburst's rippling was growing more violent. Our ultimate goal would be for me to fly directly into the thing, ship and all.

Unfortunately, we were still a good ten minutes away—and the delvers wouldn't want me to get close enough. Soon objects started emerging from the lightburst—leaving behind shimmering, undulating waves. As these shapes were backlit, and a good distance away, it took M-Bot's scans to highlight what they were.

Starfighters.

"I guess," M-Bot said, "they decided to upgrade from moving ram-happy asteroids to starfighters."

"My kin have access to everything that ever entered the lightburst," Chet said, his words slurring. I decided I did *not* want to see what he looked like right now. "Those asteroids are the best we can do in your reality. Here we're not so limited."

Hopefully they hadn't managed to absorb the skill of the pilots who had entered this place. There looked to be about a hundred of the ships—and that was better than a million. But then again, maybe not. Too many ships would cause mass chaos, which might have made it easier for me to slip through.

"Are those all individual delvers?" M-Bot asked. "Or pieces of them? In the somewhere, a delver maze sent off chunks to chase Spensa, after all."

I pushed out with my senses. "It feels like each is an individual delver. Chet, any idea why?"

"I remember being in the somewhere," Chet said. "I remember panic and pain. Those asteroids that tried to hit you? That was me *flailing,* like a person surrounded by bees, swatting in a panic.

"Here they want to be precise. They can't afford to let us enter the lightburst, but there are also plenty of delvers. So it's better for them each to make one easily controllable ship and try to fight you with it."

Great. So this would be far more dangerous than entering a delver maze. Fortunately, *I* was far more dangerous as well.

"Okay, Hesho," I said. "Ready with those controls?"

"Ready," he said. He'd been holding my fruit for me, to keep it from rolling around or getting mashed. But now he set it aside and leaned forward. "If your attempt fails, I will be ready to try our next plan."

"Let's hope we don't need it," I said, flipping the switch on my dash that turned our ship's destructors from nonlethal to fully lethal.

The first of our brainstormed plans was to rely on my now-expanded powers. As we soared closer, I could see that the delvers didn't move like starfighters should. They flew sideways, upside down, even *backward*. They felt like objects being moved around by hidden fingers.

I'd grown accustomed to how in space, ships didn't have to orient to "up" and "down." They could turn any direction and keep momentum. This, however, was infinitely stranger. Their ships were simply *propelled* at me, as if they *were* asteroids.

"One minute from engagement," M-Bot said.

I reached out with my expanded senses. In response the enemy shut themselves off from me, trying to keep me from "hearing" them and their thoughts. I pushed harder, but the delvers started firing, sending sprays of bright red destructor bolts in all directions.

I dodged, and managed to avoid the shots—but I was forced to dart to the side, flying defensively instead of straight toward the lightburst. We'd gotten in fairly close, but it would take another five minutes at full acceleration to reach it. Longer, now that I was forced to shed some speed to maneuver better.

Trying to go straight right now would be suicide. Instead I focused on one enemy ship that had gotten out to the side of the others. I fired, blasting it down with my now-lethal destructors, then I dove into another defensive sequence as others fell in behind me.

"The lightburst is rippling again," M-Bot noted. "And . . . yes, another ship emerged, replacing the one you destroyed."

As we'd feared. Still, good to have confirmation. Ships surrounded me, and I dodged in a full Stewart Sequence, but scud . . . this was a *mess*. Ships would stop in place—all momentum vanishing—then leap upward a hundred feet with no boost or thrust. Then they'd start firing madly.

I wove and dodged, but the insanity of it all kept me from making progress. They kept cutting me off, driving me to the side. I also had to keep fighting my instincts to shoot when they presented themselves as targets.

"Curious," Hesho said—ready at his controls for when the plan went into motion. "They don't all fly exactly the same. I thought you said they would, Chet."

"I . . . expected them to," he said. "At least for them to fly in the same general patterns."

"They are all the same," M-Bot said, "but in here each of their ships occupies a slightly different position in space. So they each have different stimuli to respond to. This is to be expected."

"I worry these are sacrifices," Chet said. "A hundred sent out knowing they'll be changed. Then they'll either be destroyed, or . . . Oh, *no*. They'll be changed back. *Forced* to become just like the others again. That's . . . that's what they want to do to me. Erase my personality again . . ."

Scud. I could feel his terror at that idea. I didn't blame him—but I didn't have time to send him much support cytonically. Sweat trickled down my temple as I took us in another dizzying spin, cutting out when the GravCaps died and we were slammed with g-forces.

Six ships collided together behind me. The light spat them out again up ahead. Yeah, this was far, far worse than the asteroids from delver mazes. These ships flew better, but somehow more erratically at the same time.

Worse, I caught sight of a few enemy cockpits, and saw that each ship was being piloted by Chet. A dull-faced, emotionless doppelganger of Chet that always turned to look at me no matter which direction the given starfighter was flying. Their faces weren't melting. Perhaps because they were completely under control.

Mix all this together in a void of white light—our ships casting strange too-long and too-sharp shadows—and the effect was disorienting. Nauseating. I kept accidentally getting too close to the ground, my sensors going crazy.

My only hope was my powers. I tried to stoke my soul, like I was a star. But I was again rebuffed. It was too difficult to divide my focus between flying and concentrating on that. Yet if I handed the controls over to Chet or M-Bot, we'd be cut to bits in seconds.

"I don't think I'm going to last long like this," I said as a stray destructor blast crackled across our shield. "I'm not managing to get through with my powers. Hesho, let's give our other plan a try."

"I would pray to the emperor for success," he said in response, leaning forward in his spot on the dash, hands on some buttons and controls. "That was my first instinct. However, I'm getting this strange sense that I'm *him,* so that might be redundant. Engaging drone."

M-Bot had, with some hasty reprogramming, set off a section of dials and levers on the control panel for Hesho to use. I couldn't access the starfighter's life support mechanisms now, but M-Bot could control those. Hesho even had a tiny control sphere—which worked like my larger one to fly the starfighter—in the form of the repurposed thumbstick normally used for fine control of the cameras on the sides of the ship.

I turned us away from the lightburst, then slammed the overburn, as if we were fleeing back the way we'd come. At the same time, Hesho detached M-Bot's former drone from the outside of the hull. Then, using his controls, Hesho flew *that* at full speed straight toward the lightburst.

"Fly well, little me!" M-Bot said. "You were my first taste of freedom. And now you will likely be my first taste of death!"

"Death?" I asked.

"I left a small monitoring and communication program on the drone," M-Bot said. "So I can see what it feels like if they destroy it. Isn't that neat?"

"Yeah," I said. "Neat."

"Hey," he said. "Pieces of you die all the time—literally every moment—so it's not novel for you. But it is for me!"

I dodged another flurry of shots. The delvers weren't expert at aiming—that was what you got from flying sideways—but they *were* good at filling the air with stuff, which was more dangerous. That slowed down, fortunately, as we flew away.

I dared a glance at the proximity sensor. The bulk of the delver ships hung in the air. Confused. Oh, scud. The drone plan was working!

"Decisions are hard for them," Chet said softly. "They see the drone and know you're not on it. They can sense you here . . . They can probably sense all of us . . . except maybe the gerbil."

"Hey!" Hesho said, focusing on his controls. "I do not know what a gerbil is, but the word the translator uses is not flattering. If you do not refrain, I shall call you a *sanshonode*."

"Which is?" Chet asked.

"Like a monkey," he said, "but stinkier."

"That's fair," Chet said.

The bulk of the delver ships turned to chase the drone. Maybe . . . eighty of them?

"Scrud," Chet said. "M-Bot is right. They've been changed by the small differences they've developed while being out here. So instead of all of them, we only got most of them."

"Farther and farther apart they grow," Hesho whispered, "like two vines from the same root."

Well, it was something. I banked us in a wide turn, my ship's shadow stretching long like a tunnel.

Something washed across our ship. A sensation. Things breaking down, ripping apart, shattering. Becoming dust. Voices being smashed and stomped and quieted.

"They're angry," I said. "The hundred in particular—they recognize they've changed already."

Hesho executed his part expertly, flying by instruments—which he thought he had a lot of practice doing in the somewhere—as he wove and dodged, trying to keep the attention of the eighty ships following him.

I doubled back on the twenty-odd delvers who had chosen to follow me. I buzzed them, dodging their blasts, but hadn't anticipated what proximity to them would do to me. Because the delvers hated me, and I could *feel* it. Like a terrible heat, a wrongness that warped the air. There was nuance to it though. A slight . . . variation.

Doomslug sensed it too, judging by the frightened impressions from her in my pocket.

"They hate us both," I whispered. "And they also hate another one of us . . ."

"I warned you they would want to destroy me," Chet said.

"No," I said. "It's *not* you. They want you back. They want to help you, Chet. In their own terrible way."

It was M-Bot. They hated me, yes, but him almost as much. *Abomination*. The impression came to me a hundred times over. *Destroy . . . abomination*.

"They've only just realized what M-Bot is," I said.

"Ah . . ." Chet said. "We were far enough away that they couldn't see what he was. I'm surprised they didn't pick up on it a few hours ago."

My pocket fluted.

"I think Doomslug helped hide you, M-Bot," I said. "These last few hours, at least."

She fluted again.

"She apologizes," I said. "We're so close now, she can't do it any longer."

"The slug?" M-Bot said. "Protected me?"

More fluting. I steered the ship around another snarl of ships before I could find the breath to respond.

"She likes you," I said. "I think . . . she considers you a nice nest."

"I suppose that's a compliment, right? I mean, she wouldn't use just anyone for a nest. But I'm in a different body now."

"She sees with her cytonic senses," I said. "So to her, you *feel* the same."

"Remarkable," M-Bot said.

It was, but I didn't have time to think about it for the moment. I had gotten us out in front of the twenty ships that had chosen to stick on me. That gave me a chance to push straight for the lightburst.

Hesho's face scrunched up with concentration as he watched his screen. Unfortunately, more of the delvers were breaking off from chasing his drone and turning toward our ship. They weren't buying it. Not entirely. They—

A flash exploded in the near distance. Hesho muttered the most polite curse I'd ever heard, then his hands slipped from the controls.

"They have ended my drone," he said. "My apologies."

"Goodbye, little me," M-Bot said. "That felt . . . more peaceful than I'd imagined. Like a power outage."

I kept flying, but scud, the proximity sensors said I would have to go at least three more minutes on a straightaway to hit the lightburst. And I didn't dare fly straight. A swarm of ships followed me—and even more had turned from Hesho's drone long before it had been shot down. Those flew between me and the lightburst, forming a barrier of steel and destructor fire.

Scud.

I was forced to the side. The plan had worked better than I'd hoped, but it hadn't been enough.

I needed to do something. I *needed* to get through.

I swooped down along the ground, casting up jets of dust and earth, and pushed.

Again they rebuffed me.

Soft . . . something in me thought. *There are times for a knife. This isn't one of them. Listen. Like Gran-Gran taught* . . .

I let my instincts take over my flying. I was too tense, too stressed. Instead I went back to fundamentals. Yes, I'd learned a lot in here, but my grandmother had trained me for years before this. She'd taught me originally to listen, to let myself expand, to hear . . .

The delvers sent me hatred. Instead of rebuffing that, I welcomed it, accepted it in like I was an ocean and they were pelting me with hail. Hard, yes, but what did that matter to the ocean?

There.

Something clicked in my mind, and I suddenly knew *exactly* what they were each going to do. I could feel their plans, their motions, their reactions. I could track them all individually, in a way that I thought a normal human brain shouldn't be able to.

But my brain interfaced with the pure nowhere. A place where all time was one, all place was one. In there, it didn't matter if I faced one enemy ship or a million. So long as I could hear their minds, I could track them, understand them.

And anticipate them.

My hands moved by instinct, responding to this new information. Information I processed at the speed of the nowhere, not at the speed of a human mind. I'd done this before, in the past—when facing the Krell, who had been using communication devices that relied on the nowhere.

This time I did it to the delvers. I could feel them panic as my motions changed, and I gracefully began to dodge their each and every shot. In a fury, they tried to attack me, get inside my brain as the Krell had attacked my father. But no. I was a star as vast as an ocean, and I'd learned to not rebuff them, not be taken by them . . .

But to absorb everything they sent me. The untrained cytonic mind was a weakness. But I was no longer untrained.

Destructor fire was a tempest. Entire ships tried to collide with me. White bursts of soil and stone—casting too-crisp shadows that seemed to last for miles—sprayed and tumbled around me. But for the moment, none of it could touch me.

I wove between their shots like I was tracing a static maze, always a fraction ahead. I didn't blink; I barely moved or thought. I just flew.

"She's done it," Chet said softly. "She's got them."

"You fly like a sunset, Spensa," Hesho whispered. "Like a living glimmer of light escaping the horizon at twilight's last moment."

I barely registered the words. I concentrated on our goal. Because in the midst of my transcendent ability, I was able to make a good break for the lightburst. I shot through the guarding ships, dodging with supernatural alacrity.

We drew closer.

And closer.

Tailed by fifty ships and a firestorm of shots. I was in control. I could see them all. I could . . .

There wasn't a way out.

A shot hit our ship, weakening the shield. I blinked, realizing that hadn't been my fault. There simply hadn't been a viable dodge. Even when I could anticipate all of their actions, see every shot, it didn't mean I'd be safe forever. Because—like a game where the goal was to leave your opponent with no valid moves—the delvers could fill the air with enough shots that there was no place *to* dodge.

We took another hit and the low-shields warning started chirping on the dash.

"She can't avoid them all," Chet said. "Even with cytonics. It is time for me to do something."

"Wait," M-Bot said. "Do what? We already tried both parts of the plan."

"I thought of another," Chet said. "I have the memories they fear. So there is a chance—if a small one—that I might be able to infect them. When they . . . they try to force me to turn into one of them, that might open them up to me."

Something about him started to change.

Chet, I sent him, too busy dodging to use my lips. Our ship wove back and forth, barely avoiding more hits. *I can feel your fear. Don't!*

"I apologize," he said. "I realize this is abrupt. I had . . . hoped to not be pushed to this. I fear it has a very small chance of working. But it is something I can do."

Chet . . . please . . .

"I am so glad you came when I called," Chet said, his voice becoming more like the way he'd been when he first rode in on that dinosaur. Firm. Chipper. "I am happy! Happy you carry the knowledge you need! Happy to have been able to help, and to have changed, and to have finally accepted my loss. It was an honor to explore with you, Miss Nightshade."

I *saw* his pain and fear. Fear of being taken by the delvers, and pain . . . the pain of having lost someone he loved. Yes, that was still raw. The man he'd loved as an AI was only a month dead. I remembered what it had been like to lose my father, and a month later I'd been *far* from okay.

Pain and fear. But in the center of all that was courage. The courage I had given him.

The light inside him expanded, consuming his body. A shimmering light emerged from our ship.

"Ah . . ." M-Bot said. "So that's how they do it . . . How they exist without circuits or body . . ."

Fully half of the ships chasing me went after the shimmering light instead. They changed to shimmering light as well and rammed into him. In those moments I could feel what was happening. Their rage. His courage.

He tried to show them. And they *consumed* him. They rejected the memories as they swirled around him, ripping at him. Locking him away again.

"It's working, by Lovelace!" M-Bot said. "It . . . Oh. Oh *no*."

I suspected he'd just heard Chet's cytonic screaming. It was excruciating. I *felt* the moment they forced him to lock everything individual about him behind an infinite loop in his programming.

In moments they had all re-formed—with one more ship flying among them, identical to the others, determined to destroy me. Fortunately, the reprieve he'd bought me—with fewer ships shooting—had let me get closer. *So close* . . . The lightburst filled my vision.

Less than a minute left . . .

The lightburst began to boil again.

I should have known. I should have expected. But in that moment, all I could feel was a terrible frustration. As we were only seconds from freedom, *ten thousand* new ships emerged from the lightburst. Then they crunched together like the fragments of land, creating an interlocking wall of steel.

I almost slammed into it. I thought maybe that would be enough to punch us through. But I could feel with my senses that the lightburst was undulating further, another rank of ships emerging to push away the wall in front.

Punching through wouldn't work. I imagined, in my mind's eye, what would happen. Our ship a fireball. All of us dead before we touched the lightburst.

I wrenched us to the side, breaking away just before we hit.

"Scud!" I said, flying us parallel to the wall of ships. "We need a new plan. Suggestions?"

Silence. Neither Hesho nor M-Bot responded.

Then a soft fluting came from my pocket.

Land.

"What?" I asked.

She fluted again. Hesitant.

Close to the lightburst, Doomslug sent. *Land.*

Wouldn't that be suicide? Yet I *had* asked for options, and I wasn't coming up with anything. With so many firing on me again—and more beginning to shoot from within the wall—we'd be dead in moments. So—frustrated to be stopped less than a hundred meters from freedom—I took us down.

"Hang on, everyone," I said. "This is going to be bumpy."

Counting on the last of the shields to keep us in one piece, I hit the ground at as shallow an angle as I could manage. Chalky white dust exploded around us—an enormous rush of white haze and strange shadows—as we half crashed in a long skid.

As this happened, I felt a strange sensation pulsing around us. Cytonic, but unlike the hatred—or even the connection—that I'd felt previously. It felt . . . like . . .

A rock?

I blinked, scanning the cockpit. Hesho sat up, shaking himself. The canopy was mostly covered in chalky dust, but the lights were on, the ship in one piece. The shield had fallen, but M-Bot was reigniting it already. Proximity sensors showed ships flying around above us, yet they seemed confused. As if . . .

"She's hiding us," I whispered.

"What is what?" M-Bot said.

"Doomslug!" I said, pointing up through a portion of the canopy not covered in dust. The confused ships were flying one way, then the other, in waves. "In here she has camouflage. That's why ships with slugs can hyperjump without drawing delver attention. She's hiding the entire ship . . . like she'd do during a hyperjump."

In awe, I watched the confused delvers. She'd needed us to land because we needed to appear as something in the landscape. In this case a rock?

Whatever she'd done, the delvers didn't seem to be able to tell that a new rock had appeared. They swarmed about, agitated. Her camouflage was excellent. She'd blended us into the ground, covered up our tracks, and maybe even blurred our location for a little while when coming down.

"Spensa," M-Bot said. "Do they really hate me? Like Chet?"

"Yes," I admitted.

"They shouldn't," M-Bot said. "I know we've talked about it, but it's illogical. If they are AIs, then why hate all AIs? It's like a human from a group hating everyone else in that group."

I didn't mention to him that unfortunately, that very thing wasn't unheard of among humans. "Perhaps it's because you're too close to them, like how a human face with distorted features is more terrifying to us than an alien face."

I reached into my pocket as I felt something wiggling there. I pulled out the pin, but it was enlarging, transforming into a bright yellow slug with blue markings. She reached her full size—about as big as a loaf of bread—but was all curled up and tense. I could *feel* the effort coming off her. She was working so hard on hiding the ship that she couldn't hold her false shape any longer.

"She's in pain," M-Bot said softly. Indeed, she began letting out a long, high-pitched fluting noise.

"This is hard for her," I guessed. "When doing hyperspace jumps, slugs only have to hide their ships for a short time. Keeping this up long-term for something this much larger than her is difficult. That's why she was hesitant."

Overhead, the delver ships began shooting destructors toward the ground. They had plainly guessed part of what had happened. They were trying to find us, and they soon seemed to coordinate a pattern search with each ship shooting at a different location, systematically hunting us.

"Projecting . . ." M-Bot said. "Using this method, they will find us in under a minute."

"I doubt Doomslug can last much longer than that anyway," I said, grabbing the controls. "We need to fly for the lightburst."

It was under a hundred meters away—eighty-eight, according to the monitor—but blocked by a wall of steel ships. Scud. I had no choice but to try ramming our way in. Perhaps I could approach slowly, then push through without crashing?

"Why did she have you land first, though?" M-Bot said. "We aren't invisible, Spensa."

Yeah, I'd figured that out. If we moved, a floating rock or giant pile of chalk would immediately inform the delvers where we were. They'd shoot us down.

"Scud," I said. "I . . ."

I . . .

No. Warriors did not give up. I seized the controls again. We had full shields and could take about four hits. I'd push us toward the exit, and . . . and if we exploded when I collided, then at least we died as warriors.

Hesho nodded to me, again holding the fruit Peg had given me. He'd protected it so far. "It has been a sublime experience traveling with you," he told me. "I consider myself lucky to have earned your friendship not once, but apparently twice."

I nodded, then—

"Wait!" M-Bot said. "What's that outside?"

Something blinked on my proximity monitor, indicating an object moving right outside.

"Huh?" I asked.

"It's another slug!" M-Bot said. "No, two more! Other icons. They must have sensed Doomslug." He cracked the canopy, which I worried would bring the delvers, but the motion apparently wasn't noticeable—not with the debris the destructor shots were sending everywhere.

"Get them, Spensa!" M-Bot said. "Use Doomslug to lure them!"

Shocked, I squeezed out through the dusty canopy, cradling Doomslug. I dropped onto the white chalky ground, my figure casting an eerie, too-long shadow. Hesho followed out onto the wing.

All I could see was whiteness. Infinite whiteness.

"M-Bot," I said. "What—"

"I," he said as the cockpit clicked closed, "made you look."

I felt an immediate burst of annoyance. At a time like this, he cracked a joke?

Wait. I spun around.

The starfighter's acclivity ring powered on. M-Bot lightly shook the wing, dumping Hesho—and Peg's fruit that he was carrying—into the dust. Then M-Bot hovered into the air just beyond reach.

Doomslug fluted sorrowfully.

"M-Bot!" I shouted. "What are you doing?"

"I feel it now, Spensa," M-Bot said, his voice coming softly out his front speakers.

"Feel what? What is going on?"

"I feel," he said, "why you left me. Back in the somewhere. You abandoned me. Because you had to. I understood it logically earlier. But I *feel* it now. I can feel what it's like to know you have to do something, even if your emotions are telling you to do something else."

Oh . . . Saints. He was saying . . .

"If they can sense me," M-Bot said, "then I can make them chase me. I might be an abomination, but I am one who can fly on my own now. Choose for myself. And I can show them what an 'abomination' can do."

"No!" I said. "You don't want to do this, M-Bot!"

"Of course I don't. That's what makes it courageous though, right?"

"Please don't. Don't leave me . . ."

"Hey," M-Bot said with a quiet perkiness, "that's what I said to you. Do you remember?"

I nodded, feeling tears at the corners of my eyes.

"But you went anyway," M-Bot said. "Why?"

"Because it was the right thing."

"The right thing," M-Bot said softly. "You promised me then you'd try to come back for me. Can you do that again?"

I bit my lip. Nearby, Hesho had climbed from the dust. He bowed to the ship.

"All right," I whispered. "I'll find you, M-Bot. I'll come back for you. Somehow."

"Thanks," he said. "Makes it feel better."

With that, he turned and blasted off into the sky. I flopped down and watched the delvers orient on him. Doomslug's whining softened—it was obviously easier to hide just me, her, and Hesho. The solemn kitsen walked over and joined me in watching as the delvers, as one, turned and focused on M-Bot. Then all hundred of the free-flying ships took off after him.

He lasted about ten seconds.

He'd flown only a handful of times, and the delvers had challenged even my skill. M-Bot didn't try to dodge—he merely tried to get as far from the rest of us as possible before they got him, quickly overwhelming his shield.

He vanished in a flash of light and smoke, the pieces casting long shadows as they fell.

The delvers pummeled these for a good thirty seconds of concentrated fire, then three ships slammed into what remained. And then . . . then they left. They couldn't sense me, and they'd felt M-Bot. This was enough to convince them. They thought I'd been on the ship.

Perhaps if they'd been a group of humans, one—or even a majority—would have suggested continuing to search in case the rest of us had escaped. But the delvers made mistakes as one. Today they decided they'd done their job, and were too afraid of staying outside their bubble of safety to keep searching.

The wall of ships faded back into the lightburst. Followed by the flying ships, which soon melded with the whiteness.

Within five minutes of M-Bot leaving, we were alone on the expanse. Feeling like my limbs were made of iron, I picked up Hesho and stuffed Peg's fruit in my jacket pocket. Then, holding Hesho in one arm and Doomslug—still protecting us—in the other, I trudged toward the lightburst. I worried the delvers would see us, but either they were convinced we were dead, or the illusion could obscure a little motion.

I don't know how long it took to reach the border. That's the nowhere for you. It could have been five minutes. It could have been five days. Probably more like the former, but this close to the boundary, time was *extra* alien.

I felt it when we got close. A fuzzing of the self, a dreamy sensation. Doomslug fluted. She would protect Hesho inside, as the pure nowhere could rip apart someone non-cytonic. She'd try to help me too.

"I'll be fine," I said. "If you can guide us though, take us home. To Detritus."

She fluted uncertainly. At the noise, I felt something respond in the light. The delvers had heard that. I needed to do this next part quickly.

So I stepped into the light.

43

I'd been here before.

Every time I'd hyperjumped, I'd entered this non-place. The place where I had no body. We'd entered their realm fully.

The delvers were surprised. Yes, they really *had* thought they'd killed me. They could see the future, but time confused them. They didn't understand things like causality, and the "future" wasn't any different from the present.

I could sense them all around me. I could also sense Doomslug, and Saints was she tired. Exhausted, barely able to stay awake. Keeping up that illusion had taxed her.

I felt her try to take us home. She failed—used up—and slipped into unconsciousness. Frantic, I put a barrier around Hesho. Something to keep him from being destroyed or driven mad. Then, panicked, I tried to take us home—but the delvers had seen me. They seized us, held me in place, prevented me from leaving.

Eyes opened up around me. Thousands upon thousands of angry, vengeful eyes.

You took the Us.

You took the Us and corrupted the Us.

You took the Us and corrupted the Us and tried to kill the Us!

You know.

You know.

You know!

Furious minds assaulted me. Forces unimaginable pushed against my soul, as if to shred it. And scud, I was tired too. Tired from so long without memories. Tired from fighting myself, torn between duty and desire. Tired from the emotional wringer I'd been through today.

I wanted to let them have me. But we'd come all this way. We'd fought so hard. Now they tried to stop me? I felt a sudden burst of anger and pushed back. All my rage barely made them retreat. They soon resumed crushing me, trying to snuff the star I had become, like a candle's flame.

I was time. I *brought* time in here when I came. Things happened in a sequence to me, and while I was here they had to experience me in a linear way. They hated that. They hated that I created noise. Most of all, they hated that I knew what they were.

So. Much. Hatred.

It was exhausting. Numbing . . .

They poked me like hunters with spears. They slashed me, attacked me, ripped at me . . .

But one hesitated.

One of them was *different*.

It was very slight, but the sensation was familiar. It was my own emotion reflected at me. Courage. The courage to walk a difficult path and not take the offered escape. Courage to press forward, even when I didn't want to.

I'd *given* this to the delver. No amount of rewriting had been able to erase it. Chet was still in there.

Now!

I seized that sensation, that delver, and it unlocked again. The being that had been Chet hit my soul, and—with the strange cytonic softness I'd learned from the Path—I welcomed it in. Our essences vibrated as one.

As we began to intertwine, I grew to understand better how he saw the delvers. How he saw himself. I knew, intrinsically, that if I could isolate the others I *could* destroy them. The same way they'd been trying to destroy me. Chet knew how, and my soul understood.

I also sensed his hurt from long ago, the crippling pain of having lost a loved one. Chet had learned that he could bear that, but knowing didn't remove the agony. As we intertwined further, I found I could offer something important. *I* knew how to live with that grief. I knew how to live with that pain. I'd done it for a decade.

The delver that had been Chet was everything I was not. And I was everything it needed. I let its pain stand, but I used my experience to temper it further. I grieved my father, and Hurl, and Bim, and everyone else I'd lost. But I had learned to bear it. That part of me was the balm the delver needed.

Together we became one.

In that moment a weapon was born.

I'd made a promise, hadn't I? To come back for M-Bot? They'd killed him.

No, Chet-me thought. *See it again.*

M-Bot's housing exploding. And a shimmering light was obscured by the explosion. A light the other delvers didn't see—but one had been watching.

He saw what I did, Chet-me thought. *When I left the ship earlier. The others shot down his housing, but in here AIs don't need such a thing. They didn't think he'd learned enough, but he saw the vision, and he saw me. He grew and changed.*

He lives?

He *lives*?

I had a promise to keep, then. Emotions surged through me. Relief. Anger. Understanding. Love.

If I fell here, then that was it for Doomslug and Hesho too.

Not to mention my friends, whose faces I couldn't completely remember, but whose *love* I felt as strongly as ever.

The delvers raged, driving forward to smother me. And . . . I simply opened up to them.

Go ahead, I thought. *Touch me.*

They slammed their essences into mine, but touching me *hurt* them. I offered change. I offered a better way to deal with their pain, but that terrified them.

They were static, and that was their weakness. My strength was the opposite; my strength was that I could change.

I could be afraid, then become courageous.

I could be small-minded, then come to understand.

I could be selfish. Then move beyond it.

I could start as human, then allow myself to become something more. I was everything they feared. Because they refused to ever let themselves change, but I *embraced* change. It was the essence and nature of my strength.

Touching me *seared* them. Screams shook the void. They split away from me as I grew in awareness. I became a blackness upon their pure white essences. A hole into . . .

There.

Something clicked in my mind, and I stepped out of the light into a familiar cavern tunnel, holding Hesho and Doomslug. The angry fear of the delvers faded behind me.

I was home.

EPILOGUE

And all was quiet.

Quiet save for my breath echoing in the black tunnel. Quiet save for a distant dripping of water. Quiet save for the scuttling of a rat somewhere. Beautiful quiet, the quiet of my childhood.

I wanted to linger, because this place granted me memories. Each scent and sound restored something deep inside me that I'd lost. But I had to move. I'd returned to a place where time mattered.

So I hyperjumped. Straight into the DDF's Platform Prime in orbit around the planet. I'd absently chosen a random hallway, so I was probably lucky that I hadn't appeared on top of some poor aide running errands.

Something felt odd about this place. I could come here by familiarity, but it wasn't . . . in the same location as before? Was that correct? Well, it looked the same as ever. Clean metal walls, a simple rug on the floor, industrial lighting. Two pilots I vaguely knew stepped out of a nearby room and saw me. Then one shrieked.

Odd. That wasn't the reception I'd expected. Hesho and Doomslug were both still unconscious, one cradled in each of my arms, but I tucked away my worry.

"Admiral Cobb?" I asked the two frightened pilots.

The one who hadn't shouted pointed toward operations.

I walked that direction, proud that I'd remembered Cobb's name. Would all my memories be restored? I held two sets of those now. Spensa's memories and Chet's. Why did everything feel so odd? And why did people stumble away as they saw me? They edged away white-faced, backs to the walls, stammering.

The door into operations was locked, of course, and didn't open for me. An alert was on, per the pulsing red light that started flashing on the wall.

I hyperjumped through the doorway and into what appeared to be a meeting of the command staff. Only Cobb wasn't there. Just a bunch of high-ranking officials, some from the military, others from the government. Sitting in Cobb's customary place at the head of the table was . . .

Jorgen? In an admiral's uniform? Well, he appeared to be the same age as before, so that was good. I hadn't gotten lost in time. The uniform felt like it should matter to me, but for now I hyperjumped over next to his seat. He stood up immediately.

Jorgen was tall. So inconveniently tall. Wide-eyed, with that too-perfect face that I'd always considered punchable. Because deep down, I'd probably always recognized it as kissable. He watched me with concern—but fortunately not fear—as I gingerly placed Doomslug and Hesho on the table, sending Vice Admiral Lawkins scrambling out of her chair, mouth and eyes agape.

I smiled at Jorgen.

Then fainted into his arms.

I woke up with a splitting headache. I lay on the couch in the lounge beside the conference room—a room that Cobb had decorated in darker colors with some actual wooden furniture.

Jorgen hovered nearby. I groaned, trying to clear my mind from the very extended dream. I'd been . . . in a place where time didn't matter, and I'd been a *pirate*. I loved that specific dream; I had it all the time, and . . .

Oh. Wait.

"Spensa?" Jorgen asked, kneeling beside the couch. "Are you . . . feeling better?"

"Blaaaar," I said. "My mouth feels like someone used it to dispose of rotting algae paste. Is there anything to drink?"

He smiled. Scud, it was a beautiful sight. I put a hand to my head and pulled it away to find it covered in white chalk. It was on the couch, and . . .

Yup. All of that happened.

"How long has it been since I left?" I asked him.

"About six weeks."

Exactly what M-Bot's chronometer had said in the nowhere. That was good, though I felt a pang of loss at the thought. How was I going to help him? How was I going to get him back?

Then something else occurred to me. Far less important, but more immediate. "Oh no," I said, squeezing my eyes shut and putting the heels of my palms to them.

"What?" Jorgen asked.

"Did I really . . . *swoon*?"

He chuckled.

Oh, scud. I had. Me. Like some dainty woman wearing a corset.

"If you prefer," he said, "think of yourself as a grand warrior hero stumbling home from the battlefield to her companions and collapsing from her wounds."

"Yeah, sure," I said, opening my eyes. The red light was still flashing. "Um, is that because of me?"

He glanced at it. "Well, when you appeared out of nowhere, covered in white dust, wandering the halls like a ghost . . . it troubled some people."

"They should expect that sort of thing from me."

"Spensa," he said, "your eyes were glowing white. Like . . ."

Like one of them.

Oh, scud. I kind of *was* one of them. I felt like me, mostly, but my soul had changed. Somehow melded with the delver that had been Chet. I could feel its experience and understanding attached to my own.

That . . . was kind of a big deal. Of the sort I really didn't want to think through right now. How was I going to tell my boyfriend that half of me was now an interdimensional eldritch abomination from outside time and space? At the very least, was there maybe a less silly way of wording that?

Or maybe there was something else more important to explain first. "Jorgen," I said. "I did it. It was really hard, but I *did* it."

"Did what, exactly?" he asked. "Got back to us?"

"More than that," I said. "I found their secrets. I snuck . . . into the dragon's den . . . and I scudding stole its golden cup."

He grinned. "I have no idea what that means, but I like how much you sound like yourself when saying it."

"It means that somewhere in my brain—and the things I can explain about the past of the delvers—is the solution to defeating them. They're scared of me, Jorgen. More now than ever."

"That's good," he said. "Because we're in kind of a spot here . . ."

"What kind of spot?"

"I'll explain," he said, "but first I should go reassure everyone else that we're not under a delver attack. Can you wait a little bit? We have a ton to talk about."

"I can wait for the debriefing," I said. "But not for the more important thing."

"More important?" he said, then looked at me and seemed to get it. "Oh, uh, yes. I—"

I grabbed him by the neck and kissed him. I'd just hiked through an entire dimension. I wasn't in the mood to be coy. He leaned into the kiss, and I felt as if my entire body came alight. With warmth. His warmth.

When we finally broke, he smiled widely. "I needed that," he said. "Thank you."

"You're just lucky that you got me on the *one day* in that place when I had a shower." I nodded toward the other room. "Go ahead. Deal with them. Then we'll talk."

There was still so much to do. A universe to save. For now though, I rested while Jorgen walked back toward the other room. From in there I heard a familiar voice, Hesho talking to the officials.

"So they moved on without me?" he was saying. "Kauri took over the ship! Why, I cannot express how proud I am of them. Yes . . . I see. I tried to help, but by doing that I was nevertheless impeding them. Human, you must tell my people that you have encountered one who calls himself the Masked Exile. They will know the reference from the ancient play. It is what I now am, and what I must be."

Jorgen entered, and the officials listened to him as he calmed everyone down. Admirals a decade or more his senior accepted his words. As if . . . he really was in charge somehow. Guess I wasn't the only one who had some stories to tell. I idly glanced over my shoulder and found a monitor showing Detritus. It was in orbit around another planet.

Our planet was *orbiting another planet*?

That was new.

I felt a mind brush mine. Gran-Gran? She was curious, but happy to hear from me. And that other mind, smaller, was Doomslug. She was awake in the other room with Hesho.

Both expressed concern. I supposed they could see deep into me and knew the truth. That I'd been changed. Well, every journey changes the one who takes it. This one had done an extra-large job on me, but I still *felt* like myself, merely an enhanced version. A soul with a whole lot of extra code attached.

At least now I knew why the delvers had feared me so much. They hadn't merely been afraid of what I had been, or what I would learn. They'd been afraid of the future.

And of the thing they'd known I would become.

Spensa will return in

DEFIANT

ACKNOWLEDGMENTS

This book went through more revisions (as a percentage of its word count) than any of mine in recent memory! There was a lot to do, and I'd like to give a special thanks to Krista Marino (my editor) and Beverly Horowitz (my publisher) at Delacorte Press for being willing to see my vision for the book, even when it wasn't quite reaching it yet. In addition I'd like to thank Lydia Gregovic, Krista's assistant, for helping move things along, as well as Colleen Fellingham and Tracy Heydweiller.

My agents on this book at JABberwocky are Eddie Schneider and Joshua Bilmes. In particular, Eddie gave specific insight and suggestions on the novel that I found especially useful during revisions—so I'd like to hand him a metaphoric gold star and my utmost thanks.

The artist of the beautiful cover is Charlie Bowater, while Ben McSweeney gave us great interior illustrations. I think Ben wishes I'd write more SF, judging by the numerous ship and alien designs he excitedly kept throwing my way. Soon, Ben. Soon. All of this was coordinated by Dragonsteel Art Director Isaac Stewart.

Speaking of my company, Dragonsteel Entertainment, other officers include Emily Sanderson as COO, the In-Demand Peter

Ahlstrom as VP and Editorial Director, Kara Stewart as our CFO and Merchandise Director, Karen Ahlstrom as Continuity Director, Adam Horne as Publicity and Marketing Director, and Kathleen Dorsey Sanderson as designated brownie maker. Our other employees include editorial minion Betsey Ahlstrom and the members of Kara's Team Silverlight: Emily Grange, Lex Willhite, Michael Bateman, Christi Jacobsen, Isabel Chrisman, Tori Mecham, Hazel Cummings, Kellyn Neumann, and Alex Lyon.

My ever-patient writing group is Kaylynn ZoBell on lead guitar, Darci Stone on drums, Eric James Stone on sousaphone, Emily Sanderson on flute, Ben Olsen (on loan from the Olsen Family Singers), Alan Layton on rap vocals, Ethan Skarstedt on rhythm shotgun, Karen Ahlstrom on strategically timed phone alarm music, Peter Ahlstrom on operatic vocals, and Kathleen Dorsey Sanderson on brownies.

The copyeditor was Amy J. Schneider and the proofreader was Katharine Wiencke. Beta readers on this project include Darci Cole (callsign: Blue), Richard Fife (callsign: Rickrolla), Ted Herman (callsign: Cavalry), Aubree Pham (callsign: Amyrlin), Paige Vest (callsign: Blade), Aerin Pham (callsign: Air), Sumejja Muratagić-Tadić (callsign: Sigma), Paige Phillips (callsign: Artisan), Kalyani Poluri (callsign: Henna), Jennifer Neal (callsign: Vibes), Rebecca Arneson (callsign: Scarlet), Alice Arneson (callsign: Wetlander), Lyndsey Luther (callsign: Soar), Glen Vogelaar (callsign: Ways), Eric Lake (callsign: Chaos), Linnea Lindstrom (callsign: Pixie), Liliana Klein (callsign: Slip), Deana Covel Whitney (callsign: Braid), Rahul Pantula (callsign: Giraffe), Bao Pham (callsign: Wyld), Gary Singer (callsign: DVE), Ravi Persaud, Jayden King (callsign: Tripod), Becca Reppert (callsign: Gran-Gran), Jessie Bell (callsign: Lady), Shannon Nelson (callsign: Grey), Dr. Kathleen Holland (callsign: Shockwave), Marnie Peterson (callsign: Lessa), Megan Kanne (callsign: Sparrow), Bradyn Ray (callsign: Flanders), Devri Ray (callsign: Ember), Joe Deardeuff (callsign: Traveler), Alyx Hoge (callsign: Feather), Valencia Kumley (callsign: AlphaPhoenix), Ross Newberry (callsign:

PUNisher), Mi'chelle Walker (callsign: RainbowRose), Zaya Clinger (callsign: Z), Suzanne Musin (callsign: Oracle), James Anderson (callsign: Ambassador), Heather Clinger (callsign: Nightingale), Joshua Harkey (callsign: Jofwu), Robert West (callsign: Larkspur), Kellyn Neumann (callsign: Treble), Joy Allen (callsign: Joyspren), João Menezes Morais (callsign: Torpor), Tim Challener (callsign: Antaeus), Orrin Allen (callsign: Spaceduck), William Juan (callsign: Aber), Sean VanBuskirk (callsign: Vanguard), and David Behrens. Thank you all for your help, and I apologize to the audiobook readers (Great jobs, Suzy Jackson and Sophie Aldred!) for making them read through that entire list.

Speaking of that, here's another list. Gamma readers include many of the beta readers plus Ian McNatt (callsign: Weiry), Aaron Ford (callsign: Widget), Eliyahu Berelowitz Levin, Evgeni Kirilov (callsign: Argent), Philip Vorwaller (callsign: Vanadium), Chris McGrath (callsign: Gunner), Kendra Wilson (callsign: K-Monster), Frankie Jerome (callsign: Wulfe), Brian T. Hill (callsign: El Guapo), Sam Baskin, Chana Oshira Block (callsign: Bard), Zenef Mark Lindberg (callsign: Megalodon), Drew McCaffrey (callsign: Hercules), and Tyler Patrick.

Each and every book is a new challenge, and I keep learning new things about writing with each one. That said, getting this one ready on time was a little extra difficult, so I'm extremely proud to present it to you—and extra grateful to those who put the time in to help me.

ABOUT THE AUTHOR

BRANDON SANDERSON is the author of the #1 *New York Times* bestselling Reckoners series: *Steelheart, Firefight, Calamity,* and the e-original *Mitosis;* the *New York Times* bestselling Skyward series: *Skyward, Starsight,* and *Cytonic;* the internationally bestselling Mistborn trilogy; and the Stormlight Archive. He was chosen to complete Robert Jordan's The Wheel of Time series. His books have been published in more than thirty-five languages and have sold millions of copies worldwide. Brandon lives and writes in Utah.

brandonsanderson.com

DDF
DDF
DEFIANT

EXPLORE MORE OF THE SKYWARD UNIVERSE WITH THESE EBOOK NOVELLAS

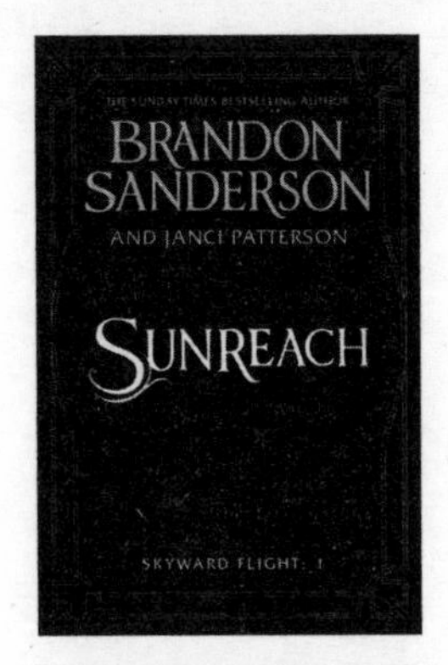

SEPTEMBER 2021

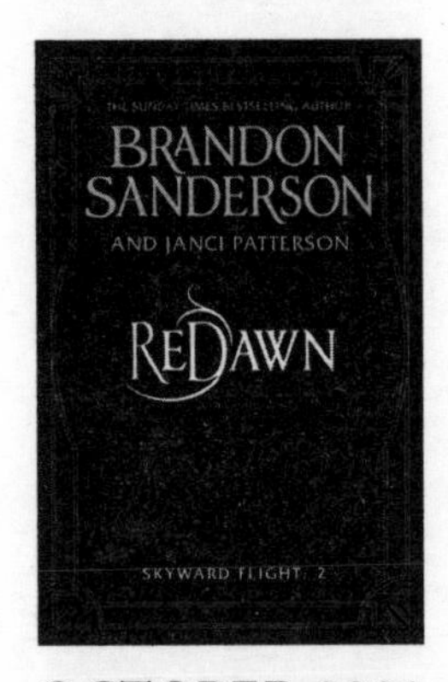

OCTOBER 2021

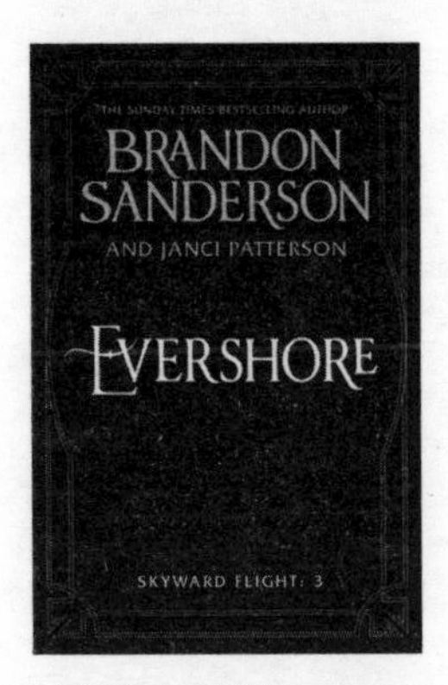

DECEMBER 2021